Satisfaction

Satisfaction

A Novel

GILLIAN GREENWOOD

SHAYE AREHEART BOOKS
NEW YORK

Copyright © 2006 by Gillian Greenwood

All rights reserved.
Published in the United States by Shaye Areheart Books, an imprint of the Crown Publishing Group, a division of Random House, Inc., New York.
www.crownpublishing.com

SHAYE AREHEART BOOKS and colophon are trademarks of Random House, Inc.

Originally published in hardcover in Great Britain by John Murray (Publishers), a division of Hodder Headline, London, in 2006.

Library of Congress Cataloging-in-Publication Data

Greenwood, Gillian.
Satisfaction : a novel / Gillian Greenwood. – 1st ed.
1. Adulthood–Fiction. 2. Interpersonal relations–Fiction. I. Title.
PR6107.R4444S28 2007
823'.92–dc22   2006034254

ISBN: 978-0-307-35138-8

Printed in the United States of America

Design by Lauren Dong

10 9 8 7 6 5 4 3 2 1

First American Edition

FOR MY MOTHER AND FATHER

There is an hour wherein a man might be happy all his life,
could he find it.

GEORGE HERBERT

Satisfaction

2004

22 NOVEMBER
HARLEY STREET

HE STOOD AT the window and thought how beautiful the city could be in November, and how no one ever noticed or said so. It was ten to four and the light was going, but the thin wash of blue and mauve between the small dark clouds still held its colors, and he felt satisfied, as he often did these days, at the way his life had gone.

He saw the woman approaching, walking down Harley Street, and he knew it was her, the one whose voice had caught his attention on the phone in a way that surprised him, holding as it did a curiosity that was absent from most of those who consulted him. She was pressing the bell now, on its fine brass plate: Patrick McIlhenny, MSc, Clinical Psychologist. And Analytical Psychotherapist, he added to himself, but that had seemed too overwhelming a title to post on his gate. As he waited to be notified of her arrival, he straightened a grimacing Honduran mask that rested against the bookshelves and picked up one of the smooth round stones that sat on his desk. He felt the tightening of apprehension and expectation that each new client delivered.

She entered the room and he saw her look beyond him, taking in the sweep of it all, as if she were making an inventory. She was a tall woman with dark hair parted to one side and pushed behind her ears. Her complexion had a natural flush, and her lips were highly colored. To his eye there was no sign of makeup, and its absence lent her an air of youth, though he estimated (with professional detachment) that she must be in her forties.

"Mrs. Marsham," he said, as he put down the stone and held out his hand to her.

"Yes—it's Amy," she said. "Hello."

"Patrick McIlhenny. We spoke, on the phone."

"You're Irish?"

"Northern Ireland. Belfast," he said.

She sat down in one of the two leather chairs that half faced each other across a small mosaic table.

"This is a beautiful room," she said.

He smiled at her.

"In what way do you find it beautiful?"

She looked directly at him, an uncommon gambit, and he was excited by the thought that here was something new, something other than the usual catalogue of depression and fear that wept before him by the hour. For a moment he thought she knew him, that they'd met before, but she indicated nothing.

"It feels safe," she said. "Insulated by beautiful things." She waved at the pictures and objects that crowded the walls and shelves. "And all the books."

"The books make you feel safe?"

"No," she laughed. "My mother writes books. Sort of."

She leaned back in her chair as if resting, her eyes closed.

"I'll never feel safe," she said. "But that's not why I'm here."

He waited. After a moment she sat forward, her hands clasped together in the soft folds of her skirt, her feet together.

"I assume," she went on, "that most people come to see you because they are unhappy, unhappy with their lives in some way."

He gave the slightest shrug of his shoulders, aware that she didn't require an answer, that she was laying out the ground before him, that her speech, her questions, though unrehearsed, were familiar to her.

"That's not my problem. Quite the reverse. I'm suffering, if any-thing, and if that's even the correct word to use in the circumstances, from an excess of happiness."

The sudden smile that followed her assertion confirmed what she said. Its warmth and sense of joy seemed to jump-start the lamps, dispatching the shadows that were starting to creep around the room as the daylight diminished. He was taken aback, unused to such pleasure in his working world, and it was almost with relief that he watched her settle back again, back, he assumed, to a sort of contentment.

He felt hypnotized by her presence, their roles reversed, and as he watched her and heard her voice, he thought it could almost be his own. And he found that he'd lost to his daydream, in a most unprofessional manner, the start of her confession.

". . . all in their best clothes and hats," he heard her say. "We'd been months preparing. I was twenty-five then, when I married him"—her voice was drifting over his head—"so young it seems now, but I felt quite old. I'd felt quite old for a long time. And he told me later that the night before and that morning, he'd been sick with love, that he'd thrown up from sheer joy." She stopped and smiled again, but this time a small contortion shaded its glow. She leaned forward and spoke quietly, and for the first time since her arrival he wondered if she was more disturbed than she appeared.

"Did he tell you?" she asked him, as if he wasn't really there. "Did he tell you? That he was sick with joy the day he married me?"

1984

JAMES WAS STANDING outside the back door of St. Mary Abbotts Church, and as he watched, entranced, a ring of exhalation from a cigarette hovered above Archie's thick brown hair. It was visible even in the sunshine, like a blessing on the day, he thought. Today he would marry Amy Fielding, as he'd known he would from the second time he met her. His certainty had shocked him. His decisions in life were usually far more considered, and he had kept the knowledge to himself for some time. But James had known it, had never had a doubt, and now the day had arrived, and 200 people were coming to wish them well.

Archie ground his cigarette butt under his shiny black shoe and clapped James on the back. They looked around them, at the more or less empty square garden tucked away behind the noise of a major city through route. On the other side of the large parish building, the main entrance opened onto the High Street, where currently a series of taxis was pulling up, causing a jam as they emptied out their excited, overdressed passengers. James and Archie could hear the distant buzz from where they stood behind the church, all quiet and green and white; a tramp was snoozing on a bench, a neat pile of empty cans laid at his side next to a zipped-up bag, an effigy of illusory tranquillity.

"I might try that in a few years' time," said Archie, who had a hangover and thought that the picture had its attractions.

"I don't think so," said James, clutching his friend's shoulder. "You would never be so tidy."

There was still just the faintest hint of bile at the back of James's throat as he breathed in deeply. He reached in his trousers for the packet of mints he'd pocketed just before he'd left the flat. He wasn't hung over, that was the odd thing. He'd insisted on staying in the previous night, just a couple of beers and a pizza while he watched Archie drink a great deal more. But he'd still thrown up before he went to bed, then again this morning. It had happened before, once or twice, in anticipation of something he wanted badly and feared to lose, but he forced himself to forget it; it was just the smallest betrayal of whom he knew himself to be this morning: a very happy man.

As Archie took the packet of mints from him, James thought that his friend seemed more nervous than he was. Archie pulled down the waistcoat, which kept riding up at the back under his long-tailed coat, and looked at his watch. They had a few brief minutes. He flung himself on a memorial bench and looked up at James, who was smiling as he stretched, his hands folded behind his head. Archie was struck by how relaxed he seemed, how different from the tense-faced grooms he'd observed on similar occasions, and he had a fleeting sense of slipping, of being now a step behind. James had always had an easy order about him, a notion of things in their proper place and at their proper time. He had lived a tidy life, from delivering his schoolwork punctually to finishing one affair before embarking on another, and Archie admired him without really comprehending the rules he lived by. James was stepping into his future with assurance, destined, it seemed, for contentment and success.

There was a sound of footsteps on the gravel path and a short muscular figure in immaculate morning dress appeared around the corner of the building.

"Everything okay here?"

"Aren't you supposed to be out front?" said Archie. "What's going on?"

Sometimes, he thought, Richard's desire to hang out with him and James could go a step too far. He was four years younger than the two of them and, like a kid brother, was oblivious to those times when he wasn't required. But what the hell. Today was glorious.

"It's amazing back there," said Richard, indicating the church. He seemed excited. "Bloody amazing. Beautiful women, all preening and smiling at each other. It's another world." He adjusted his cravat and smoothed it down, stroking it almost with affection. James and Archie looked at each other. Archie shrugged. Richard was something of a dandy. Today he had added a colorful waistcoat to his formal suit, a peacock among the gray. But when he looked over at Archie, half lying on the bench, he felt a moment's envy for the carelessness of Archie's dress and demeanor. Archie seemed to hold a certain status. Richard had registered it from the day he had met him in the agency. It was as if Archie could see himself from the outside, but from a distance, tall and good-looking, at the top of his game at almost thirty.

"Amy and her mother are about to arrive." Richard hesitated. "The sisters are here already." He shuffled for a moment, then acknowledged the privacy of James's last single moments. "I just came to tell you, that's all." He turned, one hand raised. "Good luck. It's all to play for," he shouted, and he crunched back from where he had come as Archie hauled himself up off the bench.

꒳

GRACE admired her reflection in the cheval glass in her mother's bedroom. It was her favorite mirror in the flat, and if she angled it just so, she could see her narrow back in the wardrobe door. She had insisted on wearing her hair loose, refusing to have it pinned in some unflattering chignon. She was learning fast what suited her. She was learning to enjoy herself and the startling effect she knew she could create. She was especially going to enjoy today. The day would belong to Amy, of course, her sister, the bride. But she would still be noticed, and the thought gave her an intense pleasure.

Lucy watched her for a moment through the doorway but then stepped back quickly so as not to be seen. She smiled to herself at her daughter's teenage vanity. Picking up Amy's bouquet from the table in the hall, she lifted the white roses to her face and breathed in deeply. She touched them gently with what looked to Amy, who was now standing silently beside her, like nostalgia.

"They don't really smell, Ma." Amy stood in a pose of expectancy, her elegant dress sheathing her body, her dark hair crowned with flowers. "I'm glad they don't. It might be too much."

Lucy smiled. "Yes, darling. It might be. But they're beautiful." She handed the display to her daughter, who took it in one hand.

There was a sound of footsteps from the corridor, and Lucy's sister, Jane, appeared, looking self-conscious in a pale blue dress and coat and a small feathered hat. "Will I do?" she asked, a trace of New Zealand in her voice. "The bride won't be ashamed of her provincial aunt?" Jane turned to Lucy. "Doesn't she look just fantastic?"

"She does," Lucy said, beaming at her daughter.

"You must both have said that at least four times," Amy said, "and under normal circumstances I would be wild with irritation. But today you can repeat yourselves as much as you like."

She smiled at them both. She couldn't stop smiling this morning, which felt strange to her. She had been deeply touched by Jane making the journey from New Zealand for her wedding. But as she'd spent some time with her mother and aunt this week, she had understood that her marriage was a kind of confirmation for them. It was an assurance that they'd managed to pave a way for happiness in a family that had once lost its footing.

"Where's Grace?" said Jane.

"I'm here," Grace said from behind them, picking up her flowers. She stood next to Amy waiting for her compliments.

"You look lovely, sweetheart," said her mother. "But you always do."

"Sweet fifteen," Jane offered.

"Yes," said Amy. "You look wonderful, Grace. Just try not to upstage me."

"No one could do that today, darling," said Lucy. "Could they, Jane?"

"They certainly couldn't."

Grace smiled. She was almost as tall as her sister now, and would overtake her. She loved her family. She loved Amy and their sister, Thea, who had gone on ahead to the church. She wouldn't upstage Amy, but today felt like her debut and she knew she would shine.

"Are you ready, Grace?" asked Amy. "Surely you and Jane should be going?"

Left alone with her daughter, Lucy took her hand.

"I want to ask you something, darling," she said.

"You're not going to cry, Ma, are you?"

"No," said Lucy. "Tears aren't for happiness, whatever people say. I just wanted to ask you one last time. Are you sure about me giving you away today? We could still ask Uncle John."

"I was the one that asked you, Ma. And anyway, isn't unconventional expected of us?" Amy tried to joke. She wasn't sure what had brought on Lucy's questions. Her mother was rarely given to doubt. She paused before continuing. "And I'm sure that's what Dad would have wanted."

"Yes," said Lucy, "I think he would." She looked suddenly more cheerful. "Time to go, then. We mustn't keep a good man waiting."

꒰꒱

As the two men entered the church through the small garden door, James paused for a moment, and Archie knew that his friend had at last grasped the sense of occasion. The church was almost full, the range of colors of both guests and flowers almost shocking in intensity. There was a low hum of chatter and goodwill, of anticipation and recognition as friends spotted one another across pews and families acknowledged their rarely seen cousins and newly grown-up nephews and nieces.

"There's still time to change your mind," Archie joked. He'd said the same thing early that morning when he'd found his friend throwing up in the bathroom, but James had claimed excitement rather than alcohol or doubt.

"It's okay," said James, "I'm fine. It's just . . . I want to take it all in. I want to remember it."

"Very good." Archie pushed him forward. "I, on the other hand, will be happy to forget, at least until after my speech. But it will soon be over. Then we can get drunk, or I can."

James looked across the pews, anonymous for a moment in the shelter of a pillar. These were his friends and family who were delighted for him. They trusted his choice. His gaze turned to Amy's side, her immediate family not present yet but their seats reserved, and he felt an extended pleasure as he gazed at the spaces they would fill. He loved Amy's family, not because there was a lack of warmth in his own, but because they exuded a waywardness he'd come to enjoy.

He found his way to the front pew, followed by Archie, nodding and smiling at their friends, smirking at the absurdity of their situation.

"So this is it, mate, the end of the road," whispered Archie.

"I'll still be around, you know," said James.

"What?"

"Just because I'm getting married, it doesn't mean . . ."

"What?"

"That we won't be mates."

"Well, we won't be getting drunk and picking up women, if that's what you mean."

"We haven't done that for years," said James, who wasn't sure he ever had.

"Not together," agreed Archie.

"We'll still be . . . us."

"What?" said Archie. He was worried his friend was growing maudlin. He stared at his order of service program—"Amy and James," it said on the front.

"Never mind," James said. "It doesn't matter."

"It's just nerves, Jimbo. Here she comes." As they turned to the back of the church, he, too, gazed across the ranks of their friends and family, the empty pew opposite now occupied by a single figure, her face hidden from him beneath her veiled hat, her crossed legs exposed above midthigh in her silk ruffled dress. The other sister, he thought, the one he hadn't met, the one who wouldn't be a brides-maid; well, he couldn't blame her for that. He saw, too, James's par-ents and sisters, who'd been almost his own, and Archie felt a part of it all in a way that surprised and pleased him.

The church organ's music began to inflate over the congregation, and James turned now to see his bride standing in the doorway; her mother, Lucy, next to her, upright and composed. Fussing about Amy was Grace, whose pale red hair swept artfully across the cool pale bridal dress. And now they were all three walking toward him, looking, thought James suddenly, like a benign coven that might conjure up the unexpected.

"You're doing the right thing, Jimbo," Archie whispered to him; right for James if not for him, he thought, as he watched James grin, unforced, in traditional style. "You can enjoy feeling smug," he con-tinued. "She's beautiful. I could almost marry her myself."

"Too bad for you that she's taken, then," said James, and just for an instant Archie wished it was him standing in James's place, wait-ing for the tall young woman with the stunning breasts that were curving toward him through the creamy fabric of her dress.

As Amy stopped and turned toward James, her smile seemed to encompass them both and Archie felt a rare flush of shame. She'd never aroused him before, though he could appreciate her cool restrained beauty. He preferred a more surface sexuality, something that didn't require excavation. This late moment of lust must be down to the occasion, to the virginal white, he reasoned to himself, and he wanted, just for a second, for the whole thing to stop, along with the nonsense in his head. He liked Amy, he told himself; he respected her. They were getting to know each other, as they both knew they must if they were to preserve James intact, and he knew that was what James had been trying to say, even as he had said the opposite. He, Archie, would need to be their friend now. He watched his friend squeeze Amy's hand as she glided beside him. He could feel the intense pleasure of their connection, and, though he knew it was outside his experience, he was happy for them, caught up in the optimism that now swept through the church and congregation, willing the bride and groom into a shining future.

22 NOVEMBER

HARLEY STREET

———

"DID JAMES TELL you he was sick with joy the day he married me?" she'd asked. Patrick McIlhenny wondered if he'd missed some signal or even a simple piece of information in the moment he'd allowed himself to drift away. He was unsure how to interpret this strange assumption that he knew her cast of characters.

"No," he said, "I don't think so." He was playing for time, searching her presence, her movements, even her shadow, for signs of dislocation.

"But tell me about him, why don't you?"

She'd seemed almost hostile as she'd thrown out her question, but now she was quiet again, her tone courteous.

"I married him twenty years ago," she said, her eyes sweeping the walls behind him as if looking for an exit to the past. "A proper wedding. They were all there, Ma and Thea, Grace, James's parents, their friends, our friends, and Archie, of course."

Patrick nodded. She was laying out her list, setting them up, he suspected, for the part she didn't yet know they'd played.

"I hadn't meant to talk about my wedding," she said, "but you have to start somewhere?" She looked up as if seeking agreement.

"It doesn't matter," he replied, "where you start."

"No? Why do you say that?"

Because, Patrick thought, wherever you start, it will end up at the point you intended.

"Let's just see where it takes us for now," he said.

She seemed satisfied with his answer and smoothed down her hair in preparation to proceed.

"I'll start with Archie, then," she said. "He was James's closest friend, and in those first few months, after we married, I thought that he might make things difficult. He was almost jealous, I felt, though he tried not to show it." She stopped herself and seemed to be checking her statement against some mental outline. "He had no real family here to speak of by the time I met him. He'd been at school with James, and his mother died while he was there. I've always thought how sad that was, his mother dying, him being an only child and her an American, and it all being so complicated. He and James were almost like brothers, closer if anything. He'd stay with the family sometimes, during the school holidays. And he was so handsome, Archie—well, they both were to my mind, but Archie was really very good-looking, in a confident, half-American way, and then he was rich, of course—family money. That gave him a sort of carelessness that was attractive, though he was sharp underneath. James, on the other hand . . ." She stopped for a moment and for the first time took a sip of water from the glass on the table in front of her. "James was always more . . . focused."

Her own focus was far away, thought Patrick, away through the building's fabric, to the end of the street, across the park to infinity. He watched her as she put down her glass carefully, as if the reconnection of its base with the table would solidify some fluid thought.

"I can remember so clearly walking toward them both, with my mother, and seeing their faces, seeing James so happy and then Archie's face, vulnerable he looked that day, and I made a decision that he would be part of our family, that I would take him in." As she spoke, her body softened, as if to accommodate a ghostly third party; then she sat up straight once more.

"We were so lucky. Really." She sounded as if she was pleading her case, and Patrick felt perhaps the time had come to interrupt, but she rushed on before he could speak.

"I had my children quickly, of course. I didn't mind, I was young, it was all still open to me and I had every intention of—. Then suddenly I was thirty and it was like the striking of a clock in a fairy tale, and I think that was when our life began to shift, I see now, shift very slowly at first, but shift all the same."

Patrick leaned forward to sip from his own glass, conscious of his reflective movement. The moment for intervention had passed him by, he was caught in her narrative, struggling to regain the detachment he required to assess her.

"What's that?" she asked, pointing at a small marble statue of a woman standing on the windowsill, arms outstretched.

"It's a goddess," he said, grateful for the interruption and the chance to regroup. "A minor Greek deity, I've forgotten the name, something to do with the wind. It's a copy, of course."

"The wind," she said. "How appropriate."

"So you feel, or you felt," he went on, concerned not to lose this moment, "that you were shifting?"

She laughed.

"No, not me, not at first. I had the children to ground me. It was all the others. My in-laws, my sisters, my friends, Archie especially . . . they had all started to shift around. Nothing seemed stable anymore. Except for James, of course." She stopped, making some quick adjustment to her story. "At least I'd thought he was, but by the end I'd begun to detect movement even in him. It was," she waved her hand toward the windowsill, "rather as if a wind had started to blow and they wouldn't stop whirling about, and it all went on for years until . . ."

"Until?" he said, confused by the onslaught of characters dropped into the narrative as if they were familiar to him, as if he himself were a part of their story.

"That week," she said. "Ten years ago. That's why I'm here."

1994

=====

"THE BEGINNING IS THE HALF OF EVERY ACTION."

from *Lifelines for the Living* by Lucy Fielding

AS HE SAT in the doctor's waiting room that Friday morning, Archie considered his decision to come alone. Would he have preferred someone sitting next to him, holding his hand? He found it hard to be sure, but probably yes, on balance, depending, of course, on who that someone was. He was aware of being watched by a small Asian boy who was picking his nose with one hand while hanging on to his mother with the other. There weren't many people in yet, but it was early. He picked up an old copy of a women's magazine with a smiling girl in a low-cut shirt and a push-up bra on the cover. She looked a bit like Greta; she was smiling like Greta did most of the time. It had irritated him sometimes, her determined cheerfulness, but just now the memory was appealing. He found it hard to recall the anger that had flooded him as he'd closed the door of his flat behind her on Wednesday. It was there, of course, somewhere, but the feeling had been elbowed out, shoved aside for the moment by more immediate matters.

He'd been the first person to arrive at his local clinic. When he gave his name to the receptionist, she asked him to confirm his address in such a way that he half expected her to check that his symptoms qualified for the appointment. She had the faux tough, defensive manner of people who spend their days in contact with the vulnerable and volatile, and he began to wish he'd consulted a private general practitioner, a route he'd up till now regarded as unnecessary for the minor treatments and vaccinations that had been all he required from the profession. But then he saw his doctor scurry in.

"Good morning, Doctor," said the receptionist. She handed him a stack of notes. "The first one's already here," she said, inclining her head toward Archie. Her voice was disapproving, but whether at Archie's punctuality or the doctor's lateness, Archie had no idea. It could only be five minutes either way. The doctor glanced briefly at him and headed up the stairs; there was barely time to scan his magazine for lingerie ads when the receptionist struck again.

"Mr. Morgan?"

Archie got to his feet.

"You can go up now," she said. "Dr. Sabir. First on the right."

As he emerged from the clinic, his appointment card in his hand, Archie realized it was still only 9:30, and time stretched ahead without a single fixed point to anchor it. He couldn't go home, Greta was coming. He wished now he'd put the few clothes and the bathroom stuff she'd left in a bag and dumped it outside his door, or arranged to put it in a taxi to her flat.

Dr. Sabir had been noncommittal. It might be just a cyst, he'd said, sounding unconvinced, but all the same it was to be taken seriously, one couldn't exclude the possibility of malignancy, and he'd arranged for Archie to go for a further consultation the following Monday.

"Do you have private insurance, Mr. Morgan?" he'd asked.

"Yes," Archie had said, forcing himself to be as matter-of-fact as the doctor. "At least I think so."

The doctor had waited for a further reply, this clearly not being conclusive.

"I'm about to part company with my company." Archie had smiled without conviction.

"And it's a company insurance policy?"

"Yes." Archie had thought quickly. "But I haven't gone yet so there's no problem." Another complication he hadn't foreseen, but it hardly mattered. The truth was he'd pay himself, if necessary.

"That's good. We can get you seen quickly. Today, possibly, if you like?"

Archie had considered this proposition. He probably should go today, whatever today was. It was Friday, he'd recalled.

"Would Monday make any difference?"

"No," Dr. Sabir had said. "Not really. It's up to you."

"Let's make it Monday, then."

He'd been relieved initially by the reprieve. One session of prodding and poking was quite enough, and he hoped he wouldn't have to get used to it. As he wandered up the wide avenue toward the local cafés and shops, past the late commuters on their way to the Tube station, the implications of his diagnosis began to kick in, and he considered for a moment turning back to ask to be seen by a consultant that afternoon, but it seemed too late now to change his mind. He reached Abbey Road, which looked deserted, but as he crossed he was almost knocked flat by a large seven-seater with darkened windows that swung out suddenly, at full speed, from a mansion block driveway. He sat down in surprise on a low wall, shaken by his escape, and he felt the intimations of an early demise, which had been creeping around the edge of his consciousness, sweep in and claim their territory.

An elderly woman, pulling a small, reluctant terrier, arrived at the scene of his confusion. She stood looking at him for a few moments, almost at eye level.

"You're all right, then," she said, having made her assessment. "They shouldn't have that driveway there, so close to the crossing. Not that she was looking. Foreign, I expect."

Archie found himself unable to speak. He stared back at her, trying to summon an all-purpose, public smile.

"You've had a bit of a shock, I expect," she said, as the dog sniffed his shoes. "These things upset you more than you think."

She pulled the dog sharply and carried on down the road, looking back a couple of times to see if he'd moved. As she reached the crossroads, she raised her hand before she walked around the corner. Archie stood up and waved back.

SHE'D been right, thought Archie twenty minutes later, when he'd settled himself outside a patisserie. He'd had a bit of a shock; a lot of a shock, in fact. He had hoped that the general practitioner would tell him there was nothing to be worried about, without any note of reservation, but whichever way he rearranged the conversation in his head, he couldn't make the doctor's words say what he wanted. There were further aftershocks, too, and consequences, which Archie observed in himself from a strange, detached perspective as he ordered a double macchiato. He found himself considering the possibility that the old woman with the dog might now live longer than him, something that certainly would not have occurred to him before this morning. But then again, he might just as easily have been killed by the car. He bit into a *pain aux raisins* but couldn't register its sweetness. He looked around him at the elderly clientele enjoying their coffee and pastries on this sunny Friday morning, and he tried to think logically. Everyone, of course, would die, everyone—Amy, James, the many people he knew whom he considered his friends, the people at work, his assistant, Gemma, for example, even Richard Armstrong—it was just a question of when: sooner or later. He tried to concentrate on a future he'd never given much thought to but that had always existed as part of a greater ambition. But the thought now had an independent existence and grew against his will, crowding out the good stuff in his life, like the thing inside him that had spawned it: he didn't want to be the first to die; he didn't want to go just yet; he needed time to get used to the idea.

He pulled his mobile from his pocket, ignored it for several moments, then tried James's number. He had a sudden desire to see his oldest friend, a desire for a form of coded contact, not direct conversation but a reassuring, animal backslap.

It was Katy, James's PA, who answered his phone.

"He's out," she said. "At a meeting. And then he's going straight to lunch. Sorry. He'll be back around three. Shall I say you rang?"

"Yes. No, tell him I'll probably see him over the weekend. No need to ring back."

Pity, thought Archie. He was feeling stronger now, more like himself: a dose of his friend's amused intelligence would have settled him nicely. The great thing about James was that nothing ever fazed him. Archie smiled as he heaved himself out of his seat and went to the counter to pay. You could crack a joke, even when he wasn't there, and guess that he'd be smiling.

EVEN with both windows wide open, the taxi felt unbearably hot, and as it drove through east London, James found himself thinking of his garden and the leafy road he lived on, and how glad he was that he lived in the west where trees grew along the streets relieving the city of some of its brutality. He'd been sharp enough to get by in the morning's meeting, but part of his mind had been distracted. He wasn't now, strictly speaking, going out for lunch; he was going instead, on the recommendation of an American colleague, and to his own disbelief, to see a shrink at an address in the back end of Hoxton. It was an alien wasteland full of lost souls, he thought, looking around for a ghost or two among the solid pedestrians as he paid the fare, and one that no amount of cultural spin could rescue.

James liked to think of himself, on the inside at least, as not conforming to the usual City type. His flair for finance had brought him a good living, and he enjoyed the sharpness of banking. But he was quietly pleased that his friends and his family (especially his mother-in-law, to whom he was particularly grateful on this account) inhabited a less formal, even Bohemian, world. Nonetheless, he was finding it difficult to come to terms with his current position, sitting face-to-face with a hungry-looking person called Patrick in what appeared to be the spare bedroom of a small flat. At one end of the room, there was a large leather recliner that took up a disproportionate amount of space and that James felt reluctant to occupy.

His relaxed, smiling posture veiled a discomfort. This wasn't what he had expected. He'd always imagined that shrinks dressed up their sanctums with books and totemic objects, safe, semi-ecclesiastical spaces in which confession, of a kind, came easy. But this? He looked around at the bed with its cover that looked like an old curtain and the poster on the wall of some long-forgotten exhibition. It reminded him of university life, of student trips to drug dealers, clandestine and furtive transactions.

He was far too well brought up to reveal this dismay; Patrick came well recommended, and it was James's habit to reserve judgment. He lowered himself into the chair, smiling at Patrick, a man about five years younger than him with a day's growth of beard, but Patrick didn't smile back.

"I don't know why I'm here, really," said James. *How many times must he have heard that before?* he thought. Patrick said nothing. James closed his eyes and cursed the colleague who'd sung the guy's praises. He should have realized he was mad, mad to be coming here in the first place; he should have spotted the flaw in the logic. He opened his eyes and faced it out.

"Are you one of those that says nothing?" he asked.

This time Patrick smiled.

"I say things," said Patrick, whose voice had a Belfast lilt. "I'll say this. You don't want to be here. You don't want to see a therapist, and you didn't like the look of the street outside when you came in."

"I wouldn't go that far," said James, upset that his manners had betrayed him and that he might have caused offense. Any notion of confrontation eluded him.

"I'm not a doctor, James. The symptoms that we discussed on the telephone may be specific," said Patrick, "but they are unlikely to be physical or clinical, given that you have, you tell me, already had a physical checkup. This is not a consulting room, and it's not a man in a white coat that you need. Or a pill."

"I certainly don't want pills," agreed James, glad to find mutual territory.

Patrick smiled at him again and sat in a small armchair opposite James.

"Then let's start," he said. "Talk me through the problem from the beginning."

Sitting back in the big chair, his legs extended slightly by the bar at the bottom, James remembered that he didn't like beginnings much. As he recounted the chain of recent events at work that had brought him to Hoxton, a picture of him and Archie hovered somewhere above and to the left, the two of them unknown to each other, at the start of his first term at their boarding school. He saw Archie stepping smartly up the slope in his uniform, waving goodbye at a receding car, while he stood quiet and frozen next to his mother. He'd been twelve years old.

He'd been happy living at home with his parents, but he was looking forward to a new chapter, fueled by out-of-date literature, books whose schoolboy heroes solved crimes at midnight and exposed foreign spies. His mother had bought a large green trunk to accommodate the ever-growing piles of required clothing. He could remember them packing and repacking it together, and he would sit on it expectantly, as if it contained his future. But as he'd stood on the steps that first afternoon, on the brink of the great adventure, and watched his father laughing with a group of men who swept up the trunk into the dark interior, he knew he was about to lose something precious and that it had been a mistake to imagine the future as a happy extension of his past.

James was aware of Patrick's gaze as these images floated between them. Part of him wanted to tell Patrick, this stranger, that only recently he'd dreamed about the trunk, dreamed that it had been left somewhere, stored in a distant school annex, and had to be retrieved. But he couldn't seem to find it; and when he did, it had burst wide open, and he'd been unable to force it once more to contain all the contents that had spilled out around him in a sea of anxiety. But he pushed the thought away. It would be a waste of their time to tell this to Patrick; that wasn't, after all, why he was here.

࿔

ONCE every two months, James's wife, Amy, had lunch with her sister Grace. They saw each other, naturally, from time to time, outside this routine, but Amy had insisted, in the years since Grace had left drama school, on a more regular private arrangement, quality time during which, she told herself, she could attempt to head off danger. She thought she saw in Grace an unsteadiness beneath the bright ambition. It was a trait she recognized in herself, but one that had been corralled in her own case, she liked to think, by the stability and comfort of her marriage.

She could see her sister in the distance, hurrying down the half-deserted street, and though the local population had been culled by the holiday exit, she could see that heads were turning. Ever since Grace had reached her teens, Amy had noticed that people, men especially, were watching her with increasing interest.

"You should see Grace," she'd heard James once say to Archie, soon after they'd met. "Amy's got this stunning sister. She's fifteen."

"She's quite something," Archie had said, when he finally met Grace at James and Amy's engagement party, and had felt his age for the first time as he calculated the gap between himself and the teenage beauty. "And so much younger than you," he went on to

Amy, unable to leave the subject alone. "What happened? Did your parents have a second honeymoon?"

"Something like that," Amy'd said. But it wasn't like that at all.

Now Grace was almost twenty-five, the same age, thought Amy, as she had been when she married James. They were sitting in a restaurant that opened out, in the summer weather, onto the street. Grace had been late, of course, but Amy always remembered to take a book to read so that their lunches wouldn't begin badly.

"Sorry," Grace said, "my agent rang just as I was leaving."

"And how is Maggie?" said Amy, who liked Grace's agent, regarding her as a suitable motherly figure.

"No, I'm changing agents. I thought I'd told you?" Grace adjusted her sunglasses. "I'm moving to Peter Casey. He's more . . . international."

She was wearing a pink cotton dress and white shoes, which should have looked common, thought Amy, but on Grace looked almost elegant. She was physically quite different from her sister with her red-gold hair and the look of a Pre-Raphaelite princess, and Amy was only a little bit jealous, the ten-year age gap between them being sufficient for her to take pride in Grace's glamour.

"So what's your news?" said Grace. She scanned the menu, then waved it at a passing waiter. "I'll have a Kir Royale," she said. "What are you having?"

"A Virgin Mary and a large bottle of sparkling water, please," Amy addressed the waiter directly.

Grace looked sulky. "I hope you're not going to give me a lecture," she said.

"What about?"

"Drinking at lunchtime."

"Why ever would I do that? Don't change the subject. Tell me about the new agent."

Grace hesitated, anticipating her sister's disapproval. Amy didn't care for change of any sort. It upset her. It took, she'd once said, too much time to catch up with herself, but Grace hadn't understood.

"Well, he rang me a couple of weeks ago and asked if I'd like to meet up with him. He said he admired what I was doing and—"

"Well, he would, wouldn't he?" said Amy.

Grace was under no illusions about her sister's view of her current role in a popular soap opera.

"—and—I refuse to allow you to spoil my moment," said Grace, "—and, or, 'but,' I think was the word he actually used, didn't I think it was time to move on to something bigger."

"What does he have in mind?" said Amy.

"Don't be like that."

"Like what? No, honestly, what does he have in mind? I'm not against it. Who else does he represent?"

"Good people, names. Katherine Jamieson, Sam Harris . . ."

"I'm impressed," said Amy.

"I'm seeing Sam, in fact." Grace sounded nervous and excited.

"I'm even more impressed," said Amy. She'd seen Sam Harris in the last film she'd been to, and suddenly realized it was at least three months ago. She and James used to go frequently. She hadn't noticed that their habit had stopped.

"But that's not why I've changed agents," Grace added.

"So you've said yes," said Amy.

"Yes, last week."

"Have you told Maggie?"

Grace pulled the face she always did when contemplating something unpleasant that had to be taken care of. It registered both distaste and resolution. Amy was reminded, not for the first time, that the protective role she'd assigned to herself was largely out of date.

"Let's talk about something else," said Grace. "Let's talk about you."

"Me? There's nothing to say."

"Don't be like that, there must be something interesting happening in your life." Grace sounded unconvinced.

"I think I'm pregnant," Amy said. "Well, I don't think so. I am."

She hadn't intended to tell Grace. She hadn't told anyone. She hadn't told James.

Grace sat back in the basket chair, summer issue for lunch on the street.

"No," she said.

"I'm afraid so."

"But that's great news," said Grace. "Surely?"

"I haven't decided," said Amy.

"You're not going to get rid of it?"

Amy looked shocked, but it was at the harshness of the phrasing rather than the sentiment. Why shouldn't she think about not having the baby? It was her life and she'd only just got it back. But her instinct told her to keep the idea to herself.

"I shouldn't think so. I meant I haven't decided whether it's great news or not."

Grace leaned forward and lowered her voice. "It is James's, isn't it?"

Amy laughed. "Oh, yes. My life's not that exciting."

"Well, you never know," said Grace. "You don't fool me." She smiled at her sister as she sipped her champagne.

"What do you mean?" said Amy.

"You can still pull when you want to," said Grace. "I've seen you. I'd say old James should watch out, though I suppose now he's got you pregnant again he needn't worry."

Amy had felt briefly uplifted by Grace's teasing, but the latter part of the observation chimed too closely with her sense of impending confinement.

"He's not old and I think I will have a drink after all," said Amy.

She felt scrutinized by her sister, whose antennae for complication were sensitive. It was only recently that Amy had congratulated herself on the current state of her life. Her marriage and children were on track, settled and happy, as far as she could tell, which meant in comparison with those of other people, but there'd been no sense of joy when she'd tested positive for pregnancy. She supposed she was still in shock. She looked around the restaurant at the smartly dressed, affluent customers who exuded a competence and confidence that she'd always aspired to. She felt she was one of them, about to produce another, and she wasn't sure that it was such a good idea. It was more in defiance than celebration that she found herself drinking champagne, but then one glass wouldn't shrink the baby, she thought, and Grace had something to celebrate. Amy felt, for a brief moment, like cheering. She smiled at her sister across the table, mentally willing her on to success.

"Here's to Peter what's-his-name."

"Casey," said Grace.

"Peter Casey."

"There's something else you should know, Amy."

Grace's tone raised a tension between them and Amy braced herself.

"What?"

"Thea rang me last week. She's coming home."

Amy put her glass down.

"Oh," she said. And then, "I thought she was staying on in L.A., even though—"

"Even though the engagement was off. I thought so, too," said Grace.

Amy said nothing.

"Aren't you curious at least?" said Grace.

"I know so little about it," said Amy. "It's hard to be interested."

"I don't believe you."

"We should order," said Amy. "It's half past one already."

Amy's affectation of detachment fooled neither of them. Thea was her twin.

She stared past Grace, watching the people on the street who seemed to divide into those whose steps were determined, and the rest, whose movements had nowhere to go. Despite their estrangement, she'd been going to write a letter when she'd heard that Thea was getting married. It was half drafted in her mind, a letter of congratulation and appeal, heartfelt and emollient, but that had been ten months ago, and not long afterward she'd heard that it had all gone wrong, and she knew a note from her would be unwelcome.

Such a shame, as their mother, Lucy, frequently remarked (without, it seemed to some, an appropriate regret), that no sooner had Amy and Thea discovered the fun of being twins, they'd stumbled on the drawbacks.

She took a cab home. She was hot and flushed with champagne and the exchange of unexpected news. So Grace had a new boyfriend. Amy had noted the triumph as well as the anticipation beneath Grace's usual vampish cool, and she felt a moment of envy at her sister's excitement, at the ripples of a newly engaged sexuality. For her such immediacy of experience could be only a memory, or a fantasy. She leaned back in her seat and recalled an image of Sam Harris from the film she'd seen, a teasing and erotic seduction, and she tried to put her husband in Harris's place. But he wouldn't hold still, and she found him replaced by their friend Archie, and then she wasn't sure who the woman in the picture was, but it wasn't her any longer and she didn't like to look too closely. As the taxi cruised through the warm streets, she felt suddenly suburban, old at thirty-four. She distracted herself with her mental list. She had to pick up the meat and chicken for tomorrow's barbecue, and she must remember to get some sausages. Her children loved sausages, and so did Archie, whom she would invite. A wave of nausea passed through her body. She shouldn't have drunk the glass of champagne. Her head was full of sex and flesh, and now Thea was coming home.

꙳

ARCHIE'S adult life so far had been a flow of energetic hedonism interspersed with a living that he'd tailored to suit his needs. He'd long grown out of drinking excessively, or thought he had, but the new set of circumstances that seemed suddenly against him had given him license to regress, and he was already on his third lager. He wouldn't usually have turned to Amy, or indeed to anyone, until he had constructed at least a partial challenge to the physical and mental ambush that had overtaken him. But she had rung to invite him to supper the next evening and had picked up the panic in his voice. He wouldn't tell her everything, he'd reassured himself, but he could see it might help to make a start, and James, after all, had proved elusive that day.

He'd arrived early for their rendezvous at the pub they often went to in Little Venice. Its ornate Edwardian facade and grand interior had led to the rumor that the bar had once been a brothel, but these days, thought Archie, no one got paid, except in drinks, and sex was usually off the premises. The evening was hot and humid, and there was quite a crowd on the far side of the courtyard, but Amy had found him on a secluded bench in a corner behind the raised porch door.

"So," he said, after he told her about Greta, "it's all becoming a bit of a mess. Not a great way to celebrate my fortieth."

"But you're not forty yet," said Amy, unsure how to proceed in light of Archie's reversal of fortune. "Not for ages."

"Near enough, in November," he said.

"That's ages away. You've been saying you're forty for months. Why do you keep doing that?" said Amy, whose half-drunk spritzer was now warm and flat. "It just means you'll be forty for two years instead of one."

Archie smiled at her. She was a pragmatist, he thought, like her husband, though he knew there were times when the capable Madonna could make mischief.

"That's the least of my problems," he said, and Amy was obliged to agree.

"If it's any consolation," she said, "I never really thought Greta was right for you, not long term."

"You didn't say so." Archie was used to Amy's lack of regard for his women and was often amused by it, but this evening he took mild umbrage at the slur. "I always thought the two of you had things in common." He picked up his beer and, seeing the expression on her face, took a large swallow. "I thought you got on rather well," he corrected himself.

"She's a laugh," said Amy, "and I made an effort for your sake. But James and I both thought she was a bit shallow."

Archie looked down into his glass.

"Thick, you mean," he said.

"No, shallow. She's not thick," said Amy. "If you thought she was thick you were way off."

"I didn't think she was thick, I thought you did," he said.

"No, she's smart. Smart but shallow." Amy pushed her dark hair back behind her ears again.

"Well, I'm glad we've cleared that up."

Amy pushed her glass to and fro, reluctant to drink. Archie wanted her full attention, but he sensed it slipping away, back to Finlay Road, to her husband and her children. He could usually reclaim it with ease, with some anecdote, some absurd entanglement that his curiosity or sense of adventure had led to, but tonight his supply appeared to be low. "Smart, yes," he went on. "Smart enough to shaft me before I saw it coming."

Amy raised her head, drawn back in by the confession.

"I usually like to bail out first. As you know."

She smiled at him, a warm, familiar smile. It cheered him up through his beer and growing panic.

"What?" he said. "What are you smiling at?"

"Maybe you didn't want to bail out this time?"

"No," he said, "I was just preoccupied."

It was true and not true at the same time. He was certainly preoccupied. For one thing, the business he'd started six years before, with energy and optimism, had finally run out of cash. He would shortly have to tell his staff that both the travel magazines he published were on their last issues. But where Greta was concerned he'd been unaware of any problem. He'd been quite happy, if occasionally bored, and possibly even ready to settle. And in his complacency, this cold wave had crept up on him. It was odd, he thought, how crises surfaced, though all surprises had their own history, just ones he wasn't privy to, or hadn't noticed. He looked across at Amy, and he wanted to tell her all of it, to weep in front of her, here in the pub, but that was out of the question. He raised his glass to his lips, his mind elsewhere as she comforted him.

It was easier to nurse the pain of Greta than to contemplate his business failings. She'd arrived at the flat on Wednesday night, her hair plastered to her head by the summer evening rain. "Poor baby," he'd said, kissing her as he gently patted her thick damp hair with a towel. She'd pulled it to her shoulders and moved away from him, sitting forward on a leather armchair as if waiting for her stylist in a salon. He'd squatted in front of her, pulling at the tendrils on her neck, and he remembered observing just before she spoke that the hair clinging to her scalp leant her a sculptured look, an unexpected seriousness.

"Could I have a glass of wine?" She said it without smiling, without the gaiety that usually arrived with her.

"Yes, sure. What do you want? Champagne? I've got some champagne in the fridge." He hadn't seen her for several days; she'd been away on location, for some advertising shoot. He was surprised how pleased he was to see her, and he felt like celebrating.

"No, not champagne," she said.

"What's up?" Archie tried to recall his most recent failings. He knew he wasn't good at calling when he said he would, but only because his attention had got caught elsewhere. He handed her a glass of wine.

"I can't come with you," she said. "On Saturday. To France."

Archie laughed. "Well, I'm not going without you." He was looking forward to the week, to getting out of London, to staying at the hotel in the Loire where he liked to take his girlfriends, where his mother had once taken him, after the divorce.

Greta sighed. "What I mean is, I don't think we should go on seeing each other."

He heard what she said, and he registered somewhere outside himself that he had never had this conversation before. He'd used his own clichés, of course, as he'd made his several exits. But things were different, on the receiving end.

"It's not going anywhere," Greta said, taking a large sip from her glass.

He considered her statement carefully. *She wants me to ask her to live with me,* he thought.

"But it's all arranged," was what he found himself saying.

"I don't care," she said. "You go. Take a friend. I'm sorry, Archie."

He'd thought Greta might be different. Amy was right, she was shallow, but the sort of shallow he'd decided he could live with, that he rather liked. He found it untaxing, and she was fun, a party girl without malice, and she cheered him up, an antidote to something disturbing he couldn't quite name, but that seemed to have fallen slowly into step with him over the last few years.

"I don't think we're really suited, do you?" She gulped some more wine.

"Since when?" asked Archie. Of all the things she might have said, this seemed absurd. And then his brain re-engaged and his focus returned. "You've met someone else."

"No."

"I don't believe you."

"Well. Yes and no," she said. "But it wasn't going anywhere, Archie."

"I think you'd better go," he said, and stood up.

Greta got up to face him, placing the towel carefully over the back of the chair.

"I'm really sorry, Archie," she said, picking up her bag and fiddling with the clasp.

She walked past him quickly and out into the hallway, and he shut the door behind her.

That had been on Wednesday. That was how it had begun for him. He'd drunk the rest of the bottle of wine, then almost a quarter of a bottle of whiskey, and passed out. On Thursday morning he'd overslept.

SITTING with Amy in the pub, it was just as it had often been over the last decade, sometimes with friends, sometimes the three of them, sometimes just Archie with one or the other, trading news and the small irritations of life. But tonight he felt overwhelmed by the impetus of fate, and the pub felt too small to contain the big numbness he felt.

"But you've known for a while that things couldn't continue as they were?" Amy was asking him a question, and he wasn't quite sure what they'd been talking about. He thought for a moment that they were still on Greta and was on the point of a strong denial, but then he realized she'd moved on, that she was referring to his visit to his accountant the day before, with a hellish hangover, only to be told that any idea of keeping his magazines in print was absurd. The venture was over.

"Yes, I suppose I knew," said Archie, in answer to her question. "But I'd hoped there was another chance, you know. I just needed some cash fast." He observed that he was laying his problems before her in reverse order of their significance to him.

"Maybe it's time for a change," said Amy. "Do something different."

"I just couldn't believe Richard wouldn't help me out," said Archie, who wasn't ready yet to match her pragmatism.

He was waving one arm around in the air as he'd always done, in a sort of imitation of his old self, she thought, as if he was telling her the sort of story that made you laugh and remember you were glad that he was your friend. She felt moved by his confidences, by his unfamiliar distress.

"I lent him the cash, after all, to set him up when he needed it, didn't I?" Amy nodded. "But he just sat there and said it would be throwing good money after bad, that I'd lost interest—'disaffected' was the word he used—and I'd be better to pack it in."

It wasn't the money, he thought. It wasn't the twenty grand that rankled. After all, he'd had a good return on an investment he could well afford at the time.

Richard's company, a marketing outfit, had turned out a great success. It was the success, he supposed, that made the withholding so cutting.

"It does seem unfair," said Amy, thinking that Richard was sharp and probably right. "James and I have never been quite sure about Richard. And he's probably short of money since the divorce."

"He can be a two-faced shit," Archie agreed, but he didn't believe her entirely. He was sure that James, at least, liked Richard. He'd certainly seemed to over the years, on their boys' nights out, and with James what you saw was what you got. And as for Richard's divorce—it was a couple of years ago at least, there were no children, and his wife had had plenty of money of her own. He picked up his empty glass. "I need another drink."

Amy watched him as he weaved his way through the crowd that hovered around the pub courtyard. She felt frightened for him, frightened that Archie might be tiring of his charmed existence; that for some time the effortless energy of his younger years had been slowly receding and his self-deprecation, often so attractive, had turned into something more fearful. It unnerved her and summoned a presentiment of other losses. She'd come increasingly to rely on Archie as a conduit to another, more interesting world, to flirt with her, to make her laugh when her life seemed taken over by a blood-less domesticity or when her equilibrium was hard to hold steady. This latest vulnerability touched her, disturbing some internal arrange-ment of her affections.

"The irony is I've got the money in theory," he said, returning from the bar. "But it's tied up, and the fucking trustees are of the same view as Richard."

"You'll find something else to do," she said. "You said yourself you were sick of other people traveling at your expense. Now's your chance."

"True. There's nothing much to stay here for," he said, but then he remembered the doctor's appointment and the hospital visit on Monday and had the unfamiliar sensation that he was about to crumble.

"What? What is it?" asked Amy, alarmed at his expression. She reached out across the table and took his arm.

He hadn't intended to tell her.

"I, er . . ." said Archie. "I found a lump in—I found a lump."

"Where?"

He looked slightly past her.

"Is it in your testicle?" she asked.

He looked astonished.

"How do you know?"

"Because you look embarrassed and you've just put your hand near your crotch," she said. "Have you been to the doctor?" She sounded anxious and insistent.

"Yes. This morning."

"And?"

"I'm seeing a specialist on Monday."

"Good," she said, sitting back in her seat. "It's probably nothing. Lots of people have scares."

He could see her processing the information, calculating the odds, searching for the right thing to say. She stared at him for what seemed like ages, lost in some struggle of her own, but then she smiled, as she might at one of her children, and the warmth and intensity of her expression embarrassed him.

"Look," she said, "why don't you come back with me tonight? Talk to James."

"No. Thanks. I need an early night."

She looked away across the crowded courtyard and then back, as if to withdraw a portion of her tenderness.

"Okay," she said, trying to smile. "I understand. You'll come to supper tomorrow, though, won't you? And what about Monday? Would you like me to come with you? Or James would come, I'm sure."

"No, really."

She kept on smiling.

"Then there's nothing we can do until Monday," she said.

HE walked home along the canal where the houseboats lined up beside the towpath. Once, he'd picked up a girl who lived there and woken to see a bargeful of tourists peering in through the window as they cruised toward Regent's Park. It hadn't been one of his finer moments, but he found himself nostalgic this evening. He remembered a certain erotic frenzy and the chaos of limited space. Houseboats weren't for women, or not his sort, with their knickers and stockings and small armies of tubes and bottles. The memory, in conjunction with the vodkas that had chased down his beer, brought a wet self-pity to his eyes, and he lengthened his stride as drops of rain, warm and viscous, began to stick to his hair. He wiped his face with his jacket, crumpled and damp, put it over his head, and ran.

Two streets west was the red-brick mansion block where Archie had lived for the last eight years. His flat was the most solid thing in his life and, short of major subsidence, unlikely to let him down. But in this unaccustomed state of mind, all bad things were possible, and he half expected to see a fire engine on the doorstep or a policeman at the end of the road in the aftermath of a gas explosion. He turned the corner to find all was quiet, the roomy pavements deserted; there was no one to be seen, except for Dr. Sabir in the distance, climbing into his car after a late evening appointment.

He took a beer from the fridge and sat down in front of his outsized television; it didn't matter what was on just as long as it stopped his imagination. There were quite a few messages on his voicemail, but the thought of the several social invitations it undoubtedly contained brought him no pleasure. The damp summer evening made his skin stick to the dark red sofa through his trousers, and he slipped his hand down his crotch. His cock flickered halfheartedly, as if it knew it wasn't the object of his searching fingers. Carefully he felt around his balls. He'd sworn to himself he wouldn't do this. He would leave it alone; wait for the verdict on Monday. But there it was, as he'd known it would be, a hard lump sort of around the back, which he'd thought was just part of the furniture till he noticed it had doubled in size. He pulled his hand out and wiped it on his shirt, though his palm felt dry compared to the rest of him.

"There's nothing we can do until Monday," Amy had said, and Archie had smiled back at her. "*We*," he thought. *There's no "we" in this. I'm on my own.*

2004

22 NOVEMBER
HARLEY STREET

PATRICK COULD HEAR the traffic below the window beginning to stack up as the rush hour or two began its evening expansion. A motorcycle revved and a couple of voices shouted a greeting: the blood couriers, he thought, the local ferrymen who biked your medical tests across the Styx and returned in black leather with your fate. Across from him sat Amy, caught in the stillness of dusk and framed by the light behind her.

She'd frightened him, not at first, but as she'd begun her story, with her fierce and begging question about sickness and joy that he hadn't understood, and that had now retreated. She was married to a James, that much was clear, yet her talk was now of Archie, her focus on this other man, a common and everyday triangle, he found himself assuming, but the adrenaline of her first attack refused to subside.

"When he first told me he might be ill," she said, her voice lowered, "I found myself wanting to hold him close." She folded her arms across her chest to emphasize the physicality of what she was describing. "And for some reason the words of my wedding vows came into my head, 'In sickness and in health,' but it wasn't Archie I was married to, and it smacked of betrayal."

"You felt it a betrayal of your husband?" asked Patrick.

She seemed to dismiss his echo, shaking her head, her voice growing stronger. "It would have been typical of Archie," she said, as if off on an unrelated tack, "to exaggerate his predicament for comic effect, to make me laugh, for my attention, for both those things. But I knew this time that he was frightened, and I suppose that's why he was reluctant at first to tell James. He'd held an image of himself for years as the stronger, even though he'd come to rely on James far more than he knew. James tried to explain it all to me once, a long time ago, that Archie always sort of saw himself out in front. Maybe his balls dropped first or something, I never asked. It's difficult, isn't it, to shake off your early assumptions? But, of course you would think so, that's your trade."

Her last statement had a sudden change of tone, a sharpness, and once again Patrick sensed a current of anger, an advance and retreat.

"Is that how you see me?" he said. "Plying my trade?" He drawled the last word, as she had. He shouldn't be tossing her words back at her in this way. It was a trick that he'd mostly abandoned, out of place in the sleek, affluent sanctum he'd built up through long hours and luck, except to remind his clients from time to time that he was listening.

"It wasn't that I was surprised that Archie turned to me first." She was matter-of-fact again, and he found himself disoriented by her changes of mood and pace. "He had become my best friend as well as my husband's, a part of our family, another child sometimes. And he was ill. But it was symptomatic of the state we were all in somehow, that he wouldn't or couldn't approach the two of us together. He must have had some instinct that beneath the surface we weren't quite solid. I knew, I think, when he said what he said, that all our lives might change, and not just his, and that we'd been building toward it. But I had no conception, that evening when he told me, of the speed at which it was going to happen."

1994

"THE ONLY WAY TO HAVE A FRIEND IS TO BE ONE."

from *Lifelines for a Simple Life* by Lucy Fielding

ARCHIE HAD INTENDED to see James the next morning, to call him up and meet him for coffee and a bacon sandwich, and get the whole talking business out of the way. Instead he'd spent most of his Saturday in bed. He looked at his watch and felt guilty, but as he often slept on weekend afternoons, the fact that it was four o'clock felt almost normal, just a bit of morning slippage, allowable under the circumstances, and anyway now he had so little to occupy him there would be plenty of time for whatever it was he felt he should have been doing.

He pulled the drawstring and released his made-to-order blackout blind. The light and the August heat were intense, and he was covered in an unaccustomed sweat that showed no sign of cooling. The loss of the day took on a scary dimension, and he showered quickly and made coffee and toast, as if in defiance of the lateness of the hour. He checked his voicemail. There were two messages.

"Hi. Richard here."

(pause)

"Are you still up for our game tomorrow morning?"

(pause)

"I'll be there if I don't hear from you. Cheers."

"Archie, it's Amy. You are coming, aren't you? Can you do me a favor and pick up two pints of semi-skimmed milk on your way over? See you later. Bye."

Every Sunday morning for the past few years he and Richard Armstrong had played tennis, weather permitting, at the Paddington Sports Club, a surprising oasis of space that wasn't in Paddington at all but off a quiet street in Maida Vale. But now it seemed to Archie that events had outstripped habit and surely it couldn't be assumed that this arrangement should just carry on. Richard's recent flat refusal to reciprocate his own earlier investment in Richard's now thriving business had infuriated Archie, even as he recognized the logic of his friend's position. And now Richard just took it for granted that Archie would want to see him, would want to continue, as if nothing had happened, the ritual on which their relationship was based. The late afternoon heat made it hard to think clearly and he decided to do nothing. He might just leave a message later, when Richard was sure to be out.

The walk to James and Amy's house took about forty-five minutes if he walked at a moderate pace, which he did today, not wanting to arrive hot and sweating. He was wide-awake now, and an unfamiliar blast of self-pity at his accumulating misery kicked in. He didn't want to go to a family barbecue, even to see James; he wanted to go to some wild late-night bar, or stay at home and feel wretched till Monday when something might actually happen. It was in this frame of self-absorption that he embraced James, who opened the door, arms outstretched. The two men hugged each other as they'd learned to do as adults, never without both reflecting how unthinkable it would have been in their school years.

"Come on in," said James, ushering him through. "Hard times, old mate."

From the garden at the back, Archie could hear the sounds of excited children on the verge of meltdown. James rolled his eyes. "We'll have a drink later when the kids have gone to bed." He put his arm around Archie's neck and pulled him to him. "Sorry about Greta." He sounded surprised.

"Yes, well," said Archie and laughed, though he couldn't think why. "There you go."

Amy had told him, of course. Archie knew she would. But how much?

"There you go," said James. "There you've been before."

"It's not usually me that gets dumped, though," said Archie. It was important to fix his history, as if he sensed an imminent revision.

"No. That's true. But you weren't that keen, were you?"

"No, not really," said Archie, and slapped him lightly on the back.

Amy was sitting on the terrace, which gave on to a wide garden bordered by flowerbeds and trees. She was watching her two children demolish a third.

"That's Tamsin from next door," said James.

"Yes, Tamsin," said Amy, and rolled her eyes at Archie exactly as James had done. "Her parents will be over in half an hour. You've met them, haven't you? Mike and Susie Dixon?" She got up to greet him, taking the milk cartons that he thrust at her awkwardly, and disappeared through the French doors.

"I didn't know anyone else was coming," said Archie. "I thought it would just be us."

"They're only coming to collect her," James said. "We asked them to supper but they're off on holiday tomorrow."

"Nice for them," said Archie. He was relieved.

"Hey," shouted James suddenly, "not so rough," and moved off fast to separate the bodies on the lawn. Archie, left alone, followed Amy into the kitchen and picked nervously at a plate of salami laid out on the counter.

"You told him."

"No."

"Yes. About Greta."

"Oh, that. I didn't think you'd mind that," she said.

"What else?"

"Nothing else. You asked me not to. I had to tell him something, Archie. He's my husband. I can't keep secrets from him." But she could, she thought, and she was, and it struck her that this conceal-ment was all part of something new. "So you tell him. Please. He'll be pissed off if he finds out you've told me and not him."

"Okay, later."

"Good. Stop eating the salami." She reached out to push his hand away, and as she did so she recalled the evening before, when his face had almost dissolved in front of her, and she'd touched his arm but had wanted instead to curve her fingers across the bones of his cheeks, an impulse she had felt before but never acknowledged.

She pulled the plate from his fingers and moved it to the surface behind her, then turned her attention to the contents of the fridge.

"What do you want to drink—beer?" She handed him a bottle, then unwrapped a large parcel of sausages and waved them at him as they unraveled, like a ball of string in front of a kitten.

"I bought them specially for you," she said.

There was something about the absurdity and tenderness of the gesture, the thick waxy sheen of the sausages and Amy's desire to stop his fear that made Archie more anxious. He took a swig of the beer and smiled at her.

"And sausages will make it better?"

"No, of course not," said Amy. "But you don't have to stop doing what you like just because you're miserable." She stopped herself. "Oh, God, listen to me, I'm becoming my mother."

"You forget what you like," he said. "That's the trouble."

She handed Archie a plate and a pair of scissors, and he cut through the small umbilical cords, piling up the pale stuffed sacks, snipped and separate.

"God knows what they put in them," he said.

"Don't be silly, they're organic," said Amy. "And hurry up, Grace will be here in a minute."

Archie kept snipping. He sensed that the stalling of his life was about to go public, and he wasn't sure he was ready.

"I didn't know she was coming, too," he said.

"You don't mind, do you? She wants to show off her new boyfriend."

"How much have you told her?"

"What about?"

"Me, what do you think?"

"Archie, for God's sake. She's not interested in you."

Archie picked up the plate and made off toward the garden. He thought her remark was unlikely to be true. Until recently he'd had the kind of confidence that couldn't be rocked, in any serious way, by the opinions of other people, other than doctors, of course.

"Anyway," Amy called after him, "don't worry, they'll leave straight after supper. They've got more fashionable things to do."

It was comforting, he thought as he crossed the lawn, how the chores and paraphernalia of family life could distract temporarily from personal obsession, and he was glad now that he'd forced himself out of bed and made the effort to come. He approached the three children who had been lined up at a safe distance from the brick barbecue that jutted out from the back wall. They were crouched on a low parapet, coughing dramatically while James pumped a pair of ancient bellows at the coals. They looked, thought Archie, like the three monkeys that had sat on his grandmother's dresser, hands pressed to contorted faces, warding off noxious evils. He had formed a good relationship with James and Amy's son and daughter, but they could make him uneasy, offering up, as most children did from time to time, a mixture of trust and suspicion.

"Ah, the sausages," said James, putting down the bellows. "Can you stick them on for me, Arch? I need a quick wash. Just keep the kids away from the fire."

Archie looked at the children sternly and waved a pair of tongs at their retreating father.

"You heard what he said. Don't move."

"Would you like to hear me sing the song I'm doing for the school concert?" said Rosie.

"No, no, no," said Jonny, standing up with his hands clasped to his ears. "It's shit."

"Sit down. You're not supposed to say 'shit,' Jon," said Archie. "Don't let your mother hear you."

"I only wanted to cheer you up," said Rosie.

"By singing shit?" said Jonny, whose voice had begun to rise. "Shit, shit, shit."

"I don't need cheering up," said Archie, irritated and unready for sympathy.

"Mummy said you did," said Rosie. "She said you were sad about work and things."

"What did Mummy say?" called Amy from the terrace. "Look who's here."

Standing next to her, an inch or two taller, in a high-fashion, flimsy dress, was Grace. A fair-haired man stood to one side, polite and smiling. The children leaped up at once from the wall and ran toward the terrace, calling out Grace's name, then hung back briefly at the sight of the stranger.

Amy pulled Jonny aside, gripped his hand and leaned over him.

"What have I told you?" she said. "You are not to say 'shit.' I could hear you in the kitchen."

"You do."

"But you can't. I've told you."

"Yeah, yeah," said Jonny. "I won't say it at school."

"Sorry about that," said Amy, turning to her new guest, then back to her brood.

"This is Sam Harris, Grace's friend."

"Are you in the opera, too?" said Tamsin.

"She means the soap opera," said Rosie. "*Bridewell Wharf.*"

"No," said Sam, "I'm not really on the telly."

Amy had recognized him as soon as she opened the door. It was hard not to stare at the familiar features. He was just a boy, she thought, and she wondered what it must be like to be a man and quite so pretty. Not as lucky as it first appeared, she suspected. It was difficult to get past looks like that; they were almost off-putting, though to be fair he didn't seem obviously vain.

"Come with me, Sam, and get a beer," she said, flustered despite her best intentions. "Then you can meet Archie—and James when he comes out from wherever he's hiding."

HE heard Grace's heels click as she climbed onto the brick platform, and he turned to greet her. She put a hand on his shoulder to distract him from the fire and kissed him on the cheek. Ash and smoke hung between them. He turned to look at her and was struck as always by the fine beauty of her limbs and features.

"You look amazing," Archie said. "Quite an outfit for a north London barbecue."

"We're going on to a party later." Grace pulled a face in commiseration. "Sorry to hear about Greta."

Archie sighed. Who didn't know?

"Thanks." He really didn't want to discuss his ex-girlfriend with Grace. He'd flattered himself over the years that Amy's young sister found him attractive; they understood each other, he'd often felt, and he'd certainly enjoyed their long-standing flirtation. He liked the mix of cunning practicality and wickedness that Grace embodied. She was a more extreme version of Amy, he thought. But tonight he wasn't in the mood for her playfulness and the aura of her recent fame seemed to accent his own sudden decline.

"That was quite a greeting you got from the kids," he said.

"I'm only popular since I went into the soap. They want to come to the set again." Grace pulled up a flimsy strap that had fallen off her shoulder.

"Christ, they're so venal." Archie poked at the sausages.

"All kids are like that," she said. "Weren't you?"

He tried to remember. He'd learned early on how to get what he wanted, but by charm.

"Maybe. I just played my cards closer to my chest."

"That figures," she said.

He could smell her scent through the barbecue haze, an alien mixture that he found erotic.

"Who's the new guy?"

"Sam, Sam Harris."

Archie looked around quickly only to see Sam and Amy disappearing back into the darkness of the kitchen.

"So it is. That's one way to get attention," he said. "I'm jealous, of course."

"Don't let Amy hear you flirting with me," said Grace. "She might take it seriously."

"She's used to me," said Archie.

"She's used to having you to herself—aside from your girls, of course. But she can always see them off. As I think we know." She gave him a sly look, willing him to acknowledge some secret.

"That's ridiculous," said Archie.

"It's okay for her, married to Mr. Right. She's got her cake." Grace picked up a towel that lay discarded on the wall and wiped Archie's forehead with a nurselike care as he leaned again toward the heat. "I think it's time she set you free."

"For God's sake, Grace, you've been in that soap for far too long. Can we change the subject?"

"Yes," said Grace. "If you like. Let's see, what's new? Has Amy told you yet that Thea's coming home?"

Archie almost dropped the sausage he was turning.

"Why?" was all he could think of to say in response to Grace's bombshell. "Why's she coming home?"

"Her engagement is off," said Grace.

"That was ages ago."

"I suppose she misses us."

"You, maybe. Not me," he said.

Across the lawn he could see Amy talking to a couple who were swinging Tamsin between them. They were laughing now, the three of them, a picture of neighborly harmony. He liked the Dixons though he barely knew them; they were part of Amy and James's domestic set, which he usually tried to avoid. But tonight he almost wished they were staying. It might at least have stopped Grace from being nosy. They turned and waved at him, and he raised his tongs in acknowledgment. Grace repositioned herself on the low wall, her long legs forced forward, tanned and awkward. As she spoke she wiggled her toes up and down, like one of the children. "I want you to help me sort things out this time."

"It's between them," said Archie. "And anyway, you're the one Thea talks to."

"But you can help. After all you were partly to blame."

"No, I don't think so."

"Yes, you were. You can't fudge it."

"No," he said. "No, I'm not to blame, not for that, not for them."

HE'D met her first at the wedding. He had known about Thea, of course, the twin who had almost qualified as a doctor and had suddenly thrown it all up to study law. She had still been at university, in Leeds, living with some boyfriend. He'd been fascinated, naturally, by her resemblance to Amy, though he'd been briefed by James not to make too much of it. It wasn't the physical similarity that was disconcerting. It was other stuff, like the cadences of her voice and the way she moved her hands. They'd sat together under the trees in the Orangery in Kensington Gardens. It was late on, after the speeches and the cake, in the hour when guests were beginning to think about going home, and hoping the bride and groom wouldn't be tempted to linger too long before leaving. He could remember asking her if she thought she might get married soon, and her laughing and saying that the thought gave her nightmares.

He turned back to the barbecue with extra care. There was a sudden squeal from Grace and a dull hard thud as a ball hit the side of the grill, and he heard James shout at Jonny to be more careful. He couldn't take this on now, it had been bad enough back then.

His mind returned once more to its obsession, the thing that sat inside him, between his legs and at the permanent center of his focus. Amy and Thea were the least of his problems, he reminded himself, as he stared at the half-cooked meat.

"So, old man," James said as they sat slumped together at the kitchen table at the end of the evening, "what's the story?"

The children had long gone to bed, and he and Amy and Archie had sat talking together until Amy, claiming exhaustion, had left them to it. Grace and Sam had wandered off into the summer's evening in search of their own kind, and Archie found himself half wishing he could have gone with them. James refilled his glass. The late evening was warm, and the doors to the garden were still open. They could hear loud voices in the distance, slurred and hopeful on a hot Saturday night.

"Which one?"

"Whichever one you want to tell me," said James.

"What's Amy told you?"

"That you broke up with Greta—that she left for some other bloke?"

"It's true," said Archie. "But worse than that, the accountants are closing me down. That's it. I'm finished."

James sat forward in his seat. "Christ, man. I didn't know it was that bad. Why ever didn't you tell me?"

It was an odd household, thought Archie, where the eight-year-olds knew more about his status than their father, but he was too drunk to wonder further.

"I'm telling you now. Finished—and by Richard Armstrong."

"Richard? How come?"

"Well, not exactly by Richard," said Archie. It wasn't Richard's fault that his little kingdom had fallen, but he could have stayed the execution. "I asked him to cashflow me and he said no."

"That's a tough one, mate." James paused and drained his glass. "But he must have had his reasons. Look, it happens. It was always a gamble. You can move on."

"It hasn't happened to you."

"It could," said James.

"No," said Archie. "I didn't adjust in time. I didn't care enough, is the truth." He stretched himself out as far as the kitchen chair would allow. "And you're not the sort of person who gets closed down."

"What sort of person am I, then?" James was almost staring at him. He was flushed and glassy.

"That's a bit deep," said Archie.

"Well, I'm drunk," said James. "And I'm not the sort of person you think I am. In fact I'm not the sort of person I think I am."

He raised himself from his chair with difficulty and fumbled in a drawer for a corkscrew.

"I'm not following you."

"It doesn't matter," said James, turning back to him. "We're supposed to be talking about you."

James walked carefully over to the garden doors and stood looking out. His curly black hair seemed to be growing in several different directions. It struck Archie that James was right. That tonight James seemed not quite himself. His substantial form was slightly out of focus, and not just because they'd been drinking. It unnerved Archie to think of James as anything other than his usual stable presence. But nothing seemed its usual anything at the moment, so how could he tell?

"I'm supposed to play tennis with Richard in the morning," he said, turning his chair to face the garden doors.

"Rather you than me," said James, whose foresight included tomorrow's hangover. "So he wouldn't come up with the money?"

"No."

"I'm not entirely surprised," said James.

"He could have taken a punt. He's made plenty. And out of a business that I helped to finance."

"He owed you, I suppose," James said, slurring slightly as he made his way back to the table. "It's a pity. Stuff like this can make you bitter. It's like divorce. Then people have to take sides."

"What would you know about divorce?" said Archie.

"I know people have to take sides. You have to lose someone."

Archie drained his glass as James spoke. He knew about divorce, about sides being taken. It had begun with his mother's unexpected arrival at school, on a weekday. He'd been summoned to his housemaster's study. He was eleven years old. It was the term before James arrived. That was how he placed it, when he looked back, as if his friend's arrival and easy good nature had retrospectively cushioned the blow. His mother had smelled of roses, of something soft and full-blown, a distinct rounded smell in contrast to the odor of polish and sweat that infested the wooden structures of his schoolhouse. She'd sat close and told him, in her low, American drawl, that his father was going away for quite a while, to work in Kenya, but that she would stay here, to be with him, and that, by the way, she and Daddy would divorce and she was going to marry his uncle Simon, though they both knew that Uncle Simon wasn't really an uncle at all.

Now, as midnight approached, there was still a small glow from the embers of the barbecue and a candle flickering in a lantern in the shape of Mickey Mouse.

"Is that what happened with me and Thea, then?" said Archie. It was the heat of the night that made him think of her, the sultriness of her, which he could recall in his semistupor; the languor that was absent in Amy. "She's coming back, you must know that?"

"Where the fuck did that come from?" James said, reaching for the almost empty wine bottle.

"And you and Amy sort of took sides, with me, and then she left."

"I'm not sure, mate," said James. "I'm not sure I know that."

Archie shrugged his shoulders.

"I do," he said.

After the divorce, during the school holidays, he'd gone to visit his father's parents in Somerset. It was as if his mother didn't exist.

All the photographs were of him and his father, his mother cut off, excised from their history.

"I'm not sure I want to know if it's something I can't tell Amy," James continued, slurring his words now. "Do you know what I mean? There's only so much you can have for yourself when you're married, do you see?"

"Yes, mate," said Archie who didn't, and didn't know why he'd brought it up. After all it was second nature to him to crop attachments when life required it.

They'd been sitting in this kitchen, all four of them, thought Archie, the night he'd let her seduce him. She'd broken up with her boyfriend, but James and Amy were convinced it was only a blip, that Thea and Mark would soon be engaged and she would finally settle down. Like most married couples, they were eager for others to join their party. He should never have let it happen, but he'd drunk too much and she'd looked so good, and when they'd taken a taxi home together and she'd asked if she could come in for a while, that she wasn't tired, wasn't ready to go home alone, it had felt effortless. She was familiar to him. He had allowed himself an illusion of knowing her well.

Archie's memory flow was stopped as James got to his feet again, knocking over the empty wine bottle. It rolled off the edge and, to their amazement, bounced on the kitchen tiles.

"I was just going to get another one," he said.

2004

"THEA'S TIMING WAS always dramatic." Amy shrugged in a parody of exasperation. "I suppose it makes up for the lack of singularity. It can be exhausting, you understand, the striving, all those years, to stand alone."

Patrick felt his cultivated air of dispassion soften in the intimacy of the revelation. He was relieved at least that she had introduced her twin to him rather than assuming he was already acquainted with her. She'd been with him for almost an hour. It would soon be time for Patrick to stop her, to call a halt to the proceedings in a manner that would let her withdraw intact. He was still unclear as to why she had come, but he sensed she was looking for her questions as much as for answers. He wanted to help her, convinced that the small treasures unearthed in this imprecise and blind burrowing were worth the search, but still he was puzzled by Amy's oblique approach.

"We'd quarrelled," she said, "before Thea left for America, about something trivial. Thea started it, she usually does. It's her way of making space between us. Do you know the worst thing about being a twin?"

He shook his head.

"You have to work twice as hard to stake your territory, because it's always assumed to be shared."

Patrick tried to imagine a double image of the woman in front of him, and as he did so, he thought he sensed the pain of a willful separation. She seemed to be challenging him to contradict her. He wanted to test the statement but sensed it was a diversion and stayed silent.

"So that week, of all weeks," Amy continued, dropping her confrontational manner, "Thea had decided to return, to give it all up after just two years, her West Hollywood apartment, the job in the film industry—that's what she did back then, she was a media lawyer. . . . She's very clever, much more so than me. But she's always been prone to changing her mind. And we'd barely spoken to each other in that time. So I was caught by surprise, don't you see? Her coming made me see it all differently."

As if to emphasize this last point, she turned her gaze on Patrick. She seemed to be willing him to speak, frustrated by his lack of response.

"Nothing ever stands still," she said suddenly. "There's always something new to negotiate, something unexpected to digest. Change is the natural state, I know, but change implies something gradual, and the change that really changes things is sudden. It comes right out of nowhere."

She was clenching her fists, attempting to steady the small seismic tremor of recollection, and Patrick wondered what it could be that had shaken her so hard.

"It was about my mother," she said, "the argument, before she left. But I knew, we both knew, it was just an excuse to separate again. We'd got tangled up somehow, under the surface, and not for the first time."

Patrick felt himself to be in more predictable territory. Mothers he knew about. His own, back in Belfast, tranquillized to a comatose passivity, had, after all, precipitated his career in mental health. Mothers were the wellspring of his practice. Mothers had paid for the smart consulting rooms, the flat in Marylebone, and his rising reputation in his chosen field.

"I knew, of course, that Grace kept in touch with Thea, that she'd been over to America a couple of times to see her. And I'd intended to write, I really had, to make it up, but—"

"And Grace is . . . how much younger than you?" Patrick interrupted her.

"Almost ten years," said Amy.

Patrick wrote the figure beside Grace's name.

"It was such a shame," she said, her voice suddenly quiet. "Grace was only five when my father died."

Patrick put down his pen.

"I'm sorry," he said, bending toward her. "I'm sorry that your father died. So you, and Thea, must have been fifteen. That's also very young. And sad."

"Yes, it was sad," she said, her voice lowered even further. "And it was sudden and it did change everything."

She was looking away from him, off to the side somewhere. Patrick waited to see in which direction she would go.

"But it was a long time ago and so much has happened since," she said. She brought her gaze back to him and tried to smile. "And there are other ghosts."

1994

SUNDAY 14 AUGUST

"PRAY FOR RAIN BUT DIG FOR WATER"

from *Lifelines for the Gardener* by Lucy Fielding

AS THE BALL spun just beyond his reach once more, Archie decided he couldn't be bothered to indulge Richard any further. He would throw the match. He was going to lose it, anyway; his concentration was shot, and this way at least it would be over quickly. It had been, he now knew, a mistake to come along. He watched the stocky figure of Richard prepare himself to serve at the far end of the court. As the ball went up and came over the net, he moved awkwardly to the right, extending his racket like a demented fencer, and fell hard on his side. *Good work*, he thought. It wasn't exactly what he'd intended, but it would do.

"You okay?" called Richard.

"Buggered my knee, I think," said Archie as he got to his feet. His knee was fine, but he realized that his elbow was horribly painful. "It's been playing up a bit," he said, picking up his foot and putting it down gently. "Christ. I think that's me finished for today."

"Too bad," said Richard. "Just when I was winning."

"No way," said Archie. "I was just getting into my stride."

"Your stride," said Richard, "is that what it was? Too bad. Can you walk?"

"As far as the bar," said Archie. He'd drunk too much the evening before. Long gone were the days when a Sunday morning game of tennis was just the thing to shake off a Saturday night. But the thought of a cold lager was very appealing. One drink and that was it. One drink to clear his head.

As Archie sat at a table overlooking the tennis courts, watching the enthusiastic if awkward Sunday morning players scold themselves as they missed an easy shot, then berate their partners for their backhand, he considered how best he could withdraw from this weekly arrangement. He'd assumed till recently that Richard admired him, regarded him as a sort of mentor. He'd even privately congratulated himself on his patronage. And though he knew that virtue was supposed to be its own reward, in the circumstances he felt shortchanged; he felt a sense of outrage he didn't fully understand.

"Look," said Richard as he sat down with two pints of ice-cold beer. "What can I say? About the whole business. About the company. I'm just gutted." He shifted his compact body on the flimsy chair.

A prematurely bald man in bright green shorts swaggered past them, raising his racket. "Hey, Archie, how's tricks? How's Greta?" he asked, though not appearing to want to stay for an answer.

"Simon," said Archie, "hello. Fine, thanks," then, "Prat," he muttered as the man moved out of earshot.

"I, er, I heard she . . ." said Richard.

"I don't want to talk about it," said Archie. "And don't let's talk about the company." He smiled as he took a gulp from his glass and felt himself withdraw into the colder part of himself where he could disengage with ease. "It's not your problem."

"Oh, come on. It's fucking heartbreaking and I know you're pissed off with me. But I'm right. The magazines aren't viable."

"If you say so," said Archie. He'd nearly finished his pint, which he was having to drink left-handed, though the throbbing in his elbow was easing off.

"Not in the current climate," Richard went on. He had a point, Archie knew. Richard was no fool. After all, he was still in business.

"So you think it's down to the climate?" Archie said.

"In part, yes." Richard didn't want to repeat what he'd said when they'd argued just days before: that Archie was overgenerous to his staff, that his cover prices were too low, not to mention other financial practices he considered unwise.

"Maybe," he said, "you should think about coming in with me? It would be like old times."

"I don't think so," said Archie.

CLINGING to the handrail of her cab, Grace felt sick. The driver was taking advantage of the quiet, early Sunday morning streets to drive as if approaching the finishing tape of a cut-price grand prix.

"All right in the back?" he said.

"No," she said. "Let's stop here." It was almost home, after all. He pulled into the curb, and Grace felt immediately better. She decided to call into the comforting café in front of her for a cup of coffee and an illicit cigarette. It was an odd little place, opposite St. Mary Abbotts, and it hadn't changed its decor in thirty years. The only other customers early on Sunday morning were the church's bell-ringers, and there was little danger of their taking an interest in her.

It was only in recent months that people had begun to come up to her in the street and in shops, to ask Grace Fielding for her autograph or make leering wisecracks about her role in the program that had brought her to public notice. She was beginning to sense that there was a price to pay for the attention she'd always wanted. It wasn't altogether wise, for example, to jump into taxis looking as if you'd just got out of a bed you hadn't slept in. But Grace was content to run up the debt. She was having the time she had looked forward to for years, pressing in on the perimeter of the golden circle she felt she deserved to be inside.

She pulled hard on her Marlboro Light, relishing the moments of anonymity and solitude. Sometimes, when she peered over the edge of her youth, she saw herself dancing on, unable to root or settle, and she felt afraid. She knew she had a hankering for uncertainty and for mischief, which often undermined her best intentions. Life was simply more exciting, she told herself, if you didn't close off your options. She was scared by the disillusion she thought she'd seen clouding Amy's eyes, attributing it to marriage and children, but then she thought she'd seen it creep into her sister Thea's, too, an equal disappointment with variety and freedom. Dissatisfaction, she'd decided, was a family trait, or perhaps it was just that life's sheen had some built-in diminishment. She was determined, whatever the consequences, to keep her own buffed as long as she could.

She heard the church bell begin to toll across the street. It was ten o'clock; time to go. She stubbed out her cigarette, paid her bill, and felt strong enough to negotiate the road. People were starting to collect on corners, at cashpoints, multiplying as if in a time-lapsed sequence. As she crossed the High Street, Grace's mind wandered back to the night before, to the sex with Sam, which had been the best yet. She was still surprised at how good things were between them. Sex was wonderful, of course, but she had often wondered why people were quite so obsessed with it, quite so often. After all, there were only so many orifices, only so many things you could do. She had found, in her own experience, that it could quickly get repetitive.

"If that's your attitude at twenty-five, God help you," her mother had said on one occasion. "To think we fought for you to enjoy it."

"I do enjoy it," Grace had said. "I just enjoy it with different people." But already there was only one, and she wondered what the magic could be that kept couples busy for years.

Stepping out of the small wrought-iron lift directly into her mother's top-floor flat, Grace breathed easier. Enveloped in its rural fantasy, she felt the demands of the city outside fall instantly away. Lucy Fielding had converted and transformed what had once been a workshop and then a small casino, tucked above a former bank. The apartment was filled with light from south-facing windows overlooking the churchyard and had a cottage charm that belied its size.

She could hear her mother watering the roof garden at the top of a spiral staircase, which stood to the right of the entrance hall.

"Is that you, darling?" shouted Lucy above the hose.

"Yes, it's me. Hi," called Grace. "I'm just going to have a shower."

"You're an early bird," said Lucy.

"Sam's filming."

The sound of gushing water reduced to a drizzle.

"Would you like some coffee, darling?" said Lucy from the top of the stairs.

"Decaf, please, Ma."

"We'll have it up here. The garden is looking heavenly today."

She heard Lucy's hose resume full service.

For fifteen years, the flat off the High Street and its secret garden had been home, and Grace had never moved out. Apart from her time at college and brief stays with boyfriends, she liked the comforts provided by her mother, and she relished the eccentricity of Lucy's world and the pleasure she took in it. Grace admired its artifice, its self-conscious construction, and she noted that it had gone some way in allowing her mother, unlike her daughters, to evade life's erosion of delight.

It was about 10:30 by the time she emerged onto the terrace in a pale silk kimono and a towel wrapped around her head. Her mother was right, she thought, the roof garden was "heavenly," though it would never have occurred to her to describe it in those terms. Lucy's vocabulary and sentence structure seemed borrowed from some imaginary place and time, not quite solid, if vaguely familiar, a language designed for a ruthless positivity. Nothing was allowed to diminish Lucy's pleasure in her very gratifying world.

Grace couldn't remember the early years, the years that Amy and Thea talked about, or used to—the "Lucy Lost" years, as Amy called them—but she could half remember a dark time, when her father died. She knew that Lucy had gone away for a while, and life had gotten better, or so she'd been told, and she also knew that when Lucy returned, she'd been different, but unlike Amy and

Thea, Grace had liked the new Lucy. Their shiny new mother was the one she preferred.

"So, my darling," said Lucy, who was sitting at an ornate verdigris table under a leafy trellis, pouring coffee from a china pot. "Sit down and tell me what you've been doing."

"You don't want to know what I've been doing," said Grace. "Not really."

"Of course I do," said Lucy. "I don't seem to have seen you for days."

"I saw Amy and James last night—and the kids."

"Oh, how lovely," said Lucy, "my darling grandchildren. How are they?"

"They were sweet," said Grace, "a bit noisy."

"It would be worrying if they weren't," said Lucy.

"I'm very popular, of course," said Grace, trying hard to play her mother's game. "I give them street cred at school." She regarded her niece and nephew as an interesting experiment that her older sister had embarked on. Fond of them as she was, she was almost sure she didn't want to repeat the result.

"And how was Amy?"

"A bit grumpy. She said they're coming for tea today?"

"Yes," said Lucy. "I do hope Amy will be cheerful. She's so unpredictable these days."

"Hmm," said Grace, "she's got a lot on her mind."

"I can't think what," said Lucy. "She's very blessed."

"Well, don't tell her that," said Grace. "She won't thank you."

"She was always a discontented child beneath that self-assurance," said Lucy. "Are you milk or no milk today?"

"No milk, thanks."

"But that's her path and she must tread it," continued Lucy.

"Yes, Ma," said Grace, tuning out as she often did when she felt her mother assuming a guru's mantle, though she maintained an expression of interest.

"It's just a pity," said Lucy, "that she had to drag Thea along it, too. Discontent is dangerous for Thea. Her mooring is less steady."

Grace pulled the towel from her hair and smiled at her mother's nautical reference. She doubted that Lucy had ever been near a boat in her life. She wondered if she should consider moving out when Thea arrived on Wednesday. She could live with Amy for a bit, if necessary, or maybe even Sam. Lucy was expecting Thea to stay with them in Kensington, which was fine, but somehow she couldn't imagine her sister sidestepping Lucy's eccentricities with her own lightness of foot. She couldn't imagine that at all.

"I wouldn't describe Thea as grumpy," she said, calibrating her re-entry into Lucy's flow.

"No, no," said Lucy. "Not grumpy by nature. But easily led astray. The second twin, late into the spotlight. She was ten whole minutes behind Amy, of course."

"Of course," said Grace, who had heard it all before.

"And she's been trying to overtake her ever since, not always for the good," said Lucy, reaching to snap off a dead hosta flower that was protruding from an otherwise perfect pot of yellow blooms. "But she never will, of course. She must live her own life."

"She's been in L.A. for over two years, Ma," said Grace. "I shouldn't think she's spent that time thinking about Amy."

"Two years is nothing in a lifetime," said Lucy, who had quietly turned sixty just three months before, "not to mention the possibility of several, and twins must be bound beyond the norm."

"Whatever that is," said Grace quietly.

"You may mock," said Lucy, "but she's coming home."

Grace had never known how seriously to take her mother's utterances. Lucy Fielding was no fool. But at some point, many years back, she had taken a decision to reframe her mental landscape, and though Grace had glimpsed the more cynical and sophisticated being who lay dormant and who called up from the labyrinth only on rare occasions, she had been born too late to have known her.

Amy and Thea, she knew, found their mother's relentless optimism oppressive. Lucy seemed to them to leave no room, as if the
air required to fuel their own contentment was sucked up in her
presence. They were embarrassed by the books she wrote, dispensing
her hope to the public in bite-sized pieces. They'd been thankful, of
course, that the part of their mother that had spiraled into clinical
gloom had retreated, but there had been other parts that they'd
missed, that they'd tried over the years to reclaim. Lucy was locked
in the center of a carefully relaid maze, and, as Amy was fond of
remarking, it would take more than a ball of string to retrieve her.

ॐ

THE hum from distant traffic filtered through the side streets and the
chatter on the radio as James lay in a hammock, swinging gently. He
should be doing things, he thought, things in the garden, or clearing
up last night's mess. He shouldn't just be swinging his Sunday away.
But it was almost peaceful here, and he could breathe without the
tension in his chest that had crept up on him over the last weeks,
often slight, but almost always present.

Amy and the children were out, gone with friends for the day to
a lido in South London, then back to their granny's for tea. James
was fond of Lucy, and she of him, but he'd been relieved when Amy
had agreed that he needn't come along. She'd been more disagreeable than usual this morning; not that Amy was disagreeable as a
rule, it was just, lately, she . . . they were fine. If he could just get
over the hiccup at work, that was all it was, he was sure; or he had
been until Patrick the shrink had put the question to him.

"Do you love your wife?" Patrick had asked as James sat in the
curious chair that reminded him of the dentist. He was embarrassed
at the turn things were taking in Hoxton, but the problem that
had brought him there was now chronic. After five years of untroubled elevation, his legs were refusing to take him through the doors
of the lifts at the sleek City bank where he worked; instead, he was
walking up twelve flights of steps twice a day, pretending it was part

of a new exercise regime. He feared that his phobia might soon extend beyond the bank, and who knew then what horrors the involuntary stoppage might spawn—problems with the Underground, or aeroplanes maybe. He would be jobless, shunned and ridiculed, unable to support his wife and family. The shame of visiting Patrick, he reminded himself, was a small price to pay. But could Patrick solve the problem? "Short and sharp," his American colleague had affirmed as James explained his need of some help for his wife's fear of flying. "Three sessions a week and he'll sort her out in no time. A month at the most."

"Do you love your wife, James?" James had been visualizing himself inside the lift at work, describing its pale marbled walls, its shiny buttons and inset telephone receiver for emergencies, the one that almost certainly didn't receive when the lights went out.

"What's that got to do with it?" he said, brought up short by what felt an intrusion. James was a practical man. He hoped Patrick wasn't going to resort to a crude Freudian approach.

"You're not suggesting this is some sort of womb or vagina thing, are you?" he said. "Because it isn't."

"Is that what comes to mind?" Patrick asked.

"No. To your mind, maybe."

"I'm not the one who said it."

"You know what I mean," James said.

"No, I simply asked you if you loved your wife."

"Your timing was pretty specific."

Patrick had smiled. "Possibly."

"Do I love my wife? Yes. Of course."

"Of course?"

"What's significant about 'of course'?"

"Well," said Patrick, "when I say 'of course,' I often mean, 'without question.'"

"Yes, that's it."

"You love your wife without question?"

"Yes."

"We'll leave it there, then."

Ever since this conversation, since his session, James had had a feeling of being shortchanged. He felt that having raised the subject, Patrick should have followed it through. As he swayed slowly in the hammock, looking at the weeds in the flowerbeds that seemed to multiply rather than wither in the August drought, he considered the possibility of asking himself Patrick's question again. But even to ask would be dangerous. James knew that questions could unleash far more mayhem than answers.

IT was still there, the small shame and uncertainty that had marked his new beginning, at the school where he met Archie, the sudden inability to control his tears that had threatened to blow his school life off course. Mr. Fairbrother, James's housemaster, a man who smelled of tobacco, a man with a kind smile, asked him if he loved his mother.

"Yes," James said, not looking at the man but past him, to a picture on the wall that wasn't a picture exactly, but a square of squiggly paint.

"And your father?"

"Yes," said James. It was obvious, he thought, that it was the homesick thing that made the tears.

"Very much?"

James thought about the question for some time, staring at the squiggles that seemed to have a life of their own and threatened to roll beyond the edges and down the wall.

"Yes," he said, "I suppose so."

"Then why, James, do you want to make your mother and father unhappy by crying for them?" said Mr. Fairbrother, raising his eyebrows and jutting his jaw forward across the table that separated them.

James had no idea. The concept of his parents' unhappiness had never in his short life entered his head. Unhappiness was not a part of his makeup. An odd sulk, a childish disappointment: these had colored his world, of course, but until he had come to the school, he'd existed in a cocoon of contentment. The tears seemed to be something that happened outside him. They only came with a thought or a memory, and if it weren't for the contempt of the other boys, he would have taken even these in his stride. And now here was this man with hair in his nostrils suggesting that he, James, might be the cause of a seismic shift in the home he'd left behind; that his parents may now have fallen into some black hole of his making, into this thing called unhappiness. He gripped the chair as fear and panic swept through his small body.

HE woke from the recollection with a start and looked at his watch; it was ten past four. He toyed with the idea of making himself some tea, but the thought of the journey to the kitchen was still too tiring. He imagined his children in the garden, on the roof in Kensington, leprechauns among the foliage in thrall to Lucy's magic, while Amy sat it out, willing herself to smile for her mother, because, she said, she couldn't bear to give Lucy the satisfaction of disapproval. He heaved his large frame off the hammock and headed inside. On reflection, he felt he could tell Patrick that the problem was nothing to do with his wife, that he did love Amy, that the lift business could be solved without reference to cliché. There were no ghosts in his present or his past, just the distant grief of an immature boy leaving a much-loved home.

⁊

TEA with her mother had been the ordeal that Amy expected. She'd woken that morning with a mild hangover, despite drinking almost nothing but water the night before. James looked terrible, as he did after his occasional man-to-man evenings with Archie, but, to her annoyance, it became apparent over breakfast that whatever they'd talked about late into the night, it wasn't the state of Archie's health.

As far as she was concerned, that had been the point of all her efforts, and now she, Amy, exhausted and pregnant, must continue to keep Archie's secret, as well as her own, which she had nursed to herself, refusing to share its existence.

As she drove home through Little Venice, she passed close by Archie's mansion block and thought of stopping off to tell him face-to-face that she would tell James if he didn't, that it wasn't fair to burden her alone. But Rosie complained of carsickness and Jonny wanted a pee.

"I told you to go at Granny's," said Amy over her shoulder. "Why didn't you go there?"

"I don't like Granny's loo," said Jonny.

"Why not?" said Amy.

"It's full of plants and worms."

"Rubbish," said Amy.

"Can you stop, Mummy? I'm going to be sick now." Rosie's voice was thin and high.

"I thought we'd go and visit Archie," said Amy.

"I want to go home," said Jonny.

"I'm going to be sick. Mummy, I'm going to be sick. Quick."

Amy swept into the curb and hauled the child out of the car as she expelled a torrent of yellow and white ice-cream vomit over the pavement.

Amy looked at the puddle of sick, then at Rosie, and rummaged in a bag for a handkerchief to wipe her daughter's mouth. But first, she pressed it to her own face and closed her eyes for a moment. She was pregnant, and she didn't know if she could really go through this again. It wasn't the pain of childbirth or the anxiety of motherhood; it wasn't the sleepless nights or the expectations. It was the humdrum vomit, the endless questions, and the constant noise that she dreaded repeating. She knew her limitations, and she feared her well of patience might fast be drying up.

"Never mind, sweetheart," she said. "We'll go home now. We're nearly there."

༐

THREE days early according to the family schedule, in the late afternoon, Thea Fielding disembarked from a 747 at Heathrow. She collected her luggage, washed her hands and face, bought a Sunday paper, and took a cab to the Bow Club in Covent Garden, an elegant but small townhouse hotel. She was running on her own timetable: two days to decompress, she thought, before she had to face them. She got up and looked in the mirror above the console table, turning her profile from right to left and shaking back her hair. She looked remarkably fresh after the eleven-hour flight. Her dark hair was long, much longer than when she'd left, and sleek in a new American way. She had a light tan, a patina of L.A. She looked into her own greenish-hazel eyes and saw Amy looking back at her, already privy to her inner world. She was prepared for it; she'd known it would happen when she returned.

2004

TWO DAYS LATER, Patrick was at the window once more, waiting. But this time his waiting was freighted with expectation. The light outside was flatter, diffused by an even spread of cloud, yet it still retained some of the luminous delicacy of early winter. He identified her from some distance, way back beyond the crossroads; she was striding along the pavement in a long coat, her large leather bag strapped across her chest, like the advance party of some expeditionary force. She looked up at the first-floor window as she approached, as he knew she would. He'd wanted to stand back, to hide himself from her, but he stood his ground and raised his hand. She nodded her head up at him in acknowledgment, her hands deep in her pockets as she jumped up the steps to ring the bell.

"So many books," she said, looking around his room before she sat, as she had the last time.

"You said your mother wrote books, I think?"

"Well remembered," she said, smiling at him, as if surprised and impressed, and he allowed himself a small moment of professional pleasure.

"That's if you can call them books," she said. "They're rubbish, really. Self-help and positive thinking, that sort of stuff, though the practical tips have always been sound."

Patrick looked puzzled.

"*Lifelines*," said Amy. "Lucy Fielding. The *Lifelines* series. You must have heard of them, they were on the counter in bookshops for years." Patrick nodded. He had a dim awareness of the name.

"She started them after Dad died. I shouldn't be dismissive of them, they've supported us well."

"What type of thing—" he started, but she interrupted him.

"A ragbag," she said. "A sort of combination of domestic advice and positive thinking, or that's my view of it. She started off with gardens. Lucy, that's my mother, was always brilliant at gardening, and *Lifelines for the Gardener* was a huge success."

Despite the emphasis on "huge," she looked pained at the recollection, and he raised his brow.

"Lucy took it all so seriously, her . . . philosophy," she explained.

"And you didn't."

"I couldn't. I can't bear all that. But she's a believer, or she was. She's less dogmatic now. But she believes it saved her, when she cracked up, after my father . . . and it sort of did, I suppose."

"What do you understand by 'it'?" asked Patrick. "You said 'it' saved her."

Amy considered the question. She looked down into her lap, into her linked upturned hands, then lifted her head.

"A blind refusal to live with the shadows," she said. Her voice was tight.

"But you could see them? Live with them?"

"I've had to."

The pain that he saw in her face surprised him.

"But now you're happy?" he asked. "That's what you said to me last time."

He could see her struggling to organize her thoughts, to layer the present over the past.

"That's now," she said.

"But you felt the need to come here?"

She sat in silence for a moment, but he knew that this time she would answer.

"I've come here to try to stay that way," she said finally, "and to ask you something."

He looked at her, questioning, waiting, but her features glazed over in a manner he recognized. It was the retreat of the will. She'd gone as far as she dared in the instant.

"What did you want to ask me?"

"I'm not sure yet," she said, and she stared at him for a moment, then continued quickly as if she were afraid he would stop her.

"There were other books, lots of them—*Lifelines for the Cook, Lifelines for the Office.* Lucy became a sort of cottage industry. She was the incarnation of its brand. I used to feel that she never quite forgave Thea and me for knowing her before her transformation."

"Used to feel?"

She looked at him with impatience, as if he weren't keeping up.

"I was talking about back then. She's different now. She's remarried, for one thing."

"Your mother?"

"Yes, and she really is happy now. Before, I always thought she was just pretending."

"So now you're a very happy family indeed?"

Amy tilted her head. "Don't mock," she said. "She did her best, we all did. It was just that Thea and me, we were a constant reminder of her past, and I know now how that feels and how afraid it makes you, and how sometimes you want to be rid of the things that remind you that bad things can happen; and when you love them, it's as if you're split in two."

MONDAY 15 AUGUST

"THE FIRST WEALTH IS HEALTH"

from *Lifelines for a Simple Life* by Lucy Fielding

HE WAS EARLY for his appointment. Archie stood and looked at the outsize revolving doors of the Chelsea and Westminster Hospital and thought about buying a paper and a cup of coffee till nearer the time, but the doors held his attention. Why were they so large? Wheelchairs? Bodies? But they wouldn't bring bodies out the front; they'd be disposed of discreetly around the back somewhere. After a couple of minutes, he disappeared into the Starbucks next door, then, hugging a latte, he made his way back and through the circulating glass.

He was surprised by the degree of fear that kept interrupting his composure as he walked along the corridors. It was a distinct muscular spasm that had started as a knot in the stomach and unraveled in waves that spread through his chest, over his shoulders, and under his armpits. Before now he'd found hospitals reassuring places. He'd enjoyed their institutional flavor and sense of mission, though he knew that many people, perhaps the majority, found them unsettling. Today he understood how natural that was. It was his own approach that was unrealistic; his rose-tinted understanding had never dealt fully with the connection between hospitals and death. Perhaps that was why the doors revolved, to reassure those who entered that there was an exit for the living.

"Archie Morgan?" called a nurse, a man in a short tunic with a clipboard and hairy forearms.

"That's me," said Archie, standing and folding up his newspaper. He felt ridiculous in his faded blue hospital gown, naked except for his shoes and socks. He wasn't a man with an obvious vanity, but he didn't like to look foolish.

"Mr. Graham, three doors down on the left."

Mr. Graham. He'd known, of course, that he was seeing a Mr. Graham, but he'd avoided, until now, the implications of the title. "Misters" might be surgeons, as far as he knew, but then in this game he knew very little.

He knocked on the door and another nurse let him in. Mr. Graham was on the phone, in a heated discussion about the timetabling of the operating theaters.

"Sorry about that," he said when he'd finished. "Too many patients, too few slots. I'm sure you know."

It was hardly comforting. Archie hoped he wouldn't need a slot. Anyway he had private insurance, surely that smoothed things along.

"So, Mr. Morgan, you've found a growth in your testicle."

"A lump, yes," said Archie. He didn't care for the word "growth."

"Better have a look then," said Mr. Graham.

ONE surreal hour later, Archie was back in the waiting area fully clothed, with a handful of other men, mostly younger than him he noted, and all of whom seemed anxious to avoid eye contact with one another. He'd been prodded, scanned, and drained with great efficiency. He'd half wished the process were slower, a different day for each maybe, to ease him into the medical routine. But here he was in no time, waiting, he presumed, for a diagnosis.

The nurse approached him directly instead of calling his name.

"Mr. Graham's ready for you now," he said. His name was Bryan; it was on his badge. He wondered why Bryan had bothered to come around from the desk, and if it was a subtle shift to the treatment of the seriously ill or if he was just stretching his legs.

Seated once more in front of Mr. Graham, Archie looked for clues in the man's face as he in turn carefully scrutinized the notes in front of him, the notes that Archie himself had brought, in a sealed brown envelope, straight from the scan. The office was functional but sparsely furnished, as if the surgeon were only a temporary resident. He probably had a smart set of rooms on Harley Street, thought Archie, and wondered if Mr. Graham was using his tea-breaks in the National Health Service for his private work.

"Right, Mr. Morgan." Mr. Graham sat back in his chair and looked directly at him. "I can tell you that your scan has shown up a growth."

"I thought we knew that already," said Archie.

"Yes," said Mr. Graham. He smiled. "Yes, we knew there was something there, of course. But we thought it might merely be what we call a hydrocele, a sort of cyst."

"So, what . . . ?"

Mr. Graham looked down at the ultrasound image in front of him.

"After we drained the fluid from your scrotum we found a small lump remaining."

Whatever word was used, there was something there.

"A tumor," said Archie.

"Don't jump to conclusions, er, Archie." Mr. Graham squinted at the notes, checking his name. "Can I call you Archie?"

"Yes, yes, of course," said Archie. *Get on with it*, was what he wanted to say. Get on with it or, alternatively, say nothing at all. He wished the conversation had never begun.

"We will need now to make an incision in the scrotum, under anesthetic, of course, which I have to tell you is likely to result in an orchidectomy, whatever the outcome."

"Remove a testicle, you mean?" said Archie.

"Yes. I'm sorry but it's more than likely. We could arrange to insert a prosthetic during the same procedure."

"So it's not good?" said Archie.

"Not as encouraging as we might have hoped."

⌇

JAMES was walking up the four flights from his own office to his boss's when his phone rang.

"Archie," he said, short of breath.

"Why are you breathing heavily?" said Archie.

"What's up?" said James. "I'm about to go into a meeting."

"Are you free for lunch?"

"A quick one, yes, if you can come over here."

"I've fuck all else to do," said Archie. "I'll see you in reception at one."

"Fine." James closed his phone and stopped as he reached the sixteenth floor.

Four flights were manageable, four flights could be written off as keeping fit. But now he was going out of the building for lunch, that meant sixteen down and twelve up again afterward, and then there was the meeting at Goldman Sachs at 4:30, and back again. At this rate he could give up his gym subscription. Perhaps he could claim a parents' evening and go home without returning to the office and the stairs. But that was impossible in August. He felt breathless just thinking about it. Something would have to be done.

⌇

A taxi took Archie from the hospital to Marks & Spencer's on Oxford Street, where he bought himself some new underwear and pajamas. It was the place, he'd assumed, to find a suitable pair for the hospital, plain and functional, and it was something specific he could do, something concrete and under his control. He was feeling, he realized, increasingly alone. His weekends were usually spent with

Greta and any of a large number of friends and couples who made up his world. He'd been behaving like a dog that had taken to its basket, waiting to recover or die, and was relieved this Monday morning to have caught James at his desk and forced himself back into life.

Leaving the store, swinging his carrier bag, he decided to catch the Tube to the City, to take his time and think. He walked east toward Bond Street and was about to cross the busy road, full of buses and taxis, when he suddenly caught sight of Amy standing on the other side. She was hailing a cab, and though he called to her she didn't turn, unable to hear him above the panting and the revving of the traffic.

"Amy," he shouted again, so loudly that people around him stared. She looked up and around her, then jumped in her cab, which drove five yards in the direction of Marble Arch before becoming stationary again. She moved to the window behind the driver and stared across the street until she found him in the crowd, waving and mouthing at her. She put her finger to her lips and made telephone gestures at him in a manner that seemed almost suggestive, then her face disappeared behind a passing bus. Archie stood with his carrier bag, trying to make some sense of her mime. It took him a full thirty seconds of staring across at where the cab had been, until he realized that it wasn't just the dumb show that had thrown him, it was the hair. It was too long. It wasn't Amy he'd seen; it must have been Thea.

It had always been the differences between them that held his interest. Thea was more contradictory than Amy, both amoral and high-minded, and (he indulged again in nostalgia) she had an erotic charge, an uncertainty, that he'd known in other women. She appeared to talk with the same directness as Amy, but something was kept back, protected. He hadn't considered her that first time as a girlfriend. It was to be just a night between friends—they'd both agreed. It was easy to see now that they should never have let it go further, that any interest on his part would be colored by notes of incest. He'd half forgotten her in her long absence, but now it seemed that Grace was right: she was back.

⁂

"I'M telling you, man, it was definitely her," said Archie, "and why are we walking at this manic pace?" James was striding down Lombard Street, pushing through the mass of lunchtime pedestrians, toward the wine bar they both claimed to dislike but always went to. Archie almost struggled to keep up.

"And I'm telling you she's not coming till Wednesday," said James. "My wife won't discuss it, but I know the calendar is ringed. She can't wait. She's dreading it but she can't wait."

"She said she'd ring me."

"Who? Amy?"

"No, Thea. It was her. And her hair was long. Much longer than Amy's. In fact, now I think about it, she looked pretty good."

James stopped suddenly in the City street, and the crowd behind them seemed to part on some undetected cue, moving gracefully to either side before merging again in front of them.

"I thought you didn't speak to her. I thought you said you saw her across the street."

"I did," said Archie. "But she did this." He mimed with vigor the gesture that Thea had made, then laughed at James's expression.

James looked around, embarrassed. "Come on," he said, "not here." As he followed James up the street, Archie's moment of lightness dimmed. He would have to tell him about the doctor, what he'd said; he'd have to hear himself say it. And all thoughts of Thea and her complications retreated before his own.

⁂

BY the time Thea had crossed Piccadilly and cut her way through Mayfair she was ready to find a cab. She had felt the need to walk free through the London streets, to feel herself here again, in its center, where a person could stroll along the pavements, along the Strand and down the Mall, up through the beauty of Green Park on a summer morning. And that was when Archie had seen her, as she'd turned onto Oxford Street to catch a taxi.

Thea considered, with a cool satisfaction, that he'd seemed excited, he'd been waving and shouting. But then she remembered it must be her sister Amy that Archie first thought he'd seen. A bus had passed, and he had emerged puzzled. His face had been like a series of snapshots, a strip of four—pleasure, puzzlement, recognition, then . . . yes, pleasure again. Part of her wanted the sequence to finish with negatives—disappointment, embarrassment, or regret— but he'd definitely been pleased to see her. Pleased. After everything. *Typical of Archie, generous but unfeeling*, she thought. After all this time.

The cab had taken her around Marble Arch, through Bayswater, and was now sailing toward the west of London. The windows were wide open and as they reached Holland Park Avenue she could smell the woody scents, mixed in with a hint of asphalt. The tall, leafy planes on either side spread themselves, wide and even, across the road. She'd always loved this street, loved leaving London on a summer weekend and returning to the city late on Sunday, through the big trees that seemed sometimes to be dancing in some ancient formation. She closed her eyes. It felt good, in spite of everything, to be back.

"So do you work at the studios, or what?"

The cabby had opened the connecting window and was settling in for a chat.

"No, I'm just visiting someone."

"Anyone I know?"

Thea wasn't sure that she wanted to engage in a taxi conversation. She was out of practice, she thought; she no longer knew how to deflect one with grace, and her instinct told her it would be unwise to be rude.

"I shouldn't think so, she's only got a small part. She's my sister, Grace Fielding."

"Oh, very funny," said the cabby. "Or are you being modest? Everyone knows her."

"Do they?" said Thea. "Everyone? Well, there's a thing." Life was incomprehensible.

"Of course they do. She's the Babe of *Bridewell Wharf.*"

Thea laughed, but she felt disturbed at this first warning of the adjustments she might have to accommodate on her homecoming.

"I've been living in Los Angeles, I'm afraid, for some time. She's not famous there, of course."

"Didn't she tell you?"

"She said she was getting known a bit. Yes," said Thea, "I remember her telling me someone had come up to her in the supermarket—but nothing huge."

"Well, I don't suppose she's huge," said the cabby. Thea was almost disappointed; she'd been starting to enjoy Grace's celebrity. "But she's a pretty girl, that's for sure."

Looking through the window, she saw that the landscape had changed to one of pokey streets and shabby shops, but she still liked the view. She felt comfortable here, among the solidly familiar with its scuffed and rounded edges. She considered what she'd miss in Los Angeles: the valet parking, the streamlined service that made every foreigner with a few dollars feel rich. She'd miss the delicacy of the food provided for the health-conscious, she'd miss the early morning energy of the place. But she wouldn't miss the ruthlessness that ran under its freeways.

She'd loved it to start with. It had suited the sense of dislocation she'd brought with her. She loved the endless driving and the multi-syllabled street names—La Cienega and Sepulveda, the Boulevards, Drives, and Canyons. It was a city to vanish in, to drown in while its population waved for the attention it craved. She'd savored it, excited by its throb of power; but, over time, the suffocating expectations of the film business had been exhausting.

She had tried to suppress her distaste for the life she'd chosen, a distaste that she knew stretched back beyond the simple move between continents. She'd even hoped that marriage to a man she found dull but worthy, an economics professor at UCLA, might protect her from the corrupting Hollywood shallows she swam in each day. But the compromise was too much for her. Whatever she had tried to hang on to, it wasn't enough, and she'd come home.

"Is she pregnant or not, then?" said the cabby, interrupting Thea's reflection as the car pulled up outside the West London Studios.

"Who?" said Thea.

"The Babe of *Bridewell Wharf*," he said, in a manner that implied a hostile ignorance on Thea's part.

"I've absolutely no idea," she said, tired of the subject, and she moved away quickly through the doors to reception.

She caught a glimpse of herself in the reflective glass, a tall long-haired woman in sunglasses, more sophisticated than she remembered. She felt nervous at the prospect of seeing Grace. It had been a year or more since her sister had come over to visit, and Grace's life appeared to be changing so fast. She followed the runner who came to fetch her through dingy corridors and high security to a small canteen that catered for cast and crew. Almost immediately, Grace appeared, dressed in a tiny skirt and low, tight top with heavy eye makeup.

"Don't smudge my eyes," said Grace, as she hugged her sister to her before they sat down at a table piled with plates of salad and chicken.

"You look grotesque," said Thea, and heard the too-sharp note in her tone.

"Sorry," said Grace, pushing back her hair. "It's my uniform."

"Very fetching for hanging out on street corners."

"And you look fantastic," said Grace, taking in her sister's presence. "You've lost weight, not that you needed to, but you've become so . . . so sleek." She looked down at herself. "You should see me when they really dress me up."

"I have," said Thea. "You sent me tapes."

"The papers call me the Babe of *Bridewell Wharf*," said Grace. "The crap ones, at any rate. So, how does it feel? To be back?"

Thea smiled. "Good, I think. Strange. I'm decompressing." She felt uncomfortable, distant from Grace, distant from everything around her.

"Hiding, more like," said Grace, who knew that a shyness underlay her sister's cool sharpness.

"It's not hiding. I just need to get my bearings before I face everyone."

"It puts me in a difficult position," said Grace. "They'll be upset if they find out I've seen you first."

"No, they won't. They'll pretend to be, but they won't," she said. But Grace didn't seem to be listening. She was waving at a man who had settled at a table across the room. "That's Simon Parry," she said, turning to Thea, "our best writer. He's attractive, don't you think?"

Thea looked over, but the man she saw looked pasty and middle aged.

"He's very funny," Grace said. She was waving again now, mouthing something at the man who laughed in response.

"How's the new boyfriend?" said Thea.

Grace was unfazed. "He's fabulous," she said.

"For how long?" said Thea.

Grace pulled a face. Thea understood her. As she'd sat astride Sam that morning, fooling around in bed, she'd watched him smiling up at her. His handsome features had seemed to morph between an image she found intensely desirable and something she wanted to push away. And when she'd tried to hold on to the vision she preferred, it had slipped out of focus until she closed her eyes and opened them again.

She watched now as her sister helped herself from a bowl of tomato and cucumber. Thea looked a little older, but this new angularity suited her, suited her impetuous style. It differentiated her from the softer, more curvaceous Amy, though Grace could never say such a thing. She had never understood how people could confuse Thea and Amy once they knew them, and each year that passed seemed to differentiate them further. It was true that in addition to the physical likeness they appeared to share an ironic, slightly detached view of the world, but Thea, as well as being the more clever, was the less accepting, her manner in some way more watchful. To Grace, at least, it was written on her face, somewhere under the cheekbones, she'd always thought, and at the back of the eyes. It was as if Thea saw a darkness in their world that the rest of them tried not to think about.

"You can relax," said Thea. "My secret is out. Archie saw me this morning."

"No. Where?"

"On Oxford Street."

"What was he doing on Oxford Street?"

"I don't know, I didn't speak to him."

"What? You ran away?"

"I didn't run away, Grace. I was getting in a cab. I waved at him."

"After two and a half years, you waved at him."

"I think he thought I was Amy. He must have. Then I waved at him through the window and he realized. His face," Thea started to laugh, "his face was a picture."

GENEROUS but unfeeling—that was how she'd decided to remember Archie. He'd taken her to Rome for her birthday, just weeks before they had broken up. He'd put such care into planning the trip, insisting that it be so unashamedly romantic, that she began to think that a proposal must be coming, and, though she hadn't really thought it on the cards, it seemed suddenly like a wonderful idea. They'd gone out to small restaurants hidden in ancient squares, walked along the Tiber in the darkness, hand in hand, enjoyed energetic sex in their pretty hotel tucked behind the Spanish Steps. But nothing had been said after all, and despite her own silence on the subject, and her continued pretence at being carefree, she'd felt wrong-footed, humiliated.

"We should bring Amy here," he'd said in passing, as they sat in the Piazza Navona, watching the young Romans preen and strut. "She'd love this."

It wasn't what she'd wanted to hear.

SITTING back against the wooden bench in the studio canteen, Thea rested her head on the wall and closed her eyes. "It was just like old times."

"That's not fair," said Grace. "He was really fond of you."

Thea looked at her sister.

"Who said I had to be fair?" she said. Grace's accusation hit a nerve. "Fair" was a word she had given some thought to over the last year as she'd taken stock of herself and her life. Fairness was something she aspired to, and overall, she'd decided, it was in short supply.

"Let's change the subject. What's all this about a pregnancy?"

"How could you possibly know?" said Grace. Her eyes glowed through the dark rings penciled around them.

"No big deal," said Thea. "I'm not likely to tell anyone. Don't worry."

"But how do you know? Has Amy told Ma? I thought she didn't want to tell anyone about the baby yet, in case she—"

Grace stopped abruptly, and Thea reached in her bag for a packet of cigarettes. "Ah," she said, extracting one with guilty pleasure. "So Amy is pregnant." She seemed distant, as if absorbing Grace's confusion from far away. "I would have thought two children were quite enough." She paused to light her cigarette. "It's a relief to be in a country you can smoke in," she said, blowing out a cloud furtively, to her right. "Though not for long, I suppose."

"Thea, tell me how you know about Amy."

"I don't," said Thea. "I thought it was you. Not actually 'you.' I meant in your show. It was a joke. The cabby who brought me here told me it was your hot story."

Grace had forgotten how complicated things could become when she found herself standing in the twins' line of fire. It was one thing to imagine herself as a creator of harmony, to imagine glorying in the credit. It was quite another to feel the rise in tension engendered by their physical proximity.

"Oh, God," said Grace. "Don't tell Amy I told you. I promised."

"There you are," said Thea, scraping her chair back and exhaling. She seemed almost satisfied. "More complications. Nothing's changed."

"I think," said James, when the two of them had settled down at a table, "I think you'd better keep quiet about seeing her till you speak to her, if you see what I mean."

"She made phoning signs," said Archie. "How can I call when I don't know where she is?"

"She meant she'll call you."

"Oh," said Archie. He knew he should have realized, but in the eighteen months he'd spent with her, Thea had often left him confused.

"Is this going to be a problem?" asked James, who thought it was. He felt an obligation to be twice his usual practical self, as if to compensate for the weakness of his secret visit to Hoxton. He also knew that his friend was in need of some sort of ballast, and he had a sudden image of himself hanging on to Archie's feet as he floated in space.

"No," said Archie. "It can't be a problem, I've got enough already. Why should it be?"

"I just thought. Well, you know. She left because of you."

"No, she didn't." It had taken Archie by surprise, this consensus that he was at the root of Thea's departure. "Grace said that on Saturday. I'm not having it. It's bollocks."

"It was part of it," said James.

"Bollocks. Did she ever say that? Or Amy?"

"No. Not as such."

"It's almost three years ago. It was finished by then, long before she left. And it was only eighteen months." He refused to be their scapegoat. He thought he knew Thea well enough to know it was far more than him she'd been turning her back on.

"They never forget."

Archie took a slug of his drink, ignoring James's generalization. James knew little about women, Archie had long ago decided. He'd had the good sense to allow Amy to choose him, but that was the extent of his expertise.

"It's very loud in here," he said. He usually liked the noise of the place, its atmosphere of competitive camaraderie. "I think I might have cancer."

James heard the word, but it took him a moment to move on from the question of Thea, an awkward subject in itself, but preferable now to this new one.

"What?" He pulled at his hair, at the front. It was a gesture from childhood. His mouth moved, but his brain had stopped. "Have you been to the doctor?" he heard himself saying.

"Of course I've been to the doctor." Archie was disappointed. He'd expected more from James. "What do you think I am, a bloody hypochondriac?"

"Sorry," James said, confused by this attack on his order of thought. "Sorry. Of course you've been. Where? What sort?"

"In my left testicle."

James smoothed down his hair and picked up his drink.

"Right." He thought quickly. "Right, well, that's not a bad place to get it." He thought again. "Except, of course, for the—"

"—for the likelihood of amputation and assault on my manhood. Not a bad place." Archie felt himself shaking.

"I only meant," said James slowly, "that it has a good survival rate. I've read about it."

"That's all right, then," said Archie. He poured half a bag of peanuts into his hand and stuffed them in his mouth. "Nothing to worry about."

"You said you *think* you've got cancer," said James, reconnecting with himself, with the logic and sense he'd temporarily abandoned, ready now to take this on fully, to grab Archie's ankles and plant him in the ground. "What exactly did the doctor say?"

⌇

FINLAY Road had been tranquil since the early morning when the children had been dispatched to Scotland for five whole days along with their cousins and James's sister and husband. Amy's joy at their departure was tinged with guilt at her exhilaration, but only tinged. At last she could think: think about the reality of her pregnancy, about what she really wanted, about what was for the best, and, of course, though she'd prefer not to think about it, the fact of Thea's return. Compared to many of her friends she'd had her children early, put the rest of her life on hold in her twenties. But the worst was over, the worst of the dependency, and now she had wanted to do something else; she was afraid that she might otherwise turn into one of those women who tell their children what might have been if not for them.

It had become second nature to think about other people's lives, not because she was unselfish, but because she'd had to, and she was out of practice on the business of herself. She found herself thinking about her husband in his office block in the City, and she experienced a flash of impatience and anger that distressed her. They'd had no time together at the weekend, and already he was back out in that other world in which she played no part.

Out of habit she picked up a basket of newly ironed clothes from the kitchen and took it upstairs, wondering if Archie would ring to tell her about his appointment. He was something else to think about. She was confused by her rush of adolescent sentimentality toward him. She could only think it had appeared as some compensation for her dissatisfaction, triggered by his fragile condition, or possibly her own, she thought, touching her stomach with her free hand. Whichever, it was absurd and foolish and thankfully unreturned. And if he didn't want to confide in her over his medical consultations, she could hardly make him. Yet when the phone had rung at lunchtime she was sure it was him.

"Hello, Amy?"

"Yes?"

"It's Richard, Richard Armstrong."

"Richard." Amy's disappointment was followed by a sudden sense of divided loyalty. There were principles of friendship to be upheld. Richard, she'd decided, had let Archie down.

"Haven't seen either of you for ages," he said. "How are you?"

"Ages," she said. "We're fine." There was an awkward pause while she tried to readjust her position on Richard, whom she'd always liked. She saw him as energetic and fun. She'd liked his wife, too, when he'd had one, though they never saw her now. "How are you, how've you been?" She listened to herself. She needed to make her displeasure clear. He had to know her position.

"So you're well, you and the kids?"

Amy didn't want to be bracketed with "the kids." "I'm very well," she said, "and they're growing up. In fact I'm thinking of going back to work."

"I'm glad to hear it. That sharp mind is wasted on domesticity. If you're serious we should talk."

Amy felt an unfamiliar rush of pleasure but said nothing. She would love to work with Richard, but how cruel life was in its timing.

"Actually," he went on, "I'll come to the point. I know it's cheeky of me to say so under the circumstances, but I'm concerned about Archie."

Amy knew she should extract herself or be compromised. She had to take sides.

"If you're worried about him, why don't you call him?" she asked. "Archie can more than look after himself."

"I have. I can't get hold of him. I saw him yesterday."

"Oh. I didn't know that." Why did she say that? Why should she know?

"Yes. We played tennis. We play every week."

Why should she know that, either?

"And I thought he seemed stressed—"

"What do you expect, for God's sake?" she cut him off sharply. "He's watching a part of his life disappear and . . ."

"Okay," said Richard, whose voice now held a self-conscious steadiness. "I'm sure I'm not popular in all this, but I had a thought last night, a good one. I want him to contact Frank Denny, he's a big online publisher. I doubt he'd buy him out, but he might pick up the titles, or at least absorb some of the staff."

"Well, then why don't you leave the number on his machine?" Amy said. She was aware of Richard pausing. She wondered if he was counting to ten.

"The thing is," he said, "do you know where I can find Archie? Frank wants to speak to him today. It's important to move quickly in these matters. To survey all the options. Consider his own future, too. What he'd like to do next."

"Consider the future. I need to do that." She spoke without thinking.

"Me, too," said Richard quickly, but Amy retreated from the shared confidence.

"He'll be fine," she said. She felt uncomfortable in having allowed even this small intimacy.

Richard sighed.

"Well, if you speak to Archie, get him to call me. He'll want to. He's not a fool."

Amy considered this statement. She thought that Archie sometimes could be foolish. It had been foolish, for example, to start an affair with her sister Thea; it was asking for trouble. But then he liked to feel he lived dangerously, almost as if he did things sometimes simply for the pleasure of the story he would later retell.

"I'll ask him to call you, if he rings," she said.

"Okay, thanks." Richard's tone lacked any note of finality.

"Bye, then," she tried.

"Amy?"

"Yes."

"I heard from John Holt that Thea might be coming back."

"Who's John Holt?"

"A guy who works with me. You've met him. The gay guy. He used to work with Thea, before she left for L.A. I think she's kept in touch with him, you know?"

"No, I don't know."

"Well, he mentioned she was due back, and I'd like to get in touch. Would you have a number for her?"

Amy was shocked at this affirmation of her sister's return, though Richard couldn't know that she barely knew of Thea's homecoming herself.

"She's not here yet. Not till later this week. She'll be staying at my mother's for a bit."

"Do you have the number?"

Of course she had the number.

"You want my mother's number?"

"Well, yes."

She wondered, as she rattled it off, why she felt so reluctant to give it to him.

"Thanks."

"And don't call after ten, my mother goes to bed early."

"No, no, of course not."

"And Thea's not there till Wednesday, or Thursday. In fact I'd give her till next week."

"Thank you," said Richard, and he was gone.

She had wanted to ask him why he needed to speak to Thea, why the rush to contact her, but she could never have brought herself to do so. It would be a work thing, she told herself; after all, Thea and

Richard were in related fields, they'd worked together in the past. Now that Thea was back, she would once again have to acknowledge that Thea was living a life that she wasn't; that Thea was out there, clever Thea, like James, and Grace, and Archie, or Archie until just now. They should never have let this standoff go on for so long. But she felt that she'd always been the one to give in. All their lives Thea had taken umbrage and she had had to placate. And then this last time Thea had gone altogether, decamped to the West Coast in a cocoon of resentment, and for once Amy had refused to make the conciliatory move before her twin had disappeared.

THE High Street was less frantic than usual. Those who lived in the streets and backwaters that threaded its borders were away for August, and only the shop assistants and office workers of Kensington remained. Lucy had been out shopping for food. It wasn't the experience it had once been, for the area had little to offer in the way of fine fresh produce these days. She very much regretted the loss of the greengrocer who'd once picked out the best for her, but now she made do with Safeways and the patisserie on her route back home. She had taken to using an old-fashioned basket on wheels, which she pulled behind her with a lightness lent by her upright deportment. As she approached the front door of her building, fumbling for her key in a pocket, she saw a fair-haired young man standing on the step, looking up.

"Can I help?" she asked, standing the basket to attention and clutching her handbag under her arm. She wanted to be trusting, but one could never be quite sure which way strangers would jump.

He turned to her and looked relieved. "You must be Mrs. Fielding."

"Yes?" Lucy thought how young he seemed. With his curly hair and blue eyes he looked like a beautiful child, almost holy, she considered. He seemed to her to have a sort of innocent strength.

"I'm Sam, Sam Harris, Grace's friend."

"Sam? Yes, of course. How nice to meet you. But Grace is at work."

"I know. But she asked me to pick up a suitcase. She said she'd tell you."

"Ah," said Lucy. "Well, she didn't." She looked at him and smiled. "But I don't suppose either of us is surprised, are we?" She put her key in the lock and pushed the door open.

"Come in. I presume she's packed it."

The two of them squeezed into the tiny lift, together with the basket. Sam's head almost brushed against the ceiling. Lucy beamed up at him.

"So, you're Sam."

"Yes," he said. He found Lucy's inquisitive, mischievous smile disconcerting, though it reminded him of Grace, and their proximity seemed too intimate for speech as the lift creaked slowly up through the three floors.

"Here we are." Lucy pulled open the iron gate, and Sam maneuvered the basket through the door that opened out into the flat.

"Bring it into the kitchen, Sam," said Lucy, "and I'll make us both some coffee."

"I really ought to get back," he said. Lucy looked at him, disappointed.

"I've got Danish pastries," she said. "And I'm sure you'd like to see my garden. Everyone does."

Sam was more compliant than his youth or profession might suggest, and he began to take the bags and parcels out of Lucy's basket and load them onto the wooden worktop.

"I knew it was you," said Lucy, "on the step. At least I thought it might be. I've seen you in a film. I'm afraid I can't remember what it was called."

"I hope you enjoyed it," he said. He wanted Grace's mother to like him. He had decided, after some reflection, that Grace was a woman worth his love, despite her tendency to behave sometimes as if her life were a continual performance. He, on the other hand, had known from the start of his career where to draw the line.

"I think I did," Lucy said. "I saw it on the television at Christmas."

"*A Postcard from Palermo?*"

"Yes!" Her smile seemed to compliment him on his memory. "That's right. It was most enjoyable."

"I was very young when that was made."

Lucy laughed. "You're very young now."

"Let me take that," he said, reaching out for the tray that Lucy was about to lift.

They sat together under the foliage canopy up on the roof, and Sam began to relax, seduced by the pastries, the prettiness, and the sheer comfort of Lucy's domain.

"Grace is going to find my place tough after here," he said, thinking of his minimalist apartment and licking his fingers. Lucy passed him a napkin.

"Sorry," he said, as a flake of pastry escaped onto the tiles.

"Don't worry, the pigeons will have that. Lick away."

She sat back in her elegant wicker chair.

"Do you really want to be an actor?"

Sam felt wrong-footed.

"I suppose I already am."

"Yes, and a good one, no doubt. But I'm sure there's more to you."

He felt as if she'd stolen his clothes. That without him noticing, she'd slipped beneath his skin and taken liberties. He should have been offended, but instead he found her directness more disconcerting than unpleasant.

"Well," he said, looking around at the abundant pots of white and purple flowers behind him, anywhere but at Grace's mother who wasn't much like a mother at all. "Actually," he forced himself to face her, "I think I'll direct, eventually, when I've got more experience."

It was the first time he'd said it aloud, but he knew it was true, that the job was merely the means to an end. Lucy smiled at him again and made a small, comforting noise, as if she were winding a baby. He sat back and took another bite of his pastry. Lucy filled up his cup.

"So don't be seduced," she said. "Flattery can be very destructive."

Sam swallowed in silence.

"You'll get what you want," she said.

Sam thought he knew a dramatic pause when he heard one.

"But?" he said.

"No 'but,'" said Lucy. "I must give you one of my books before you go. You might find it helpful." She lifted her cup to her lips, its blue and cream saucer held delicately beneath. Sam shifted in his chair and leaned forward.

"You don't mind, do you, Grace coming to stay with me?" he asked. "I'm sorry she didn't tell you." It was thoughtless of Grace, he felt, but he was too engaged by her charm not to assume that the world would forgive her most things.

"No," said Lucy. "I don't mind. I'll miss her, of course, but Thea will be here for a while. And she's got to go sometime."

"It's only temporary."

"Is it?"

Sam hoped it wouldn't be, and he knew that Lucy knew.

"That's the plan," he said.

"Plans are just maps for your journey, Sam."

He looked perplexed.

"They take you somewhere, that's all."

She watched him as he drained his cup. She'd frightened him a bit, she knew. She liked his good manners and the way he moved his head as he listened to her; it was something her husband had done. She tried, as always when the past crept in, to shut the door in her head, a heavy door that stood on the boundary between her two lives. But it wouldn't quite close today, and she had a sudden memory of the time before Grace, of just the four of them, her and Tom, Amy and Thea, in the car together, driving through the countryside. She could see the twins through the mirror on the back of the sun visor, sitting in the back, two identical faces dressed in clashing colors.

They'd been on their way to a local agricultural show, an outing for their ninth birthday. Amy was animated, overexcited, but Thea was sullen. She had wanted to go to the hospital fete in Maryfield. The sick people, she'd told them, were more important than the animals, and though they'd promised to call in on the way home, she wouldn't forgive them for settling on what had been Amy's choice.

As she watched Sam finishing his Danish, his head framed by the yellow rays of early chrysanthemums, Lucy could hear Tom's voice singing in her head: "Run, rabbit, run, rabbit, run run run." He was tapping his hand on the steering wheel of the car, and Amy was singing along, too loudly.

"Don't give the farmer his fun fun fun."

Lucy saw herself twisting in her car seat to look back at Thea, and the melancholy evident in the child's face touched her own, then and now, releasing it from its confines until she felt drenched.

"Cheer up, darling," she'd said at the time. "You'll love it when you get there, I promise."

"Bang bang bang bang goes the farmer's gun," father and daughter sang on.

Thea had turned her head away and looked out of the window. "I'm going to be a vegetarian when I grow up," she'd said and then had put her head down into the book on her lap.

Lucy gathered up the coffee cups and put them on the tray. She forced the door on the scene in her head tight shut, but as she did so she could see a small sulphurous cloud seeping under it, and it frightened her. She couldn't and wouldn't return to that time. It was these comings and goings that were stirring up the old silt, the grains left behind that could, on odd occasions, cloud her view. But they would soon settle. She willed herself to examine a fine clump of white begonias for signs of greenfly, then smiled across at Sam.

"You've indulged me long enough," she said. "Let's go and fetch Grace's case."

2004

24 NOVEMBER
HARLEY STREET

—

AMY'S FOOT, PATRICK noticed, was drawing small circles on the rug as she spoke, moving slowly, a silent counterpoint to the fractured rhythms of her voice. The foot, he fancied, was determined to see this through, and, with surprising speed, she found a way back, beyond her marriage and the more recent events that she'd claimed were her purpose in visiting him.

"When our father died," she said, "I think that we both felt as though we'd been swept aside. It was as if we'd been edged to the walls of the house by my mother's depression." She was speaking on waves of her breath, depositing the past, and though it was clear to him that she'd said the words often before, there was a fear in her voice that her story might never really be heard.

"For three months we were shut up with a mother who could barely function, and Grace who cried and cried. For two weeks we didn't go to school. We steered Lucy through the funeral, then we took her home, and she made a sort of encampment in her bedroom and would barely come out. My father's sister, Sylvia, arrived, supposedly to take care of things, but she was hopeless; she'd spend the day sipping sherry and talking on the phone while we got on with the household stuff, going to school from time to time, cooking and cleaning, taking care of Grace."

As he listened, Patrick watched for his own response. He found himself interred with her, as she spoke, in the darkness she described, the isolation, three children locked away from the world in a vault of grief. Amy was staring into her lap, one thumb stroking the other, sealed for the moment in a past as concrete as the room they sat in.

"It was my mother's sister, Jane, who saved us in the end. She flew from New Zealand to take charge. She sent Sylvia home, then she threatened the local doctor until someone came to assess Ma's state of mind. It was soon after that, one morning, a Sunday I remember, two nurses took her away in an ambulance. She cried and cried when she left, hugging us all, not wanting to go. It was terrible to see her so upset, but even we could see that the crying was better than the blankness that had been there before." Amy reached for a tissue from the box placed discreetly on the side table and blew her nose.

"Where did they take her?" said Patrick, mesmerized by her gothic detail and unable to resist a professional inquiry. "A hospital, a nursing home?"

"A hospital at first, I think. I didn't much care at the time," said Amy. "Things were so much better after Jane arrived. She was wonderful. It felt like a sort of golden age, and it lasted for about four months. She opened up things in some way, and people began to come and visit us, friends from school. She'd play music, quite loudly, Frank Sinatra and the Beatles, and whatever we were keen on, David Cassidy probably, and there were always flowers, I remember, and wonderful food."

She stopped to sip water like a marathon runner at a pit stop, and then she was off again.

"Jane took us to London, to the theater and museums. It felt like a resurrection. And she had a knack of making Thea and me feel for the first time that it was all right for us to look the same, that we were part of each other. We began to experiment, and we liked the attention we got, especially from boys. Thea cut her hair to match mine and we started to share our clothes, but then, suddenly, it was over. Ma was much better. She would be coming home, and it was time for Jane to go." She raised her hands and put them for a moment on the top of her head, then, self-conscious, returned them to her lap. She took a quick breath in, and held it, and paused before she went on.

"I can remember in clear detail the day that Lucy came home. She arrived like a star in a comeback, her hair all newly colored and waved. She was dressed in a sort of pastel blue and smelled of lemons. Whoever this woman in the doorway was, she was different, she wasn't anyone we could remember. She stood, her arms outstretched, and said to us, 'Everything's going to be all right now, darlings. We're all going to be happy. I'm going to be just like Jane, you'll see.'"

Amy stopped and laughed.

"Outrageous," she said, her foot tapping now rather than circling, "it was an outrageous performance. Lucy really confused us. I thought she was quite mad, and I still do. And so did Thea, which was why I got angry when she sided with Ma before she went off to America."

"Sided with her?"

"I told you."

"Not exactly," Patrick said.

"I wanted Ma to face the truth about what had happened, with Dad. I felt it was time, that we all should, but Thea said Ma had a right to protect her happiness."

She appeared to be opening up to him, but, despite her frankness, he felt there was something hidden, something she was keeping from him, not the usual half-conscious hesitancy of most of his patients, but a deliberate withholding.

"Like you, you mean," he said. "Isn't that what you said you were doing, by coming here?"

"It isn't the same," said Amy, but she looked defensive. "My mother wasn't protecting anything, I told you, she was pretending."

"Explain to me the difference," said Patrick.

1994

FOR THE VERY last time that day, James climbed down the back stairs at Fortson Payne. He felt his leg muscles tremble as he neared the ground floor. Against his better judgment, he had rung Patrick the shrink that afternoon, after lunch with Archie, to ask for another appointment. The climb upstairs after his meeting, the third and a half of the day (that was forty flights in one morning, not counting the descents), had driven him to make the call.

To his surprise, Patrick had offered him a consultation at 6:30 that evening. It would be preferable, of course, he had said, if they could fix a routine, but while they were both still "on a mutual trial basis," as he put it, and it was August, he was happy to see James in an impromptu fashion. James's reaction was less considered. He'd thought he'd better go while he was still in the mood, and Amy, he knew, wouldn't be home till eight from her yoga class. They were due to go out for dinner to celebrate their first evening alone without the children.

As he walked to the Underground, he forced himself to stretch out his contracted leg muscles. He could feel the sun on his face and was more conscious than usual of all the bare flesh on display, jackets slung over shoulders, freckled arms and tanned cleavage, even a few hairy legs under shorts threading through the uniforms of the City. There was a not unpleasant smell of bodies, of an erotic vitality.

It was sexy, and the street seemed to sway a little and shimmer. His legs relaxed, and he regretted making the appointment with Patrick. He wanted to stay here, in the bars and verandas with their hedonistic promise, love-bombed by a cult of money and aspiration, where death was not admitted other than as a tax to be avoided.

The idea of Archie dying was, of course, unthinkable, but the faintest possibility had now been seeded. Archie had been part of James's life for so long that his permanence as a fixture was unquestioned. It wasn't a refusal on James's part to admit death in principle; he'd sensed the fragility of life in respect of his wife and children. He'd taken out insurance, made a will. He'd woken from nightmares, distraught and bereft, having to get out of bed to go and check that they were alive and breathing in their beds. But he'd never thought of death in connection with Archie, and as he tried to absorb the idea, standing on the escalator in the station, he felt as if he'd disappeared himself. He scanned the unfamiliar faces opposite, searching for something, willing one at least to turn and acknowledge his humanity, however briefly, but they passed like ghosts on the other side, floating upward to the light he'd left behind.

FORTY minutes later he found himself trying to explain his fear to Patrick. He sat in the big chair, with his legs out in front. It was certainly good to put his feet up after the day's exertions.

"I just couldn't imagine it, him dying," he said.

"Couldn't or can't?" asked Patrick.

"Sorry?"

"Well, can you imagine it now?"

James closed his eyes.

"No, sorry, it's completely blank."

"That's quite logical," said Patrick.

"Is it? Why?"

"Well, death is a blank, I suppose. Unless you have strong religious beliefs."

"I'm an agnostic," said James.

"What does a blank mean for you as an agnostic?"

"I don't want to get off the point. I don't want to get into religion."

"What is the point?" said Patrick.

James pulled at his hair. He wanted to leave but felt he owed it to Patrick to answer.

"I want to know if it means I would rather my wife and children died than Archie. That's the difference. I can't see him dead. But I've seen them dead in my imagination."

There, he'd said it.

"Is that the right question?" asked Patrick.

Oh, God, thought James. He knew it would end up like this.

"I knew this is what you'd think," he said.

"What would I think?"

"That I'm a repressed homosexual."

Patrick smiled.

"Because you have feelings of love for another man?" he asked.

"Because we went to an English public school, because you think we're all repressed homosexuals."

"Really?" said Patrick. "I was thinking more along the lines that perhaps you identify with Archie and it's your own death you fear." He warmed to his theme. "You're approaching forty, after all. This new sense of mortality is common."

"Oh," said James. He thought for a moment. "You might be right about that," he said, and then he heard himself saying, "There were girls in the sixth form, as a matter of fact."

Patrick paused, and James wondered which way he would jump.

"Were you and Archie close—before the girls arrived?"

James looked up. He thought maybe Patrick was laughing at him, but he saw in his face what he'd been looking for earlier in the Tube station: a reflection of his own being, and something in him gave up the fight.

"Yes," he said, stretching out. "Yes. We were close, not in that way, but very close." He saw an image of Mr. Fairbrother sitting across the desk in his study.

"WHO'S your best friend here at school, James?"

"Archie."

"And why do you like Archie?"

James was nonplussed by the question.

"I just like him."

"But you're friends with the other boys, too?"

James wasn't sure. He was uncertain of his standing at the school. The threat of bullying loomed over him because of his tearful outbursts, and there were a few who prowled around him, as if waiting for their opportunity. But so far Archie, who was tall and physically mature for his years, had held them off.

"Sort of," he said, staring past Fairbrother to the picture behind him that seemed to drip. He could feel it dripping now as well as see it; it was dripping down his cheek, the involuntary leak that brought humiliation and grief.

⌘

THE grand doors of Archie's mansion block hid an interior that was in need of redecoration. They were sheeted with copper and polished every day by an ancient Romanian, who spoke no English but who smiled and wiped vigorously as she nodded to the inhabitants. Amy took the red-carpeted lift up to the fourth floor and rang Archie's bell. It was quite the normal thing, she told herself, for her to come here to see Archie as she had on several occasions, to express her friendship and concern. But it didn't feel normal, it felt like trespassing. She was here, if she was honest, because she felt compelled to be; it was something to do with him confiding in her, with his condition; but why his weakness should have crossed a boundary between them was not clear to her. She seemed now to have little choice but to see this through, to see Archie through whatever would happen, however complex her motives. She didn't want to scrutinize her excited compulsion too closely; it was as if Archie's crisis had allowed her one of her own. She would keep it in control. After all, that was her style, she told herself.

It took several rings before he answered the door, sleepy and disheveled. He was wearing boxer shorts and an old baggy T-shirt, and she was surprised at how young he looked in the afternoon light, young and vulnerable. She wanted again to put her arms around him and feel him against her, too close, but instead she offered her cheek for him to peck.

"Come in," he said. "I half thought it might be you. What time is it?"

"Six. I was worried."

"You needn't be. Sorry, I know I said I'd call you."

"Never mind," she said, "it doesn't matter." She looked around the wide room with its expensive but distinctive furniture and the striking 1960s American abstract paintings that Archie had inherited from his mother and to which he claimed a philistine ambivalence. Today the room felt uncared for; there were unwashed cups and plates on the table, clearly left from several sittings.

"I've told him," said Archie. "I've told James."

"Good."

"Sorry about the mess—Maria's on holiday."

Amy said nothing. This air of neglect was new, even allowing for the fact that his cleaner was away. She felt absurdly shy, standing here with him, her dear old friend. She could remember when their friendship had taken off, when he'd first begun to get used to the idea of her. They had been in Paris, about six months after her wedding. There were supposed to have been four of them, but Archie had just parted company with yet another young woman whose soft blond exterior had hidden her ability to exploit a weakness. As she stood now in front of him, in his large London sitting room, ten years later, the conversation returned to her intact.

"SHE kept claiming I was immature," Archie said, seeming both out-raged and amused.

They were drinking coffee together in a café. James was off visit-ing a museum that neither Amy nor Archie could face.

"And are you?" said Amy.

"No, not really. A bit, maybe. She meant I didn't want to take things further."

"So are you sad?" she said.

"No, not really."

"A bit, maybe," she teased.

"She was fantastic-looking," he said with a note of regret. "I'll miss that."

He'd never talked to Amy about his girlfriends before, or about anything significant, in fact.

"What else did you like about her?" she asked him.

Archie watched a chic Parisienne as she walked past their table into the café.

"All the girls in Paris look like lesbians," he said. "Pretty ones, of course, but I don't suppose they are."

"I asked you a question," she said.

He seemed to think about it as he watched the French girl sit down and take out her cigarettes.

"I used to look at her," he said, "when she was asleep and not complaining about me, and I just wanted to hold her and look after her, and stop anything bad happening to her." The confession appeared to surprise him.

"And when she woke up?"

"She was still very decorative," he said, "like you." He smiled at her and leaned forward, too close, and stroked her face. She pushed his hand away gently and laughed.

"You don't have to flirt with me," said Amy. "I'm your best friend's girl."

He was embarrassed for a moment, then relieved. It was as if he'd forgotten where he was or, more to the point, whom he was with.

"So," said Amy, "nothing else?"

"No. Yes, of course other things. But I do like beauty. I admit it." He raised his cup again. "Here's to the future." They sat in silence, not wanting to abort the moment, the click of recognition that heralds friendship as well as love. Archie was the first to speak.

"And what about you, Madame Marsham?"

"What about me?"

"Are you going to make my friend James happy?"

"Are you anxious for him?" she asked.

He considered her question.

"I think," he said, "that you might be too cool for him."

Amy looked at him, amazed. Then she pushed back in her seat and smiled.

"Thank you," she said, "for the compliment. But that won't be a problem."

FROM time to time over the years, as he moved from girl to girl and she teased him, she had pulled out his comment from some recess of her mind and pondered it. She'd never considered herself to be cool. That was more Thea's style. But whether he'd meant cool in the fashionable sense, or just cold, she'd never liked to ask. She hadn't wanted him to know she still thought about it. She'd prided herself on seeing through Archie, beyond the charm that James had once described, in a rare fit of annoyance with his friend, as pathological.

And now, here she was, another of his conquests, though he didn't know it, her self-control slipping, part of her wishing she could give way.

"I could make some tea," she said, forcing herself from her fantasy.

"Or we could go out," said Archie, looking around at the uninviting chaos. "We could go round to the deli." He looked more cheerful at this prospect, and Amy agreed at once.

"Oh, yes. Let's have ice cream, it's so hot. But you'd better put some clothes on, don't you think?"

He looked down at himself and seemed puzzled. "I'm sorry. I didn't realize I wasn't dressed."

He disappeared up the stairs into his bedroom, and she resisted the impulse to clear up the plates from his table. She checked her reflection in the mirror that hung at an angle, sloping forward into the room, refracting the light from the window. She was pleased with what she saw and she smiled at herself, at this rise of her foolish and inappropriate excitement. She was about to call out to Archie, to tease him out of domestic decay, when the telephone beside her rang and she half moved to pick it up.

"I'll just leave it," he called.

The message clicked on and Thea's voice carried through the flat in an eerie imitation of Amy's.

"Archie, hey. It's Thea. No, you weren't hallucinating. It was me you saw. But Ma and Amy don't know I'm back yet, so if you haven't already told them, I'd appreciate it if you didn't. I'll explain some time. I'm at the Bow Club, should you want to call me. Bye."

Archie stood in the doorway from the hall to the sitting room, his hands on either side of the frame. He looked at Amy frozen in the middle of the room.

"I was going to tell you," he said.

As James walked up the hill to Finlay Road, he felt exhausted. It wasn't just his legs but his whole being. He wanted to lie down. He'd been looking forward to this dinner, alone with Amy, but now it seemed an ordeal to be weathered before he could get into bed and fall asleep. He felt cheated, cheated of an undisturbed evening with his wife, and of a satisfactory conclusion to his appointment with Patrick. He felt he'd bared his soul, told him things that no one knew, himself included, till this evening. But the session had ended, time had run out, and there had been the inevitable producing of

Patrick's diary and a fresh appointment made. There had been no catharsis.

Amy was standing in the hallway smiling at him as he let himself in, smiling, he noticed, a little too brightly. She kissed him.

"You look exhausted, sweetheart," she said. "Hard day?"

"I saw Archie," he said. "He told me."

"Yes, I know. I saw him, too, briefly, this afternoon." She was aware that her careful tone might strike the wrong note.

"Is there anything else?"

"Whatever do you mean?" she said, turning to go back to the kitchen. Her husband's tone was almost sharp, and she wanted at once to reassure him, to restore him to his geniality. "Let's have a drink, sweetheart," she said. "There's half an hour before dinner."

"He tells us, or rather he tells you," said James as he followed her in, "about Greta, and you tell me. Then he tells me about the job, and now he tells me this, for God's sake. What else?"

"Nothing," said Amy, uncorking a bottle of cold white wine. "It's quite enough."

"So when did he tell you?" asked James.

She turned her head away as she poured him a drink.

"I wanted him to tell you on Saturday night."

James slammed his keys down on the table.

"You've known since then and you didn't tell me?"

"He made me promise. I told you about Greta. He couldn't handle it all at once."

"He's not the only one." James picked up the glass and almost emptied it.

"Don't take it out on me," she said.

THE weight in James's legs seemed to spread through his body. By the time they had walked the quarter-mile to their local restaurant, he felt he might slump through the warm damp air. The sight of people on the dark, sultry streets, running and calling to one another, as if changed briefly by the heatwave into exuberant foreigners, exhausted him. He was relieved to reach their destination, the entrance hidden down a narrow alley and lit by a single lamp over the door. It was a popular place, and in summer, weather permitting, its ivy-covered walled garden was always full, even in August.

"Señor James, Señora James. Welcome, welcome." The maître d' greeted them, his regulars, and waved them through to the back where the table tea lights struggled for oxygen. They smiled at each other, but only out of habit, as they ordered, as almost always, grilled calamari for Amy and *bistecca* for James. Amy watched her husband's face as he fought to subdue his weariness.

"Archie will be fine," she said.

"How do you know he'll be fine?" asked James. "How could you possibly know?"

"The consultant said it was probably nothing," she offered.

"That's what he told you?"

"Yes, this afternoon; we had tea. He seemed quite cheerful." She felt she could live with the simplicity of this statement. For that was all it had been, tea between friends.

James pulled a face, and the reassurance she'd garnered retreated.

"What did he say to you, then?" she said.

"That the doctor said it was probably something."

"What? What something?"

"You know." James lifted a piece of bread to his mouth. It felt thick against his tongue.

"Cancer?" she said. "Definitely?"

"A tumor." He swallowed the dough as he spoke. "Maybe."

"They don't tell you that till they know, do they?" Amy was disbelieving, her bafflement growing to catch up with her husband's.

"He thinks they know," said James. "The things they said."

"He didn't tell me that."

"Didn't want to worry you, I suppose."

"No."

"He's having an operation on Wednesday."

Amy poured herself a glass of water. She could hear James talking, but she sat unsteady and far away. She'd had tea with Archie. He hadn't told her any of this. He'd eaten his cake and teased her. It had been almost like it used to be, before Thea, she thought, when they used to be able to flirt without an undertow. It was Thea's fault. That was when things had changed between her and Archie, and she'd withdrawn without noticing; and now, when she wanted the old Archie back, it was so much more complicated. Thea had stolen their innocence.

"Wednesday. This Wednesday?" she said.

"Yes. He just wants to get on with it, though he claimed the doctor said it would make no difference, this week or next."

Amy put down her fork and pushed the food on her plate to and fro.

"No difference to who? Bloody doctors. They're hopeless. What a thing to say. It makes a lot of difference to Archie. He has to live with it. Can you imagine what that's like for him, the waiting?"

James smiled, then let out a croaky uncharacteristic laugh.

"What are you laughing at? How can you laugh?"

"You look just like Rosie."

"I'm her mother. It's hardly surprising."

"You look like her when she's cross." He reached over and tried to take her hand, but she pulled it away.

"Now you're taking it out on me," he said.

For just a brief moment she hated him beyond all rationality. How could he laugh? Ever since he'd gotten home, James had been detached and crabby, a mood he'd imposed on her with increasing frequency over the last months, and suddenly, halfway through dinner, he was trying to revert to his usual self, to make things all right when they weren't, and expecting her to follow.

"I know how fond you are of Archie," James said. He leaned forward and spoke quietly as if the other diners might be listening, though the tables were well spaced. "I could almost be jealous sometimes."

Amy looked up at him, alarmed, but he was smiling as he spoke. "We all love Archie," he went on. "I do, too. I love him."

Amy's petulance retreated in shock as she heard his words. It might seem a small thing, quite natural, for James to say that he loved Archie, but he'd never said it before. He could tell her he loved her, and would say it to his children. She knew he'd loved his mother, though she'd never heard him use the words. But she'd never expected him to say it of Archie. It was much too high-flown for the two of them.

She leaned toward him.

"You really are upset, aren't you?"

He looked at her in surprise.

"Yes, of course I'm upset. Did you think I wasn't?"

"I just thought you had a funny way of showing it." She offered him the hand she'd refused him before. "Sometimes," she said, almost to herself, "I think we're all a bit too fond of Archie."

James took her hand, but with his other he was reaching for his wallet. "I've got a thumping headache," he said. "Do you mind if we go home?"

He'd been going to tell her about Patrick tonight, about work and the lifts, but he felt unable to set off into uncharted waters. It would surely, he told himself, be selfish under the circumstances to talk about his own problems, and he didn't want to think any more about Archie's, not tonight, though it was hard to stop the darkness creeping in. He wanted to lie down, to forget it all, for Amy to help to make it better; but she, like him, was out of soothing reach.

"No," said Amy. "Let's go. We both need an early night."

Walking back, holding his hand, she was glad the evening was almost over. She was beginning to acknowledge, for the first time, that her husband's steady disposition was in a state of flux and had been for a while, and it frightened her to think so. And yet she hadn't even told him she was pregnant. She felt as if she were someone else.

She would usually confide everything in this man who was walking beside her, so who could she be, this separate creature whose will seemed independent of her own? But she couldn't tell him yet. She could still think she had options. She would get this difficult evening out of the way, and then things would be clearer. He hasn't even mentioned Thea, she thought, though she knew that Archie had told him about the Oxford Street moment. But then neither had she.

2004

24 NOVEMBER
HARLEY STREET

"It was so much easier," she was telling him, "to indulge myself with these thoughts of Archie than to face what was happening to me. It was easier to imagine myself even a bit in love with him, under the guise of my concern, of course. I didn't want another baby, and I suspected that James might not want one, either. I didn't want to think what that might or might not mean." She was standing by the window as she spoke, and she turned to look at Patrick, who read the fear of an accusation in her gaze. "It's not always easy to take your bearings," she went on, "when you're supposed to be happily married. Sometimes you have to read your cues from other people, and I was having trouble. James was usually so open, his emotions had always been easy to follow, but he'd closed off from me."

She had asked him if he minded if she stretched her legs, and as she'd taken a turn or two around the room, physically examining his select objects, her eyes absorbing everything, Patrick had watched her, feeling voyeuristic and at the same time exposed.

"Remind me who this is again?" she said, picking up the small green figure on the windowsill.

"Alkyone," he said. "I looked her up. She's the goddess of the wind, or one of them."

"I like her," she said, putting it down and striding back to her seat. "I used to like the idea of the wind changing things. When you're a child they tease you, they tell you that if the wind changes you'll stay as you are, get left behind. I suppose there's something in that."

"Did you get left behind?"

"Oh, yes," she said.

"When?"

"Back then, that week . . ." She took a breath, and he wondered if she would spit out or swallow what she wanted to say. They gazed at each other across the low table.

"The week your twin sister came home?" he said.

She frowned at him as if he were willfully obtuse, ignoring his question.

"Yes," she said. "The week my husband came to see you."

1994

Tuesday 16 August

4:00 a.m.

Toward dawn, James woke up, thirsty and anxious from a dream of loss that he could not recall. He'd slept badly, blaming the heavy restaurant dinner and his growing inability to be comforted by his wife. He got out of bed, went for a pee, and then pushed open the door into Jonny's room, forgetting that his son and daughter were away. The bed was empty and he was back in the nightmare, and, just for a moment, all the pain and emptiness of the universe were exposed to him by the absence of the small breathing body under its red striped duvet. He sat on the single bed, his head in his hands. He supposed this was the sort of stuff that Patrick would like if only he could remember it. He tried to recall the dream, to shake out its meaning. He felt like a dog with a bone. He'd been crying in the dream, he was sure of it, but when he put his hands now to his eyes, they were dry.

On his way to the kitchen to get some ice for his whiskey, Archie stubbed his toe hard against the corner of the large professional oven that had come with the flat and was rarely used other than for caterers to heat up canapés for the parties he used regularly to give. As the pain registered, he swore and almost dropped his glass. *Four o'clock in the fucking morning,* he thought, *and fate is awake and against me.* He half hopped to the fridge and held his foot against the inside of the freezer door while he extracted some ice from the dispenser, then limped back to the sitting room and slumped on the sofa. *This time on Thursday*, he thought, *I'll be asleep. Then I'll wake up and my life will have changed.* But he knew that it already had. He was almost exhilarated by the notion of a laundered sheet of a life, even if it were to be a short one. He felt an unfamiliar relief and fell asleep.

SAM and Grace had been making love for the second time that night, and it had dwindled now to a sleepy embrace, more of an inability to separate than a search for sensation, an alchemical mingling of whatever sits just above the human surface, binding beyond the skin.

"I'm so glad you're here," said Sam.

Grace smiled, close up to his face.

"Me, too," she said, and realized with relief that at this moment she meant it. "What time is it?"

He pulled the upper half of his body away and reached for the clock.

"Ten past four."

"Oh, God," she said. "I must sleep. I've got to leave by eight."

ACROSS the city, Lucy sat in her dressing gown and a wrap, among the flowers, above the roofs of Kensington. It felt like a ritual, this sitting in the cool stillness, the strange quiet of the streets, on her first night alone. Grace had gone now, she knew that, even if her daughter didn't. And she was glad. It was time, and she liked Sam and hoped that Grace would let him make her happy. She listened to the clock bell striking in the distance. She was sixty, sixty years old. She'd spent so long maintaining a world from which bad thoughts were banished that simply to hope on Grace's behalf, rather than to know, seemed like failure. She sensed that with the exit of her last child, her gremlins saw their chance. They were knocking at her door. Something or someone was calling out her name.

2004

24 NOVEMBER
HARLEY STREET

PATRICK WAS STROKING the back of his left hand with the fingers of his right as he looked at her, playing for time, shocked by the baldness of her statement: "The week my husband came to see you." So it was there between them now: that James was their hidden point of connection, their frame of reference.

"You've remembered," she said.

It was dark outside, and he got up suddenly and went to draw down the blinds, to shut out the squares of yellow that hung in the darkness across the street.

"You've just told me," he replied as he came back to face her.

"But you remember."

"In a manner of speaking."

Why, he thought, *why deliberately hide this from me?* But he knew better than to ask the why question. You couldn't trust the answer. It had started to come back to him during this second session. He'd begun to suspect it as she continued to repeat the litany of names. This woman was the wife of a former client. He did remember now, it was his job to remember things, a man who had come in the middle of the summer, years ago, when his regular and rather small clientele was away, and Patrick was young and broke and would take the work where he could. The man had come to see him only briefly, three or four times, and never returned, believing himself, Patrick assumed, to be cured. And perhaps he had been. It was a phobia that had brought him, after all; Patrick could remember that: panic attacks, symptoms that could come and go. He also remembered that he'd liked him.

"I don't think, then," said Patrick, "that under the circumstances, I'm the right . . ."

"No," she said, "I thought you might say that. But now I'm here I'll continue, if I may?"

Nothing in his training or experience had prepared him for this type of infiltration into his confidence. He felt himself for a moment to be her hostage, until the concentration left her face. She smiled at him almost shyly and the reassurance overrode a moment of fear. He would allow her to continue for the hour, he decided, but decline to see her again. The room had grown darker, and he moved to switch on another light. He wished it were summer, that he could throw the windows open and let in the air. He felt formal and constrained, and he wanted to feel the pulse of an everyday existence, of the life in the city, far away from this shadow she'd brought up the stairs and inside.

Tuesday 16 August

"Colour Outside the Lines"

from *Lifelines for Parents* by Lucy Fielding

As the train to Brighton left Victoria, Richard Armstrong pulled out his mobile, opened his coffee, and began making calls. He'd taken the day off work to visit his mother, but certain aspects of business still had to be taken care of. He rang his office, imagining Lynette, her willowy torso sitting behind her desk, immaculately dressed in black-girl chic. He imagined her waiting for his call, her function to carry out his bidding, to make his life smooth and collude in his swift ascent.

"Richard," said Lynette, "give me a break. I thought you were taking the day off."

Richard was never quite sure if Lynette was teasing him. But she was a good worker, even if she didn't always deliver the respect to which he felt entitled.

"Just a couple of things, then I'm off your back," he said. "I want you to call Frank Denny's office at Denny Publishing and ask them to bike over their prospectus and any other company information they can give me."

"Then what?"

"I'll dictate a letter to go with it, and I want you to bike it around to Archie Morgan's home address. Have you got it?"

"I have," said Lynette. She liked Archie, who flirted with her on the odd occasion he came into the office.

"Good," said Richard. "Now put me through to John."

THE train rushed through the Sussex countryside, but Richard hardly noticed. It was difficult for him to sit still. He wanted to be in the heart of things, his energy urging him on to the next task and the next. He looked around the carriage, which was only half full. His busy mind began to calculate the price of first-class tickets and number of occupied seats. August wasn't good for business, he thought, and his own wasn't growing as fast as he would like at the moment. It was just one of the reasons he wasn't prepared to lend Archie money to chuck away. But he'd been feeling an unexpected nostalgia for the time he and Archie had worked together years before in advertising. They'd rush around their agency, wielding campaigns like small boys with light sabers, junior lieutenants in a world of contrivance. They'd stay late in the office, laughing at the foibles of their clients, thinking up new games to offer them. But they couldn't go back to that, and he'd been foolish even to suggest on Sunday that they might join forces. Not that Archie would consider it.

He heard himself sigh and forced his head back into the seat. He would miss Archie if this quarrel took a bad turn. Richard had liked Archie right from the start, had admired his relaxed self-sufficiency, a trait that Richard wished he could emulate and that he'd noticed even at his interview, when Archie had been one of three men sitting across the desk from him. The meeting hadn't gone well; he'd been nervous, and Archie had been the most sympathetic. They had struck up a rapport, playing a matey game that had allowed Richard to shine between rounds of sparring with the doubters. He'd found out later that Archie had swung it for him, had said they should take a gamble, that Richard had an edge they needed. A couple of years ago, reminiscing one late night, Archie had confessed to Richard that it was an edge he felt he now needed, or one he was looking to regain.

He had tried to warn Archie that business was getting tougher, for everyone, that cleverness and originality were no longer enough. The days of quality for its own sake were over, and short-term profit was the holy grail. Archie had slipped out of step. Richard couldn't help but feel a little smug when he thought of his own success in comparison. His money was hard earned and not for gambling. It hadn't come easy as it had for Archie, he thought, as he justified yet again his decision not to "invest" in Archie or, more truthfully, delay what was certainly coming. What was the point? Archie was sharp when he concentrated, and his charm was never in question, but he didn't seem to use it where it mattered, he didn't seem to care. Richard took out his newspaper and closed up his phone, resolving not to use it till he was on his way home.

The carriage was almost deserted, and he spread himself across the first-class seat, considering the day ahead without enthusiasm. His mother would be waiting for him, in her new flat in Hove. She'd been a widow now for almost nine months. His father, a Manchester cabby, had dropped dead on retirement, and now his mother had come to Brighton, to live near his auntie and uncle. At least she'd been left well provided for, which proved, his mother often told him, just what a good man his father had been, but Richard knew this view was rose-tinted by widowhood. Death made people sentimental, and his own recollections were harsher.

He took a taxi from the station to the flat. The smell of salt and warm seaweed hung in the air as he paid the driver. He wondered what it would have been like to grow up here, by the sea. There were worse places than Blackley in the seventies and eighties, but it had been a district on the losing side in the battle for upward mobility.

"I've brought you a present," he said, after he'd kissed her.

"What is it?" she asked.

"Open it, Ma, and see."

She fished in the carrier bag, pulled out the parcel and felt it, smiling at him.

"Open it."

He watched her peel off the wrapping paper with hands that seemed older than he remembered. Her engagement and wedding rings were looser below the swollen knuckles.

"Oh," she said, "I've wanted one of these for a bit."

"I know."

"Does it . . . ?"

"Yes, it turns itself off. You can go to sleep listening to it and it shuts off."

It was what she had asked for, not too complicated, a digital clock radio encased in silver Bakelite.

"It's lovely, Richard. Thank you. It's just what I wanted." She put a hand to his cheek and kissed him, and he saw that her small blue eyes were still keen and seemed to accuse him of something unspoken.

"Happy housewarming, Mum. Sorry I couldn't make it sooner."

"You're busy, love. Our Patsy sent me those flowers," she said, pointing at a pot full of fading pink and white blooms, "and Paul rings every week."

"That's nice. What's he up to. Behaving himself?" His younger brother had been regarded as difficult, but was now in the army in Germany.

"He's going on exercises."

"That should keep him out of trouble."

"He's a good boy. We're all proud of him."

Richard felt momentarily excluded, chastised in some way. For what? She was needling him already. He pushed the irritation aside.

"Right. Are you ready? It's a brilliant day. Let's go out."

"But you've only just got here. You're always in a rush, Richard. Have a cup of tea first." She disappeared into the kitchen, and he sat down in front of the mute pictures dancing on the television screen.

ARCHIE closed the door of the building on the river behind him. It had been a scene of unreality that paralleled his visit to the consultant just the day before. First he'd sat in his office and listened, while an accountant and a company lawyer, dressed in a variety of grays, outlined his options. Not that there were many, and, of course, unbeknownst to the pair across the desk, he was concerned that there might be even fewer.

There weren't many advantages to be had from living with suspected cancer, but the knowledge that his tormentors, if that wasn't too strong a word for the man and woman seated opposite, would soon be twitching with guilt was one of them. ("How awful. Have you heard about Archie Morgan? We couldn't have known. He sat there and never said a word!") But it was essential, he'd decided, that he go ahead with this meeting quickly; there were too many other people involved to stall the decision any longer. His staff would need to look for other work. He would sign the papers today, before he went tomorrow for his biopsy, snip, reconstruction, or whatever it was going to be.

His colleagues were gathered together, a dozen or so who worked in the small offices, three intersecting rooms facing the river, in a former warehouse. Their faces were anxious, though they knew what was coming. Archie sat on a desk in front of them as he had so often before when he'd had more uplifting news, a rise in circulation, a trade award or two. But there had been nothing like that for a couple of years, and the demoralized group in front of him induced an overwhelming guilt at his lack of foresight, at his own complacency.

"It's a tough business," he heard himself saying. "And it's through no fault of yours. We created an excellent product." On and on his voice went, and he wondered if they were really listening. They seemed patient and sad, though one or two were sullen. At the end of it he shook their hands, promised them fair notice and a party to bid them farewell. He'd let them down.

He walked toward the riverbank feeling he had put his life on hold. One signature and the whole business of staff dismissals, payments to magazine contributors, and cessation of trading was now in the hands of the lawyer and accountant. They would act for him in the short term. It felt cowardly, but events had overtaken him and in his lack of choice there was a freedom, a lightness that displaced some small part of the fear he now carried with him.

BEING in a soap opera was much like being at school, Grace thought, as she registered the slightly more than usual interest she was attracting from her colleagues on the set this morning. There were the toadies and the bullies, the hard workers and those who got away with sleepwalking through the daily fiction of adultery, confrontation, and derailed lives. There were the back row one-liners who were nowhere to be found when required, and the bad boys and girls who lived with the threat of expulsion and press exposure. Presiding over all was the executive producer, the headmaster, who must be obeyed and placated if a decent story line was to be had, or a pay rise in the offing.

Today there was a rumor that Grace Fielding might be moving on to better things. She'd no idea where it had come from. She'd admitted her grander ambitions to no one but her family and Sam, and her new agent had told her to keep everything under wraps. She'd had, however, to inform the headmaster that she'd changed management, and that must have been the giveaway. She'd rung her agent in a panic; the toeholds on the climb up were so easy to miss.

"Don't worry about it. Just keep quiet, deny everything, and enjoy it," he'd said.

"But how do they know, Peter?" said Grace. "I haven't as much as hinted, I promise."

"New agent, high-profile boyfriend, stand-out performances; it's the obvious next step. They're not stupid."

"They might fire me."

"They won't. But we need you to go out with a bang."

A bang. That was the thing with life in a soap, she thought, it couldn't resolve until you were dead.

She wondered sometimes if she'd been a fool ever to get involved in *Bridewell Wharf.* It might prove to be a curse that would follow her about like an embarrassing relation. When she'd first had the offer, she'd turned to her family for advice, but Amy and Lucy had pleaded ignorance, while Thea had been appalled, feeling Grace should aim higher. It was James, oddly, who had given her the push she needed.

"It's a launching pad, Grace. If you're any good, you'll fly beyond it. You've got the looks. Give yourself two years max, then get out."

And he'd been right so far. The public loved her, the press loved her, it was eighteen months. All she needed now was a great part to go to. And, of course, there was Sam.

When Grace thought about Sam she experienced a pleasure and a warmth that was new to her, but also the beginnings of an anxiety that she could never live up to what they had started, never be what he supposed her to be. Most of the time she loved being with him, and she recognized that their union had many advantages. But in her darker moments, she was unsure in what order she would put them. He was very attractive and without duplicity, he was successful, he was sought after, his cool and his profile coated her, gave her a sheen of unearned glamour. He was also faithful. It could be argued that fidelity could hardly be measured at three months, but her instincts told her that whatever temptations he encountered, Sam would mate for life given the chance. In these same dark moments she suspected that, though she'd meant it when she told him she loved him, Sam might not keep her straight.

She sat in her dressing room trying hard to concentrate on the lines for her next scene, distracted by the real news that her agent had lined up a reading for her with a Hollywood director who was coming into town that weekend. As she answered the insistent ring of her phone, there was a knock on the door. It was her call to the set.

"Hi, Sam, sweetheart," she said, "where are you? I'm on my way through as we speak."

"At rehearsal, but we're on a break. Listen, there's a late-night screening of *Fire at the Kat Club* tonight, are you up for it?"

"I'm exhausted," she lowered her voice, "by you. And I'm supposed to go to Ma's and see Thea."

"Fine, it won't start till late."

"I've got an early call, Sam."

"Why don't you call me from your ma's and we'll take it from there? If you don't want to go, we won't."

"But you can go, you can go without me."

There was a pause.

"I don't want to go without you, it wouldn't be fun."

"Sweetheart," she said, "I've got to go. I've got to read these lines."

Grace's life so far had been rather promiscuous. She'd lost her virginity at fifteen and never looked back. Amy and some of her own friends were disapproving, and she'd learned to keep her lovers hidden, except from Thea, of course, whose own history was almost as louche. Not that it was difficult; the older, married kind, the kind she had preferred, were only too happy to stay in the dark. But she'd grown bored with secrecy and promised herself a more public affair. Sam had proved perfect casting.

She hadn't thought through this moving-in business, just jumped before she could change her mind, and it all felt too quick. It went against her image of herself as a free and Bohemian spirit. Married men were trouble but at least they kept their distance. She forced her attention back to the lines in front of her. They seemed predictable as she read them, but only, thought Grace, because everyone is. She thought about Thea, discontented and elusive, with an American fiancé she'd run away from; about Archie, whose girlfriend had given up hope of pinning him down and had looked for love elsewhere; even Amy and James, happy for so long, but now Amy was unsettled and looking for trouble, even if she didn't know it yet herself. They were three of a kind, Grace thought, she and her sisters—restless women driven by life's inconsequence—and there were times when she wished she could submit to something firmer, even to the tightly meshed structure of the script that she held in her hand.

⌁

So Grace had decided to move out just as Thea was coming home. An interesting departure, thought Lucy, as she viewed the rooms of her apartment through the shift of perspective brought on by an imminent arrival. What would Thea see tomorrow as she moved through the familiar theater of her mother's flat? Might she now regard the welcoming and colorful clutter as too old-world and claustrophobic? Lucy had a special tenderness for her most difficult daughter, which, over the years, had been reciprocated. She willed herself to believe that Thea's homecoming signaled its continuation, but arrivals sometimes heralded change, she knew that. Her own return home from the hospital, years ago, had changed them all. She had been surprised, for one thing, by the new solidarity that the twins had displayed. She'd always believed Amy and Thea to be separate creatures, a pair of cats from the same litter who lived together and walked alone. But as she'd watched them grow apart once more as they grew older, she'd considered that they were simply returning to themselves, and ultimately to her.

As she placed a small vase of flowers from the roof garden in Grace's room, the room now to be occupied by Thea, and removed and tidied away the debris left by her youngest daughter, she acknowledged to herself that the twins' return had never been complete. She found herself again looking back against her will, and as she watched, through the years, the setting pattern of the bonds between them, she saw Amy hiding her discontent beneath her pragmatism, and Thea, furious and clinging in turn. They had all been glad when the dark time was over, but the twins were confused by her resurrection and haunted by the years before it, their lost childhood already made golden in their memory, a gilded fiction that Lucy's renewal had stolen away.

IT was eleven when the telephone woke Thea. She could see the bright sunlight through a tiny crack in the curtains, and she thought for a moment she was still in L.A.

"Hello," said Grace, "I thought you'd want to know. Amy knows you're back."

"Ah," said Thea. She clutched the sheet to her naked body as she sat up in bed. In this state of drowsiness, she felt unarmed and exposed.

"She thinks you should meet up," Grace went on.

"Does she now. When?"

"Today."

"No," said Thea, lying back on her pillows. "No can do."

"Why not?"

"I'm busy."

"No, you're not."

"I don't want to see her today. I don't have to justify it."

"What shall I tell her, then, Thea? She wants to make things right."

"On her timetable. Tell her I'll call her tomorrow, after I've called Ma. And tell her to keep quiet about me being here, for now. She can at least do that for me."

"Are you going to pretend you've just arrived?"

Thea heard the annoyance in Grace's voice.

"No. I'll tell Ma what I've done. But let me be the one to tell her. She'll understand."

Grace yawned down the phone.

"You make too much of a meal of everything. I'm exhausted. Too little sleep. I'll speak to you later."

Thea lay back on her pillows. She hadn't really intended to make things more complicated, and now her impatience both to resume and change her life was becoming pressing. She wanted, she knew, to live in a different way, to have a life that made more sense to her than the one she found herself in, the one she'd thought she wanted. But she was embarrassed to think that in the last few years she had taken a wrong turn. She didn't want to admit it, and especially not to Amy. But if she was to settle back home and change direction, she would have to resolve things with her sister. If only she knew more precisely what it was that Amy withheld from her, she might be able to fill up the space she felt she only outlined in her presence.

In danger of falling back into sleep, despite the sunlight, she forced herself out of bed. It had always seemed to Thea that Amy could beat her to any source of satisfaction. Despite her academic superiority, despite her more obvious sexuality, she felt that Amy usually won out. Even on that terrible day when their father had died of a heart attack, it had been Amy who arrived home first from school, her arms already around their mother. She'd hated Amy in that moment, and hated herself even more for thinking it. They'd both been daddy's girls, but Thea more so; her grief was keener. In her experience of loss for once she'd been running ahead.

As she showered and dressed, she decided she could wait no longer. She would check out now and go to her mother's—take Lucy by surprise. It would be simpler that way, and there would be no time for Lucy to wonder where she'd been. She'd explain everything later, in the afterglow of the surprise, and all would be forgiven. Who would be forgiving whom was not a question she asked herself. When she chose a course of action, she was single-minded.

The matter of Archie's failure to propose to her, for example, she'd decided was simply a failure of nerve. All he'd needed was encouragement. Two weeks after their trip to Rome, when they were lying entwined in his bed one Sunday morning, she had given it to him.

"Is this a leap year?" she'd said.

"What?" Archie had rolled over toward her, his face smiling down at her from above. "What are you on about? I haven't a clue."

"Just that if it were, I'd ask you to marry me," she'd said. She had kept her tone light. "I'd wait for you to ask but as you're the shy type . . ."

His face had barely registered a change. His smile had increased to a grin, then to laughter. He'd kissed her cheek.

"It's true," he'd said. "Who wouldn't be shy with you? You're beautiful." He'd kissed her again. "And talented, and intelligent, and solvent. Every man's dream." He'd moved on top of her and down her body and as she'd felt his mouth on her thighs and a wetness between her legs, she couldn't help feeling she'd been left high and dry.

She ordered a cab, packed her bag, and paid her bill. As a child she'd been regarded as willful, but willful had its uses in the grown-up world, and, so far, she'd always been able to retrace her steps, when necessary, to clear up what she'd knocked over en route, if with painful consequences to herself. She wanted now to pick up the pieces of the life she'd left behind, and it wasn't just Archie and Amy she'd fled from, it was from something further back and more consuming.

It only occurred to her halfway to Kensington that Lucy might not be in. For the two and a half years she'd been away she'd held a mental image of her mother caged in the rooftop apartment. So etched was the picture that it seemed self-evident that Lucy would be there when Thea got home. Thea looked at the two suitcases propped against the taxi's flip-down seats. She must still be jet-lagged not to have foreseen herself sitting on the doorstep till God knows when. She fumbled in her bag for her phone and reluctantly dialed Lucy's number. No answer. She dialed Grace's mobile. Likewise. Leaning forward, she opened the partition to speak to the driver.

"I'm very sorry, but I need to go back."

"Back to the hotel?"

"Yes, sorry."

He swung the cab around on a sixpence, scattering pedestrians.

"I've left something behind," she said, anxious to mollify him.

"Makes no difference to me, love."

She found the sentiment depressing. She'd hoped today to make a difference, to delight and surprise Lucy and be received as a prodigal child. Maybe Lucy was away; after all she wasn't expecting Thea till tomorrow. She was probably shopping, shopping for her: food for her delectation, soaps and sprays and candles. She knew her mother's style. Lucy would swamp her with sweet smells and tastes, wrap her in a sort of love, and she would sink back and respond until it cloyed. She tried her mother again.

"Hello," answered Lucy.

"Ma? I thought you were out."

"Amy? No, I was upstairs."

Thea forced herself not to react to this early provocation.

"No, Ma, it's Thea. I'm here a day early."

"Thea? But I wasn't expecting you—why—where are you?"

"I know, Ma, that's what I'm saying. I'm early. I'll explain. I'm on my way to you now."

"From Heathrow?"

"Er, no. I flew into Heathrow, yes. I'll explain. It's okay if I come now, isn't it?"

"Of course, of course. What time will you be here?"

"In about twenty minutes."

She opened the partition to the driver.

"Sorry, sorry, but I need to go back to Kensington."

He executed the turnaround with all the assurance of a nimble fat man dancing.

"Sorry about this," she muttered, "all this changing direction."

DESPITE leaving his home and his wife that morning with a passing desire never to return, James was feeling more himself. Like Richard Armstrong, he was watching the world go by from a comfortable first-class train seat, but James was headed in a different direction.

He was on his way to Aylesbury to discuss a potential merger with a company chairman, one who liked to conduct business from home in August and whose wealth allowed him to do so. He was aware that his mood was mostly due to the prospect of a day away from the City, a lift-free day. Or at least he hoped it would be. Almost on waking it had occurred to him that Andrew Buxton was the sort of man who might have installed some sort of elevator, to show his guests the view from the roof perhaps. He pushed the thought away. It was a grand house and he'd never have got planning permission; but then again, Buxton was a man who invariably got what he wanted. James looked out to see a herd of cows running from the train, and, determined to dismiss his paranoia, he picked up his newspaper.

He scanned the front page, then turned to the back out of habit, to work his way through the day's reports. He'd come back to the sports page later. Mid-August—and the business pages were quiet. He soon reached the obituaries, where his eye was caught by a small paragraph, tucked in the bottom left: "SIMON FAIRBROTHER OBE. Distinguished headmaster and rugby blue." Well, that was a turn up. Old Fairbro dead. James checked his age: seventy-six. Not a great age, but a decent one, he supposed. He thought of ringing Archie to tell him their old housemaster had kicked the bucket, then reconsidered. News of death, however natural in the scheme of things, was probably not what Archie wanted to hear on the eve of his operation.

He'd encouraged himself to forget those first-term chats with Fairbrother, whom he'd otherwise grown to respect. It had been easier to decide that the blundering questions were well intentioned.

"So you're telling me, James," Fairbrother said, "that you haven't cried for six weeks now."

James nodded, his eyes trained on the crinkled sockets in front of him. He knew that his form master and house matron had confirmed his story.

"How are you getting on with the other boys?"

"Well, sir, I've been put in the first junior football team," said James, who was learning the skill of deflection.

"Very good."

"I've scored four goals so far."

"Do you like girls, James?"

James blushed. Only days before, he'd had his first wet dream. He'd thought, when he woke, that he was crying again, but then realized what it was with a feeling of relief and pride. He was one of them. He'd listened to them talking about it.

"I like my sister, sir."

"Then don't get too close to other boys. Boys shouldn't have special friends, James."

James glazed his eyes, blocking out the man's intention, which he understood. *Wanker,* he thought to himself. *Total wanker.*

He closed his eyes as the train shuddered through a dull suburban landscape interspersed with remnants of what was once the countryside.

From time to time he'd entertained fantasies about writing to Fairbrother, to tell him how cruel and clumsy he had been, whatever his intentions; and now the man was dead and his chance was gone. He was surprised by how angry he felt, surprised at the images of revenge that flooded through his mind, violent and bloody. Could he really want to do those things? Yes, he thought, even though it had only been a short blip in an otherwise careless youth.

Outside the window, time and place seemed speeded up as the train increased its pace. James stared out, amazed to uncover his feral core and to discover that, after the initial shock, it pleased him.

Amy had woken early with a feeling of resentment and nausea, which she feared might be with her all day. She'd pretended to be half asleep as James got up, but she was aware he'd been awake in the night, pacing. She lay with her face turned into the pillow.

It seemed to her that the children might as well be here for all the enjoyment she and James were getting out of their break. She'd offered to make some breakfast, but he said he'd get something on the way and left, closed off again in his new private world.

She woke an hour later, and to her astonishment the irritation and sickness of the early morning seemed to have vanished, her spirits resurrected. Her day rolled out before her, uncluttered and fresh, and she was young again. This was what it used to be like, she thought, but today possessed a keenness that only the brevity of her freedom could supply. She would phone her old friend Cassie who lived out in Richmond now, since her divorce, and see if she was free. They hadn't met up for ages. She might even tell her everything, and get her advice.

She could go for the whole day if she wanted. What was to stop her? Amy almost jumped out of bed, dressing carefully, making up with her old attention, enjoying her rejuvenated reflection in the mirror. She felt she could be preparing for an era that was full of promise. She picked up the phone when it rang, without any of the resentment of intrusion that made itself felt in her darker moods.

"I can't talk long." Grace was brisk. "I'm back on set in a minute. I just wanted to tell you I spoke to Thea and she said can you leave it till tomorrow, after she's spoken to Ma."

Amy had almost forgotten about Thea. Forgotten that today was the day she had decided to sort things out. But now she remembered that it was part of her plan.

"I'll ring her myself," she said.

"I wouldn't, if I were you. Just leave it. Another day doesn't make any difference."

Amy felt the day losing some of its freshness as the sun began to climb high.

"She always makes such a meal of everything."

Grace was slightly surprised to hear Amy use the very words she'd spoken herself. In the mouth of her sister they sounded unforgiving, she thought.

"You can be just as bad," she said.

"What do you mean?" said Amy.

Grace sighed. "You can't make it better overnight, even if you want to. Why don't you drop her a note or something?"

"I thought of that," said Amy. "You mean at the hotel?"

"Yes. Tell her you're looking forward to seeing her. When she's ready. In her time and so on."

"Hmm." Grace was becoming bossy, she thought. Amy was used to giving advice, not taking it, but she had to admit that this course of action had its merits.

"Okay, then," she said, "I will. I'll do that. I'll write her a letter."

"Just a note," said Grace, and Amy laughed.

She got out a pen and paper to make a list, a way, she'd discovered over the years, of stopping her brain from jumping from one thing to the next without focus or progress. She wrote:

1. *Baby/Pregnancy—three weeks to consider*
2. *Thea*
3. *Career*
4. *James*

She wasn't sure exactly what about James but there was something. He was buzzing about in her brain with as much insistence as the rest.

5. *Richard Armstrong*

He shouldn't be there at all. He'd muscled in.

There was something else just out of reach but she couldn't catch it. It was probably innocuous, like a need to make an appointment for the children with the dentist. But she knew in a moment that it was Archie who was missing, and that in some way he was relevant to every other heading, and that his image was permeating her thoughts, just below their surface. He wasn't on her list because he was too big for it. But the thought frightened her and she reduced him to an item and put him in at number six.

~~~

RICHARD sat with his mother in a pink and gray restaurant with ruched curtains at the windows. They faced each other, watching the day-trippers walking up and down the esplanade outside, children in tow in various stages of sunstroke and exhaustion, crying with fatigue or frustration at some minor deprivation. Richard felt a smug reassurance as he observed them. He had so far no desire to reproduce himself, and there was little in the passing parade to make him change his mind. But it was clear to him that his mother saw something different as she looked out of the window. She laughed with pleasure when a screaming boy was pacified with an ice cream, or a parent was tugged across the busy road toward the beach by its frenzied offspring.

"I miss Tim and Molly," she said, suddenly sad at the reminder of her daughter's children, left behind in her progress south.

"Patsy will bring them down for the holidays," said Richard. "They'll love it."

"Yes, they will, of course they will. They'll like the Pleasure Beach."

"The Pier," he corrected her.

"Yes, the Pier. They'll love it. We took them to Blackpool for the day last year, before they went to Spain. Tim was over the moon. So excited we couldn't get him to bed."

Richard was glad he hadn't been there. His mother was on a roll now.

"Patsy wants to know when you're going to settle down."

He looked at her. "You mean you do."

His mother could barely bring herself to mention his divorce. She'd been uneasy with his former wife, a sharp, intelligent woman who'd been a partner in the agency where he'd worked with Archie.

Neither of them had wanted children and the marriage had just fallen away after several years, with no hard feelings.

"Yes, well, I would like to see you settled. After—you've done so well." She leaned across the table. "We're very proud of you, you know."

He recoiled a fraction as he tried to smile. He felt unaccountably angry with her, as if it were her fault that he hadn't yet found someone else whom he could imagine being with long term.

"And now you want me to saddle myself with a bunch of kids?"

She withdrew behind a large card menu.

"What shall I have?" she asked him.

"What do you fancy?"

She looked up and down the menu, unfocussed through her glasses. "Fish. I like a bit of fish."

"Just don't get a bone stuck in your throat like the old Queen Mum did," he said smiling, tipping her card down with his finger so he could see her. "I don't fancy an afternoon in the ER."

She smiled at him. It was an old joke.

"I'm sorry, love," she said. "I shouldn't have said anything about . . . It's none of my business."

"No."

"I just want you to be happy."

"I am happy."

His mother smiled at an elderly couple who had come to sit at the table close by. "This seems a nice place," the man said to them, stowing his umbrella under the table.

"Very nice," said Richard's mother. "I'm sure you won't need that brolly." Richard hoped that this wouldn't be the start of a prolonged conversation. His mother's capacity for involvement with strangers was a further trial.

"He just likes to be prepared," his wife said, smiling at him indulgently.

"My husband was the same," Richard's mother answered. But then she picked up the menu card again and leaned across the table.

"Patsy says she thinks you've got a girlfriend, Richard." She knew she was pushing her luck but his face maintained its expression of bland appeasement.

"No one special," he said, which was true, but he smiled at her as if he might be holding out.

"What's her name?"

It was easier to name someone than not, he calculated.

"Amy," he murmured behind his menu, as a picture of Amy Fielding came into his mind.

"Who?" his mother said, leaning forward to hear.

Amy Fielding was married. She wouldn't do.

"Thea," he said. That was okay.

"Thea," she repeated. "That's an unusual name."

The desire to please and at the same time aggravate his mother was perpetuated by an inner confusion that had refused to settle with the passing years. Settle, he thought, settle down. It was the phrase she always used. And if only he could, though not in the way she meant. He'd like to settle in the sense of quelling the racing anxiety that often drove him, the busy antennae that probed each world he entered, constructing the map of his ascent.

They sat side by side after lunch, in deck chairs, above the sands, staring into a sea whose unusual warmth was strictly a surface affair. Snatches of familiar tunes floated on the breeze toward them, along with cries and whoops from the fairground hidden at the far end of the pier.

For as long as Richard could remember, he'd felt himself shoving involuntarily against a door that refused to give way. His desire to break through had driven him from his roots, his family, and his class, and he winced at the thought of the small disloyalties and betrayals that his desire to move on had engendered.

He'd often argued with Archie and James, who teased him, saying he was a throwback to a bygone age, claiming hierarchies that no longer existed. But he didn't believe it was bygone altogether. He'd studied it up close and he knew better. It wasn't about money, not entirely; there was still a subtle changing of manners and taste. It was a territory whose precise definition continued to elude him.

He found his eyes resting on the children playing below him, toddlers with spades, arms in the air as if dancing a reel. It struck him that his own children, were he to have any, would naturally absorb the cartography he'd tried to teach himself, they'd know it already. They would know the way. He looked at his mother. She'd been right all along for the wrong reasons. He should settle down. He could and should have a child—children—who would be what he could not be. He felt as if his whole life had changed in an instant. He reached across and pressed her arm gently to wake her from her doze.

"Fancy an ice cream?" he said.

⌒

DEAREST *Thea*, wrote Amy, sitting at the table on the terrace, concentrating on the task in hand, ignoring the claims of domestic existence she'd earlier been unable to shake off. She crossed out "Dearest." "Dear Thea." That was the easy bit. Just a note, Grace had said, but how could she convey in a note what she wanted to say?

> *Dear Thea,*
>   *Welcome home.*

She wasn't sure if that sounded patronizing but decided to leave it.

>   *Grace tells me you've taken a couple of days out to acclimatize. It makes perfect sense to me.*

Or at least it did if you were dealing with Thea, she thought.

>   *I'm sad that we haven't spoken for so long and really hope we can straighten things out now you're back. I'll call you at Ma's tomorrow, then, when you're ready—if you're ready—let's meet. And chat.*
>
>   *Love,*
>   *Amy*

She read it through, wrote it out again changing the last word to "talk," then put it in an envelope and sealed it. It didn't express what she'd hoped, but that was hardly surprising since she couldn't work out what she felt herself. It would have to do. She thought through her day once more and decided not to phone Cassie after all. It would be too confusing, she reasoned, to involve another person in her problems. Instead she would take the letter herself, go down to Covent Garden and deliver it by hand; and it seemed only natural in that case to phone Archie to see if he wanted to meet her there for lunch. She doubted he'd much else to do today, and he was on her list.

～

LUNCH was laid out ready on the terrace at Hansford Park. Andrew Buxton was a man who enjoyed life, enjoyed his ventures and dealings, sailing close to the wind but staying just the right side of the law. Buxton also enjoyed the money he'd made and was proud of his house, a large Jacobean manor set in thirty acres of Buckinghamshire with an unbroken view across the woodland. James was enthralled, high on the experience of doing business with a man whose unashamed pleasure in acquisition was softened by a cultured generosity.

There were no lifts in the house. James had felt foolish even as his anxiety receded soon after his arrival. He'd been ushered up a smart staircase to the third floor where an air-conditioned suite of offices had been constructed in what must have once been a congested servants' quarters. There, over the last couple of hours, he'd sifted through the architecture of Buxton's latest takeover, a chain of fast-food restaurants whose menus its new owner was unlikely ever to have sampled.

Away from the office and the thick City heat that seemed to have generated an unaccustomed torrent of domestic trouble, James had felt a fresh interest in the fine detail it was his business to pick through. In recent weeks he'd felt jaded and begun to wonder if his time had come, if this was the premature arrival of a midlife crisis, as Patrick had seemed to suggest. He'd seen his older colleagues go through it. Some weathered the storm, some ran off with a mistress, and others simply dropped out of sight. One, he'd heard, was running a hotel in Scotland when he wasn't drinking his own bar dry of malt whiskey. But today James felt reinvigorated. The sweet stillness and the picturesque beauty of Hansford Park might have the look of another century, but it was maintained and fueled by the pump of City money, and he was happy to be part of it.

At 1 p.m. precisely, he waited, as instructed, on the terrace. A young man in a white shirt offered him a glass of champagne, which he refused. His host had disappeared somewhere in the house, and as far as drinking alcohol at lunchtime was concerned, James felt he should take his cue from the top.

"Hello."

He turned around and saw a pretty blond girl in her early twenties standing in the frame of the French doors.

"I'm Kitty. Dad—Andrew, that is—said I should lunch with you. I hope you don't mind."

James held out his hand.

"I'm James. Of course not. Do you live here?"

"No. I'm just here for a couple of weeks. I'm working in Paris."

"Lucky you." He imagined himself for a moment, a bachelor in Montmartre, a feline French girl smiling through a bar window. The thought was incongruous in this English summer setting.

"Not really," Kitty replied. "The French are so difficult."

"Oh," said James. He wasn't sure if the "difficult" was ironic.

"To work with, that is. They're charming otherwise." She turned and, to James's amazement, winked at the boy serving drinks.

She looked back and smiled at James, a direct, knowing smile, a touch confrontational. Even in the shade of the veranda he began to feel rather too warm.

"How's your French?" he asked, shifting his eyeline slightly to the left of her.

"Not good enough." She turned to the boy again. "Philippe, je parle français très mal, n'est-ce pas?"

"Aussi bien que je parle anglais," said the boy, his face passive but fixed on hers.

"Not a great compliment," said Kitty. "That's half the problem."

"And the other half?"

"I'm working on the launch of a new magazine."

She seemed very sophisticated for someone who appeared to be so young. "What sort of magazine?"

"The French edition of *Your Destination*. One of Dad's, I'm afraid."

"Sounds fun." James was appalled at how weak he sounded, like some old uncle.

She sighed and took a glass of champagne from Philippe's tray.

"It should be. But you have to consult the unions about everything. Even the cover price. It's difficult to get decisions made."

The sound of steps drew their attention.

"Difficult? What's difficult? Not a word in my vocabulary." Andrew Buxton appeared from the dark interior. He'd changed into a pair of shorts and a polo shirt, and James felt overdressed.

"Take your jacket off, James. We've finished for the day. You'll stay and have a swim after lunch? Kitty, get James a proper drink. He's done a good morning's work."

James slipped his jacket off and loosened his tie. He smiled at Kitty, holding her gaze as she handed him a glass. The compliment from Buxton had the sudden effect of making him feel part of all this, part of this sleek oasis that functioned so smoothly and whose domestic cracks could no doubt be papered over with pounds or dollars.

"Cheers," said Andrew.

"Cheers," said James. The day just kept on getting better.

Sitting by the Thames in the sun, with his back to the building from which he'd operated for the last twelve years, Archie was close to sleep when his phone rang. He'd been contemplating the traffic passing up and down, human on the embankment, maritime on the river, and marveling at its flow, its constant movement, going nowhere about its business. He fished in his pocket and answered without checking the number; he was beyond interest in who was calling.

"Hello."

"Archie? It's Amy."

"Amy? How are you?"

"Fine. More to the point, how are you?"

He breathed heavily.

"Not great."

"No?"

"No."

"Are you free for lunch?"

He felt his spirits, if not exactly lift, attempt an upward movement.

"Definitely. Definitely free for lunch."

"Where are you?" she said.

"On the South Bank."

"Good. Can you meet me in Covent Garden?"

"If you like. I'm just across the bridge. I've been at the office, sorting out stuff, you know. It was pretty bad. I had to tell them all."

"Oh, Archie, I'm sorry," she said. "It must have been awful. You can tell me the whole thing if you want to. Where shall we go?"

He thought, as he often did when asked this question, that he'd like to live in a place where life offered fewer choices, a place where the simple matter of lunch didn't require a consultation of options.

"Luigi's," he said after a moment. They wouldn't see anyone they knew there. It was a secret held by an older generation, retired politicians and theater people who remembered its heyday.

"If you like," she said. "I haven't been there for ages. Can we make it twelve thirty?"

"Fine."

He snapped the phone shut and looked at his watch. He had over an hour to kill.

He heard the phrase repeating in his head, "an hour to kill." It was one he'd used often over his not quite forty years, and it now struck him as unfortunate. He wondered at what point in life people stopped saying it, if ever. By seventy, seventy-five? Surely by then its terrible significance must have broken through? Words that had implied leisure, a hedonistic squander, now chilled him. He got up from the bench by the river and went to lean on the rail overlooking the wet bank below, an urban beach lapped by the dirty wake from the boats. Wrapping papers, a plastic bottle, and what looked like potato peelings but couldn't be, surely, bobbed against the grit and sand while a seagull made tentative forays in their direction.

It was nearly a week now since his life had begun to unravel. And yet he was starting to understand that this timing was illusory. The sense of disengagement from life he felt now was merely an exaggeration, perhaps a compression, of how he had been feeling for some time. He knew, for example, that Richard was right when he'd accused him of being disaffected from his professional life, and that he had been for a while. And, if he were honest, it went deeper. It was a disengagement from his own self that had crept up slowly, and he couldn't quite work out when it had started or what part of him had got left behind.

The doctor's words came floating back to him for the umpteenth time: "You mustn't assume it's cancer until you know for sure," he'd said. Every time Archie remembered this, his incredulity at the doctor's lack of understanding increased. It was the most absurd piece of advice he'd ever heard. He reran the scene in his imagination, contradicting him: "No," Archie heard himself saying, "you've got that wrong. You've got it completely wrong. We will always assume it's cancer until we know for sure that it isn't." But he'd said nothing of the kind as he'd listened from his new position of distance. Now he needed to reclaim himself, to push himself on and through, but a dark moment of fear had washed over him and extinguished his will.

The seagull seized a bit of potato peeling, half choked, and spat it out on the bank. Archie leaned over the railing further and was amazed to see it was a ribbon of videotape. He looked up the river to Westminster and beyond and decided to head that way, to kill time or whatever.

Fifteen minutes later he found himself walking over Lambeth Bridge and through the stately Victorian doors of the Tate Gallery on Millbank. It was one of those things he'd meant to do far more frequently, ever since he'd come to work within striking distance. He could have come any lunchtime, any evening, but as his life had rolled out in front of him and as exhibitions came and went, his proximity coupled with the barrage of images in papers and magazines had somehow persuaded him that he'd already been.

As he walked through the octagonal entrance, he looked upward to the airy glass dome that spilled the sunlight across its empty floor. Now that he was actually here, he was at a loss as to what to do next. Other people were bustling through, bent on an endgame. He tagged along behind a smart gay couple who looked as if they knew a thing or two and found himself walking through a room of graceful red-haired women, of naked nymphs and ethereal girls. *Spirits in an enchanted dream*, he read, and as he stared at the maidens poised on their golden stairs, for a moment he felt disembodied, as if he, too, had left the earth behind.

The gay couple were a few meters ahead. They were tall and languid, one blond, one dark, in similar but not identical gray T-shirts and jeans. They were smooth and almost chiseled, with light tans that evened out their skin tones. He could almost find them attractive.

"Shall we do the late Turner seascapes?" said the blonde.

"No," said his partner, "too cold and turbulent for a sunny day. Too much form in the service of light. It's definitely a winter room."

Archie was astonished. He had no idea that pictures or objects could be classified by season.

"Let's go to the Bacons. But round the back way. I can't bear to walk past the Stanley Spencer."

"All those awful little men with bad bodies," said his friend.

Spencer rang a bell at once for Archie and he knew he'd seen it before, that it had been a favorite of his mother's, a weakness he remembered her saying, in her passion for less figurative art. They had been here together to see it, more than once, but it was a part of his life he'd mislaid. He needn't see the Turners, now he knew what to say, though he had to admit that cold sounded fine in this weather. The winter business was bollocks of course; he knew enough to know that.

As he approached the gallery where the Stanley Spencer hung, he turned to look back. He caught sight of himself in the reflective surface of the door. He looked fragile, a ghost framed between two uniformed guards. As he pushed on into the long room he had a sense of déjà vu, that he was sailing into unknown but familiar territory.

There was a party of schoolchildren in front of the picture, and he had to jostle through them to find a position. The cool feel of free floating that he'd had since he entered the building now dissipated. He listened to their teacher as she expounded on the theme of Resurrection, and he saw through childhood eyes the picture that he remembered as a crowded and terrifying vision, demons and changelings disguised in human form, climbing from graves to fetch him. But the children around him were laughing. Their teacher was describing a cozy world that he didn't recognize, a world of family and mothers and just a little bit naughty, as if these escapees from the underworld were climbing from their cots. He looked again and his attention was caught by a naked man, standing in front of his tombstone, his arms resting across it. He looked, thought Archie, quite indifferent to the turbulence that surrounded him, and this image seemed to empty him out as he tried to make sense of it. He felt light-headed again; he was just a body in a crowd, a reflection of the man on the wall, with his unfettered vulnerability. He willed himself to turn away and left the room.

⁓

THE hotel doorman beamed at Amy as she climbed out of her taxi, her letter for Thea clutched in her hand. She stepped carefully onto the pavement, unaccustomed to the high-heeled sandals she'd decided to wear. Feeling like her younger self, she adjusted her sunglasses and smiled with a determined glamour.

"We thought you'd left us," the doorman said. "It's nice to see you back so soon. And your haircut looks very nice, if I may say so."

Amy turned away and paid the driver. This confusion was the problem in a nutshell, the bare fact that she and Thea hadn't learned to live with. It wasn't the affront to their individuality that upset them, or the leering sexual interest they could inspire, they had once concluded in a high-minded (and not entirely truthful) moment. It was the shocking and constant reminder of the superficiality of most human encounters, of how people glanced, typed, and made assumptions in such an unconsidered fashion.

At the desk there was more of the same until she established that Thea had checked out an hour ago.

"Well, that's just typical," said Amy, waving her letter in his face.

The desk clerk looked puzzled, and quickly punched information into his computer.

"There's an address here," he said. "We could forward your letter."

"Thank you," said Amy. "I know where my mother lives." She left the hotel quickly, without a look at anyone. *This is what you do, Thea,* she thought. *This is the sort of mess you always leave behind you.*

She walked up along the Strand, past its eclectic mix of gift shops and men's outfitters. It was nearly time to meet Archie. She'd go straight to the restaurant, sit down, order a drink, and wait for him;

and she would calm down. All that had happened was that Thea had checked out of the hotel. There was no reason why she, Amy, should have been informed. If it had been anyone else it would have been merely inconvenient; this was not Thea's fault. She made herself take deep breaths, but as she breathed, a small fury constricted her chest. Who else but Thea would have her chasing across London in taxis to deliver notes of appeasement?

In the restaurant cloakroom she combed her hair back from her face, tucking it behind her ears. The doorman at the hotel had clearly thought it looked good, even if he had thought she was Thea. So Thea must have grown her hair. Well, that was something. Amy had taken extra care getting ready that morning, because, she'd told herself, she'd had more time, with the children away. And it wasn't unreasonable to want to look her best for lunch, even if it was just with a friend. She reapplied her lipstick and pressed cold water to her face. She began to feel a little better, allowing the possibility that her anxiety wasn't all about Thea. But the day was hot and she was pregnant, and Archie was about to arrive, and then the thought of both him and Thea circling within this small radius of central London produced such fresh confusion that she considered, briefly, running away. She felt an urgent need to tell him everything that was on her mind, as if in doing so she would release herself and absolve him in some way, and perhaps Thea, too. She could sense it growing stronger by the moment and it frightened her. It was in these last few days, she told herself, since he'd told her he was ill. The sudden shift in closeness between them seemed to have stirred up fury along with desire, and she was unnerved by the degree to which she now felt that he and her twin had transgressed.

He was already at the table as she walked into the dining room. He shouldn't be there yet. She needed more time.

"You're early," he said.

"So are you." She kissed him and sat down opposite, fiddling with her napkin as she did so.

"You look as if you're about to cry." Archie was looking at her closely. She was flushed and seemed tense. He was used to a variety of moods when seeing Amy, most of which he disregarded, but she rarely cried. Now her expression reminded him of the sad faces of his employees from earlier that morning, and he felt a bit like crying himself.

"No, I'm just hot," she said. "It's lovely to see you. You must have had a dreadful morning and I've been so worried about you, about the hospital. James told me you were . . ."

"Don't be silly."

She looked at him. He sounded almost sharp.

"Sorry. It must be, er . . . difficult." She struggled for the right thing to say. "I realize it's not something you want to talk about all the time."

"It's not something I want to talk about at all."

Archie surprised himself by the coldness of his tone. He'd been looking forward to this lunch, hoping that he'd left the worst of this particular day behind. He'd walked out of the Tate on a high and taken a taxi to the restaurant in a weightless daze, but confronted now with Amy he felt resentful, forced back to the morning's desolation and the reality of his condition. To his horror she began to sob into her napkin.

"Amy?" he said. "What is it? I didn't mean . . . Wait there a minute." He sat up, pushed back his chair, and hurried off to ask the waiter for water and a bottle of wine. He came back and crouched down beside her. It was still early for lunch and the restaurant was almost empty. A woman seated at a table halfway across the small room was reading a newspaper, waiting for her companion, and tried not to look as if she was listening.

"I'm so sorry," said Amy, clutching the napkin to her nose and mouth. "I'm all right now. It's not you."

Archie didn't believe her.

"I really didn't mean to grouch at you," he said. "I'm just a bit . . ."

"It's Thea," she said. "It's silly, I know, but I brought a letter for her, she's staying at a hotel to avoid us, but you know that, and then she wasn't there, she'd gone, checked out, and I was so cross. And I'm being completely unreasonable, she can check out when she wants to, she didn't know I was coming. I'm so horrible. No wonder she hates me."

Archie returned to his seat and filled their glasses.

"I'm sure she doesn't hate you," he said. He wanted to tell her to pull herself together, to snap out of it.

"Are you pleased she's back?" Amy's voice was still shaky.

Archie hadn't given Thea's return any considered thought. There simply wasn't room in his schedule of crises. He shrugged.

"I just wondered," Amy said, trying to smile and seem light-hearted. "You're both single again, after all. I wondered if you . . ."

"Don't be ridiculous," said Archie. "Come on now. Drink up."

Amy hesitated. "I can't," she said. "I shouldn't."

"Why not?"

"I'm pregnant."

The information seemed to reach him from far away, and he searched for a standard response. At least it explained the topsy-turvy of her logic.

"That's wonderful," he said, but to his surprise the tears came again. "James must be thrilled," he tried.

"He doesn't know yet," she said, looking at him anxiously. "And I don't want you to tell him."

꒰Ꙭ꒱

A large glass bowl of strawberries, blueberries, and raspberries was placed on a side table by a young woman, a sallow copy of the boy who had brought champagne and who now busied himself serving the fruit.

"This is Adele." Andrew Buxton indicated the girl, who was tending to a tray of coffee cups, as if he owned her. "She and her brother are here to study English. Their parents look after my house in France. Thank you, Philippe," he added as an iced dish was set in front of him.

"Merci, Philippe," said Kitty. "That means 'I don't want any,' Dad, in French. *J'ai mangé déjà des fruits, au petit déjeuner.*"

"I know what 'merci' means, Kitty. You speak too much French to Philippe. He's here for his benefit, not yours." Andrew's tone was sharp, but his smile indulgent.

James wondered what sort of benefits had so far passed between Philippe and Kitty, and whether her father knew.

A telephone rang inside the house, and Philippe ran in to fetch it, then presented it to Andrew, still ringing, as if it were a gift. He answered, rising from the table and turning his back. "Yes, yes," he said. "I've got James Marsham with me now. It's done." He turned to James. "Excuse me, won't you? I'll be a few minutes. Carry on."

James looked across the table at Kitty. She was staring at him and grinning.

"What is it?" he said. "Have I got cream on my nose or something?"

"You're James Marsham."

"Yes."

"The James Marsham."

He was disconcerted. No one had ever referred to him as "the James Marsham" before. She was mocking him.

"I don't know what you're talking about."

"Grace," she said, "Grace Fielding. I was at school with her."

"Oh," he said, relieved. "I see, Grace. Amy's sister."

"Amy's husband?" said Kitty, whose stare and grin had remained fixed and were taking on a gargoyle quality. James was unnerved despite his initial relief. He sensed there was more.

"Amy's my wife, yes."

"You know she was completely crazy about you."

James's brain fizzed and seemed to short-circuit. He couldn't focus on what she was saying; he paused too long.

"Amy?" He knew she didn't mean Amy.

"Grace. She was crazy about you. For three years. She drove us mad at school with it. I can't believe you're here."

"Grace?"

"Yes. She had pictures of you everywhere. In her bag, in her desk, in her bedroom at home—she had to hide those, of course."

James felt his face grow red. He hadn't blushed for years; it must be the heat and the champagne.

"I don't know what you're talking about."

"Oh, come on. I can't believe you didn't know. Grace said you flirted with her all the time when Amy wasn't around."

James felt compressed in a collision of alternative realities.

"That's ridiculous. I had no idea. And if it's true, it could only have been a schoolgirl crush."

Kitty leaned across the table in a parody of conspiracy. "Are you sure you didn't come on to her? Gorgeous girl, still at school, and mad for you? Most men would be tempted."

She was right about that. He looked at Kitty again. How did he know she wasn't teasing?

"You're having me on."

Kitty pushed her chair back. "She said you had a special relationship."

"That's right," said James. "We always said that."

"There you are, then."

"Not like that. I was like a big brother. I still am."

"Well, big brother, if you don't believe me, test it out."

"What?"

"I'll have a bet with you, if you like?"

"And why on earth would I want to do that?" James knew that his earlier suspicion was right; Kitty Buxton was trouble.

She shrugged her shoulders, got up from the table, and fetched the bottle of champagne from its bucket. Philippe was nowhere to be seen.

"If she did have a crush on me, it's long forgotten. You should see the bloke she's with now."

"Sam Harris, I heard. He's cute." Kitty leaned over his shoulder, a little too close as she filled up his glass. "But you don't just get over crushes like the one she had on you," she whispered. "In any case, believe me, Grace likes older men, she always has, she just keeps it quiet."

She stood up straight as her father reappeared, without the telephone. He wore an expression of triumph and self-satisfaction, and James wondered briefly if that was how he looked after sex and whether young women found him attractive.

"Sorry about that," said Andrew, taking his seat. "But it's all done and dusted. Cheers." He raised his glass to James. "We'll do business again."

2004

24 November
Harley Street

Patrick was struggling to maintain his concentration. His thoughts kept slipping back to Hoxton, to his old flat and his old self, as he pictured the man James, her husband, sitting there all those years ago. The moment of hostility he'd felt toward Amy when she revealed her secret had passed, and, though he felt cheated by her concealment, he was drawn to her again, as he had been toward her husband. He was convinced now that he had sensed their commonality from the start. They sat together in the dark room, lit gently in its corners, and he thought, as he waited and watched her, that she was, for this moment, another one of the room's treasures, an object on loan, unique but representative of a time and its culture. He would let himself enjoy her presence, indulge himself briefly. It was an idea that brought him satisfaction, and he rolled it through his body, enjoying the quiet while it lasted.

She was slightly flushed, he noticed, and she leaned forward to take off her cardigan. Her pupils, Patrick noted, were a little dilated.

"You're too hot?" he asked.

"I feel wicked," she said, "perhaps that's why. I feel wicked now that you know, about James. I know you disapprove. That I should have told you."

"Not disapprove," he said, "but I have to respect the fact that your husband was my client. That he came in confidence."

"Yes."

"So you know we can't talk about that? You understand that? It's the condition on which we can continue today?"

She stared at him, her lips parted, and nodded. She seemed, he thought, to be pleading in some way, pleading to share some secret, private knowledge.

"Don't you want to know if he discussed it with me?" she said.

"I'm presuming he did, as you're here."

She looked thrown for a moment, as though this basic observation had tripped her up.

"I thought," she paused, her eyes scanning his face for a signal to start, "I thought I might tell you about the time he came here—"

Patrick inclined his head a fraction, against his will.

"Not here," he said. "He never came here. I used to have a practice in north London."

She went on. "I thought that if I tell you what I know, how I saw it, then, without betraying your principles, of course, you might, or rather I might then know in some instinctual way, without your ever saying anything . . ."

He should stop things here, he knew that, stop this now.

But she stopped herself, smiling up at him, happy with this odd summary of her position, then settled back, expelling the air from her lungs as if having negotiated some tricky first maneuver.

"Does your husband know you've come to see me?" asked Patrick, in what seemed a natural break in her flow.

"No, not exactly," she said, her eyes moving away from his face. Her ambivalent response made him suspicious of a direct pursuit.

"But you're happy, you say?"

"Oh, yes," she said, nodding her head. "It's been hard, but things are very good now."

"Then, forgive me, but I don't understand why you . . . why you've come here, to see me in particular." There, he'd said it. He'd asked the why question and for once he felt it was justified. Why was she here?

1994

TUESDAY 16 AUGUST
1:30 P.M.

DESPITE THE COOLNESS of the interior, very few people had come to lunch in Luigi's; its usual clientele were away at the beach with their children or, more possibly these days, their grandchildren. Amy couldn't eat. She sipped at a glass of wine between swallowing large amounts of mineral water, presumably, thought Archie, as he watched her across the table with an almost cruel dispassion, in the hope that this tidal wave would allow the alcohol to bypass her fetus. Her face was red and blotchy, and the two of them couldn't seem to slip into their usual easy exchange, taking up from where they'd left off the last time they'd met. Archie knew she felt he was shutting her out as she tried to talk over the gaps in their conversation. It was almost, he thought, like the end of an affair, the tears, the tension, the fear of silence.

He felt upstaged, temporarily, in his moment of crisis, and the less he said, the more Amy talked. It wasn't that he wanted to talk about anything in particular, certainly not Thea or the magazines or his operation. He didn't want to talk at all. There was nothing to say. The more she talked, the more he retreated into the role of a distant prompter. The waiter came and went, delivering then collecting plates of food that were barely touched, his manner indignant at their failure to appreciate what he had brought them. But neither was hungry. Failing to draw Archie out, Amy talked about her sisters, then her mother and her children. She talked and talked, clinging to the subjects available to her in the vacuum left by his reticence. But in all this, he noted, the subject of James and her pregnancy were avoided, and it made him cross.

"I simply don't understand you, Amy." Archie could bear it no longer. "You really haven't told James about this baby?"

"No, not yet."

"Why not?"

"I've told you." She wanted him to understand. She felt he ought to understand without her saying.

"No, you haven't, and I feel terrible, knowing before he does."

"Now you know how I felt," said Amy, "when you wouldn't tell him you were ill."

"It's not the same. I'm not married to him."

"It's because I don't know what I want." Her voice quavered again. "I want to keep my options open." As she said the words she felt the opposite, she felt her options slamming shut.

"You mean the option to, er . . ." said Archie.

Amy was finding it difficult to keep up with herself. Could she really be discussing aborting her husband's child, and with Archie, who was quite ignorant of the recent disturbance of feeling he had caused her?

"Yes, but only the option—I couldn't, obviously." And even if he did have an inkling of what she felt, what difference would it make? She'd just told him she was pregnant. And he was ill. It was hardly a guaranteed seduction. It was absurd.

"Well, not obviously," he said, irritated by her evasion. "It is an option." He could see out of the corner of his eye the woman who had witnessed Amy's first outburst of tears. She was talking to another woman opposite her. They were both attractive and smartly dressed, dressed for business it seemed. But as they spoke her eyes checked out his table. She caught him looking at her and then looked away quickly. He couldn't decide if it was curiosity or flirtation.

"After all, women do it all the time," he went on, distracted from the implications of his statement.

"I've thought about it, I admit," she said, not looking at him. "Part of me would consider it, but I don't suppose I could live with myself if I did. I'm not sixteen, or even twenty-five. And even if I could, James couldn't."

Amy fished a handkerchief from her bag on the floor and blew her nose.

Archie was out of his depth, and despite his appearance of objectivity he was aware of a creeping sense of shock at what she was saying.

"How do you know that till you talk to him? He might not want it, either."

"Shh," said Amy, though no one could hear them.

"He might not."

"He might not," she said, "but it's more complicated than that. You don't just . . . just throw babies away. It would be like flushing a part of our marriage down the lavatory." The idea brought on a fresh fit of tears.

"I'll have to have it, or him or her." She sipped more wine and downed a glass of Evian. "There, I've made the decision. I'll tell him tonight."

Archie should have been relieved that she'd settled for the inevitable, relieved that her concerns were a distraction from his own. Instead he felt cheated of the happy hour he'd spent on his own before lunch, with its illusory horizons, unshadowed by unwelcome pregnancies and hints of marital strain. He wanted to get away from Amy, to wander off on his own and recover his thread, but her tears came again as they left the restaurant and he suggested a walk across the bridge before they went home.

They walked in silence, the cars roaring by, the boats and the birds on the river flattened and muted by the heavy sun. It was more than ten years they'd known each other now, and he had grown very fond of her. She had never resented his friendship with James in the way that some wives might have done. She was one of the few women he could relax with, a line he had almost never thought to cross. And James trusted him with Amy, or he had until the business with Thea. That had made them all uneasy if he was truthful. It had changed things, though no one actually said so. He'd liked to think that in the last couple of years, since Thea had left, life had settled back to how it was before, and it was almost true. He turned toward Amy as she walked along beside him. She was looking down at her feet, bare in their fashionable sandals, showing off high arches and neat unvarnished nails. They were Thea's feet.

On occasion he'd tried to imagine what it might have been like to marry Thea, to be part of the Fieldings and all that that entailed, but it felt as if that part of him was buried and dead. He was still unsure how serious she had been when she asked him the question, and had taken him by surprise. Not so serious, it had seemed. After all, it was only weeks later that she'd decided to go back to Mark, to the boyfriend who'd hung around for years.

"I made a mistake," she'd said. "It's not what I want. It's been such fun, but I don't think we should spoil it."

He'd made a gracious protest and she'd been reassuring, but he'd sensed that she felt the decision had been his, that his reticence had spoken, and she was sad.

He and Amy now stopped to stare across the expanse of the Thames, down toward Westminster Bridge. Two red double-deckers followed by an open-topped bus rumbled across, too big for its proportions, like toys lifted from the wrong play set. "Let's go down," he said, when they reached the stairs that led to the river's edge, and as they did, the traffic noise behind them receded to a background hum.

"That's better." Archie looked back at Amy as she followed him down the last few steps.

"The water's so dirty," she said.

He didn't care. Gazing into it he felt less anxious. He took her hand and squeezed it. Amy found herself staring back up at the bridge, overtaken by a sort of vertigo despite the fact that she was standing below it.

"Do you remember Paris, Archie?" she said.

"Yes," he laughed, "when you thought I was making a pass at you. I probably was."

She thought he'd say no, or why, or what are you talking about. She didn't expect him to know what she was thinking. She pressed on, hearing her words at a distance, too embarrassed to connect them with herself.

"You did, almost. I sometimes . . . I sometimes wish you had."

"What?" Archie let go of her hand.

His tone had changed and she felt panic rise in her chest, but it was too late to stop now.

"Well, not then, of course, I'd only been married six months, but sometimes . . . I've wished . . ."

Archie was stunned. This was a conversation he had never antici-pated.

"Amy, don't do this, you're upset."

"Yes. But I need you to know. When you and Thea . . . I had to wonder if you . . . you know what I mean."

He wondered what she could possibly want him to say. He couldn't fully take in her words, but he sensed their direction. So he did what he always did when uncomfortable confrontations with women arose: he took control and flattered.

"You know what?" he said. "I think you're just really upset, con-fused about the baby and about James, and I think it's just the shock . . . of everything, and . . . if you want to know if you're still a desirable woman, then yes, a very desirable woman, and married to my best friend."

She took his hand again. She had heard the clear deflection in his statement.

"Thank you," she said. It was all she would get and she knew it and it left her sad. She'd almost made a fool of herself. Maybe she had, but if so she had erred just this side of idiocy.

"Everything will be fine, you know," he said. It was a ridiculous thing to say, but it was what he was left with.

"I suppose so," said Amy. "I could say the same to you."

He looked at her and smiled. "We'll both just have to wait and see."

She put her arms around him and hugged him to her. It felt awkward and unnatural but he kept his hand on her shoulder as they drew apart and stood side by side.

Across from them was the huge, hideous facade of St. Thomas Hospital. He imagined the people inside, the patients in their beds, looking out at the sky; some of them would never stand outside in the air again.

"Do you ever think about dying?" he asked her.

She turned to him and rubbed his shoulder.

"Archie, you're not going to die."

"I hope not. But do you?"

"No. Sometimes in an aeroplane."

"But we will all die."

"Yes," she said.

"I suppose if I was ill, am ill, really ill—I've thought about it—it would just be sooner rather than later."

"I suppose so." She leaned into him with a sort of nudge. "But you know, I'd rather it was later. You know that, don't you?"

"Yes," he said. "So would I."

⳥

TWO pigeons were performing a mating dance on the top of Lucy's small garden shed, which sat like a doll's house in one corner of the overflowing roof garden.

"Shoo, shoo," cried Lucy, clapping her hands in their direction, waist high among flowers, shrubs, and pots. "They're such a nuisance," she said, more to herself than to Thea, who was sitting at the table sipping tea. The birds flapped in the air for a moment, then returned to their game.

"They make such a mess."

Lucy had taken Thea's early arrival well; more than that, she had seemed delighted. More than that even, she had treated it as the surprise that Thea had hoped for.

"You could shoot them," said Thea.

Lucy laughed and came and sat down. Thea looked at her mother in the afternoon light. She does look good, she thought. It was hardly surprising since she'd barely allowed herself a moment's stress for twenty years. No wonder the public bought her books. They might be crazy but they cheered people up.

"You look great, Ma. I just hope I look as good as you when I'm sixty. I'll save a fortune in plastic surgeons."

"It's only just sunk in," said Lucy, "the sixty business."

"I'm sorry I missed it, your birthday." *I should have come over,* thought Thea. *I should have made the effort.* Her habitual guilt, ever close, pricked beneath her skin.

"It was very quiet," Lucy said. "I didn't want a big fuss."

She looked across at Thea, searching her face for clues, for something to clutch onto and pull her close, but her surface was smooth and closed.

"Don't stare at me like that," said Thea. "It makes me feel uncomfortable."

"I'm sorry, darling. I just haven't seen you for so long."

Thea folded her arms across her chest.

"Well, you'll see plenty of me now."

"You can stay as long as you want, you know that. I'm just so happy to have you here."

"Thanks, Ma." Thea felt herself soften.

"You are staying? I mean in England, not here. I know you won't want to be here forever."

"Yes, I think so. That's the plan."

"And what—" Lucy stopped herself. "More tea?"

"What's the rest of the plan, for the rest of my life?"

"You've just arrived. There's plenty of time for that and it's certainly none of my business."

"No," Thea said. "I mean yes. Plenty of time, Ma."

It occurred to Lucy that her daughter seemed bruised in some intangible manner. The thought hung over her, refusing to be dismissed, and she observed, as she had more and more in the last few months, that her own will to happiness was slipping from her grasp.

"If you need anything, money I mean, I can always help out."

Thea smiled at her. "I don't need money. I made plenty in L.A. And I've been offered jobs back here several times in the last year . . . I'm just . . ."

Lucy waited, her face composed in patient interest.

"I'm just not that sure about things anymore."

Lucy made no comment. Lucy didn't think that Thea had ever been sure about anything except in those moments when her need was greatest, but she sensed that her daughter was changing. Lucy claimed not to understand any of her children's apparent ambitions, they were so far removed from her own concerns, though it was true that her books had earned her a small spotlight of her own.

Thea knew that her mother was curious about what had gone wrong in America, but she felt she couldn't explain it to her, not until she had a firmer grasp on where she was heading. There had been the plans for celebrations the previous Christmas when she and her fiancé had intended to come to London to visit Lucy, and then, suddenly, it had all been over, a relief in the end, for both parties, a rebound engagement, predictable and messy. Thea couldn't get over a feeling of awkwardness about the whole business. She wanted to move on, to jump over the explanations and sympathy. She was convinced her decision to return home was the right one, but it was hard to shake off the feeling that she trailed a slick of failure.

She stretched her head back to take the full force of the sun. The smell of the azaleas behind her pushed into her nostrils as if she'd just crushed them. A bee hovered by her ear and she sat up. Her mother was still watching. Here, in the roof garden, she could feel the past two and a half years slipping away almost as if they'd never existed.

"I'm not going to pry, Thea," said Lucy. "As I said, I'm just glad you're here."

"Thanks, Ma. Me, too."

"The best is yet to come."

"Which of your books is that in?"

"I forget."

Thea smiled at her and reached for her sunglasses. Lucy's determined optimism was at least consistent.

HER decision to leave London had been impulsive, and veiled behind a torrent of logic like most of her choices in life. When she'd been offered a job by the production company she worked for, helping to set up an office in Los Angeles, she'd said no. Her family and friends weren't surprised. She'd seemed settled at last, after years of upheaval. She'd recently bought a new flat and was set for promotion at home. She'd appeared to be well over the affair with Archie and back with her long-term boyfriend, a man far more dependable, more what she needed, she'd said.

But Thea knew exactly the moment she'd changed her mind. She was at a party at Richard Armstrong's. It was late October, Halloween perhaps, though of course the Brits didn't go in for masks and costumes the way her American colleagues did. Her boyfriend, Mark, was wrapped up in a conversation with James on the potential for some share flotation. Amy wasn't there for once, which was a relief. Their relationship was in a private freefall.

She was talking to Richard in the kitchen, indulging in the sort of banter and flirtation she relished. Richard made her laugh, he was clever and funny, with a drive to him, a hunger that was attractive. He was teasing her about a trip to an alternative health clinic she'd confessed to.

"Come on, then, what did you have done?"

"I'm not telling you."

"Crystal stuff? That sort of thing?"

"It's personal."

"Colonic irrigation?"

"No."

"I bet it was. Is it sexy?"

"Richard!"

"What's sexy in here, then?" Another voice chimed in. It was Archie. The charge in the atmosphere shifted from positive to negative. Thea's natural languor seemed to ossify. Richard swigged from his glass and picked up a bottle.

"Want a drink?" he said.

"Yes, please." Archie turned toward Thea and made as if to kiss her on the cheek. She ducked under his arm.

"Mark and I are leaving shortly," she said. "See you later," and headed for the rest of the party. But a moment later, realizing she'd left her bag behind, she turned back. She was almost in the doorway when she heard Archie swear.

"Fuck," he said. "I can't seem to get it right around Thea."

She leaned against the hall wall for a moment to compose herself.

"She'll get over it," said Richard. "She's back with Mark, isn't she?"

"So what's her problem?" Archie sounded irritable.

"What was your problem? She's gorgeous."

"It was too complicated."

"Only because of that prima donna of a sister. She treats you like one of her kids."

Archie poured himself a fresh glass of wine from the bottle that Richard held out to him.

"I hardly think so," he said, "and it had nothing to do with Amy."

"She didn't like it, you being with Thea."

Richard was getting drunk, thought Archie, but he smiled as he listened.

"She didn't like sharing you with her sister," Richard went on. "She likes you."

"Of course she does."

"No, I mean I think she really likes you. Know what I mean?" Richard raised his glass to Archie and drank.

Archie laughed, embarrassed.

"She's my best friend's wife."

"Ideally placed, then."

"You're sick."

"That's rich. You fuck the twin because you can't have the original and call me sick. That's sick."

"Now you're being a cunt," said Archie. "Just leave it alone."

She felt ice cold standing in the corridor. On the wall opposite hung a mirror with an ornate black frame. As she caught her reflection, the ironwork around the glass seemed to soften and extend its tentacles toward her. She wanted to move, to get back to the noise and light, but her back and shoulders were stuck. She wanted to look away but she couldn't turn her neck. She knew the woman in the mirror wasn't her and that if she could move she'd smash it, find a brick, a shoe, or an ashtray, and reduce that mocking image to a rubble of refracting shards.

SHE felt cold now, too, here in the afternoon heat of her mother's terrace. She could hear Lucy chattering on like a bird or a running tap. She was telling Thea about her grandchildren, Thea's niece and nephew, so much changed in her absence. Thea's eyes were half closed against the light.

That night, she'd decided to go. She'd signed a contract the next day, put her flat up for rent, and dumped poor Mark yet again. She'd refused to discuss the reasons for leaving with Amy, and then picked another fight that she didn't want to win. Archie was another matter. He'd invited her out to lunch to say good-bye. They'd both been on their best behavior. He'd held her hand across the table and said he wished things had ended better.

"If wishes were horses, Archie."

"What?"

"Never mind. I was such an idiot to even think of it," she'd said. "We're neither of us cut out for marriage, are we?"

"We can be friends, though, can't we?" he'd said.

"Distant friends."

"Yes, distant friends."

She thought he'd liked the sound of that as he waved her good-bye.

Lucy was still talking, and Thea could see a picture of Archie as if he were signaling to her through the wavy lines of heat that crossed between her and her mother. She realized he was standing on Oxford Street as he'd done yesterday when she'd watched him through the taxi window. Strange that her last and first glimpses of him were with his hand in the air, seeking her attention. And now, according to Grace, he'd been dumped by his latest girlfriend and had taken it badly.

"He's in a midlife crisis," Grace had reported.

"Don't be silly, he's not even forty," Thea had said.

"Almost. Life's not what it was for men. Over forty's just as tough for them these days."

How ruthless Grace had sounded, and it frightened Thea to know that a bit of her relished the thought of Archie's decay. When she'd floated the idea of getting married, she had been sure, in the moment, he would agree. She had tried to interpret his teasing and complimentary replies as enthusiasm, and his fondness for her had seemed undiminished. But she didn't believe it compared with hers, and the disparity hung between them, unmentioned, along with the rest of her family baggage. She'd taken the only route out she knew, and while Archie had been sweet and forgiving, she was sure that he was secretly relieved.

THE small epiphany he'd had on Brighton beach had stayed with Richard all through the journey home. It had been a difficult start, but after the uncomfortable accommodation that had to be made with the mother he saw infrequently, the sense of duty to be summoned, the self-conscious patience the reunion required, they'd settled into a semblance of mother and son togetherness that had surprised them both. He relaxed in his seat, feeling pleased with himself. The only small needle in his smug contemplation had been his mother's parting shot.

"Bring Thea with you next time," she'd said, waving at him as he left her flat in a taxi for the station.

He'd forgotten until she issued the invitation that he'd fibbed about having a girlfriend, fibbed about a name. He'd said it to shut his mother up, and it had worked. Why he'd used the Fielding twins was a mystery to him, though he was forced to admit to himself that a pleasing, if out-of-date, vision of both Amy and Thea Fielding had floated into his mind, as it did now. And in fact, the explanation was simple. He'd been talking to Amy on the phone only this morning, and he knew he wanted to talk to Thea about her experience in L.A., to pick her brain about contacts and opportunities. And besides that, he liked them both, he always had.

He'd met them through Archie, intrigued as everyone was, as men were especially, but he was always able to tell the difference between them. It was quite clear to him. Thea, for a start, was more sexually overt than her twin. Amy was married now, of course, but it was more than that, he thought. Thea seemed to carry a charge that was obscured in Amy, hidden beneath a controlled exterior. It was a charge, he'd thought more than once, that he'd secretly enjoy unearthing.

As he finished his warm railway buffet gin and tonic, he began to feel restless. The train was much more crowded than on the journey out, and it seemed to slow down every fifteen minutes. He longed to be back in the city. It was 6:30 by now, and Lynette would have left the office, so there was no point in ringing her, though he could feel his phone burning a hole in his pocket, begging to be stuck to his ear. He tapped his foot under the table and debated whether to stagger to the train bar and queue up for another drink. There was no sign of the boy of indeterminate nationality who had been pushing a refreshment trolley up and down the aisle. He pulled out his notebook to check his "to do" list. Halfway down he'd written, "Call Thea Fielding (Thurs/Fri)." It was only Tuesday. He couldn't remember if Amy had said exactly when she was coming back. If she wasn't back already, he could leave a message. It would be friendly and welcoming. Or he could pretend he thought she was back. Aware that he hadn't thought this through with quite the care he should apply, he rang Lucy's number, which he'd scribbled down beside Thea's name.

The rings went on forever. There was no machine. He was about to give up when a voice answered.

"Hello?"

"Mrs. Fielding?"

"Yes?"

"This is Richard Armstrong. You might not remember me—we have met once or twice, at Amy's. I'm a friend of James and Amy—and Thea."

"I do remember you," said Lucy. "You played hide-and-seek with the children in the garden."

Had he really? He must have been trying to impress.

"I was wondering if I could leave a message for Thea. A 'welcome home and give me a ring when you're up and running' sort of message."

"You don't need to leave a message, you can speak to her now, she's here."

"But I thought . . ."

He could hear her calling Thea's name. It sounded as if she were calling upstairs. He hadn't planned this far, it was only going to be a message. What on earth should he say to her? In the background he could hear footsteps getting closer.

"Who is it?" he heard Thea say.

"Richard. That charming boy who played hide-and-seek with Jonny and Rosie at Amy's birthday."

"Who?"

"Richard."

She took the receiver from her mother.

"Hello?"

"Thea, it's Richard Armstrong."

"Richard!" she said in recognition. "I couldn't think who Ma meant. I thought she was talking about a child." He sensed her turn away to speak to Lucy: "He's hardly a boy, Ma." Then she turned her mouth back to the receiver: "She called you a boy. You should be flattered. . . . So, Dickie boy, how are things with you?"

"Fine. When did you get back?"

"Sunday," she said. She seemed to have lowered her voice.

"Right," he said, stalling.

"Is there something in particular?" said Thea. "I'm not being rude, I just wasn't expecting you to call."

She was being rude, he thought, but it amused him.

"Yes," he said, becoming brisker, "I wanted to catch you before everyone else does. I want to know what you're up to and pick your brain, if I'm honest. John—you know, John Holt, he works with me now—he told me you were back. You've been in touch over the last couple of years, haven't you?"

"Yes, sure, we've done some business." She could hear herself adopting her L.A. voice.

"Why don't we meet up for lunch?" said Richard. "It would be great to see you, and I'm interested to know what you're going to do next." It was the gin that had done it. The gin and her flirtatious tone. He hadn't intended to suggest lunch, not so soon, but she was an attractive woman, after all.

There was a pause at the other end, and he wondered what was going through her mind.

"Yes. Okay," she replied. "That might be useful. You can fill me in on what's happened here." She didn't want to reveal her own uncertainty. "When?"

What the hell, thought Richard, whose instincts had always served him well.

"I'm free tomorrow," he said, crossing through a meeting in his diary. "Any chance?"

~

Amy lay on the bed, gazing out at the sky, which was all she could see. She shut her eyes and reran her lunch with Archie in her head. It had hardly been a success, and the truth was that she had been quite self-obsessed, if not a bit crazy. He'd certainly thought so. She wished she had something to distract her from her thoughts. It had been strange as the afternoon wore on not to have the children return from school or activities, not to have to collect them or focus on what to feed them. It was alarming to be without structure, for time just to pass without an allocation for things outside herself. She thought of calling next door, to see if Susie Dixon was in, for a cup of tea and a superficial chat. She thought she could hear Tamsin in the garden, shrieking as she chased some hapless friend. But then she realized it couldn't be the house next door, that they too were away, gone off to Brittany for Tamsin to run wild on the beach.

Her head ached. She must have drunk at least a couple of glasses of wine at lunch. She'd have to stop that now. She'd have to stop her fantasy life with Archie, as well. It was only an image of Archie, she knew that, though it didn't make it any less potent. An idea of him had taken hold of her in her panic, a clinging to the freedom of spirit he used to display like some arrogant bird. But he was no more free now than the rest of them. He was restricted by his body just as she was by hers.

She wanted to cry again but the tears were too far out of reach. She could only see her unborn child as putting an end to any ambition she might have had. She knew that what she'd said to Archie at lunch was true, that she had made her decision, but she still wasn't ready to share it. She sat up feeling sick and wondered what time James would be back. She might tell him tonight if things felt right. It was different from her first two pregnancies; they had been an expected surprise. This one would take life in an unplanned direction, and she wanted to choose her moment. If she told him, it would be settled. She could then tell her mother, and Thea, of course. Perhaps it would be a sort of peace offering. But what if Thea was envious, because now she would have three children and Thea none. She caught a shadow at the back of her brain and pushed away the thought that a part of her wanted Thea to envy her. She didn't want to believe that was true.

SHE couldn't remember exactly how it had started, this feeling of the two of them in competition, pulling away but needing each other. She could picture them sitting around the kitchen table one winter afternoon after school. They must have been about eleven. They were doing their homework, always a competitive moment, the relative merits and honor of the separate schools they attended at stake in the difficulty and amount that had to be done. Thea got up from the table and pressed her legs and back against the radiator, arms folded.

"Where do you think Ma is?" she said.

"I don't know. I think she's still at work." Lucy had a part-time job teaching horticulture at a local college.

"No, she's not."

"How do you know she's not?"

There was silence.

"Where is she, then?"

Thea turned around and studied the lists and bits of paper pinned to a corkboard on the wall.

"Thea!"

Amy threw a pencil at her sister's back. It bounced to the floor and rolled over the lino back under the table. She didn't know if she was annoyed or alarmed.

"Stop being a bitch, Thea. Tell me."

Thea turned around, her eyes were watering.

"I heard Penny Adams's mother talking this morning. I heard her say Ma was pushing her luck, that people were starting to talk."

"What about?"

"I don't know."

Amy pushed her chair back and stood up. It was a moment that had remained with her down the years, a trace memory that fluttered over her skin every time she left a table.

"I do," she said.

She wasn't sure how she knew. She'd known for some time but it wasn't till Thea had opened the box that she understood her secret knowledge. The simple facts flew out. Lucy was having an affair with one of her father's legal colleagues. Her father was unhappy. Lucy was unhappy most of the time. They would probably get a divorce like Sarah Pinsent's parents, and she and Thea and the baby would shuttle backward and forward between Lucy and their father. There would be new stepparents who treated them badly and all sorts of horribleness. This vision of their life hung over the kitchen in the half-light of a late winter afternoon, a damp miasma. She looked across at Thea, through the future, and she knew that they must call a truce, that they must rope themselves together to survive.

JAMES woke with a start as his train pulled into Liverpool Street. He'd slept for most of the journey, or rather slipped in and out of a postlunch coma. Dreams of a startling intensity had been punctuated by a rattling nasal whine, which, to his embarrassment, he realized was emitting from his nose and throat.

It wasn't till he reached the end of the long platform and entered the busy shopping mall that now passed for a railway station that he became fully aware of his condition. He was moving slowly, to the rhythm of a lethargic throbbing that he dismissed as the sun overheating his body through the train window. But a flush crept up his face as he now recalled the eroticism of the images that had flooded his brain in his afternoon torpor. Grace naked astride his lap. Grace, her legs wrapped around his body. Then a door had opened, in the dreamworld, behind them, and a figure had entered the room and he'd known it was Amy.

The combination of lust, shame, and dehydration made him dizzy. He diverted into a supermarket and bought a bottle of water from which he drank with vacuum strength. It was just before six. He couldn't go home yet, not until he'd shaken this off. It flashed through his mind to ring Patrick, but when Patrick had said he could make impromptu appointments, James doubted he'd appreciate quite such short notice. In any case, he wasn't sure that he wanted to tell Patrick this stuff. It was too new and much too close to home.

The person he wanted to tell was Archie, because Archie would laugh it away, but he might not want to know. It was the big day tomorrow—the hospital, the moment of truth. And Archie had made it clear he wanted to go in there on his own. Still, James reasoned, that was tomorrow, and after all he wouldn't be much of a friend if he didn't check in to see how Archie was the night before a major life event. He found his phone and pressed the buttons.

"Hi, it's James."

"Hi, man. How are you?" Archie sounded far away.

"Fine. I'm on my way home. From Liverpool Street. Fancy a quick drink?"

There was a hesitation, then, "Shouldn't you get home?"

"I'll call Amy and tell her. She wasn't expecting me till later."

"Er, okay, then. Why not? Prince of Wales?"

"Yes. I'll be forty minutes at the most," said James, oblivious to Archie's lack of enthusiasm. "See you there."

THERE was almost never a time when Archie didn't want to see his friend, but tonight he would have preferred to be alone. He was carrying secrets for Amy and he felt like a traitor. She'd overstepped the mark between them today, voicing what he'd always told himself was natural, what he knew was natural as long as it remained unspoken; it was just part of a man and woman being friends. It must be the pregnancy, he told himself again, and he felt a recurrence of the anger she'd provoked in him earlier. He knew she hadn't meant to tell him, but she had, and now he knew about the baby before James did, which was unforgivable, and he knew something else, that in the space of these few uncertain days things had gone awry. His anchorage had failed to hold, and he seemed to be pulling away, unsteered, and unsettling whoever else was close by in his chaotic slipstream.

THE Tube was hot and full, and James wished he'd taken a taxi. But an August traffic jam across London had been the less appealing option. As he hung from the rail a man in vest and shorts lurched against him, delivering the full blast of a day's odor. James shut his eyes and tried to breathe through his mouth. But behind his closed eyelids there danced still the lewd images of Grace. He fixed his eyes on the red line of the Tube map and mentally repeated the stops on the Central Line. Bank, St. Paul's, Chancery Lane, Holborn, Tottenham Court Road, Oxford Circus: only six more to go before he could escape onto the Bakerloo Line. It made no rational sense, he knew, but the brown route through to the northwest of London had always seemed less frenzied, as if the broad leafy avenues of Little Venice called down to the travelers beneath the surface, easing the cramped compartments with their promise of light and air.

It was 6:45 when he reached the pub, and though business was brisk as the day's workers stopped for cold beer on their way home, the atmosphere was heavy and disgruntled. There was an air of resignation and of lingering resentment toward colleagues lucky enough to escape the August city heat while those left behind saw out the dog days, manning phones, sifting information, and stalling decisions till the great September return. There was no sign of Archie. James bought a pint of lager and found a seat outside just vacated by a couple who left holding hands. He watched them as they lingered on the pavement and kissed and went their separate ways. An office romance? Was one or both married? His curiosity was perfunctory, just something to occupy his mind, to keep it busy and hold off its prevailing obsession.

"James."

Archie stood in front of him. James had been sufficiently preoccupied not to see him coming, and now he barely noticed the reservation in his manner. He stood up and clapped his friend on the back.

"Hey. Good to see you. What do you want to drink?"

"I'll get it—do you want another?" Archie waved his hand toward the interior.

"No. I've only just got here. I'll have a packet of crisps, though."

Archie disappeared into the crowded bar, and James willed him to get served and return as quickly as possible. The information that had come his way had a significance for him, for whatever reason, beyond its surface. If he could joke about it, dilute it down, he could surely get it into the perspective it deserved. After all, it was a good story. Archie was going to enjoy it.

"You'll never guess what," he said, when Archie returned.

"What?"

"What happened to me today."

Archie almost smiled. It was a long time since he had seen James so pumped up with news.

"Tell me, please. It will make a change from wondering what's going to happen to me tomorrow."

James hesitated, then plunged in. He was doing the right thing. It was a distraction for Archie. It was just what he needed.

Sitting here in front of James, who was talking nonstop in a state of childlike excitement, Archie was reminded of a time way back at school, when James had broken a leg falling off the gym block. James had sat against the wall, waiting for the doctor, gabbling to conceal the pain. Archie could remember imagining the cracked bone beneath the flesh; and looking at James across the pub table, he had the same sensation. How had he not seen it sooner, this stress fracture in his friends' marriage? Had it just materialized, or had it been a weakness, a misalignment that had been waiting for years to emerge? For what else was Amy's girlish nostalgia, and the midlife maundering that was coming out of James's mouth? So, gorgeous Grace had had a crush on him when she was still a schoolgirl. Well, he could have told him that. He'd always assumed James knew.

"That's a bit of a turnup," he said.

"You can say that again."

"Made your day, I should think?"

"Yes," said James. As he took a drink from his glass, he appeared to deflate as he swallowed. His shoulders sank, his mouth moved slowly, fishlike.

"Actually," he said, wiping his face with the back of his hand then pulling his hair, "actually, to be honest, I wish she hadn't told me."

He looked beyond Archie to the crowd of customers at the tables. A couple of drinks on and they had miraculously reanimated, the noise level steadily rising. Archie turned to follow his gaze and wished he could be part of the crowd again, men and women with their overfull glasses and laughing faces, part of their hour or two of forgetfulness before the retreat to face another day.

"Why?" he asked. "You should be flattered. Most men would be." *I would have been*, he thought. *It should have been me.*

"She's my sister-in-law."

"And she was just a kid. It's pretty standard stuff."

"I suppose so." James crumpled up the empty crisp packet. "The weird thing is I'd never thought about her like that before."

Archie looked at him, amazed.

"What? You mean you'd never noticed that Grace is a complete stunner?"

"Yes, but, you know, not . . ."

It took him a moment but then Archie understood it all.

"I get it. You're running porn movies in your head."

James looked sheepish.

"Something like that."

Archie laughed. He felt relief. James's natural prudishness was suddenly reassuring.

"Don't worry about it. It'll wear off. Enjoy it while it lasts." He drained his glass and watched James's face relax. "Another?" He picked up the two glasses with an air of someone who had just discovered conviviality. "Then you can tell me more."

James smiled. "One more, then home."

THE sound of sirens wailing in the streets roused Thea from her stupor as she sat in the warm evening sun. For a moment she forgot where she was and thought herself back in the small terraced garden outside her Hollywood apartment. The heat of London had surprised her and she longed for autumn, with its sharp mornings and mist that would tell her she was home. She was sitting once more on Lucy's rooftop as her mother worked below, the smell of something in the kitchen signaling advance preparations for a celebration supper, and it felt as if her time away had dissolved, finally, into the unreality she'd suspected it to be. Perhaps it was the nature of expatriate life forever to live a few feet off the ground, but she needed these sounds and smells, the vowels, the colors that stretched back for better or worse through her existence, to know she took up space, to know that the roof over her head and the rain that fell on it were proofs of some solidity.

It had been quite a shock to hear Richard's voice on the phone, a voice she had pushed from her mind long since. But the words he had spoken that evening in his kitchen still resonated. It was as if they'd been inside her for much, much longer. It was as if Richard had voiced them, but she had punched them through, had forced their articulation in some way. She wondered if it was something he remembered. It was unlikely, though he might recall the sentiment. He was a shrewd guy. There had been a time when she would tease Archie about Richard's devotion to him, to joke that Richard's girlfriends were just a cover for a secret passion. Archie was embarrassed, had said it was an outrageous suggestion. He was right, there was no doubt. Richard was straight. She'd seen the way he'd appraised her and other women—and Amy, of course—but she'd also noticed how he'd sometimes look at Archie, as if he were studying him.

"Late developer," Archie had said when she'd brought it up again. "Went to a mixed-sex school, never did the boy thing."

"What?" she'd said. "I rest my case."

"It's not about sex," he'd said. "It's about bonding, so I'm told. Dick's never really done that. He's always struck out on his own."

"And you have?"

"Yes. Me and James. We're bonded." Archie had laughed at his statement, clamping his hands together in a gesture of solidarity, and she'd stared at the double fist he'd made. Her boyfriend was bonded to her twin's mate. She'd known it since she met him, but their passionate enjoyment of each other had stopped her from admitting it, and she had felt a moment of indecency in the lack of space between them.

⁓

A suspicious smell of burning reached Archie through the sharp spray of his bathroom shower. He'd meant to turn the sausages down to the grill's lowest setting but had forgotten. It was always a mistake to try to cook, and he preferred to order in, but tonight he hadn't wanted to wait. As he rushed toward the kitchen, stark naked, the phone rang, and he made a dash into the sitting room to answer. It was Richard. Fuck, he thought. Still naked and dripping, towel and phone in hand, and hoping the woman whose form he'd been known to scrutinize in a window opposite couldn't or wouldn't reciprocate his attention, he turned off the grill, wiped his head, then wrapped himself around.

"Richard. Sorry about that. In the shower. Bloody hot. Just been to the pub with James."

"How's tricks?" said Richard.

You tell me, Tricky Dickie, thought Archie, but breezed on.

"Under control."

"Thought you might like to come out for a drink on Thursday night? There's a few of us up for it."

It was the sort of evening that he could only now admit to having tired of quite some time ago. Forced banter out in the clubs. But you weren't supposed to be there at forty. You were supposed to go home to your wife and children.

"I can't make it. Meetings and stuff."

"Meetings?" Richard said with new interest. "Quick work."

"You've got to fight while you're fresh," said Archie.

"Good for you. Tell me more. Have you phoned Frank Denny? I had the company prospectus sent around to you. Have you got it?"

"Yeah, yeah. I'll think about it."

"Look, come and join us later on Thursday. Or we could meet up on Friday. I'll give Martin Seddon a ring. It's about time we persuaded him to have a night out."

Archie had forgotten about Martin Seddon along with the rest of the cast of his usual life. He'd also forgotten how tenacious Richard could be.

"Another time. Drink to my health."

He said it without thinking. He could smell the sausages smoking next door, burning bread and meat.

"No," he said. "Don't drink to my health."

"What?" said Richard. "Are we on for tennis again on Sunday, then?"

"Drink to my future," said Archie. "I've got to go, there's someone at the door."

He turned off the sausages, which spat from the griddle, gobbing fat onto the hob. He couldn't face eating them now, there was too much of the crematorium about them. He forked them one by one, with difficulty, onto a plate, dumped them in the rubbish bin, and drank a large quantity of milk straight from the plastic bottle.

He sat in front of the TV and wondered how to stop himself from thinking about tomorrow and how soon he could go to bed. The flat was full of distractions—videos, books, and games of all kinds, a small amusement arcade in the hallway, machines he'd collected over the years—but nothing appealed. It was only 8:15. He flicked channels and found Grace standing behind the bar of a pub in a low-cut blouse, speaking in an accent broader than her own. He listened to her cascade abuse at a man with more hair on his chest than his head. As he watched her parry and thrust he began to forget who she was, Amy's sister, the looker, the girl who only this afternoon had caused a rush of new blood through her brother-in-law's body. She was very convincing. She made him forget who she was even within the constraints of a nightly soap. She was good.

He felt warm as he watched her, paternal even. This emotional generosity seemed to be a by-product of his crisis. He was happy Grace was talented, happy for her that she had a career before her and a good-looking boy at her side. Such feelings were unfamiliar to him, and he sank into this new sensation, as if his edges were curling like heated wax. He wanted to be there in the pub, with Grace, the one on the television. It looked inviting, even with all the shouting. Perhaps he should ring Richard back and go out with a crowd on Thursday after all. But then he remembered he couldn't go on Thursday, that he would be in no fit state to go drinking. They were singing in the pub now, something he would never do, but somehow it was all right tonight, all right for them in their local, even aged forty and over, and he wished he was there with them.

Archie was gripped. He couldn't think why he'd always been so snooty about Grace's soap. He could see its point. It was perfect. It meant you didn't have to go to the pub yourself, or have arguments, or resign from your job. It was a public service. He looked at the TV page of the evening paper. There was a hospital drama on next. Perhaps if he watched that, the worst of the things that could happen to him tomorrow would be performed in advance. He could have the experience without the blood and knives. He felt suddenly hungry and went and fished the burned sausages out of the rubbish bin. They'd be fine if he wiped them clean. He ate them quickly, standing up, with a large quantity of tomato ketchup, thinking as he did so that at his age it felt a strange and lonely thing to do.

SEARCHING for cucumber to make a sauce, Amy confronted the contents of her fridge. It definitely needed a clear-out, but now wasn't the time to make a start. She'd had a bath and dressed herself for her husband's return, taking the same degree of care that she had that morning, to reduce her guilt. She had poached some salmon, which was cooling off, and found a half bottle of champagne in the cellar, which she'd hidden in the freezer. If they were going to have another baby, which they were, and if this evening was the right time to discuss the subject, then they must surely celebrate (she would merely sip at a glass now, of course), until the congratulations that would come their way extinguished their apprehension. She heard James let himself in and sensed him pause in the hall, though she couldn't imagine what for. It was summer, there was no coat to dispose of.

"I'm in the kitchen," she called.

He stopped in the doorway, his jacket slung over his arm and his tie spilling out of a trouser pocket. It seemed to him a lifetime since he'd left this morning. Amy's body language, he noted, suggested they were back on track.

"You look exhausted, darling," she said. "How was Archie?"

"You had lunch with him today, I hear, you must know."

He came over to where she stood chopping up dill. He put his arms around her waist and kissed her neck.

"But," he said, "to answer your question: shit scared, I think. He still doesn't want anyone to go with him. However . . ." Amy opened her mouth to protest. "However," he went on, "the good news is he'd like us to visit him tomorrow evening."

She put down her knife.

"Thank God for that. I couldn't bear to think of him waking up there. . . ."

"I know. He still won't know anything, I shouldn't think."

"Yes, but someone should be with him."

"We'll be there."

"Yes."

She put her arms around his neck.

"Are we okay now?" she said.

"Feels okay to me." He pulled her close. "I'm sorry about last night. I must have been worried about my meeting. Don't know why. It went brilliantly."

"That's because you are brilliant," she said, smoothing back his damp hair. She should tell him. This was a perfect moment.

"Can that wait?" he said, nodding at the chopping board.

"Yes," she said, "and if it can't I'll throw it away and start again."

He kissed her with a passion that he hadn't been able to summon for months.

"I need a shower," he said. "Come up with me."

SHE was going to tell him, as they stood naked together under the running water in the smoky-mirrored bathroom. But as he kissed her and soaped her back, she closed her eyes and felt a freedom and a return to the eroticism of her youth. There was an iridescence about her, no room for a baby. As they clung together first on the old chaise longue in their bedroom, a wedding present from Lucy, then graduated to their bed, with the door wide and unlocked for once, they felt themselves recapture the lightness of spirit that had been such a part of their early life together, when their laughter seemed to infuse the more serious business of sex, without ever breaking its spell. Amy pushed the thought of the new child away as she clung to her husband, reclaiming him from the stale exile to which she'd consigned him. This was the answer. This she must maintain to save them.

JAMES was transformed. He could feel his anxieties recede and he felt like a king. He'd make it into the lift tomorrow, he was sure of it. And then, just as he was about to come, just as his body was thrusting on a track that should have bypassed his brain, his head filled with visions of Grace in positions that a man would once have been pressed to find in the back of a porn shop. He slumped on top of Amy, on top of his loving playful wife, shagged out and ashamed, and he could feel the sticky dampness spreading beneath their thighs. He was not the sort of man who fantasized about other women when making love to his wife—or not often, or at least never before about his sister-in-law, not even Thea, and surely a man might be tempted by a twin? He looked at Amy's contented face. Whatever else was going on he knew he loved her, but for the first time in his married life he acknowledged that family could be a fragile affair.

2004

24 November
Harley Street

Patrick considered himself an effective member of his profession. He had, after all, developed a strong reputation among an affluent clientele and was soon to give an important paper on attachment in Boston. He even worked pro bono one morning a week to offset the corruption of his substantial charges. But now this former client's wife was sitting in front of him, against all good practice, and he couldn't seem to let her go. He should send her away with kind words, refer her to couples counseling, the usual sort of thing. He thought he could recall her husband's features as he'd sat in the old leather recliner, furniture bought in a sale when he'd first started out all those years ago. He found himself looking back on the curly-haired figure in the chair with affection, and guessed his nostalgia was less for a man he barely knew than for an earlier simplicity of purpose.

Amy placed her hands on the arms of her seat, a gentle but deliberate, determined gesture.

"I need you to listen to me," she said.

Patrick waited. The silence between them magnified the thud of a heavy bass from a car stereo pulsating at the lights on the corner. He was aware of an anger rising in him, of his heartbeat increasing to match the sound outside.

"Are you married, Patrick?" Her question and the use of his name took him by surprise, and he wanted to divert her as he normally would, to ask what relevance his marital status had for her, but instead he shook his head.

"Then you might not know," she said, "how hard it is sometimes to see beyond the life you live with someone else, to see that there are other lives that they might long to construct without you; and when, sometimes, you do see, then not to mind too much, to understand. I think that's what happened with James and me." She put out her hand quickly, as if to stop him from interrupting her. "Let me talk about him, please."

"I didn't say you couldn't speak about him," said Patrick, his attention only in part where it should be, "I said that I can't."

"I understand," she said. "After all, I sometimes feel the need to keep his secrets, too."

He was caught by her statement, by its simplicity. He wondered if she was challenging him with her more intimate knowledge, establishing her prior claim, but she seemed happy to accept his terms.

"Up till that week I'd always thought we were happy," she went on, "and in most ways we were, or we had been, but you can't always . . ." She stopped for a moment, then, like a train starting up, she accelerated. "It's just not easy to stay still, in fact it's impossible. And you can't always move forward. So I think we were in a bit of a backslide, which was, to say the least, bad timing. I couldn't bring myself to tell him about the pregnancy. Once I'd spoken the words out loud to him, that would be it, and I knew that at first we'd pretend it was marvelous and then it would be. My mother is right, sometimes you can pretend what you've got is what you wanted all along, or you can with babies because biology takes over and makes it so. But most times, in my view, you can't do that, you can't pretend, and I think we might have been pretending to be as happy as we once had been."

As he listened to her, he felt again her fragile stability, her searching for a safe harbor.

"But that's what everyone does to some extent, isn't it? Act the part?" She was talking to herself now. Her questions weren't requests for answers.

"Pretending makes it so, that's what my mother says. My sister Grace is brilliant at it, she does it for a living. She's an actress. You'll have heard of her—Grace Fielding?"

He nodded, and as he did he remembered more. It was a name that everyone knew, a name even back then.

"But you have to stop at some point," she was saying. "It's unsustainable. You have to stop and face the truth."

James Marsham had talked about Grace Fielding, Patrick remembered that. And he'd talked about his friend Archie. But as far as Patrick could recall he had barely mentioned his wife.

"I really think," he said, "that you should talk to your husband." Patrick wasn't averse to prescribing common sense when all else failed. He was pleased with himself for taking this maverick line. But she seemed to dismiss this possibility, shrugging her shoulders.

"I've tried," she said. "Really, I've tried."

1994

WEDNESDAY 17 AUGUST

"IT IS A CHARACTERISTIC OF WISDOM NOT TO DO
DESPERATE THINGS."

from *Lifelines for Hard Times* by Lucy Fielding

THE DOORBELL HAD rung at 6:30 that morning, the abrasive electric
sound of the buzzer, and then the odd sensation once again of hearing her name called from inside her head. Doorbells were mis-
named, Lucy always thought, they no longer rang, or chimed, but
savaged their way into consciousness and, when unexpected, signaled demanding strangers or unwanted news. She was already
awake, drinking tea and watching the sun come up over the roof of
the church on the corner. She'd been feeling at peace with herself, a
state, she reflected, that was eluding her more frequently this side of
sixty. Thea was home, asleep in the bedroom under Lucy's feet. Amy
and Grace were safe and well. Her demons had settled back behind
the door, and she'd almost forgotten they were restless.

Lucy knew she should answer the door, though it might be just a
passing tramp. It buzzed again. As she climbed down the spiral staircase back into the flat, careful not to tread on the hem of her dressing gown, she saw Thea heading toward the intercom, hair over her
face and wearing an old T-shirt.

She picked up the receiver and turned to face Lucy, raising her
eyebrows.

"Who is it?" Thea asked, and a moment passed as she listened to the answer.

"Yes. Why . . . ? Come up, I'll get it for you."

She pressed the buzzer and turned to her mother.

"It's Grace," she said, sounding surprised. "She's got no money for the taxi."

"But she's got a key," said Lucy.

"Well, clearly not this morning," said Thea, moving toward her bedroom.

"It's okay," said Lucy. "My handbag's in the kitchen." She disappeared up the corridor and returned a minute later to find Grace standing in the doorway. She thrust a twenty-pound note into her hand.

"Thanks, Ma. I'll explain. I'll just go down and pay him."

Lucy and Thea looked at each other.

"I'll put the kettle on," said Lucy.

They sat, the three of them, in the kitchen. There was an air of crisis that dictated that the impromptu meeting should be held indoors despite the beauty of the August morning. Grace looked exhausted, her red hair pulled back in a ponytail, her face pale and shadowed from lack of sleep.

"I just had to get out. Get away," she said.

"Without your bag," said Thea. "There's drama for you."

"I suppose I had quite a lot to drink last night."

"Poor darling," said Lucy. "You look so tired."

"I've had two hours sleep, Ma."

"We'll ring the show and tell them you're ill," said Lucy.

"No," Grace almost shouted.

"No," said Thea. "She can't do that."

Lucy shrugged her shoulders. "The show must go on," she said.

"It's not that," said Grace. "It wouldn't be fair on the others. It's a nightmare if someone doesn't turn up."

"Does Sam know you've left?" asked her mother.

"No. Well, I don't know," said Grace. "I've turned my mobile off."

"So what exactly did he do?" said Thea. "Turn into an axe man? Shoot up?"

"Nothing," said Grace, but she almost smiled.

Lucy and Thea exchanged glances.

"It's me," said Grace. "I just felt too claustrophobic. Well, we'd had a bit of a row, I suppose, but we'd sort of made up."

"I think you should both go back to sleep for an hour," said Lucy.

"Fat chance," said Thea, getting up from the table and pulling her robe around her. She was irritated by Grace's performance, but she recognized it as something she once might have done. No more of that, she promised herself.

"I'll wake you up in time for work, darling, I'll book a cab," Lucy continued. "Can we put her in your bed, sweetheart?" she asked Thea. "The small spare's not made up yet."

Thea nodded as Grace got up without speaking and walked to her room, her mother and sister hovering behind her.

"Wake me at eight fifteen," she said, "and if you could, book a cab for eight thirty?"

She stopped on the threshold and turned around. "Thanks, Ma. It's okay." She sighed as she adopted a pose of resignation. "It's just happened again, that's all."

"So what do you think that was all about?" asked Thea when they had crept up the staircase to the roof with a fresh tray of coffee. Lucy stroked the leaves of a plant with a finger, soothing herself to regain her serenity.

"Your sister has a penchant for unhappiness," she said.

"I've never noticed," said Thea. As she said it she knew it wasn't true.

Lucy smiled. "She's good at hiding it," she said. "She had to learn early."

"She's had a row with her boyfriend, that's all. They'll make it up."

"Maybe," said Lucy, "but maybe the struggle is greater."

"For God's sake, Ma, don't go all Zen on me. I had enough of that in California."

Lucy said nothing. She couldn't prevent the door in her head from opening a fraction. She could hear the voice calling faintly. It was as if her daughter's confusion had begun to bleed beneath her skin, softening the barriers to the past. She knew that guilt lay behind the door along with an unspeakable blankness. She turned to Thea and smiled, a forced well-being that seemed to cross her face before it crinkled into lines and reached her eyes.

"Sam seems such a good thing," said Thea. As she said it, she heard the flaw in her challenge.

"Yes," said Lucy, "he is. I expect that's the problem. It takes time to appreciate what's in front of you instead of what's ahead."

"Is that in one of your books?"

Lucy turned to her and smiled with just a trace of some old cynicism.

"No," she said, "it's in one of my lives. This one."

❧

His tongue was sticking to the roof of his mouth, and Archie longed for a cup of strong coffee. He realized he'd spoken to no one that morning apart from the cab driver, and the self-imposed isolation that accompanied his new existence was increasingly oppressive. As he made his way up to the fifth floor of the Queen Elizabeth private hospital, he felt like a condemned man.

The building itself was labyrinthine and had the air of a cruise liner, but rather more hushed. There was none of the obvious hospital paraphernalia that had characterized the big National Health Service block where, for reasons too bureaucratic to comprehend, he'd been sent to see his private consultant. Looking around, he almost wished he was back there. The hospital on television last night had looked a lively place, and despite the high rate of cardiac arrest there had been something cozy about it. This kind of nonsense had been spinning through his brain since he'd woken up. He'd had no coffee, no breakfast, as instructed, and he'd been alert since five, sick with anxiety. No one ever warned you, he thought, that almost worse than an illness were all the small sufferings that surrounded the main event. He should have let Amy come with him, or even James. James would have come if he'd asked. He'd phoned his father in Nairobi the previous evening, to let him know, in case . . . His father hadn't offered to come over, but he'd wished him luck. To be fair, he'd sounded concerned, thought Archie, and nothing, after all, was settled. He wasn't frightened exactly, or not in a way he could recognize; in fact, he was surprised to find himself feeling self-consciously brave. But then he'd never faced actual danger before, and that was what this was, the calculated risk of allowing yourself to be put in a coma and sliced wide open.

The operation was scheduled for noon, and it was only just after eight. A middle-aged nurse with bleached hair and a big smile met him as the lift doors opened. She introduced herself as Judi, Judi with an "i"; she was emphatic on the point, though he couldn't imagine at the moment that he'd be writing to her. He followed her down the carpeted corridor till they reached his room. Apart from the high-tech bed frame and its single nature, and one or two clinical fittings on the walls, it bore a strong resemblance to an average decent hotel, with a bathroom tucked neatly away at the side and a large TV on a trolley.

"Just slip into this gown, Mr. Morgan," said the nurse, presenting him with a highly laundered blue garment, "and get into bed. You can keep your briefs on for now." Even through his self-preoccupation, Archie registered that she was able to talk and smile at the same time. He took the gown and held it out. Tapes hung from its opening.

"You do it up at the back," said the nurse. "Buzz me if you need help." She pointed at a bell push at the side of the bed.

He put the garment down on a bedside chair as she left the room and went to the window, which overlooked the buildings across the street. He could see directly into an office, white and modern, whose occupants wore muted colors, nothing primary. He looked down at his own similarly toned jacket and trousers, and vowed to buy a loud shirt as soon as he got out. He noted his positive attitude and breathed deeply before taking off his clothes. It was no wonder, he thought, that the nurse had suggested he keep on his shorts: the theater gown simply brushed the top of his thighs, and he appeared to be wearing a dentist's smock with no trousers. As he climbed beneath the covers of his bed, he realized he'd forgotten his new pajamas, and the sudden thought of Thea on Oxford Street made him feel lonelier still, as if he might have thrown all his chances away. He'd stuffed the pajamas in his briefcase at the last minute, then forgotten to bring it with him. He would get the nurse to ring Amy and ask her to fetch it. He sipped from the glass of water as Judi had instructed ("just wet your lips") and switched on the TV.

The images that paraded in front of him as he surfed the channels were taking on an ever increasing immediacy, and he wondered why he hadn't observed their significance before. What had previously seemed tacky, sentimental, informative, or shocking now related clearly to him. A mistreated dog filled him with a personal guilt; a neighbors' quarrel seemed a small but perfect tragedy, and when the news came of a car crash on the M25 and two dead, he wanted to shout out to the newsreader, to press a button and halt the flow of information. "This is death you're talking about. You have no idea what you're saying. They're dead, dead, dead." As the news items passed by, only one thing made sense to him and nothing else mattered. Life mattered. Pictures of refugees fleeing, their homes on their backs, left him strangely unmoved. They were alive, therefore they were lucky. And if his number was up, he knew he'd trade places.

⌇

AT 9 a.m. on the dot James rang Patrick the shrink to confirm an appointment for lunchtime. Patrick couldn't be doing very well, he thought, if he could fit James in at such short notice. On the other hand, perhaps Patrick regarded him as an important client. The thought gave him some satisfaction, though he doubted it was true. James might have romantic impulses, but he was a realist at heart. Only yesterday afternoon he'd been convinced his anxieties were a blip and that Patrick was already a moment in history. But from the moment he'd woken from an overheated sleep, the thought of a visit to Patrick had been on his mind, and it seemed that only a phone call could clear it.

En route to the office, he'd concentrated hard on his copy of the *Financial Times*, forcing analyses and projections into his renegade brain usually so untroubled by imaginative flights of fancy. By the time he arrived at Bank station he felt he was getting a grip and had recovered some of yesterday's buoyancy. He willed himself toward the doors of his building, through the turnstile, across the marble floor to the lifts. He stood among the throng of employees, all dressed in dark suits, some red-eyed from the night before, some tapping their feet from their morning adrenaline, all focussed on the day ahead. He saw people he hadn't seen for weeks, forced to avoid their company on his lonely climbs up the emergency stairs. He smiled at them now and nodded his head in greeting. He would let them carry him through and up to the twelfth storey.

He lasted three floors. As the doors opened to the fourth, he stepped out, having positioned himself at the center front as a precaution. He felt absolutely certain that had he stayed in the lift, he would have blacked out, slumping, not exactly to the floor—the lift was too tightly packed for that—but against the woman next to him, causing mayhem and panic and drawing too much attention to himself. It was better surely to anticipate the problem, nip out safely here, and climb again to the office.

As he slogged up the stairwell, he tried to reassure himself that three floors was progress. But he felt unmanned, and he replanned his day. He'd need to cancel a lunch with his opposite number at Levison's. That was easy. Pressure of work would do for a postponement, then a trip by cab to Patrick and back to tie up Buxton's deal.

There were loose ends, contracts back from lawyers, but he should be able to sort that out by the end of the afternoon, then he could leave for the hospital to see Archie. He pushed out of his mind any thoughts on Archie's prognosis. After all, what could he do? He could wish it away, hope for the best, keep his fingers crossed, but the answer to the question was fuck-all. He could do fuck-all about it.

As he reached his floor he noticed that he was barely out of breath. The daily hike had its compensations. He was healthy and physically strong, and he felt bad that his trifling anxieties should make such inroads when his friend was facing less fanciful threats. As he pushed open the door to his department, he knew that he felt guilty, too, because he was relieved it was Archie and not him in the hospital bed. The thought left him feeling diminished.

In an office half emptied by the summer vacation, Lynette was fielding calls and watching her boss, Richard, through the glass walls of his corner room. He was closeted with John Holt, his recently appointed head of international formats, and their stiff torsos and small ugly movements suggested that the error she'd made yesterday was about to cause trouble. She'd thought it was nothing. She'd only clipped a document by mistake to the papers that had come in for Archie. She'd sent the package around as Richard had told her to. And now they wanted it back, immediately, and Archie didn't appear to be in.

It would soon be time, Lynette thought, for a change of scenery, and as she answered the phones in as polite a manner as possible, she studied the pages of PA vacancies at the back of her newspaper.

"He's in a meeting at the moment," she said into her mouthpiece. "Would you like me to put you through to the head of press? . . . No? . . . Well, I'll tell Richard you rang."

She thrust the newspaper into a drawer as she saw the meeting draw to a close. The door opened, and she kept her head down as

John Holt made his way out and left, followed by Richard, who appeared uncharacteristically anxious.

"Great start to the day," he said. "Any luck yet?" She shook her head.

"Keep trying."

"Shall I say what it's about?" asked Lynette.

"No," he said. "Just put him through when he rings."

Lynette, lent courage by the appointments vacant column in the paper, stuck her tongue out at his retreating back, then she dialed Archie's home number again and his mobile, without success.

Richard returned to his blue padded chair and put his hands on the desk. He swung himself slowly from left to right and back again, in an attempt to calm down. This was uncharacteristically stupid of Lynette. But if he hadn't been so keen to appease Archie, it would never have happened.

"He's still not in," Lynette told Richard when he put his head around the door to check on her progress.

"Fuck," he said. "Did you leave another message?"

"No."

If Richard noticed her unusual if timid attempt at insubordination, he said nothing.

"Ring back and leave a message, on both numbers. Tell him it's very important."

꜀ꙅꙅ

It had been impossible for Thea to go back to sleep after Grace's early morning entrance. By ten o'clock she'd drunk enough coffee to kick-start an army and was feeling tense. Grace herself had crawled out of bed at 8:20, appeared briefly in the kitchen, said she'd phone them later, then jumped into her waiting car. Now Thea stood against the counter, stirring her cup, as Lucy tried to read her proofs on the kitchen table.

"What's this one about then, Ma? Lifelines for daughters? Or the over-sixties?"

Lucy took off her glasses.

"No, it's a collection of letters that readers have sent me."

"You've taken to recycling your fan letters?"

Lucy smiled patiently.

"Not exactly. I'd say they were about the triumph of attitude over adversity, personal stories, that sort of thing. I find them very moving."

"I'm sure they are," said Thea. "So where are we all sleeping tonight, then?"

"We'll manage," said Lucy. "We'll make up the small bed. Or one of you can go to Amy's."

"One of us?" said Thea. It was typical of her mother, she thought, to assume that one awkwardness canceled out another in a convenient fashion. She could write a book about it.

"Grace could go, if need be," said Lucy, a pair of black-rimmed glasses almost falling off her nose. She looked up at her daughter. "I thought you were going out to lunch."

"It's only ten, Ma," said Thea. She could feel the old exasperation undermining the feel-good of her homecoming.

Lucy took off her glasses, her concentration interrupted by Thea's restlessness.

"Do you want to walk around the pond," said Lucy, "like we used to?"

Thea knew her mother was humoring her. She leaned across the sink and looked out of the window at the blue sky.

"That," she said, "is a first-class idea. But I can go on my own if you want to get on."

"No, no. These can wait," said Lucy.

As the two of them approached the expanse of water, edged by small figures and a rabble of birds, Thea couldn't believe it hadn't occurred to her during the last couple of days to come here. It was the perfect place to think. There was a quiet continuity about the

Round Pond in Kensington Gardens, bequeathed, she supposed, by the generations of children who had played there. It hadn't been her own childhood park, but when her mother had moved nearby fifteen years ago she'd adopted it, and now, even after two years' absence, she felt it had been part of her forever. She was as familiar with its seasons and changes, its ice-cream vendors and resident eccentrics as any veteran of the borough.

She walked a pace or two ahead of Lucy, exhilarated by the sunlight on the water. As she turned to wait for her to catch up, she was struck by how intriguing a figure her mother cut. She was wearing an old but shapely straw hat and linen trousers and jacket. Her sleek gray hair was cut to below her chin. But it wasn't just her clothes, it was her bearing. Lucy walked not so much as if she owned the park, but as if they all did. It was both magnanimous and embracing. Her mother, Thea acknowledged, was something of a one-off, admirable in many ways, especially from a safe distance. Up close her unique brand of impermeability could hang you out to dry.

"They're all French, of course," Lucy said as she caught up with Thea.

It was true that they'd heard not a word of English since they'd entered the gardens.

"That explains it," said Thea.

"What?"

"It looks so very composed today. Neat little groupings of people. So European. Like pictures."

"French pictures," said Lucy.

"Exactly. In fact you look rather French yourself, if I may say so."

Lucy laughed. "I could never be so groomed," she said, indicating with her head an immaculate crop-haired woman with a nanny and child in tow.

"Still," said Thea, "you look chic."

"So do you, my darling." Thea, she'd noticed, had taken on an American style that suited her tall, slimmer body, a cleaned and pressed look that seemed to hold in the confusion underneath. She looked almost angular, towering over the two Japanese students in full punk regalia who overtook them as they walked.

"They're a bit out of date, aren't they?" said Thea. "Or have I missed something while I've been away?"

"I think the correct term is retro," said Lucy. "I think I've decided that I shall be retro now I'm sixty. Much better than being old."

"Sixty is not old, Ma."

"No," said Lucy, "you're right. But it is a bit of a shock."

Thea laughed as they sat down on a bench at the water's edge. Close by a middle-aged man was launching a model ship onto the Round Pond. A younger man stood crouched behind him, fussing with its sails. A passing swan, well used to bonsai yachtsmen, craned its neck toward them in a gesture of contempt.

"I should have brought some bread for the birds," said Lucy.

"They're fed so much I'm surprised they don't sink," said Thea, retrieving some of her cynicism. But she wasn't interested in the swan; it was the two men who had her attention. What were they? Father and son? Lovers? Maybe just friends. Whatever they were to each other was strengthened by their passion for their hobby, and she envied them.

"I've been thinking," she said, "about going back to medicine."

Lucy said nothing.

"I said I thought I might go back to medicine, Ma," she repeated, disconcerted by her mother's silence.

"Yes, darling, I heard you. And I don't know what to say."

"I thought you'd like the idea."

"I do. I thought you might, one day. But I'm afraid that if I say I like it, you'll change your mind."

Thea took her mother's arm.

"I feel such an idiot, Ma," she said. "Whatever have I been doing? I felt left out, back then, I think."

Lucy put her arm around her daughter and pulled her close.

"Everyone seemed to be having such a glamorous time, with lots of money, and all I could see was a series of hospitals. But medicine was what I always wanted. It's what I want now."

"Then that's what you must do," said Lucy. "And you mustn't regret the past," she said. "It will be part of your future."

LUCY had taken off her hat. Her eyes were closed now behind her sunglasses, and she allowed the features of her dead husband to form in front of her. They weren't recalled from life, but from one of the photographs she and Thea had been looking at together the previous evening, one taken a year before his death. Tom was holding Grace, a child of four, astride a small tricycle, one hand on the handlebar, the other on her back to steady her. He was looking up at the camera, smiling, though she knew it hadn't been a truly happy day. They'd been alone in the garden, the three of them, Amy and Thea upstairs together.

Lucy felt the sound in her head, a sort of rattle and a call. Perhaps it was Tom, knocking after all these years. She felt cold as her imagination embraced the idea that perhaps he'd come to collect her, to gather her up. She opened her eyes and dismissed the thought as superstition despite the fact that it was the sort of intimation to which she usually liked to give credence. Why, after all, should he want to come after her when she'd caused him so much pain? She shut out the thought. He'd been smiling at her in her memory. He'd been smiling in the photograph.

⁓

THE pre-meds had begun to take effect, but Archie was disappointed. He'd been expecting a pleasant legal high but felt instead fractious and out of control. The nurse had shaved off his pubic hair, and his nakedness under the short gown had been complete. He felt like a baby. They wheeled him on a trolley through the corridors and down in a lift, and he wished someone was with him besides the nurse and the porters. He found himself staring at a picture on the ceiling. He was in some sort of theater anteroom and was aware of staff on either side. The picture was a copy of an Impressionist painting, a Cézanne, he thought, mountains and trees, placed above to focus the attention. He turned his head from side to side. The anesthetist spoke to him quietly.

"Mr. Morgan, I want you to count back in a moment, from ten down."

"You should have had apples," said Archie.

"Sorry?" said the anesthetist.

"Cézanne. Apples. On the ceiling."

"Oh, I see. Well, just keep looking at the mountain."

"It's the left one," said Archie.

The anesthetist was bent over him, and Archie saw his eyes swivel to a nurse on the right.

"Has he had his pre-med?" he asked.

"Yes," she replied.

"You will get the right one, won't you?" said Archie. "I mean it's the left, left testicle."

The anesthetist picked up a set of notes, scanned them, then bent over him again.

"Don't worry, Mr. Morgan. The left, certainly. Now . . . count down from ten."

⁓

RICHARD had never known Archie to be so elusive. It was possible, of course, that he'd left his phone at home. It was also possible that Archie was cold-shouldering him. The quarrel between them threatened to be more serious than he'd realized at first. Whatever the reason, Archie couldn't be located, and it was time to hunt him down. The piece of paper that had been stuck so unfortunately to the back of the Denny material was a contract, already signed by a client of John Holt's. It had been sitting on Lynette's desk awaiting Richard's countersignature. Holt was understandably cross at its disappearance, as Richard would have been in his position, and if they didn't return the contract countersigned by close of play today, a substantial financial penalty would be enacted and that would be their commission lost.

Richard had given up on Lynette, whom he could see in the outer office, shuffling papers. He was angry with her but couldn't help but blame himself, and he wasn't prepared to lose money over something so stupid. He picked up the phone and punched in the numbers for Amy Marsham.

"Amy. Hello. Richard Armstrong here."

"Richard. Again."

He sensed that her manner was cooler than yesterday. He was definitely out in the cold.

"Sorry to bother you, Amy, but it's really important. I need to get hold of Archie. Do you know where he is? I've already phoned a couple of his other friends. Toby Sachs says he's left him a couple of messages but Archie hasn't replied."

She thought for a moment. It hadn't occurred to her she might have to lie for him, but she was sure that Archie wouldn't want Richard, of all people, to know he was in the hospital.

"He's gone away for a few days." It was almost true.

"Where?" said Richard, sounding indignant. "I spoke to him last night. He didn't say anything about going away."

There was a pause.

"Something came up," said Amy. "A family thing."

"But he's not answering his mobile."

"Ah," said Amy.

"Look, I hate to ask you this, but . . . I've sent him something by mistake and I've got to get it back, quickly. We desperately need it. It's a work thing." He took a deep breath. "You haven't got a key to the flat, have you?" He was surprised at himself for asking her, but he thought that she might understand, that the fact that he'd asked such a thing might convey its importance.

"You want me to break into his flat?"

"Not break in . . ." he said. "He wouldn't mind, I'm sure. I mean he'd understand. It was a mistake. It's no use to him."

"Can't it wait till tomorrow? I can probably get hold of him then."

"No. It can't, Amy. It really can't."

There was a silence while they both considered their positions.

"I can't get involved," Amy said finally. "Archie's very angry with you at the moment. I couldn't let you into the flat without his permission. You must see that?"

"That's ridiculous," he said. "You're being unreasonable."

"And you can be a complete shit sometimes," she said, and put down the phone.

He should have known he wouldn't get past her, that she would be unbending in her alliance with Archie. He looked at his watch and realized he would have to leave if he was to meet Thea on time. Maybe she could suggest something; she might even know where he'd gone. A family thing, Amy had said. Archie had no close family now, as far as Richard knew, except for the distant father. Maybe Thea would have a number for him. It was worth a try.

As Archie stared upward, semiglazed, at the Cézanne mountain, he began the countdown as instructed: "Ten," he said. "Nine . . ." An image of his mother seemed to float before his eyes. He'd been thinking about her the previous night, as he lay in bed, hot and restless beneath a sheet, his eyes closed, heart beating. He remembered her lying in the big bed at home in Richmond, his stepfather, Uncle Simon, holding her hand and trying not to cry, his uncle Ed, his mother's brother over from New York, talking on the phone downstairs and sending out for exotic food she couldn't eat, distraught that all their money couldn't save her. He'd been brought back from school just three days earlier, and each day he'd stood or sat beside her as her cheeks sank a little further beneath her bones. He was fourteen and he'd had no idea she was so ill. They simply hadn't told him. They, his grandparents, his stepfather, his father, all in their separate compartments, had somehow conspired to black out the news, censor the information that his mother was dying.

She'd seemed fine only weeks before in the Easter holidays. He knew that she'd been in the hospital for an operation. She'd written to him in a shaky hand, claiming she was writing on her knees. When he'd looked at the letters, years after her death, at the thin strokes of the pen as they crossed the page, they'd seemed to him, in hindsight, unsure of a destination. There were jokes about friends and neighbors, the usual suggestions of treats for the summer. But each anecdote had tailed off, each potential trip or outing weighted with equivocation.

He'd spent most of the summer that followed with James and his parents, thankful to escape from his father and grandparents, who continued to ignore his mother's existence. It made no difference to them if she was dead or alive, and this was a policy now to their mind doubly justified. After all, what point, they reasoned, could there be in upsetting poor Archie further? His time in Scotland had been strangely happy. He remembered moments, out on the moors, of near delirium, a feeling of intense and heady freedom. There were unfamiliar rushes of energy, shadowed by guilt, but he'd found it easy to evade his latent misery, engulfed in a family's love and attention and in particular the flattering mockery of James's older sister.

"Eight . . ." he managed, still looking at the ceiling and its blue-black mountain. He was kissing Liza at the foot of a Scottish hillside, kissing with tongues. He'd had an intimation then, compounded by the attention from the girls in the nearby village, that women were a treasure trove that would open to him easily. It was a game whose rules were instinctive to him, and he'd begun to tease and retreat, whisper and withdraw, and watched his effect with growing confidence. The blue of the mountain above him now bled into black. "Seven . . ." He was out.

As Thea approached the small French restaurant tucked away in a lane behind Oxford Street, she felt a desire to turn and run. It wasn't from the thought of seeing Richard Armstrong, but from what he represented. Her family was one thing, they existed in a limbo of their own, and although it was certainly strange to be sleeping in her mother's house in London once again it felt transitional, à gentle way back. Meeting up so soon with a man who had been more a friend of her sister's, a man who was nonetheless acquainted with the details of her past, to discuss a future she didn't want, that was another matter. She felt hothoused into a life she was almost sure she would leave again, but then this, she told herself, might be a good way of making absolutely sure.

She almost bumped into him in the doorway. He had seen her from the other side of the road and rushed across, not wanting her to arrive before him. He thought at once how vital she seemed, more immediate than he remembered.

"Hello," he said, and bent awkwardly to kiss her cheek.

"Richard," she said, "how nice to see you." She felt fraudulent. She wasn't sure it was nice at all.

"You look wonderful," said Richard, with total sincerity. His morning had been so fraught that he hadn't had time to consider how to approach the rendezvous. It had been a spur of the moment invitation to Thea, prompted by some combination of his Brighton epiphany and a hazy recollection of something he'd once found seductive and complex.

As Thea watched him sit down opposite her, putting away his phone, fiddling in his jacket pocket, adjusting his collar, she realized he was nervous. She was surprised; she'd always had an impression of Richard as confident, a man with a puppy arrogance that amused rather than offended. He smiled at her and knocked over a glass as he picked up the menu.

"Oops," he said. "Clumsy."

"Good to get it over with, I'd say," said Thea.

"What?"

"While it's still empty."

"Oh. Right," he said. She seemed to be staring at him.

"Let's get a drink," he said. "That's if you still do, after living in L.A.?"

"Oh, yes, I do," she said, smiling at him, and he smiled back, trusting that a glass or two of wine would help to settle things down.

⌇

THE front door of Patrick's small terraced house opened, and a man of about forty emerged quickly and sped down the short path. James waited a moment to let him get through the gate under the impression that his exit hadn't been witnessed. He, too, had felt the urge to pull up his jacket collar and put his head down when leaving. He looked after the man as he walked away up the street. Same age, same social group, he guessed. He wondered what had brought him here: work, a failed marriage, a simple phobia. But phobias were not simple, it seemed; his was proving resistant. He would make Patrick get to the point.

"This lift thing, you've got to help me sort it out," he said to Patrick, before he even sat down.

"I had the impression when you rang that something else was bothering you," said Patrick.

"Yes, no. Yes, there is something else."

"Would you like to sit?"

"But I'd like to deal with the lift first."

"Fine," said Patrick, whom James suspected of suppressing a smile. "Tell me about the lift."

"I can't get in it. Or rather I can't stay in it."

James sat in the chair and loosened his tie.

"Is it worse or the same?"

"The same. I got in this morning, but I had to get out."

"What did you feel?"

"A sort of silent panic."

"Can you be more specific?"

James forced himself to remember the morning's event.

"I did feel as if I was going to die," he said.

"Good."

"But I'm not going to die in the lift. Or at least it's highly unlikely."

"Exactly."

"So how does that help?"

Patrick smiled at him. "Think about it."

James thought.

"It's not the death," he said. "It's the dying."

Patrick nodded.

"It's the trapped and not being able to get out."

"So it's about being trapped."

James sat up.

"I know where you're going with this," he said. "And it's not that. I love my wife. I love my children. We're happy. Or I think we are."

As he said it, he regretted the qualification. He knew it was a mistake.

"You see yourselves as happy, you and your wife?"

James's picture of life at Finlay Road seemed to be reassembling its composition with a queasy speed. He saw Amy pressing at a window as if it were jammed, and she was trying to escape.

"I suppose," James said, surprised at himself, "that it's possible that my wife might be the one who's trapped." He looked at Patrick. "But then why is it me who has the problem?"

They sat in a thoughtful silence for several moments until Patrick spoke.

"Tell me about the other thing. The thing you were anxious about."

James looked at his feet.

"It's embarrassing," he said.

"That's why you're here, presumably, telling me rather than anyone else."

"Well, I did tell Archie, you know, my friend Archie."

"Well, now tell me—if you'd like to."

"It's my sister-in-law Grace. Grace Fielding. You might know her, she's an actress. Actor, is what I'm supposed to say."

Patrick nodded again.

"Do you know her?"

"I've heard of her," he said. "She's a bit of a celebrity."

"Yes, I suppose she is."

"What about her?"

James stumbled through an account of his meeting with Grace's school friend.

"It sounds so silly," he said, "so naive."

"Why? That you didn't know?"

"That, yes. But also that I was so absurdly pleased. I couldn't stop thinking about it."

"You were so pleased that you rang me?"

"Yes. No." He looked at his feet again. "I was having fantasies about her. I can't stop thinking about her. I was making love to Amy last night, and I couldn't stop thinking about her. Even then."

"It doesn't sound uncommon," said Patrick. His tone was careful.

"You don't understand. She's my sister-in-law. I feel like a pedophile."

"You feel guilty."

"That's an understatement." James paused. "These fantasies, they were, are, wild. Out of character."

"That's an interesting phrase."

"It's not me, I mean. I mean I have fantasies, of course I do. But not like these. It's as if they're coming from somewhere else—from someone else."

"From her?"

"Yes." James looked at Patrick with new respect. "How did you know that?"

Patrick smiled. "Trick of the trade," he said.

"They're not, of course." James made the statement a question.

Patrick said nothing.

James closed his eyes and saw Grace bending over, naked, in front of him. He opened his eyes immediately.

"She's like a siren, waving me on. It's not really her, I know that. But I don't want to go."

"Where? Where don't you want to go?"

"Nowhere."

"You want to go nowhere?"

James felt as if the lift doors were closing.

"I want to stay where I am." He contemplated his answer and was pleased. He felt his anxiety receding.

"That's not always possible," Patrick said.

BY 1:45, Richard was able to congratulate himself that lunch was going tolerably well. He was enjoying himself. It was extraordinary how a passing thought, an unsought image, could result in material fact. If Thea's name hadn't emerged from his mouth in a small white lie to his mother, the two of them probably wouldn't be sitting here now. He noticed how her skin was lightly tanned, and she seemed different in some way. She had a slinkiness about her. He'd always liked her, liked both the twins. As he looked across the table at Thea, he thought of the fun they'd all had a few years ago, before things and people had begun to drift. This new Thea was fresh and smart and amusing, with a sense of the absurd that matched his own, yet she seemed to withdraw as he turned the conversation to ask her why she'd come back.

"I couldn't settle," she said. "Not there. It's too alien."

It was pretty much the truth. She made light of her engagement, a moment-of-madness sort of thing. And that was true, too, but she didn't reveal the months of upset that the moment had engendered, the anger and upset that her fiancé had endured when she'd told him it was over.

"And what about you?" she said. "I'm surprised you're still single. It's a few years since you separated, isn't it?"

"Divorced for two, in fact," he said.

"I thought you were the marrying kind. Was I wrong?"

Richard felt a flush rising up his neck. It was as if she had uncovered an indiscretion. He wanted to ask her what she meant, but it felt too intimate. He hadn't seen the woman for over two years, and he hadn't known her that well even then.

"Well, I'm straight, if that's what you mean," he said.

She laughed.

"No, that's not what I meant. I know that."

He raised his eyebrows at her. She was looking directly at him. It was pleasantly disconcerting.

"Welcome back," he said.

"I heard about Archie," she said. She seemed to let go of her hold on him as she changed the subject. "Grace told me."

"You mean Greta, or the company?"

"I never knew Greta," she looked away, "nor would I want to. I meant the magazines."

"I'm in the doghouse. You probably know that, too," he said.

"Yes. I imagine that's no fun."

"Ah." He couldn't protest. She was staring at him again. He had an urge to tell the truth.

"It was the right decision." He paused. "But I wonder now if I couldn't have done more. I've been trying to help, but he doesn't want to know."

She leaned toward him, conspiratorial and reassuring.

"Archie leads a charmed life, Richard. Neither of us needs to worry about him. He'll emerge unscathed, he always does."

Richard took a mouthful of his double espresso. "And now I've got myself in quite a mess."

Through most of lunch he had managed to push away the nagging thought of lost commission, but now her friendliness was a straw to clutch at, and he outlined the story to her. He tried to turn it into a joke and succeeded in making her laugh as he mimicked the distinctive outrage of John Holt.

"It's not really funny," he said. "John's justifiably upset, and we both stand to lose money. Archie has completely disappeared. Have you got a number, any number, that I might be able to reach him on? What about the father?"

Thea shook her head. She'd never even met him.

"He lives in Nairobi."

"What about Amy? Could you talk to her, ask her?" said Richard. "She's barely speaking to me. I asked her to let me into Archie's flat if she could, that it was an emergency. No chance."

Thea shrugged. She would have liked to help him.

"My sister and I aren't, well, we aren't currently on the best of terms."

"That makes two of us, then," said Richard. "Must be difficult, sometimes, having a twin."

"Most people think it must be fun," said Thea, gratified by his insight.

"You never looked as though it was fun, exactly," he said. "I always thought there was a bit of tension when you got together."

He knew, she thought. He remembered.

She sat back in her chair, her flirtatious manner subsiding.

"I think," she said, "part of the problem is that people can't help but compare."

Richard looked at her over the rim of his coffee cup. He'd never really spent time with her alone before, even though he'd known her for years.

"But there must be an upside," he said.

"You sound like my mother."

Richard burst out laughing. He'd forgotten the lost contract for a moment.

"Me, sound like Lucy Fielding? That's fantastic." He emptied his glass. "I rather like your mother, actually, even if she is a bit nuts."

Thea winced and Richard kicked himself.

"Sorry," he said. "Not nuts. Eccentric. You should meet my mother."

He was amazed to hear himself mention his mother. He couldn't remember talking about her since he'd left home, except to his brother and sister, and he hoped the reference would fall away without her noticing, but Thea was smiling back at him.

"Tell me about her," she said.

He told her just a little at first. He handed her some fragments he'd digested and made sense of. But as Thea listened to him, Richard was surprised to hear himself talking more freely. He told her how stifled he'd felt as a boy, how different he was from his sister, who seemed to relish the family constraints. He even found himself telling her about his young brother, Paul, who was more like him, but without his resources, and who had got into trouble with the police. His life, he imagined, had been quite different from hers, but as he talked on, he began to see it through her eyes, a complex and substantial story, and he felt euphoric at its easy flow, at the words that wouldn't stop.

"Sorry," he said, as they finished their coffee. "I don't usually talk about myself."

"I did ask," Thea said. In truth she was touched and charmed by the way he'd confided in her. Her instinct told her it was something of a first for him, and she was flattered by his new vulnerability. Perhaps it was the wine on his part, or the jet lag on hers, but she sensed a certain headiness as they smiled at each other.

"Next time it's your turn," he said.

"You don't want to know."

"Yes," he said, signing the bill. "I do."

⁓

THE fan whirred quietly beside the bed where Lucy lay on her back, her head on the white linen pillows that in turn rested against a carved French headboard. She tried not to think. The room was silent apart from the fan; subtle double glazing and wooden shutters had screened out the city noise. It was painted the palest of greens, and if she turned her head she could see the large gilded mirror and in it the soft reflection of an ancient piece of embroidered fabric she'd found years before in Morocco. But it hurt to turn her head, and if she moved she feared a tearing, a renting of an internal veil.

If she tried to sleep she saw him. Trapped by pain and fear, she could neither turn her head nor close her eyes. She stared upward, blinking. Tom would have been sixty-four now. They'd never believed such an age would come, and now it was here; it had come but he had gone, and she had behaved so badly. Her chest constricted, and she forced herself to breathe, willed herself from habit to expel the guilt, to inhale an opiate cloud from her imagination. She must get up. Get up and get on. She had the sense of being needed, being called. She lay still on her bed. She wouldn't get up, not just yet. She would wait for the pain in her head to subside, wait to see which one it was whose need was pressing in, calling in advance on her reserves.

It was after 3:30 when they emerged, with a certain awkwardness, into the bright sunshine of the street. There were a few shoppers off the beaten track of Oxford Street but little traffic.

"So what will you do now," she asked, "about Archie? You could always hire a detective."

Richard felt elated and free.

"Fuck it," he said. "There's nothing I can do. It's only a deal." He wasn't convinced by this posture but it would do for now.

"Well," she said, sticking her hands in the pockets of her linen jacket, "I really enjoyed that."

"Yes," he said, "so did I. Can we do it again?"

"We'd better," she said. "You haven't told me yet if I've got any job prospects."

Richard's light-headedness subsided.

"I'm embarrassed," he said. "You should have stopped me talking. I got carried away."

Thea smiled at him, almost shyly, and his discomfort was replaced by something more pressing.

"It couldn't matter less," she said. "And I don't even know that I want to go back to work for the moment—well, not our sort of work, anyway." She pulled out a large bunch of keys from her pocket and fingered it like a set of worry beads.

"Don't they weigh you down?" he said.

She held them up, and they dangled in front of him like a promising fetish.

"No. Well, yes—but at least I can find them in the bottom of my bag."

"I can see that would be an advantage," he said, noting the large leather sack weighing down her forearm.

"I keep them as mementos, I suppose," she said. "That one," she splayed them out on her palm, "that's the key to my Hollywood Hills apartment—and see, there's even one from my old Leeds house. It's ironic considering I haven't a home to go . . ." She stopped suddenly and looked up at him.

"I've got a key," she said.

"I can see that."

Thea's voice rose in pitch. She seemed excited.

"To Archie's flat. I've still got his key. It's this one. We could go if you like, that's what you suggested to Amy, isn't it?"

Richard looked at her, astonished, and surprised at her willingness to transgress.

"Look," she said, "he'd get it back to you if he was around, wouldn't he? If this silly quarrel wasn't happening. He might be pissed off with you, but he's not vindictive." She was enjoying herself. She felt she could stand outside them all for a while and try to readjust the picture. "We'd just be doing what he'd do himself. As far as I'm concerned, that's good enough."

He'd been almost ready to drop the pursuit of Archie—or at least swap it for that of Thea Fielding. Lunch had made him reckless. But maybe he could have both. He took her arm.

"Come on," he said. "Let's go."

At his desk twelve floors above the City, James felt reinvigorated by his visit to Patrick. He'd walked back up after his lunch outing—it would have been foolish to dispel his sudden mood of optimism by attempting the lift again today. The white noise of the air-conditioning soothed him, shutting off the overanimated part of his brain and allowing him to think. He studied the analysts' reports in front of him and found he could sift through them, just as on a good day, like a knife through butter, he thought, self-satisfied. He floated on through the afternoon, working through his list, making calls, smoothing wrinkles, and bridging trenches. He felt invincible but calm. He rang Amy to hear her voice but found her irritable and complaining of feeling unwell, so different from the night before, he thought, and the intensity of his disappointment surprised him.

"I'll see you at the hospital at seven thirty," she said, "and don't be late."

"Okay, and I love you, too," said James. "Bye, darling."

He had no explanation for what he did next. He'd intended to spend the last hour of his day wrapping up the paperwork on the Buxton deal in readiness for a final trip there tomorrow. He'd then climb down the twelve flights, catch a Tube to Bond Street, and walk to the hospital. Instead he found himself punching the number of his sister-in-law Grace.

"Hi, James," she answered. "This is a charming surprise."

"How are you?" he said.

"I've been better," she sighed. "I've had a bit of a row with Sam."

"Oh."

"And I've had a horrible day at work. The only good thing is that I finished early and I'm lying in the bath."

James became aware of the echoing quality of the line, and his imagination went into overdrive.

"What can I say?"

"You could tell me why you rang?"

He didn't know, was the truth. Or he couldn't say that the truth was he'd spent twenty-four hours thinking about her, apart from a couple of hours' respite while making love to her sister.

"I, er, I wanted to talk to you about something."

"Fine, what?"

"Well, not now, I'm in a rush. It's a sort of surprise thing. Look, I'm meeting Amy in town, but not till half past seven. I thought . . . on the off chance . . . you might be around, for a drink?"

"Well, now," she said. "And what's it worth?"

"What?" he said. Flirting didn't come easily to him.

"Never mind," she said. "Where could we go?"

He hadn't a clue. Then he remembered meeting a client in the Dorchester bar.

"The Dorchester?" she said, making the idea sound faintly ridiculous.

"Yes," he said. "I don't want to go to any of the noisy places you go to."

She laughed.

"Okay. This should be interesting."

"It's fine, I promise you. It's quite nice, actually."

"'Quite nice, actually,'" she repeated. "For God's sake, James."

He began to feel a creep of humiliation and fought back.

"Do you want to come or don't you?" he asked, with a degree of sharpness.

She backed down immediately.

"I'll be there. What time?"

"Six fifteen," he said.

༂

THERE was a silence in Lucy's flat that wrapped itself around Grace as she emerged from the bathroom. Behind her she could hear the gurgle of water vanishing down the pipes. In the hallway she sensed an absence and felt frightened. Wrapped in a towel she crept to her mother's bedroom and put her head around the door. To her relief, Lucy was there, lying down, eyes open.

Her mother smiled without turning her head.

"It's okay, darling, I'm just feeling a touch dizzy."

Grace crept in a little further.

"I'll make you some tea."

"Thank you. That would be lovely."

Grace withdrew, confused. She couldn't remember the last time Lucy had been ill, or even indisposed. Her mother was health and happiness's representative on earth, her stock in trade, her raison d'être—for her to be forced to lie down was significant.

She found the clothes she'd left at home amid the jumble of Thea's in their now shared room and pulled them on. What did you wear to a date in the Dorchester? Well, not a date exactly, not with your brother-in-law. The ritual of dressing to please distracted her; she selected her wrappings, a fitted black vest, a short pink skirt, high-heeled sandals. As she admired her reflection and relished the prospect of the hour to come, she remembered the tea she'd already forgotten and tottered into the kitchen to put on the kettle.

On the table was a picture of her father, lying on top of Lucy's proofs. She picked it up and wondered what had prompted Lucy to keep it out from the box they'd been sorting through the previous evening, a part of Thea's homecoming. Lucy didn't have pictures of Tom around the flat. She said it was retrogressive. Grace had some, of course, but she rarely looked at them. He was a fantasy stranger to her. If she tried very hard she thought she could remember his presence, but she'd been only five when he died. She thought she could remember this moment—her on the tiny tricycle steered by her dad—but she knew that it was only the photograph she recalled, a seeded recollection based on a piece of treated paper.

She made tea and took a cup to her mother. Lucy had forced herself to sit up and was staring directly ahead toward the window.

"Could you open the curtains, darling?" she said. "And the shutters."

Only her mother, thought Grace, would have curtains and shutters. When Lucy wanted to close herself off she did a thorough job. She put down the teacup and let in the afternoon light, moving slowly. Her instinct told her that her mother was returning from somewhere far away and shouldn't be rushed.

THEY sat side by side in the back of the taxi, Thea holding onto the hand bar above her head, her body turned toward Richard. Up close she could see the small freckles below his eyes, which were brown and deep-set and gave off an energetic gleam. He was slightly exotic, she thought, and unpredictable, and she felt she was on an adventure, here in a black cab speeding through the city toward the mansion block where Archie lived.

As it drew up outside, Thea gazed at the building. She was glad she was fortified by half a bottle of wine. She'd spent more than time here. Richard paid the driver, and she fished in her bag for her keys again, fingering through the set. But as she looked toward the front door she realized their plan was flawed.

"I haven't got the one for the front door."

"What?"

"The key to the actual building. I threw that one away."

Her logic defeated Richard, and he couldn't work out if he minded or not. He didn't know what he felt, except for an underlying excitement in her presence, a feeling that he wanted to touch her.

"Oh, well. It was worth a try," he said. Perhaps he could persuade her to come home with him. It wasn't far.

"I'm not giving up now," said Thea, and strode toward the building. She'd intended to ring a bell or two, but the need for subterfuge disappeared as a distinguished-looking older man emerged. Seeing her on the step, with keys in her hand, he immediately held open the door.

"Thank you so much," she said, smiling, and swept past him, followed by Richard, who nodded a half greeting, amazed at their luck.

As the gates of the lift opened and they piled in, they waited only for the doors to close before they started laughing. Thea put her hand on Richard's arm.

"I haven't had this much fun for years," she said.

"Me, neither." He tried not to show his pleasure at the gesture.

"You'd better ring him again," she said, "to make sure he's not there."

Richard tried Archie's number. He heard the familiar answering-machine message as they crept out onto the fourth floor.

"Has he got a burglar alarm?" asked Richard.

"Never used to. I doubt it."

She put her key in the lock. As it turned, a series of images of her and Archie blurred together above her left eye, then passed across her forehead and was gone. The door opened to her touch, and they moved through as if in slow motion, irrationally fearful of what might meet them on the other side.

Stepping into the apartment, Thea felt her stomach not exactly turn over but certainly quiver. Here she was, standing in Archie's flat after all this time and nothing appeared to have changed, except that there was a new air of disorder. She looked around, checking a mental inventory dredged from her memory. The pictures, yes, the walls the same color, the blinds. She wasn't quite accurate. A new glass table had replaced the old pine one, but the bookshelves looked almost untouched; the newspapers and magazines were the same, if updated. She could smell him.

Richard moved in behind her and took in the scene.

"It's a mess in here," he said. "Not like Archie. Still—at least the cleaner's not been, that's a plus. Nothing's been thrown away."

He began to rummage through a pile of papers on the table. Thea sat down, but upright, on the edge of the sofa, her hands clasped together.

"It's weird being here," she said.

He looked over at her. She looked younger and her expression was almost vacant.

"Are you okay?"

He put down the pile of documents and sat down beside her, taking one of her hands. She turned and looked straight at him, and he took a tress of her hair in his fingers and knotted it around them. Their heads moved closer together and then they were kissing, gentle narrow kisses at first, then wider, until Thea pulled away. He had the odd sensation that only a part of her was present.

"We shouldn't be doing this here, I suppose," Richard said.

She smiled, but said nothing.

"But I don't think Archie would mind," he continued.

"I don't think he'd care," she said.

"Do you?"

"Do I what?"

"Do you still care about him?"

She looked away for a moment then turned back to him.

"No," she said, taking his hand. "Not in that way, but we do have history."

Richard lifted her fingers to his mouth and kissed them.

"I'd better look for this contract," he said, "then we can get out of here."

She got up and smoothed down her skirt, then wandered through to the kitchen and up the short flight of stairs. Archie's bed was unmade and had clearly been slept in on only one side. It looked chaste and lonely, she thought, and she had an urge to rumple the untouched half, but instead she sat down on the edge as she had on the sofa; she longed to imprint herself on it, to remind herself she'd once lain there, not because she still loved Archie, but to reclaim something of herself that she'd left behind. Her dignity, perhaps, her self-respect. But Archie had been only part of her loss, and she'd clung on to him in increasing panic. The noise of a clock ticking on the bedside table cut through her thoughts, and she saw, half kicked under the bed, a large brown envelope.

"Richard," she called. "Up here."

He came up and through the door, and she pointed to the floor.

"That's it," he said. "And he hasn't even opened it." There was sadness in his voice. "Do you think I can just take it?" he asked.

"You've already broken into his flat. It's no time to go squeamish now," she said, watching his movements with detachment.

"No," he said. "I just hope he'll come around."

"Would you mind, if he did the same? If your positions were reversed?"

Richard thought about it.

"Yes, probably," he said.

He knelt at her feet as he fished out the package. She had kicked off her shoes and from the corner of his eye he could see her brown feet and the pale coral varnish on her toes.

"I feel like a spy," said Thea, "stealing secrets." And she grabbed the lapels of his jacket as he crouched before her and pulled him toward her as she leaned backwards on the bed.

"Thea, for God's sake."

"What?"

"This is Archie's bed."

"So? I wasn't married to him."

"No, I suppose not." And he gave in to the sensation of her arms around him, her legs beginning to entwine around his, his lips on her skin.

"Who'd have thought?" he whispered to her. "Thea Fielding."

He said her name with a certain awe.

"Yes, it's Thea," she said. "Thea Fielding." She was starting to feel aroused by him. It all felt so easy and straightforward, and she felt she could indulge herself with him without fear of complication.

"Thea," he said, "there's no mistaking that."

As he held her, a corner of Richard's mind couldn't help but calculate his situation. He was in Archie's flat with Archie's ex, Amy's sister, James's in-law. It was as if he were penetrating to the core of something. He slid his hand up her skirt, and she didn't resist. He undid the button at her waistband, slid down the zip and pulled up her linen shirt.

She half pushed him away, but without conviction.

"We can't do this," she said.

Hadn't that been his line? But he didn't care.

"I think we are," he said. His hands moved to her breasts, and she made no effort to stop him. He pulled her closer still to him and unbuttoned her blouse, unfastening her bra to leave her quite naked above the waist. She stretched back, then put her arm around his head, bending his mouth down to her nipple as his hand found its way to the top of her bare thigh and inside her loose French knickers.

"It feels so bad," she whispered, "to be here." But she made no move to stop him as her body responded, and she knew that her excitement was enhanced beyond measure by the badness that reached into her and found its shadow. One more time, she thought, one more bit of wickedness, just for the memory. And she kicked off her panties as he pulled them down over her thighs and calves.

"Thea," he said, looking down at her, smiling, his breath short.

"Have you—," she said.

"A condom?" He was reaching for his jacket on the floor. "Yes, but it wasn't . . . intended for you. . . ."

She giggled. "I didn't think that."

"Good," he said, "because you're one of the best surprises I've ever had." He kissed her, then stood up quickly beside her, throwing off his shirt, unbuttoning his pants and stepping out of them, smiling at her, locked into her gaze as he did so. He knelt over her again, lowering himself, and she ran her hand over the defined muscularity of his back.

"You're in good shape," she said, as her hand moved around to feel his erection. "Fuck me," she said, pulling him to her, "I want you to fuck me."

As he moved on top of her he felt her catch his quick rhythm, and as the heat-filled moments passed, and time seemed to race to keep pace with them, he wanted to shout out loud that this felt like the best moment of his life so far, that she was . . .

"You're . . . beautiful, you're. . . ." He paused for a moment, as if paying lip service to speech.

"Don't talk. Don't stop." She sounded as if she were begging him.

"You're amazing," he whispered and pressed on and on until he felt her sigh and shudder and he too let himself go with a strange guttural sound that felt foreign to him.

THEY'D barely spoken or moved in the ten minutes or so since they'd collapsed together.

"We should go," she said.

He lay half across her still, stroking her hair, exhausted. He rolled off to lie by her side and pulled her close.

"Let's just stay a minute." He kissed her head. "I'll have to get back, anyway," he said. "I'll have to put Holt out of his misery."

"Ah. That's all I'm good for," said Thea, sated and happy for the moment.

"That's right," he said. "No other use."

She sat up in mock indignation and knelt over him.

"I'll make you pay," she said.

"Shh!" he said. "What was that?"

They froze still as they heard a key turn in the front-door lock. Their eyes met, pupils enlarged with sex and fear. She moved away from him, pulling the bed sheet around her as they heard a pair of heeled shoes walking across the wooden floor below them.

"It's a woman," Thea mouthed at Richard. He nodded.

He guessed it was Greta, or the cleaner. But something about the way those heels had clicked across the polished boards undercut the latter theory. His mother had been a cleaner once, for a short while, when his dad was out of work. She would have slid in her stockinged feet across such a floor, in reverence. It must be Greta, come to collect something, in Archie's absence. The heels set off once more, this time up the stairs. He sprang off the bed and reached for his trousers.

In the slow moment that the door opened, Thea knew who it was. She sat on the bed, close to where Richard was standing as he pulled on his shirt. She made no attempt to dress. Richard veered between the shame of discovery and a frisson of excitement and pride at being caught with his conquest. In the infinity of waiting, he found himself wishing the intruder were a man, any man, so long as it wasn't Archie. He watched, with detached horror, as the stranger appeared through the doorway.

"Er, Amy," he heard himself say, "we were, er, we were just . . ."

It was as if he didn't exist. The twins stared at each other, each shocked by their reflection, like a cat in a mirror.

It was the last thing Amy had expected. As she'd walked up the stairs, she'd thought it might be Richard she could hear, that he and Archie's cleaning lady might have found each other, or that it was Greta collecting a final batch of forgotten bits and pieces. But now, in the doorway of Archie's bedroom, she stood in shock, flustered at first by what she had interrupted, but feeling her rage about to outstrip her embarrassment.

"I don't believe this." Her voice seemed to speak from somewhere outside her. She watched her sister draw herself up, tucking the ends of the sheet around her as if it were a sarong and she'd just had a swim. She saw, in her mind's eye, a naked Thea beneath a man on this bed, Archie's bed, and for a moment the woman wasn't Thea but her.

"How could you, Thea?"

Thea said nothing. She seemed to be waiting. *But for what?* thought Amy.

"And how on earth did you get in?"

Thea looked up and ran her fingers through her disheveled hair.

"I had a key. I always had a key."

"I see."

The sisters stared at each other, both shocked but curious, both looking for the small changes that the years apart had brought.

"It's my fault, Amy," said Richard. "I talked her into it."

"I don't doubt that," said Amy without taking her eyes off Thea. She felt herself trembling. She wanted to hit out. How dare they come into Archie's flat, have sex in Archie's flat, when he was lying in the hospital?

"It was important, really," Richard went on. "I told you. That I picked up the contract. He wouldn't mind, I know he wouldn't."

"He wouldn't mind?" Amy turned on Richard, mesmerized for a moment by this man whose pursuit of what he wanted dazzled her. "He wouldn't mind that you break into his flat, then get up to God knows what with my sister in his bedroom?"

"That's none of your . . ." said Thea. She took a deep breath. "Look, that's irrelevant. But the coming in here, it was important, an emergency."

"He's already tried that one on me," said Amy.

"Well, then," demanded Thea, "you should realize it's true. It's in Archie's interest as well as Richard's."

"That's probably right, Amy," said Richard, though he was unsure of the validity of her claim.

"Oh, I give up," said Amy. She turned her back on them and made her way downstairs. Thea and Richard looked at each other.

"What now?" said Richard.

"Wait here."

"Wait?"

"Give me a minute." She let the sheet drop to the floor and began to pull on her clothes. Then she followed her sister through the door.

Amy was sitting on the sofa, her head in her hands. She felt out-maneuvered by them both. She'd never imagined she would have to encounter this unlikely alliance.

"I'm sorry if we embarrassed you," said Thea. She stood in front of Amy, her hands clasped, a penitent. "I suppose we shouldn't have come, and we shouldn't have, you know . . . or not here." She sat down beside her sister. "It was just that I suddenly realized I had the key and I'd had a bit to drink and . . . I like Richard." She paused to see if Amy would speak but there was nothing. "And I think I deserve a bit of fun after—"

"Fun?" Amy lifted her head, furious. "You've been back two minutes. You know nothing. You know nothing about what's been going on."

"No."

Thea put her hand on Amy's shoulder, but she shrugged it off.

"Amy, please."

"What were you doing in there anyway?" she whispered. "With him?"

Her voice was fierce and Thea felt crushed. She'd been in a sort of pink limbo, in transit. It wasn't just the jet lag, there had been an ecstatic optimism that somehow, in her absence, life had reshuffled itself and fallen out in a different spread.

"What do you think we were doing?" she answered. "I've told you. It was just—a bit of excitement maybe? Nothing serious." It had been, she reflected, very, very exciting, and now, as always it seemed, there was a price to pay.

"Excitement? Fun and excitement?" Amy's incredulity was scorching, but Thea knew her well enough to detect a note of jealousy underlying her distaste. How quickly, she thought, the family grid resurfaced. Here she was, berated by Amy, in the wrong, in the wrong place, with the wrong man, feeling like the wrong twin. She felt her resistance seep out like a puddle on the floor.

"There's nothing I can say," she said. She could feel tears behind her eyes, but she was determined not to let them out. "You're right.

We shouldn't have come. You're right, of course. You're always right, aren't you?"

Amy turned and looked at her. Her anger at Thea went beyond the farce she'd innocently unleashed. All her plans, her good intentions toward her sister had never stood a chance. They hovered above her just out of reach while she sat, submerged, struggling once again to breathe free.

"You are unbelievably selfish," she said. "You make a mess of things and then you feel sorry for yourself. How could you do this to Archie? Is it some sort of revenge? Surely you're over him by now?"

She saw her sister's face, so similar to her own, compose itself and regroup for a more subtle counterattack.

"I am over him," said Thea quietly. Amy's accusation had steeled her. "And what are you doing letting yourself in here, anyway? Still can't leave him alone?"

"What do you mean?" Amy's voice was defensive. She knew it was difficult to hide herself from Thea, that every tic and gesture was understood.

"You could never leave him alone. Or anyone else who liked me, for that matter. But Archie in particular, you always wanted to keep him for yourself."

"He's my friend. Mine and James's. I knew him long before you did," Amy said. She stared back at Thea, who was looking at her closely, as if she could read her desires.

"He's more than a friend for you," Thea said.

"What do you mean?" Amy said. "You're not suggesting I've had an affair with him?"

"How would I know? I guess it's unlikely. But you might if you got the chance, and I think you'd rather no one else did," said Thea.

"Especially you, I suppose?"

"You said it. And that's what it felt like."

She watched her sister digest her words and thought what a relief it was to have said them. But as she saw Amy struggle with her cut and thrust, she almost wished she'd had the self-control to leave it alone.

"If you must know," she said, playing her trump card, "I'm picking up some things for Archie—to take to the hospital. He's in the hospital, though it's no business of yours." She pulled herself up from the sofa. "And I think you two had better leave."

Richard was standing in the doorway, the papers he'd been looking for in his hand, and he looked from one sister to the other.

"He's in the hospital?" he said. "What's wrong with him?"

Amy said nothing.

"What's wrong with him?" asked Richard again, his voice rising. "You might have told me, Amy. I'd never have bothered . . . with this," he said, waving the sheaf of paper at her.

Amy took a bottle of water from her bag and drank deeply from it as they waited for her answer.

"He didn't want anyone to know," she said. "He's having an operation. They think he may have cancer. But we don't know what's happening yet."

As she took a step toward them, she began to sway slightly and was forced to sit down again on the sofa, shaking visibly, her face draining of color, and looking as though she might faint. Thea moved quickly to support her, putting her hand over hers, waving at Richard to disappear. He stared at the sight of the two of them together, unable to keep up with the flow between them, and retreated into the kitchen.

Thea leaned in even closer now, still holding Amy's hand.

"I know you're pregnant," she whispered, then, turning her head, "Can you make some tea, Richard?" she called.

The door closed behind him and the twins sat in silence, Amy sipping at her water, Thea trying not to think about what she'd just revealed.

"I'm sorry," she said after a moment. "For all this." She waved her hand around the apartment.

"I suppose Grace told you," Amy said. "About the baby. I keep feeling dizzy. It was such a shock seeing the two of you here."

"If we'd known about Archie, I promise you, we would never have . . ."

"No. But let's not talk about it."

"How pregnant are you?"

"Only just over two months. And I haven't told James yet. So don't say anything."

Thea squeezed her sister's hand again. It was an automatic gesture, but Amy grasped her fingers in return. She had a sense of déjà vu. They'd been sitting rather like this, on an old and battered kitchen sofa, when Lucy had told them she was expecting a baby. It had been a surprise. Their world was so complete, if constrained by being part of a pair, that they'd never contemplated a third party. Lucy must have been about four months gone with Grace. Amy could remember her showing them her rounding stomach and their private worry that their mother might burst.

"So," said Thea, "let me be helpful now. What about Archie? What does he need? I'll get it."

"He wants his pajamas," Amy said. "He forgot to take them. They're in a briefcase."

"It's over there," Thea said, pointing to the front door. "He must have put it down just before he left."

Amy watched Thea's face. There was an anxiety behind the eyes that she recalled from years back. It would appear after a fight between them, a fight Amy often believed herself to have lost. But then, in a gesture or a look, Thea would betray herself, displaying a small surrender, a depletion that signaled submission.

There was a tentative knock from the kitchen, and Richard maneuvered himself through, carrying two mugs of tea.

"Here you are," he said, putting them down in front of them. "I think I'd better be off now."

The twins remained silent.

"Which hospital is Archie in?" he asked.

"The Queen Elizabeth," said Amy.

"I won't take this if you think I shouldn't," said Richard, fingering the envelope under his arm.

"Oh, what does it matter?" said Amy. "Do what you like."

He leaned in to kiss Thea on the cheek.

"I'll call you," he whispered. She nodded, and he was out of the flat in a moment.

"That man," said Amy.

"I like him," said Thea. "I always have, and I know you do." She whispered in her sister's ear though there was no one there to hear. "I seem to remember you once telling me you fancied him."

Amy almost smiled. It was true that she'd often enjoyed flirting with Richard, that she'd always been flattered by his obvious attention.

"I do, or I did. But he's been a shit to Archie."

"Maybe," said Thea. "But it's bound to be complicated. I'll tell you one thing, though: he's a great fuck."

"Thea!" But Amy laughed, and Thea was triumphant.

"I'll spare you the details. Let's go home."

⌇

LUCY heard the front door close. Grace had gone. She looked at the clock—it was almost five—and she eased herself out of bed, pulling on a silk kimono embroidered with birds in flight. Her head felt better now and her mood had lifted. She went to the kitchen, washed up her cup, and sat down once more at her proofs. The photograph of Tom was upside down on the other end of the table. Grace must have moved it. She picked it up and turned it over and wondered for a moment what her daughter thought and felt when she looked at the picture; what it must be to have a father you'd never known.

She worked on, systematically correcting her proofs, changing a word here, a phrase there. The task was simple and reassuring, almost mechanical; but as she progressed, the stories that had so touched her now began to pall, to distress her even. They were naive in their hope for the future, and she felt sad for all the accrued optimism that would inevitably falter; worse, she felt a faint flicker of guilt for having encouraged it. Perhaps people were better left to their despair.

This was so alien a thought to Lucy that it jolted her out of her late-afternoon torpor. She got up and splashed her face with cold water. She wouldn't sink down a second time in her life, not now, not after all she'd achieved; it would be a betrayal of twenty years. She went to her sitting room and stared at the bookshelves, looking for something to distract her from her thoughts. She looked along the shelves of biography and memoir and history, searching for something to weight her down; but as she looked all these lives seemed so much fiction to her. Even the physical reality of the books' boards and covers appeared insubstantial, their titles indistinct, dancing before her eyes.

She sat down in a worn blue velvet armchair, a favorite seat. This might be the onset of a migraine, an ancient, dreaded symptom before the fact. And she knew that the fact, the headache, was a symptom in itself, one that would have to be dealt with. She sat back and practiced breathing deeply as she had frequently advised others to do. The books settled on the shelves, the tension in her head dissipated—until the telephone started to ring.

She let it ring six times, then remembered she'd turned off the answering machine. She wanted to let it go on but was afraid it might be one of her daughters. Even now that they were grown up, a phone left ringing might mean a cry unanswered.

"Hello," she said, picking up the receiver on the table beside her.

"Is that Lucy Fielding?" It was a man's voice.

"Who is it?" Lucy was guarded.

"Lucy? Is that you?" The voice was familiar.

"Yes, who's that?"

"It's Michael."

Lucy was silent.

"Michael," the voice repeated, then, "Michael Richards."

"Michael," said Lucy. Her speech felt involuntary, as if some other Lucy was making the reply.

"Yes. Look I, er, I know this must be a bit of a surprise."

She forced herself to concentrate, and then to smile.

"Yes, sorry, yes. It is a surprise. . . . Michael. It's been . . . a long time."

"Twenty-two years."

"Surely not." She knew how long it had been.

"Yes, twenty-two," he said.

He paused for her to reply but nothing came. She forced herself to speak.

"How are you—after all this time?"

"I'm well. I retired last year. We came back, to England. We're, we were, living in Devon. And you?"

"Yes, well, pretty well."

"Your children?"

"Yes, yes, all well. Thea's just back from America, as a matter of fact." She paused. "And Jenny? How are you both?"

"Jenny's dead, Lucy," said Michael.

"Oh." The books and the shelves, the wall even, seemed to recede into the distance as she stared ahead.

"She died six months ago," he said.

2004

24 November
Harley Street

SHE SEEMED TO Patrick to be starting to slow down, as if exhausted by her story. He looked discreetly at his watch. It was a movement he'd learned to perform without his clients noticing. Fragments of his own memory were surfacing, reversing the order of things in a way he found hard to process, and he had become still more concerned for his professional position. He could recall now not only James Marsham's face, but his anxiety, his reluctance, and, of course, the claustrophobia, the lifts at the workplace. But of what had brought the phobia on he had no memory. That was far more elusive, as it had no doubt been to them both at the time.

Amy's words were carefully enunciated, as if she were reaching for a summary. "It was the compression of events that was startling," she was saying, "and not the events themselves. Each thing, each problem, each statement of fact, they were just the usual, more or less alarming things that happen to us all in life. But that only seemed to make things worse, as if we were screaming inside at the commonplace. And they all came together, piling one on top of another like . . ." She turned her head away from him.

"Like what?" he asked, but she ignored the question, leapfrogging it with one of her own.

"The people who come to see you," she said, "are their lives so dramatic? I suspect rarely so. It's the everyday detritus that usually trips people up, don't you think?"

Patrick inclined his head a fraction, acknowledging her point as he waited.

"But the strange thing was, as the events of our lives increased in scale, the more they seemed part of the natural order, and whenever I tried to make sense of it, all I could think was how everything had happened before and would happen again, over and over, and part of me was in the thought, anxious and frightened, and part of me was outside it, floating free." She stopped and looked at him, undecided which way she would steer.

"There's something else I ought to tell you," she said.

"About your husband?"

"Yes. And about what he said to you. And why I need to know."

"Why you feel the need to know," he corrected.

"If you prefer," she said. She sounded tired.

"I think," said Patrick, crumbling under the ethical strain, "that you should tell me why you feel the need to know. I don't see that that would be a problem."

She gazed at him, he thought, like a world-weary cat, with the same hint of seeming dislike, if you looked carefully.

"I could tell you that, and more," she said. "But it can wait."

He ignored her teasing, and he looked at his watch again. He would have to stop her soon, he thought, relieved to know there was someone else downstairs, waiting for his own hour to sit with him.

"The only person who really understood, I think, was Grace," she said. "Though I don't think we talked about it at the time. About me not wanting another baby then, about me not telling James."

"Grace," he said. And now he remembered how Grace had danced through James's landscape, and he felt a resurgence of anxiety at his compromised position. Her voice had thickened, and she reached for the box of tissues that sat on the table in front of her.

"Grace never wanted children and she has always said so. So she understood—understands—how I felt then, about my pregnancy, my panic. It's hard to imagine it now. I found myself hoping it would all go away, that I'd have a miscarriage. It was a terrible thought, I know. I even looked up the number of a clinic. Lots of women do it, you know, and certainly think about it, married women I mean, but they're not allowed to say so."

"We're talking about you here," said Patrick at once, keeping the lines straight between them, "about what you weren't allowed to say."

"About what I couldn't say," she corrected. "To him. And what he couldn't say to me that he needed to come here and tell you. And I'm trying to put it right."

1994

IT WAS STILL only six when James arrived at the Dorchester. He checked out the bar and regretted at once his decision to make it the venue for his meeting with Grace. It was large and currently almost empty. He walked back into the entrance hall and headed toward the armchairs where people were finishing tea. The lounge area had an air of anonymity, a pit stop for people in transit. He walked past the windows of expensive gift shops full of presents that no one except business travelers would buy, men mostly, guilty of some adulterous fling, fleeing to safety with a token for safe passage.

The doorman looked at him, questioning his furtive behavior. James checked his watch and moved toward the revolving doors of the entrance.

"Can I help you, sir?"

"I'm waiting for someone. She's, er, they're late."

The uniformed flunkey was impassive. James felt guilty. Did the chap think he was waiting for a tart? Why would he, James, even think that, let alone the doorman? He was waiting for his sister-in-law.

"My sister-in-law actually," he heard himself saying.

"Very good, sir. If you want to wait in the lounge, I'll direct her to you."

"Thank you."

But how would he know who she was?

"She's got long red hair."

"Very good, sir."

James found himself a seat facing the entrance and pretended to read the *Evening Standard*. If it weren't so close to 6:15, he thought, he'd cancel the whole thing. Now that he was here and sitting down, he felt hot and grubby. He should go to the men's room and comb his hair at least. But he didn't have a comb. He pushed his palm across his short thick hair. He'd probably made it worse. He should never have suggested meeting in a hotel. What would Grace make of it? Nothing probably. She'd just think he was her sister's husband and a bit out of touch. He found himself staring at the sports pages in the paper, and he wished he could talk again to Archie, who made so light of these things.

The thought of Archie only compounded his shifty feeling. He'd barely considered his friend all day, and now it was only in the context of his own selfishness; James prided himself on his friendships, particularly that with Archie. They went back, they'd looked out for each other, and he smiled to himself at the memories. But actions were the thing and he'd be there again for him. Later. After . . . He saw her come in through the doors and watched as the doorman assessed her. Her skirt, James noted, was very short. He stood up and walked toward her. Grace put her head on one side and smiled at him. Here she was, Amy's sister. She was lovely, but she was the girl he'd known for the last eleven or so years. What was he doing? What had he been thinking? He leaned to kiss her on the cheek.

"What a treat," she said.

"A treat?"

"To have you all to myself for a change." She took his arm. "I'd love a drink."

⌑

So Jenny was dead. Perhaps it was Jenny who was weighing on her mind, literally, a mass pushing in on her brain. Jenny and not Tom. Or perhaps they were in there together. Lucy smiled at her fanciful absurdity. She was up now, up and on the roof, in the soft late-afternoon light, as she began the evening ritual of watering her garden. She liked to fill the can from the hose and pour the water softly into the pots, clearing debris as she went. The scent from the blooms intensified as she approached, and the roses, in particular, smelled so strong she could detect in their sweetness the start of their decay.

Michael had brought her roses for their very last time. They had been white and perfect, and she'd thrown them away as soon as her car had traveled out of his sight. It had been twenty-two years ago, but she could still see them, through her rearview mirror, strewn all over the road as she drove home, away from the country hotel, back to Tom and the children, as Michael would go to Jenny, for good, as they'd agreed. The image flared above her eyes and for once she let it stay there, those seconds as she accelerated away until she could no longer see the flowers, no longer even imagine they were still visible.

Five years their affair had lasted, if she counted the year's break to try to mend her marriage with a baby. Five years that had seemed, against logic, to infect all her memories up to the point she met him, to fragment her picture of her life into shards. And afterwards, after the years of disintegration, and Tom's death, she'd rebuilt herself on that foundation, a light, ethereal construction untroubled by the shattered lovers below. It had been an act of survival for her children's sake. She liked to portray it now as a kind of damascene conversion, and perhaps it had been: a turning of the will, steeled by conviction.

She emptied the watering can into a pot of lobelia and turned back through the tunnel of flowers to the hose outlet. She would agree to see Michael. He'd said he would ring again, tomorrow, and she had not protested. He'd said what she'd always known he would say, that there was no one to hurt now, and it was time to make things right.

⌘

THE bar had filled up considerably since James had first put his head around the door. It was an exotic crowd—hotel guests, many of whom were refugees from the blistering heat of the Gulf states, along with an odd City type like himself indulging a whim. Grace was stirring a martini and talking excitedly at him while he picked at a plate of crisps. She seemed to like the place after all. It was certainly dramatic, with its rounded booths dwarfed by elaborate plasterwork and heavy chandeliers. A piano played a sad tune far away across the ballroom expanse of the long bar. He wished he felt more excited. He'd thought her presence might move things on for him in some way, though he wasn't sure how. Now that she was here, he felt brotherly toward her. The phantom sex goddess had vanished. He tuned into her and realized she was talking about Sam, and then wondered if that was why his ardor had dampened. He tried to listen but found himself staring instead at the gap between her thighs that opened up at the hem of her skirt.

"The thing is," she was saying, "he's a great guy, I know that. But this is new for me, and, if you want the honest truth, I've always preferred men older than he is."

James raised his eyes to her face.

"What? Sorry?"

"Am I boring you?"

"No, no. Absolutely not. You were saying?"

"You haven't heard a word I've said, have you?"

"Yes, I have. I'm listening." She reminded him for a moment of Amy and a complicated rush of shame rippled through him.

"What did I say?"

"You were saying you like older men."

"Oh."

"See," he said, "I'm with you. And I knew that. I've seen you with enough of them."

She stopped and looked awkward.

"Do you think I'm strange?" she asked.

"No. Some women just do. But you should ask yourself why."

"I never had a dad, I suppose. I don't need a shrink to tell me that."

James wondered for a moment if she knew about his visits to Patrick, but that was impossible.

"How old, in general, are we talking about?" he said.

"Well, older. I mean, not like fifty or something," she paused for a moment and reconsidered, "or sixty—that would be pushing it a bit."

"Fifty? You mean you've been out with someone of fifty?" James gave her his full attention. This wasn't quite what he'd imagined. Older had meant ten or fifteen years, around about his own age.

Grace flicked a peanut at him.

"You'll be fifty soon."

"I'm thirty-nine, for God's sake."

"I used to have such a crush on you," she said.

Used to. How cruel a tense could be.

"What?" he said.

"Don't tell me you didn't know that?"

"No, I swear. When did you?"

"The last couple of years at school. And you did know. You used to flirt with me. And then, suddenly, you didn't anymore. I remember exactly when it stopped. It was after Rosie was born."

He thought back and tried to remember her at that age, on visits to Lucy, on outings when Amy was in a mood to treat her younger sister. He'd wanted Grace to like him, wanted to win her over, for Amy's sake. Her schoolgirl eroticism hadn't escaped him, he could remember joking with Archie about it. Perhaps he had flirted with her; he'd never really known what flirting was, after all.

"It was a serious crush," she went on. "If I could have nicked you off Amy then, I would have."

"Don't be ridiculous."

"I was like that. I worry I still am."

"Like what?"

"Bad. I'm a bad girl." She toasted him with her glass.

As he sat there clutching his beer, looking up her skirt, his brotherly detachment evaporated. It was as if he were suddenly naked—naked with a rising hard-on. How crude he was. "Bad girl," she'd said, then a big smile, and that was all it had taken to open up a grubby vista of possibilities.

"I'm flattered." James felt as though he was leering at her, but he still sat forward.

"You should be. I shagged my history tutor because of you."

He tried to remember if he'd seen Grace in quite this light before. She'd always been frank, foul-mouthed Amy would say, though Lucy always laughed. Her language now seemed spoken just for him, a twentieth-century Circe's call, potent and dirty.

"How old was he, your tutor?"

"About thirty-five. He reminded me of you."

"You never said."

She laughed.

"You mean I never told Amy. She wouldn't have approved. I told Archie once. I'm surprised he didn't tell you, about the tutor I mean. I never told him about you, he would have been jealous."

James was out of his depth. He was confused by how he could simultaneously want to have sex with someone he shouldn't, yet help her at the same time. He definitely wanted Grace to be happy, and with someone else, Sam probably, but just in this moment he'd like her to make him happy, too.

"So, if you prefer older men," he asked, "what are you doing with Sam?"

Grace sighed and tugged at her skirt.

"I'm changing my ways. That's what I was trying to tell you."

James wondered if it was acceptable to take off his jacket, the hotel seemed so formal. He was warm despite the air-conditioning.

"He's a good-looking guy," he said.

"He's a sweetie," she said.

James was sure that Sam would not care to be called a "sweetie," but he said nothing.

"So," she went on, leaning forward again, "why exactly did you ask me to meet you? Was it because of Kitty?"

"Kitty?"

"Kitty Buxton. Come on, James, I know you met her yesterday, with her dad. She rang me."

"Right. Kitty." James picked up his glass but didn't drink. "I liked her. She was good fun. You were school friends?"

Grace was smiling at him with the condescension conferred by superior knowledge. "She told me she'd been teasing you."

Why, he thought, did women have to ring each other all the time? He'd assumed he'd have at least a day's grace. He was hopeless at this. He'd wanted to indulge himself, that was all, to be flattered by a pretty girl even if she was his sister-in-law, especially because of that. He took off the jacket and thanked God for his expensive shirt, which never showed sweat.

"So how long did it go on, your crush?" he asked.

"On you?"

"Yes." He felt bold.

She looked straight at him.

"First love never dies," she said.

That was what Kitty had said, or something like it, and he felt himself blushing. It was becoming a habit. He wanted to ask Grace again, to hear the words a second time.

"There's a name for girls like you," he heard his voice say.

She crossed her legs and leaned back, and as she performed the movement, he saw, as if handed the secret of a magic trick, that she was playing a role. He'd been fooled. This was what she did for a living. When her line came back he almost applauded.

"I can't help it," she said. "You're forbidden fruit."

He passed up his cue. The moment was gone.

"Don't be silly, Grace," he said. "This is me, James. Your brother-in-law."

Grace looked discomfited. He felt suddenly fraternal again, in control and deeply relieved.

"Can I give you some advice?"

Grace shrugged and gulped her drink.

"I feel a lecture coming on," she said.

"Stick with this guy Sam," he said, his sudden understanding lending him courage. "He's in your business, and he's got you worked out, hasn't he?"

Grace tugged at her skirt again, her siren sheen retired. She looked exhausted.

"Just relax and let him look after you. You might find you grow to like it and he won't run away."

Grace opened her mouth to speak, but she thought better of it.

"Because that's what you're scared of, isn't it?" James wondered if he was pushing this too far.

She smiled at him as if in surrender, leaning back against the soft darkness of her seat.

"Wait there a minute," he said. "I need a pee."

OUTSIDE the house on Finlay Road, a gardener was loading empty crates into his van when Thea pulled up in front, with Amy in the passenger seat of the family car. He stared at the two of them through the windscreen, then waved. Amy felt suddenly self-conscious at the sight of her employee.

"He only comes twice a month." She turned to Thea. "I just can't manage the garden on my own and James is hopeless." She was searching through her bag for her key. "I really don't have any other help, apart from the cleaner. We did have an au pair, but she's gone for the summer."

Thea stepped out of the car, her crumpled jacket in her hand.

"Why ever should you think I'd disapprove?" she asked across the car roof as Amy emerged on the other side. "Am I supposed to believe you do everything yourself?"

"No, but even to me it all looks rather managed and dull. Especially to me, in fact. I'm afraid I've become suburban. A bit . . ." Amy let them both into the house, and they walked through to the kitchen. Thea laid her jacket over the back of a chair.

"A bit what?" she said.

"Not what I imagined for myself," said Amy, waving her arms to indicate the saucepans and the electric kettle. "I suppose I used to imagine myself as more glamorous, more . . . Bohemian."

"You were never Bohemian. You've always liked your comforts," said Thea, delighted to have fingered a bona fide difference between them. "I was always the one on the floor in the sleeping bag when there wasn't enough room."

"You asked to be, if I remember," said Amy.

"A natural martyr," said Thea and knew it was true.

Now that her sister was here, in her home, in her world, Amy could stand outside the spacious three-storey house, the garden, the detritus of children. There were clean surfaces, evidence of silent help, and the tanned cheerful face of the young man who had followed them back in and was now saying something about bringing winter plants next week. She nodded at him and waved good-bye.

"Well," said Thea, "that's the garden sorted. So what's the problem?"

"Nothing. There is no problem as such. I don't know."

She couldn't tell Thea about her misgivings about her future, not so soon. She couldn't tell her that she too would have liked to be able to run off as Thea had done, that she too would have liked a change but now, if there was a new baby, there would just be more of the same. It would inevitably be seen as an accusation.

"I just wish sometimes," she said, "that I'd had a bit more of the other life, the single life, I suppose, before all this." She paused, looking around her. "I envy you. This afternoon . . . you know . . ."

Thea laughed.

"I know," said Amy. "Pity we can't have both. Do you want a drink?"

"No, thanks, I had quite enough at lunch," said Thea. She leaned on the table and faced her sister. "So is it the general or the particular that's bothering you?"

"What do you mean?"

"Well, is it the pattern of your life, or its components?"

Amy looked suspicious. "I know you're cleverer than I am, but I'm not quite with you."

Thea had now unlocked the French doors to the patio and stepped outside.

"It's very stuffy in here."

"Make yourself at home, why don't you," said Amy. But she followed Thea through.

"I suppose what I mean is," said Thea, "are you fed up with motherhood and marriage, or with James?"

Amy sat down. They seemed to be slipping back, despite themselves, into a semblance of an old intimacy. She found herself wanting to confide in Thea, to pick up from where they'd once been, close and trusting, but she wasn't quite ready. She was still feeling vulnerable from their earlier exchange.

"Neither." She looked at her watch. "I'll have to go to the hospital soon, Archie will be waking up."

"I'm coming with you," said Thea. "I'll order a cab."

Amy looked across the garden, noting that the hammock had split at one end.

"I'm not sure that's a good idea."

"I don't mean I'll come in and actually see him. I'll wait outside, just till James comes. To make sure you're all right."

Amy was surprised by Thea's new concern, by her seeming to want to make up for the events of the afternoon.

"It's just that Archie will be all groggy."

"Yes," said Thea. "He might think he's hallucinating. Ghosting."

Amy looked at her sister and frowned. She wasn't sure she liked the sound of that.

"Having double vision, you mean?" said Amy.

"Yes," said Thea. "He might think one of us isn't real. Which do you want to be?"

ARCHIE thought he might be awake. A nurse was taking his blood pressure, but he blinked and she wasn't there. He was lying on his back in a haze of pethedine and could see his left hand, unfamiliar outside the bedclothes, attached to a drip. He felt absolutely nothing. It was extremely pleasant. He made a bid for consciousness, but it was too much effort and he drifted back into oblivion.

TOGETHER they walked down a gray carpeted corridor toward Archie's room, behind the nurse, who stopped suddenly in front of a door with a large push-down handle.

"I'd better go in first and see how he's doing," she said. "Just a moment."

Amy looked back at Thea.

"My sister's going to wait for me," she said. "She's not visiting."

The nurse looked surprised and pointed along the corridor.

"You can wait down there. There's a visitors' area."

"Thanks," said Thea, and strode ahead without looking at Amy or the door behind which Archie lay. After a few seconds she heard it close, a dull thud of exclusion. She found herself turning around and walking back past the room to the end of the corridor and the lifts from which they'd come. She couldn't bear to be sitting so near. She'd get a cup of coffee or something downstairs, anything not to be alone.

AMY stood for a moment at the end of Archie's bed. He appeared to be asleep, lying on his back, the drip stand to his left. In his short-sleeved, round-necked blue gown, he looked as youthful as when she'd first met him. As she watched him sleep, she thought that she saw the boy whom James had known, the boy who had it all but belonged nowhere; and she felt, though she knew it was foolish, as if she'd been there, too, in their boyhood, a third party waiting in an adjacent dimension. She moved around to the side and stroked the back of his hand with her fingers. The body in the bed turned slightly and Archie opened his eyes. She felt tender toward him, nothing more pressing. As she watched him she searched for the stirrings he'd so recently caused her, but it was as if they had been temporarily mislaid.

"Thea," he said, and smiled.

SHE was standing over a coffee machine in yet another deserted annex, watching the muddy liquid dribble into her cup and wondering how long she would have to wait. Thea was shocked by the way that time appeared to have condensed in her absence. Like the characters in Grace's soap, her friends and family seemed to be hurtling through events at a ludicrous rate, and this afternoon she'd joined them. She'd missed the buildup, of course, that was part of the confusion. She needed the back story to help her fill in the narrative of her life.

A thin, middle-aged woman in a droopy lilac dress approached the machine. She smiled at Thea, but it was only a gesture. There was a collected sadness about her, months, perhaps years of extinguished hopes.

"It's terrible, waiting, isn't it?" she said.

"I'm waiting for my sister, who's waiting," said Thea.

"Is it her husband?"

"No," said Thea. She wanted to say, *It's my ex-boyfriend, in fact, whose body I knew intimately, whose existence I was once a part of, and now all that means nothing. Isn't that absurd?*

"It's a friend," she said.

The woman watched as the coffee ran slowly into her cup.

"It's my husband."

"Ah," said Thea. What could she say? She couldn't ask, Is it serious? Is it terminal?

"It's the last time they'll operate." The woman lifted the cup to her dry lips.

"I'm sorry," said Thea.

"Don't be. It's best it comes to an end." She sat down and picked up a magazine. She was like a ghost, shrunk within its ectoplasm, its moment of contact with the human plane passed and gone.

Thea left the room, and the hospital. She loitered on the corner of the street, smoking a cigarette. The evening was very warm, and still light, though the imminent sunset made the distance blur into shadow, and a large dark cloud was moving forward, driven by an accelerating breeze. A car drew up beside the curb.

"Hey, looking for business?"

She looked around toward the rolled-down window and smiled.

⁂

THE small fair-haired nurse answered Amy's call for help down the corridor, but not in any great hurry.

"What's the matter?" she said. She stood in the doorway, staring just above Amy's head.

"He seems very agitated," said Amy. "I thought he might have a temperature."

The nurse looked at Archie, then directly at Amy. She felt his pulse and put a thermometer in his mouth.

"It's normal for postoperative patients to have a temperature," she said, taking it out, looking at it, and putting it back on its stand in one movement. Archie babbled something, opened his eyes, and gazed at Amy.

"Amy," he said, "thanks for coming." He shut his eyes and once again began rolling his head. Amy challenged the nurse.

"See?"

"He's just dreaming," said the nurse. "He's not shaken off the anesthetic."

"So, he won't know yet?"

"Know what?"

"What's happened—in the operation?"

"No. The consultant will be in first thing in the morning to talk to him."

Amy stared at the nurse, willing her to divulge her privileged mysteries.

"I'm just the night nurse," she said. "I couldn't tell you anything even if I wanted to." She smiled at Amy. "I'll bring you a cup of tea, if you like?" she said.

"No," said Amy. "Thanks. I'll go and wait for a bit with my sister."

RICHARD'S unexpected arrival in his smart BMW outside the hospital was tantamount to a rescue.

"Hey, Dickie. What are you doing here?" Thea said.

"I came to see what was going on. I was worried. I only got half the story."

"Let me in." She rattled the door handle. "You cannot imagine what it's like in there."

Richard felt his stomach clench as she climbed in next to him. The combination of excitement and drama was a heady mix.

"Archie?" he asked.

Through the windscreen Thea noticed the movement of the wind in the trees that lined the street. She shook her head. "Not him. I think . . . I mean, I don't know what's going on. Amy's still up there. No, it was a woman in the waiting room. She was tragic."

He put his arm around her and kissed her.

"I wasn't allowed in," she said.

"What?"

"Amy thought it would be too confusing for Archie to see both of us."

Richard laughed.

"Well, she's got a point."

Richard shifted in his seat. He leaned across her to the glove compartment.

"Do you want some chocolate?" he asked.

"Chocolate? I don't believe it. You've got chocolate?"

"If I'd known you were so easily pleased . . ." He unwrapped the bar, thin and dark, and broke off a piece.

"It was on my way," he said. "I came to find out how Archie was doing. But it's a real bonus to see you."

She tried to smile and pointed at her mouth.

"Lost for words? I have that effect." He stuffed a double piece of 70 percent cocoa solids in his mouth.

Rain began to drop on the windshield.

"Oh, no," said Thea. "Where did that come from?" She turned to find the window button, and as she looked outside into the escalating shower she saw Amy standing on the hospital steps scanning the street.

"Amy," she shouted. "Here!"

Amy looked over and squinted at them. She took one step down as the drops became a deluge, then Thea saw her hesitate, on the brink of retreating into the hospital.

"Get in the car," she shouted. Richard leaned over into the back to open the door and suddenly Amy was there, on the backseat, a few beads of rainwater trickling down her bare arms.

As he left the rehearsal rooms in Shepherd's Bush just after six, Sam checked his mobile. Calls from his agent, from his latest film's publicist, and from his mother, but nothing from Grace. He'd rung her several times since she'd slammed out of his flat some time early this morning, and as he opened the door of his new convertible he found himself wondering whether she was worth the trouble. He caught himself in the rearview mirror and appraised the blond hair and blue eyes that drew both sexes to him and had made him something of a box office favorite. He hadn't been driven to act by neglect or neurosis but by a pragmatic acknowledgment that his looks and talent were exploitable. It had been a calculated gamble that had paid off.

He had the best of all worlds, his pick of roles and women, but now he wanted Grace and he was baffled by her opposition.

His journey back from west London would take him up Kensington High Street, or rather this route was an option open to him and one he decided to pursue. He would buy some flowers and go to Lucy's, which was no doubt where Grace would be—and if she wasn't, he would leave them as a peace offering. He wondered, as he had done all day, what it was about Grace that made him want her. She was capricious, which he only quite liked, and sometimes venal, which he didn't. But she was also passionate, with a core of sunny goodwill that he loved, even if it was overcast from time to time by her ambition. He hoped they could make it work between them.

"Grace isn't here, Sam," said Lucy into the intercom. She was standing in her gray silk dressing gown. "She went out about an hour ago."

"Sorry to disturb you," his voice crackled at her. "I've brought some flowers for her. Can I leave them?"

"Flowers?" said Lucy, who held a watering can in her left hand. "Coals to Newcastle," she continued, more to herself than to him.

"Sorry?"

"Nothing. How lovely. Yes, do bring them up." She buzzed him in, hoping that he wouldn't want to wait. But as the door of the tiny lift opened into the apartment and Sam stood before her, holding white roses in his outstretched arms, she tried to speak and then fainted.

❦

STANDING in front of a lavatory bowl, James aimed his stream of urine against its back wall. He didn't realize he'd drunk so much. There'd been the cups of tea in the afternoon, and now he was on his second beer. He should be leaving soon if he was to get to the hospital on time. He washed his hands carefully, looking into the mirror. He wasn't prone to examining his reflection and was surprised at the suave image that stared back at him. His curly dark hair for once seemed to sit in line with the contours of his skull. He recognized himself for the older man he now was, and liked what he saw. He'd grown into himself without noticing. He stood up straight and breathed out, expelling all the air in his body. He was forty next year and married with two children. His life was going somewhere good, and he would not hang back. He did not need an ego massage, or a set of directions, from a little girl whose role as a tart had got out of hand. He loosened his shoulders, raised his fist in victory at his reflection, and made his way back through the corridors to put this business to bed once and for all.

Grace was putting on her jacket when he returned. On the table in front of his seat was a padded leather folder containing their bill.

"What's going on?" said James. "Are we leaving?"

"Your wife has just rung me." Grace looked accusing. "She's with Archie, at the hospital, and Thea. She tells me you're on your way?"

"To the hospital, yes." James was noncommittal. He checked his watch. "I'm not late," he said.

Grace picked up her bag. She was definitely out of character now.

"Why didn't you tell me about Archie?"

She sat down again beside him. It was hard to continue a real-life dialogue standing on four-inch heels.

"He didn't want people to know. He's had an operation," said James. "But he's going to be all right."

"What for?"

"A lump. To see what it is."

"How do you know he's going to be all right?" she said.

He didn't.

"Did you tell Amy we were here?" he said after a moment.

She got her purse from her bag and took out a credit card.

"I'll get that," he said, but she slipped it inside the folder.

"I told her I was having a drink with a friend," she said.

"Oh." He sat up in his seat.

"I lied for you."

"There was no need to. Anyway, it's not a lie."

"No? I suppose not. You never told me about the surprise."

He smiled at her.

"No. It will keep."

She raised her eyebrows and slipped her arm around the back of his neck, across the thick white cotton shirt, and leaned around to place her mouth on his cheek.

"You're the surprise. Go to the hospital," she said. "And thanks, you're right, about me and Sam actually. You usually are—right about things."

He flushed with pleasure, the good sort, he thought to himself, and took her hand.

"At least let me pay the bill."

"Okay," she said, retrieving her card from the folder.

"See you soon."

"Later."

And she was gone.

OUTSIDE the hospital the sound of the heavy rain on the soft top of his car put Richard in mind of a school camping holiday he'd once been on. It was one of just three times he'd slept away from his family, until he'd broken out at seventeen and never gone back. He hadn't much liked home, but as a child he'd liked being away from it even less. The noise of the raindrops on the school tent's canvas had made him suddenly want his mother, sick for the familiar, however insubstantial. Now he felt safe here, sitting with the twins, eating chocolate, as water poured down the windows of the car. It was almost companionable, in a ceasefire sort of a way.

"I ought to go back inside," said Amy. It was odd to find herself here with Richard and Thea, after the farce of the afternoon, but to her surprise it now seemed not only a distant memory but, as Thea had made clear, none of her business.

"I'd wait till it stops," said Richard.

"We might be here all night." Thea looked over her shoulder at her sister. "Do you want me to come back in with you?"

"No. It's okay. I'll stay here for a bit."

Richard pressed the CD button, and the car filled with the sound of an old Herbie Hancock track. He turned it down low.

"Boys' music," said Thea.

"Nice though," said Amy.

For the second time that day Richard felt caught between opposing forces, but here in the car's humid interior the truce among the three of them was holding. He was aware of being meshed in a family web that felt warm and friendly. It was a place he felt he wanted to stay.

"When do you think he'll come out?" asked Thea. Richard didn't understand the question. Her voice seemed far away as his mind wandered within the confines of their metal cocoon.

"What?"

"Tomorrow or the day after," said Amy. "They don't hang about."

"Don't want to pay for the bed, you mean," said Richard, who'd caught up with the conversation. "The insurance."

"Will he be okay?" Thea asked Amy. "I mean, will he have recovered properly?"

"He'll come and stay with us."

"Does he know?" Thea said. "No, I thought not. He won't want to do that."

"I know," said Amy, "so you've both got to help me persuade him."

Richard was flattered to be included in this command, implying as it did that his rift with Archie was not regarded as permanent. He listened to the two of them as they chattered, and it struck him how naturally Amy took the lead in their conversation, how she exuded a quite different energy, one which had the effect of sometimes pushing her sister to one side. He felt disloyal even as he thought it and winked at Thea.

"I doubt he'll listen to us," she said.

"I doubt he'll even want to see me," said Richard.

"Well, there is that," began Amy. "After all—"

"He'll come around," said Thea, interrupting quickly. "Archie doesn't bear a grudge."

"No," said Amy. "It's just as well someone doesn't."

Richard's mind wandered again. He could hear the twins trading lines, but it was lightweight banter, nothing to disperse the overall goodwill that stemmed, he supposed, from the proximity of someone else's trouble. If only he'd known about Archie sooner. But then Archie hadn't known about Archie, it seemed.

ABOVE Park Lane, warm air and car fumes hung about with nowhere else to go, and the sky was clouding over, shrouding the city in heat. Grace stood on the hotel steps and looked across at the heavy trees along the border of the gardens opposite. She thought how nice it would be to cross into the rose walk, hidden away on the other side, where London might offer an illusory coolness. But she couldn't see a way of weaving through the layers of traffic. She felt hot and sticky despite the hotel's air-conditioning, and she felt mentally disheveled by the last hour with James. He'd seemed so unlike himself. He'd started off by shuffling and wriggling like a boy on the school bus and ended up behaving like her father. He was smart, though, James, and his sense of preservation far outstripped hers, she knew. She'd think about his advice, or some of it. It was fun to play games, to not be yourself; it was okay some of the time, but she knew that she sometimes went too far.

She supposed that James was the nearest thing to a father that she'd had. It was true about the crush she'd developed, true that she'd tried out her effect on him, her special effect that as a teenager she'd honed daily, but it had never elicited a result. She'd put him on a pedestal, and she was glad that he was up there still, despite this afternoon's clumsy foray into flirtation. She had set out to tease him, sensing he'd made an excuse to see her, that he wanted to know, in his middle-aged vanity, if what Kitty had told him was true. But she didn't want the stranger who had met her in the hotel. She wanted Amy's husband to remain out of reach. She wanted them to stay together, a family, a happy benchmark for all the rest.

It was still early in the evening, and she knew she should ring Sam to make up the morning's quarrel, but she didn't know what she should say. She took out her phone from a pocket and as she turned it on, it began to ring. "LUCY" said the letters on screen.

"Ma, I was going to call you," she said, answering.

"It's me."

A man's voice—Sam's.

"What on earth are you doing at Ma's?" she said. She thought she could hear her mother calling out in the background, but it was hard to hear.

"Your mother's been taken ill," Sam said, sounding disorientated. "A doctor's on the way. How soon can you come?"

"What's the matter with her?"

"I don't know, she collapsed on me."

"I'll be ten minutes."

Grace hailed a taxi and opened the windows wide. The cabby, as usual, turned over his shoulder.

"You're in *Bridewell Wharf*," he said.

"Yes. Look, I don't mean to be rude but I've got something on my mind."

"Okay, love, no problem."

She was relieved by this display of acceptance. One small consequence of fame was the loss of anonymous taxi rides, quiet time when you could think. It was curious, she thought, what you missed. She should have realized how unwell her mother was this afternoon; she'd thought it was just a headache. And what had Sam been doing there? Come to find her, presumably. She wondered if Lucy had been working too hard. Grace had been so preoccupied with her own life in the last few months that she had taken her mother's contentment for granted: calm, benign, occasionally maddening Lucy, happy with her books and garden. But perhaps she wasn't really happy at all. This last thought was quite new for Grace, and it took hold quickly. Its implications seemed to stretch ahead of her. She felt the heat of the city evening ignite, a bridge burning into the future.

⌇

WALKING through the doors of the Dorchester, out into the sultry light, James caught sight of her as she was climbing into her cab. The air felt damp now, and dark clouds were encroaching on the white haze of the afternoon sky. It looked like rain, but James needed to walk for a while, to digest his folly. He'd extricated himself from potential disaster, but he still tried to bring a logic to bear on what his motives had been. It must be possible to see the track he was moving on, and if he could see it he could get a grip, step on the brake. He had wanted to find out if Kitty Buxton had been right about Grace's schoolgirl crush, but, in truth, he'd wanted more than the fact. So what was that? Excitement, yes. Flattery, yes. A sort of escape. But there was something else. He'd asked her to meet him because he'd wanted something from her. Was it as simple as sex? Archie would probably say so and think no harm done as long as it went no further than fantasy. But James thought it was more complicated. He and Archie had never agreed about women, and James had always conceded that ground, at least in the days before he met Amy. Archie had been, quite simply, better at the whole business.

He walked on up to Marble Arch, lengthening his stride as he looked at his watch. He'd occasionally speculated on what might have happened to them all if Archie and Thea had stayed together. He'd thought at first that it might work out, that it might suit them all, a family affair. Not that the end had ever really been discussed beyond a quick acknowledgment. Women came and went with Archie, he'd reasoned, and in any case it was too awkward, too close to home to talk about. Amy had found it difficult from the start, but she'd tried not to mind. Now he knew he hadn't much liked it either. After all, it was strange to see your best mate kissing a copy of your wife. It did make you wonder.

❧

Now that she was reclining on her sofa, her feet up and a small brandy in her hand, Lucy felt a great deal better. In fact she felt better than she had all day. Sam was sitting beside her, watching. She rested her eyes on his face and speculated, as Amy had done, what it must be like to grow up with the kind of looks that draw incessant attention. He felt shifty under her gaze. He was used to people staring at him, but her scrutiny was ruthless.

"The doctor will be here soon," he said, for something to say. It wasn't the first time he'd said it.

"Yes," she said, and sipped her brandy, still looking at him.

He wished that Grace would arrive. He wished he'd never come. Lucy seemed so strange. He'd met her only twice before, and then she'd appeared both carefree and controlled. Today he'd had to pick her up from the floor and make her sit on a chair with her head pushed forward. It had come back to him from some long-forgotten school first-aid class. She'd kept pointing to the flowers he'd brought and insisting that he put them in some water. "They mustn't die this time, you see," she'd said.

"I'm feeling much better now." Lucy smiled as she raised her head to face him. "So don't look so worried."

"The doctor—" he began.

"Yes," she said. "He's coming. You told me. I expect he'll say it's my blood pressure. It does fluctuate a bit." She seemed to ease even further back into the chair. "Tell me about your day, Sam. Distract me."

"My day?" he said. He hesitated. There was something about Lucy that demanded the truth, and his day had not begun well.

"I was rehearsing today," he said, skipping over the early part. "For a new play."

She inclined her head slightly in encouragement.

"I'm a journalist having an affair with a Cabinet minister. An older woman—obviously."

"How old?"

"Thirty-eight."

"Young," said Lucy.

"Yes, young for the Cabinet."

"I meant young full stop," said Lucy.

"I suppose so."

"Not to you, of course. I understand that."

She was teasing him, but at least, he thought, this was more typical of the Lucy he'd met before. He was about to continue, but she seemed to sink further into her chair and lose interest.

"I've never been that keen on politics," she said. "None of us are, except for Thea. She's the one who really cares, you know. About people. I've always thought that. All this wheeling and dealing. I never thought it was right for her."

Sam sensed that no reply was expected, but he was surprised at this new light on Grace's sister.

He had met Thea for the first time the previous evening when he'd come to pick up Grace. She was sitting on her own after supper, looking through old photographs.

"Don't show him the one of me in the paddling pool," Grace shouted from the bathroom, where she was readjusting her makeup before she went out into the night.

"It's too late," called Thea.

"Cute arse," called Sam. "Ooops. Sorry," he said, looking at Thea and then toward the kitchen where Lucy was pottering about.

"Don't worry," Thea said, "'arse' is fine." They looked down at the pictures in front of them.

"Who's that?" said Sam, pointing to a man standing behind the tiny Grace on her bike.

"That's our dad, Tom. He died."

"Oh, yes, sorry. Grace told me."

"She never knew him, really," said Thea. She pulled the picture from the pile and held it up. "She was only four, I think. It was a long time ago. How long have you been seeing each other?"

"About three months," said Sam. He felt wary; Thea was catlike, he thought, changeable with a hint of something dark.

"Hmm," said Thea. "Not bad."

"What?" he said, unsure of her tone.

"Grace gets bored easily."

"I'll remember that," said Sam.

"I just mean she obviously likes you."

"For now, you mean?" he said, unsettled by her directness.

"Certainly for now, maybe forever for all I know."

"For now will do," said Sam, on his guard.

"WHERE is Thea?" Lucy's voice seemed to lose force and she leaned forward again. "She said she was coming back." Sam stood over her, holding her shoulders, and then they heard the lift, whirring gently as it moved, at its slow pace, up to the flat.

"Don't move," he said. "It will be Grace."

He waited with Lucy until he heard the gates opening into the hallway, then went to the door. Grace squeezed his arm as his lips brushed her face and went through to her mother.

"I'm perfectly all right, darling," called Lucy, now sitting up. "Sam's been marvelous."

"I think she almost fainted again," he said, hovering behind. "The doctor's on his way."

"Which doctor?" said Grace.

"Dr. Speakman, darling," said Lucy.

"That old quack," she said.

"I didn't know . . . ," said Sam.

"I told Sam to ring him. I like him," said Lucy. "Anyway it's not serious. I only fainted. Blood pressure, I'm sure."

"Thank God you were here, Sam," said Grace, smiling up at him, and her obvious gratitude made up for the morning's exit and more.

"I stopped by on my way home," he said.

"He brought you the most beautiful flowers, darling. They're in the kitchen."

Grace walked past Sam out of the room, pulling him by the hand as she went.

"She passed out on me. Practically as she opened the door," he said in a low voice as they stepped over the kitchen threshold. Grace put her arms around his neck and kissed him. In her heels she was almost exactly his height.

"I'm glad you came," she said. "Glad for Ma and glad for me."

"I thought it was my fault," he said. "She just looked at me in a funny way and then she collapsed. She gave me a real fright."

"It wasn't you. Why would it be you? She had a headache earlier." Grace didn't say that she felt guilty for leaving Lucy, that she was ashamed that she'd left her to tease her sister's husband.

"She looked so shocked," Sam said. "She looked at me as if she'd seen a ghost."

Grace smiled and stroked his cheek.

"If Ma had seen a ghost, she'd be thrilled. She'd have invited it to stay."

She hugged him to her as he leaned against the table. His body was firm and hot, and she wanted to hold on, to keep herself still. Over his shoulder she caught sight again of the picture of her father, the tall figure holding her bicycle, smiling at the camera, a picture of other people's memories.

"Why did you run out on me this morning?" he said.

She dropped her arms gently and shrugged.

"Because I'm not good enough for you."

"Bollocks."

She thought what she'd said was true but let it go.

"Well, let's say I don't always know what's good enough for me," she said. "I'm sorry."

"Don't fuck it up, Grace."

She leaned her head on his chest. She knew what he meant.

He kissed her hair, then pushed her away.

"You should ring your sisters," he said, "and tell them what's happened."

❧

THE sound of the door opening brought Archie back to consciousness or something like it. Things were definitely a bit clearer. He saw Amy coming into the room followed by James and tried to sit up, but they seemed to swoop over him, willing him backward.

"I'm fine," he said. He saw them look at each other. "Just groggy." His arm waved toward them. "I might fall asleep on you."

"That's okay," said Amy. "We'll just wait till you wake up again."

"You look rough," said James.

"Thanks. Have you got my pajamas?"

"Yes," said Amy, "they're in the briefcase."

"I didn't know you owned a pair of pajamas," said James.

"I bought some. I told you. That was when I saw Thea. I told you that, too."

"Thea sends her love," said Amy. "I saw her today, finally." *In your flat*, she thought.

"Really?" said Archie. He closed his eyes and saw her across the street, through the taxi window, waving. "I thought she was you," he said, and as he said it he knew he had a temporary dispensation to speak carelessly.

James thrust a carrier bag at him.

"I bought you some grapes."

Amy grabbed them off him and put the bag on the side table.

"Thea would love to see you, when you come out," she said, feeling generous.

"I am coming out, then?" said Archie.

"Of course you're coming out," said Amy, "and we want you to stay with us for a bit."

"I don't think so," said Archie. "It's very kind of you."

"You can't look after yourself," said Amy.

"I always have so far," he said. Archie felt he was floating above himself. He knew his detachment was drug induced but it was heady.

There was a knock on the door, and the nurse put her head around.

"Can I have a word, Mrs. Marsham?"

Amy looked uncertain, shrugged her shoulders, and followed the nurse out.

"They do look very alike, though, don't they?" said Archie. "I'd forgotten."

"They do," said James. He lowered his voice as he said it. He felt a conspirator.

He sat on a chair beside the bed, rummaged in the plastic bag, and pulled off some grapes.

"Do you want one?"

Archie shook his head and James put a couple in his mouth.

"You don't mind if I do?"

Archie smiled and shook his head again.

"I don't want to be rude," he said. "But I'd rather go home when I leave. I'll be fine."

"Okay," said James. "Don't blame you. The kids are a pain in the arse."

Amy reappeared. She looked puzzled and irritated.

"It's Ma," she said. "She's fainted or fallen or something. I'm going to have to go over."

James stood up, swallowing his grapes. He took a stem out of his mouth.

"Is she all right?"

"Yes, and Grace is there. You stay here with Archie. I'll ring you."

She bent over Archie and kissed him.

"Sorry about this, Arch. I'll come back tomorrow. You're sure you're okay?"

"No problem," said Archie, almost asleep again.

"This would happen now," said Amy. She looked cross again. "Lucy's timing. Do you think it's attention seeking?"

"Jealous of me, is she?" said Archie.

Amy smiled. "I'd better go."

As the door closed behind her, James sat down again. His hand moved toward the grapes, but he pulled it back. Archie was staring upward. His attention was fixed on the briefcase, which stood on the chest against the wall. It was a soft leather one, given to him when he left school by his maternal grandfather. He remembered that his father used to call the old man "the Mississippi snake oil salesman," yet another way of belittling his mother. But his grandpa, like his mother, was dead now. And so might he be soon. He could hear his grandpa's voice, the soft Southern accent that it had been hard to feel was related to him. He waved his hand as if in greeting toward the chest where the briefcase stood and realized his anesthetic, or his painkillers, or both, were starting to wear off.

"I'll put the TV on, shall I?" said James, attempting to interpret his signal.

The wisdom of this seemed to Archie, at that moment, the answer he'd been seeking. As James pressed the remote, unleashing sound and color into the room, the universe cohered for him. He sat up slowly, while James adjusted his pillows and his drip stand.

"That's much better," said Archie. He picked up the remote himself and began to surf the channels.

༃

THEA was almost home in any case when she got the call from Grace. Richard had insisted on driving her after James had arrived, finally, at the hospital. She'd been very pleased to see her brother-in-law, who'd greeted her like a prodigal daughter, but she thought he seemed weary beneath his bonhomie.

"Lucy's been taken ill," she said to Richard, who looked in her direction and then quickly away as a cyclist swerved in front of him. He braked hard.

"Fuck me," he said. "That was close."

"It's not serious," said Thea, her hand on the dashboard to brace herself. "It doesn't sound serious. The doctor's there."

"I hope not," said Richard. "That it's not serious, I mean. It's been quite an afternoon." The traffic was quiet as he dropped Thea off. The brief storm had barely cleared the air, which hung still and warm. It was hard to imagine Archie in his hospital bed, or Lucy needing medical attention. Illness seemed unseasonal, it felt a winter thing, unlit in the imagination. His own father had died at Christmas, or just before. Richard had been on his way home, and if he'd started out just a couple of hours earlier, he would have been there when it happened. Everyone told him there was nothing he could have done, nothing to say, but he wished he'd been there all the same. He pushed the thought from his mind and filled it instead with the image of Thea on Archie's bed only hours before, a picture that produced a combination of satisfaction and desire. But its eroticism was outshone by the other memory, of him sitting in the car with both the sisters, the dark rain hammering down on them. That had seemed the more perfect moment.

❧

As Lucy watched all three of her daughters move quietly in and out of her sitting room, walking through the flat in a harmony she hadn't witnessed for years, she knew the game was up. The doctor had been and gone, pronouncing her in no great danger. He'd also asked her if she'd had some kind of shock. "Yes," she'd said. "I found out that an old friend had died." "I'm sorry to hear that," he'd said, and left. It was true, she thought, in more ways than one. Michael's call and Jenny's death, these had been shocks; but it had been when the lift door had opened into the flat and she'd seen Sam standing with roses in his arms that she'd felt the past surge forward and stake its intention to stay.

She could hear Thea and Amy talking in the kitchen, their voices low against the tinkling of spoons and plates. Grace appeared in the doorway, her absurdly short skirt covered by her mother's kitchen apron so that she looked naked beneath it.

"Do you want sugar on your strawberries, Ma?" she said.

"No, thank you, darling," said Lucy. "They really should be sweet enough."

"They need sugar," said Grace. "I'll put a teaspoonful on for you."

I'm losing control, thought Lucy. *Well, so be it. What's a spoonful of sugar? What's a bunch of white roses, come to that?* But she knew that both were precious, that both were tokens of love, and as she closed her eyes briefly she wept for both her selves who lay now merged together on the sofa in preparation for their future.

SHE woke from a doze and could hear the sound of water gushing from the hose upstairs; she wondered which one of them had remembered to water the garden. And if the daughter who remembered had taken the action or ordered it. As she lay on her dusky pink sofa listening to the running water, it occurred to her that the rain and her own earlier efforts had made the watering superfluous. There was still a hum of voices next door in the kitchen, a comforting childhood sound, though the family roles were now reversed.

Years ago, when the twins were small, and before her affair, she'd sat talking to Tom at a small rusty table they kept on the flagstones outside the back garden door. This image was filled for her with their self-satisfaction: two beautiful daughters, an existence screened from unpleasantness or torment. Their talk was inconsequential—Tom's day at the law firm, their friends, and their delight in the smallest of school triumphs brought home by the twins. She'd heard a sneeze and looked upward to the window of the room above, where the girls, she'd thought, were asleep. Tom had followed her eyes and together they saw two dark heads at the open frame, looking down.

"Don't stop," Thea had called down, half whispering, "don't stop talking."

"You should both be in bed," Tom had said.

"In a minute," Thea had replied. "We like listening to you."

"It's like a story." Amy's voice had chimed in. "Like the stories you used to read us before we were big."

Lucy felt now, as she had then, a sudden shadow, an encroachment on the evening light. It had been the last time in her life she could remember a happiness uncomplicated by passion or calculation.

She guessed it was the twins still talking in the kitchen, and that it was Grace who had been sent upstairs to water the garden, or perhaps she'd volunteered to escape potential friction. But as their conversation drifted through, it sounded intimate and agreeable. She was pleased to hear the harmony, though she'd long since relinquished any authority over their quarrels. For twenty years, Lucy had regarded family squabbles as far too enervating to enter into. She had smiled her way instead, through the twins' grating separation. But now, lying down on a hot August evening, she was troubled by her long passivity. Poor Thea, for one thing, steaming off to America to escape them. Lucy's eyes moved involuntarily under her eyelids. She saw a part of herself walking back and forth, pacing out the rights and wrongs she'd avoided for years. How tiring it was, she thought, to be so unsure, to relinquish her faith in the best of all possible worlds. It gave her headaches and raised her blood pressure; it made her anxious. But she could see, in the half-drawn pictures her mind threw forward, that these symptoms admitted a fresh humanity, and she opened her eyes briefly. She could hear two sets of footsteps tread up the spiral staircase and felt grateful that all three of her daughters were up on the roof, in her bower, safe among the flowers. Her doze deepened, and the pictures receded as she slept.

❧

"This is a bit like being back at school," said Archie. "You and me, hanging out, watching TV." He was feeling really much better now, clearer-headed if still detached. There were fourteen messages on his phone—word had somehow got out—and although he hadn't read or listened to any of them, he was cheered by their number and thought perhaps he'd been foolish this difficult week to have isolated himself from most of his friends. James had pulled the chair up close next to him and had his feet up on the bed.

"More like university, I'd say," said James. "I don't remember watching telly in bed at school, remind me."

"We did once. When you broke your leg and you came back from the hospital, and talked Fairbrother into bringing us the little portable, and we watched England play Germany."

"We lost," said James.

"Of course we did." Archie was scathing. He shifted in his bed and winced.

"Are you okay?" said James.

"Yes. But I'm going to need a leak soon."

"Shall I get the nurse?"

"No. Not yet." Archie wasn't keen to initiate the process, but James was oblivious to the medical detail.

"Fairbrother's dead," James said. "I saw it in the paper."

Archie picked up the remote and switched channels away from the white-water rafting they'd settled on as the best option available.

"Shame," he said. "He was okay." He was surprised at this new information, but at a distance. A proper response was not quite in his grasp tonight.

"End of an era," said James. "He was old school, I suppose," he smiled at the unintentional pun, "a dying breed. He always—"

"For God's sake, James, not now," said Archie. "Perhaps you better had get the nurse."

"Sorry," James heaved himself out of his chair, "I didn't mean . . . I wasn't going to tell you but then you mentioned him. I thought you'd want to know." He put his head around the door. The corridor was empty and silent. He had expected a bustle, a sense of mission and importance to fill its length.

"It's deserted," he said, turning back into the room. "Haven't you got a bell or something? Yes, you have, look, here." James took a step toward the bed and pressed the red buzzer on the wall. Nothing registered, no sound, no pressure. He wondered how you'd know if it was working.

"It's weird here," said James. "You'd think there'd be more action."

"It's private," said Archie.

"Perhaps they drug the patients."

"Clients," said Archie.

The word made James think of Patrick.

"I'm seeing a shrink," he heard himself say. "Don't laugh."

Archie closed his eyes.

"A shrink," he said, when he opened them again. He had a sense of information swimming by in small shoals, that he was in some sort of aquarium.

It was the corridor that had forced the confidence. It had seemed to stretch away into the future, away from all that was close.

"It's, er, it's stupid really," James said. "I can't use the lifts at work."

Archie flicked the remote back to the white-water rafting.

"That's surreal," he said.

"Bad timing," said James.

"No, no. Not bad at all. Interesting, in fact. And I'd rather talk about that than talk about me, or Fairbrother." Archie was starting to register an irregular surge, a worry that was creeping around his chest. And pressing on his groin. There was a knock on the door and the blond nurse appeared, a bedpan in her hands.

"You must be psychic," said Archie.

"I was right, then?" she asked. He nodded. She bustled around him.

"You'll excuse us a moment, won't you?" she said, smiling at James.

"Of course, of course," he said. "Sorry," and scuttled from the room.

Out in the corridor, James felt that he could be in space as the glimpse into pure isolation repeated itself. He strode down toward the waiting area, willing himself to fill it, and sat down on a chair that looked brand new.

It suited his mood in some ways, he thought, to sit here. He felt himself to be in some kind of limbo, but at the same time he was impatient. He wanted to push his way through whatever came next. He hadn't really wanted to sleep with his wife's sister, or anyone else for that matter, he'd just wanted, for once, to see what would happen if he tried. He knew he was a reasonable man, but for the first time in his life he was excited by a moral ambiguity. He felt sudden compassion for the many foolish actions his friends had put before him over the years. He could see their follies now for what they were, a probing for signs of life, proofs against death or a moribund existence.

"All clear."

The voice echoed toward him down the corridor, and then the nurse's blond head popped around the corner, as if her body had been parked much further back.

James jumped to his feet. He felt she might see through him, this pretty woman who burrowed in blood and piss every day and came up smiling.

"He's almost himself again now," she said.

"Oh, right, thanks. Is he, er . . . ?"

"I don't know," she said. "The consultant will be in first thing. Don't stay too late."

James opened the door without knocking. Archie looked almost cheerful.

"I've still got two," he said.

"Two what?"

"Balls."

"That's good."

Archie looked at him. "But one of them might not be real."

James was confused. He wasn't sure that Archie had explained this part to him. "But you were expecting them to take one off?"

"They might have put in a new one."

"A new one?" James's hand moved toward the grapes but all that was left were stalks.

"Never mind," said Archie, "let's not talk about it. You were saying, about the shrink?"

James thought he'd forgotten.

"It's nothing, just a phobia. Temporary."

"Why a shrink?" said Archie.

"This guy at work suggested him, an American."

"Ah," said Archie. "Like me."

"It worked for him," said James. "What do you mean, like you?"

"Did he have trouble with lifts? Or 'elevators' as we Americans say."

"I don't think so. You mean 'Americans' as in your mother?"

"So what does he think it is, the shrink?" said Archie.

James stood up and went to look out of the window. There were still people working in the office opposite. It wasn't that high up. They could probably all use the stairs.

"God knows. My mother, my wife, my dick."

Archie held his hand over his crotch above the bed covers.

"Don't make me laugh," he said.

James turned and smiled at him.

"You may think it's funny," he said, "but I'm exhausted. Twelve flights at least twice a day, and usually four times. And it's not even that. What if it gets worse? What if I can't do the Tube or planes?"

"What does Amy say?"

"I haven't told her."

Archie stopped smiling and frowned. He'd forgotten about the gaping blackness he'd glimpsed beneath the two of them, and he didn't want to consider it now.

"I didn't want to worry her."

"So you went to a shrink instead," said Archie. "I don't get that. Unless . . ."

"No, it's not what you think," said James.

Archie looked at him. "I don't think anything, mate," he said. "It's what you think." He picked up the remote and aimed it at the TV screen without actually changing a channel.

James took it from him.

"The shrink says it's what you can't think yourself that matters," he said, flicking through the numbers methodically.

"Hmm," said Archie. "That's a bit deep for me. Stop, go back. It's *Bridewell Wharf.* Let's watch it. Let's watch Grace."

"Okay," said James. "I can live with that."

꒰ꙫ꒱

"I'M going to go, if that's okay," said Grace as the twins emerged onto the roof terrace. "I'm going to meet Sam."

"Fine," said Thea. "I take it you've made things up."

"Yes. For now anyway." She put down the watering can and ran her hands under the hose, wiping them dry on the jeans she'd changed into. "Ring me if there's any problem with Ma."

"There won't be," Amy said. "She just needs a good night's sleep."

The three of them stood together, tall women rising above the blanket of flowers, Grace's fair skin a contrast with her sisters'. She put her arms around their necks and hugged them to her. "I'm so glad you're both here," she said, "that we're all here, together."

"That we're speaking to each other, you mean," said Thea, but she smiled as she said it.

They watched her disappear from view, her red head winding around as she descended the stairs.

"I suppose I should go home soon," said Amy. "I could stay if you want?" She sat herself down in Lucy's white wicker chair and put her feet up on a stool. Her sister was watching her with an expression she found hard to define—concerned, perhaps even compassionate.

"No need," said Thea. "Ma seems much better. Don't you think?"

"Yes, but . . ."

"Go home. Rest. It's been quite a day. For everyone." But she could see that Amy was reluctant to leave, that she felt there was more to say.

"Look," Thea spoke softly, "I want to say I'm sorry. Again. What I said, about you and Archie, in the flat. It was in the heat of the moment."

Amy found it difficult to look at her directly.

"I know," she said, "but the thing is—we can't duck it. When you and Archie . . . it's hard to explain . . . in one way, I think it took a bit of James away from me."

Thea bent her head to inhale the smell of a large pot of lilies, but their decadent sweetness forced her back.

"And Archie had always been so much a part of us," Amy went on, "that I'd come to rely on him. I've needed him, for the excitement in our lives, I suppose."

Her words seemed to form in spite of her, Thea thought, as if they would no longer be contained.

"Not that James isn't fun, but Archie was always wilder than us, especially since the children, so much more buccaneer, flying off for weekends, everything such a good story, and he brought it all back to me. I suppose it made me feel special."

Thea listened to her sister. She'd often imagined the confession she was hearing. She'd wondered how it might sound, what form it would take. Now it was here, she knew that it was no more Amy's fault that things hadn't worked out with Archie than it was hers. It had been a mistake to play so close to each other. They could agree on that.

"I suppose," she found herself saying, "that he and I might be paying a price for all that now."

"Whatever do you mean?" Amy sounded shocked. "It's not his fault he's ill."

"Not that. I didn't mean that," Thea said. She sat down on the stool in front of her sister's chair, anxious to explain. "I meant, maybe he's been running around all these years, afraid of what will happen when he stops."

Amy smiled at her sister.

"A bit like you, you mean?"

"Yes. Exactly. So it suited me, too, for a while, to be part of it, and I suppose I thought for a moment that life could be like that forever."

Amy sighed and looked away. "I hated it," she said, "if I'm honest."

"Don't I know it," said Thea. "It was too close to home, but perhaps home was what I was after."

"It's what you want now?"

"Home, yes. Not Archie."

It was still warm on the roof, though fresh after the rain, with an earthy smell rising from the sodden pots, and everything seemed possible again. She pressed her foot against Amy's and felt her sister push back against her, both their chairs sliding backward across the slate tiles, each staring at the other till their legs were fully extended. They were like two dolls, Thea thought, cut from folded paper, joined at their extremities. Each was a part of the other; it was absurd to deny it.

"You should go," said Thea. "Get some rest."

"It's cool here," said Amy, "and this garden is so much nicer than mine."

"It's like a hothouse, it's almost too much."

"I like it," Amy insisted.

Thea didn't press her point. She noticed she didn't even want to.

"Whatever are the two of you doing?" Lucy's head emerged above the staircase. She was wearing her kimono pulled around her, her pale gray hair tucked behind her ears. She looked like a younger woman, made up old for a movie. It was the way she moved, thought Thea. They both sat up, swinging their legs off the stool.

"You should be in bed, Ma," said Amy.

"Soon," said Lucy. "But I want to talk to you first. There's something I feel I must tell you."

2004

PATRICK CHECKED HIS watch as he walked up the steps to the front door, shiny black and newly painted, his plaque cleaned and almost sharp in the weak setting sun. It was just after four on a Friday afternoon, the last appointment of the day. He'd forced himself out of the building, determined not to be drawn to the window; not to be caught again waiting, wrong-footed before they began. She was sitting on the oak armchair outside his door on the first-floor landing, reading a book, and looked up only as he approached. He should not have agreed to her coming back.

"I'm late, I apologize," he said.

"You're reluctant to see me, I suppose," she answered. "This is the last time, I promise."

He opened the door and gestured for her to enter before him. She was wearing a smart red jacket and more makeup than usual. She looked relaxed and oddly festive, as if today was special. He'd agreed to see her only on the condition that she contacted a colleague for the future. This afternoon was to be their last, a sort of disengagement.

As she eased into the chair, her air of celebration faded, and she seemed more subdued than she had on the previous occasions. "How are you?" she asked.

He smiled at her and said nothing. Then, after a moment, he relented. "And how have you been?" he said.

"It's only two days since I was here," she said.

"A lot can happen in two days," said Patrick. "You should know."

She laughed, but he thought that a resolution had crept into her voice.

"I'll just go on, shall I?"

Her words were not really a question, and he nodded.

"We went, James and me, to see Archie in the hospital," she began. "We were oddly happy that evening, in spite of it all. I'm not sure if we really believed that he could die of this thing, but when we saw him alone in his room, we were taken aback by how vulnerable he seemed, and we knew, I think, that things had already changed and would never be quite the same. It wasn't just Archie, of course, but he seemed at that moment to be holding the center of the chaos we were in. He was the eye of the storm, so to speak."

She crossed her arms and hugged them to her, trying to fold herself inward.

"But it made us feel closer, the caring for Archie, despite the secrets and my mother, and . . ."

"Your mother," said Patrick, reluctant to pass up a familial opening, even though the clock was ticking. He sensed she was anxious to proceed, to get her business done and leave. She wanted to unburden herself, to justify herself, but not, he suspected, to him. She said she'd come to him looking for something, information perhaps, but it seemed more likely that she wanted to offer it up, to trade it for her freedom.

"We'd known, of course, vaguely, about her affair, though not the details. But she'd convinced herself that we knew nothing."

"We're talking about you and your sisters?"

"Well, me and Thea really. Grace was too young."

"But it must have been difficult," said Patrick, "for you, at the time?"

Her smile disappeared in both irritation and pain.

"I suppose it's part of your job to state the obvious," she said. Patrick recoiled behind his still exterior and reminded himself that he'd set this up by agreeing to see her and that after today he would be unlikely to see her again.

"I'm sorry," she said. "That was rude. But I've thought about it over and over, whether I mind, whether I'm angry with her, but I seem not to be."

Patrick almost laughed at her willful denial but said nothing, and she turned her head to look out into the darkening sky.

"Lucy's turned it into a fairy tale, of course. And now they're married, in fact, and it is a romantic story, don't you think? Getting together again after two decades." Amy smiled up at him, willing him to forgive her and agree. "She's been so good to me these last years. We're so much closer than we were; I suppose we have more in common."

"But it was painful for you?" he said, refusing to allow her to blow him off course.

"Yes," she said, more obliging now. "We knew. We heard things, and my father, he was so sad. And then he died, and she thought it was her fault, and I suppose it sort of was."

She was creeping toward something, and he felt the need to avoid sudden noise, a breaking of metaphorical twigs underfoot. There was a silence, and he sensed her about to veer down a different path.

"You feel it was her fault?" he asked, hoping she would hold to her line for once.

"No. Not really. But she thought so. She definitely did. She cracked up, I told you. And I didn't understand it for years."

"But you said—your words were, it sort of was her fault, your mother's fault."

"Fault, blame, guilt, punishment, all that stuff, that's what happens when someone dies, isn't it?" she said. "And it's true and not true. You kill people in your heart. You wish for a split second that they were dead. And then you have to live with it."

"That's what happened to your mother?" he asked her as she raised herself out of her fetal position, uncoiling like a waking bird.

"That's what happened to us both," she said.

JAMES LET HIMSELF into the silent house. Two days without the children, and the novelty of their absence had subsided. They had taken a part of life with them, and he wanted it back. He'd spoken to them on the phone before he'd left the office; they'd been excited by a day on the beach with Grandpa, thrilled to hear his voice, to tell him about their discoveries and small adventures with crabs and shells and excitable dogs. Then they'd told him they loved him, in the way that children do, as an automatic part of saying good night or good-bye, seemingly untaught in their spontaneity. But they had, of course, been taught; the surprise was that the lesson was learned so completely, as if they'd merely been reminded of some instinct they'd temporarily mislaid and would mislay time and again as their lives went on.

He opened up the back doors, poured himself a glass of wine, and sat out in the garden, realizing he was hungry but too lazy to do anything about it. He'd watched Archie try to eat a plate of food earlier, and his mind had run across the notion of condemned men and hearty breakfasts, even though the meal concerned was a plate of chicken and rice. Now that Archie was in the hospital it was easier to digest the idea that he might be seriously ill. The shock had gone, replaced by helplessness; something else for Patrick, he thought.

He didn't entirely buy Patrick's line, he'd decided, but he liked him. If Patrick could just get over his predictability, the shrinking would be almost viable. Patrick should come off piste with him, derail for ten minutes or so instead of plodding ever backward to the family grail. Shrinkage should get flexible like everything else. It was oddly conservative in its position, he thought, like a business theory, once radical, that had long gone bust. But despite these observations, when he sat in the big chair, sharing his thoughts, James felt himself to be a great deal more interesting than he had for some time.

He noticed something lying on the grass in the semidarkness, toward the back edge of the lawn, and he stood up to investigate. As he strolled across, glass in hand, he felt expansive, pumped up with a fresh concentration that encompassed his home and all that it represented. It encompassed his beautiful wife, his City life, his expensive children, and now it encompassed a small dead black rabbit, half eaten, one fogged eye turned upward, that lay at his feet on the grass.

WHEN Amy reached home she found her husband quietly weeping. He stood up as she entered the kitchen and put his arms around her, clinging to her tightly.

"It's only a rabbit," she said, with the foresight to know that its death would be a short interruption in her children's exuberant flow.

James blew his nose hard on a piece of paper towel. She hadn't seen the rabbit's remains, she hadn't shoveled it into a hole. She hadn't sucked its grisly end into her brave new world as he had.

"It was Peter," he said.

Amy wanted to laugh.

"Yes, darling," she said.

"It must have been a fox, or maybe a rat."

"A rat?"

"Probably not a rat," James said quickly.

"Not nice, whatever it was," said Amy.

The remark made James think, for some reason, of Archie. Not nice. Not nice what was happening to him. But it might be all right. He still had a chance. But the rabbit . . . He put his arms around her again and pressed his buffed nose in her soft hair, her sweet familiar smell mixing with the new taste of salt water, still foreign on his lips.

"I love you," he said.

"And I love you," she said, "and I'm going to cook you steak and fried potatoes."

His face was relaxed now, and his features seemed young again as he smiled at her. She could see their son in him, in how easy it was to restore his nature, to snap him back to his equilibrium.

"And we won't talk about Archie," she went on. "Because there's nothing more we can do for now." She held him close. She would tell him about the baby, of course; she wanted to, but she wanted it to be special. She would save it till tomorrow. He was too upset, and she had had enough confession for one night.

⟡

A nurse whom Archie hadn't seen before knocked and entered his room. He was sitting up in bed, fully awake now, his supper tray finished on the table beside him. It was late, about ten, but he was waiting for his consultant who, to accommodate an early morning operating schedule, had changed his plans and would now call at the hospital on his way home tonight. His heart fluttered and his stomach churned. He could almost be waiting for a woman he wanted. But not this woman in her pale blue buttoned-through dress. He barely looked at her as she straightened his sheets and smiled banalities at him. He'd eaten his supper, that was good. The sun would shine again tomorrow, she added, and no forecast for rain. Would he like the window open wider? She lifted his tray and moved to leave the room. And the doctor was on his way. She'd seen him come through reception just moments ago.

Now that he knew the time had come, the churning subsided. Archie felt himself slipping back into a braced resignation. He thought of James and Amy in Finlay Road. He pictured his flat, empty apart from ghostly images of Thea and Greta floating through it. He saw his office, his old office now, occupied by a skeleton staff in a decimated limbo. Were these the four points of his compass? If so, his world had shrunk very small. Though it might be, he thought, that it had been this size for some time and he'd just never noticed; perspective was relative, particularly from a hospital bed.

There was a short knock on the door, and almost at once a large man, dressed in a suit, was at his bedside.

"Good evening, good evening."

Archie cringed. The repetition of the greeting felt uneasy. The surgeon pulled the bedside chair to an angle and sat down facing Archie, his hands folded between his knees. His expression was warm but detached. Archie wanted to hold the moment in suspension, for the man not to speak. This man had power; he had entered his body, his intimate parts, but Archie couldn't remember his name.

"Don't look so worried," said the stranger. "It's good news after all."

Archie stared through him. He hadn't allowed himself to prepare for this.

"Absolutely no sign of cancer or precancerous cells, just a growth, quite benign. We did an analysis in theater and it's been sent off to the lab for confirmation, but there's no problem, I assure you."

Archie let out his breath. The surgeon was still speaking, elaborating on his reprieve. He thought for a moment he was going to cry.

"Quite a relief, eh?" said the surgeon.

"Well, yes," said Archie. "Yes, a relief. I . . ."

He couldn't think what to say.

"Now. Let's just have a quick look to check the wound."

The surgeon pulled back the bedcovers and raised the blue gown. Archie remembered suddenly that he was called Mr. Graham and that he was a truly marvelous man, and he wondered if he would ever now get to wear the pajamas that still sat in his old briefcase. His life began to flash by him, his mother in the forefront against a whirring context of forty years. This was supposed to happen when you died, not when you got a stay of execution.

"That's looking nice and clean," said the surgeon, reinstating the bedclothes and standing up. He seemed to be conducting a routine. Archie expected him to look at his watch next, but he didn't.

"You can go home tomorrow, I should think, Mr. Morgan."

"Thank you," said Archie. "Thank you. I, I . . . ." *And I'll never complain about anything ever again,* he wanted to add, but didn't.

He sat speechless in his bed. There was no one to speak to in any case. And he knew that even if there were, the words wouldn't come.

2004

IT WAS TIME to leave now. He looked through the glass at the blackness and was shocked, as always, by the dark expanse of a seeming nothing between him and the lights on the other side of Central Park. The vast apartment was silent, though he wasn't alone. There was a maid who slept in, on the floor below, their only house staff apart from a secretary who had gone ahead to London with his wife. Archie turned around and looked over the clean and polished surfaces of his life. He liked the feel of it. He liked the newness and perfection of everything. Even the antiques that were scattered among the contemporary design were immaculately restored. He'd enjoyed these last years in New York, his mother's country. It was his home, and he wanted to reassure himself that he would be back soon.

He tipped the doorman as he left the building and climbed into the large and comfortable car that would take him to JFK. He was a rich man now, though it was true that he'd never been poor, and New York had been good to him. But Archie knew he had come to New York to escape, to flee from the aftermath of that terrible week, a week that seemed in memory to have existed for years before it finally happened.

He watched the buildings, then the bridge speed by as the car crossed the river, and he realized, with relief, that until this summons to London for the wedding, the past hadn't troubled him for quite some time. He sat back in the warm darkness, the smooth motion of the car interrupted almost imperceptibly by the changing lights and turns. He'd been angry, he remembered, a natural reaction, they said, but one that seemed cold and abnormal to him. He'd been so happy, he felt cheated.

THE flight was delayed by thirty minutes, and he sat in the first-class lounge with a glass of champagne that he'd picked up more out of habit than desire. The relative puritanism of New York had come to suit him, and these days he rarely drank. As he sat looking at a copy of *Newsweek* he felt apprehensive. This was a special return. They'd been back to London many times over the years and seen their friends and family, of course. They'd been to the christenings of the children and spent Christmas there from time to time, but this trip would mark more than its purpose.

"ARCHIE!" A voice called out his name, then again, louder, excited. "Archie!"

He was walking across the concourse toward the gate, and he turned to locate the sound.

"Archie! Here!"

Then he saw her, and the sight of her made him smile, and the darker thoughts that had hovered about him receded. She was tanned and smiling, her dark hair, flecked with gray, was scraped back from her face.

"I thought you were already in London. Are we on the same flight?" she asked him. "That's marvelous. Though I suppose you, fat cat, are in first class. Bahram and I are in economy, back of the bus, I'm afraid."

"Thea." He looked around, as if anxious to locate someone who was lost.

"Bahram's gone to get some water. He's just over there." She pointed in the direction of the shopping mall, and, as she did so, a short skinny figure emerged, dressed in jeans and a light jacket, a man of about forty who passed in the distance for a boy.

"Bahram," she said, as he approached, "look, it's Archie. We're all on our way."

She put her hand on Archie's arm. "You're looking well. Very young and handsome."

"Good genes," said Archie, "and a full head of hair. Where have you sprung from?"

"Belize. But our flight was delayed." It was Bahram who spoke now, his English slightly inflected. "The TB program down there."

Archie looked perplexed.

"I thought you were in Guatemala," he said.

"We were," said Thea. "Keep up."

He smiled. It was hard to keep up with them, harder still sometimes to equate this contented woman with the troubled girl he'd once known.

1994

"NATURE ABHORS A VACUUM."

from *Lifelines for Spring* by Lucy Fielding

IT WAS A late start for James that morning. Amy had left early to shop for tomorrow and then go down to the hospital as she had promised. He sat out in the garden drinking tea and savoring the peace of his last childless day, but the arrival of the cleaning lady shattered his solitude, and he decided to walk down to Marylebone station, to enjoy the morning's freshness, which would thicken soon, he thought; it would go off, like stale milk.

As he walked through the streets and crossed the busy main road at the traffic lights by the American school, he saw children playing softball in the yard, some holiday event, and he thought of his own children who would be back tomorrow. As he pictured them, laughing together, an image of Lucy seemed to float up above them, kind, but immensely sad.

"AND then she started to cry," Amy had told him as he sat in the kitchen the night before, watching her as she cooked for him. "Ma. Crying." She said it with such a breezy dispassion that James had almost wept again on Lucy's behalf. It was such a sad story, this story of love, universal in its facts of adultery and guilt.

"But really, it was wonderful," Amy went on. "She was this real person for once. I know you think I'm hard on her, but when you know, like we did, that she was really always in there, it's infuriating."

James had heard this complaint many times before.

"We knew there'd been someone, but we thought that Dad didn't know. And we'd no idea it had gone on for so long."

"Grace?" said James. "She's not . . . ?"

"No, she's not Michael's. That's his name. They stopped it and then she got pregnant, and she thought it would be all right but then it started up again. Can you believe it? After another baby with Dad? I just wish she'd told us before."

"She must have loved him. Michael, I mean," said James. He looked at Amy as she chivied the fried potatoes, and he felt an overwhelming gratitude for the simple fact of loving his wife.

"And he loved her, too," said Amy. "He wanted her to leave Dad, but she wouldn't, so he took a job abroad, to try to save their marriages."

"And now he's come back?"

"Yes. And I don't know whether to be pleased for Ma or whether to hate him."

"Pleased for her?"

James couldn't get the dead rabbit out of his head. Amy left her cooking to settle and sat down beside him at the kitchen table.

"Thea and I think he's come back for her."

"What?"

"Well, his wife's died. They're both free now."

"That sounds like romantic tosh to me," he said. "It was twenty years ago. What does your mother think?"

"She thinks he's come for her, too, to make it right. That's what he said."

"To make it right?"

JAMES had been confused by this statement the previous evening, and it was no clearer to him now on this bright sunny morning as he walked past the eclectic collection of villas that lined the streets of St. John's Wood. On reflection, James thought, he did know one thing. It was easier to keep things right than make them so later; easier to stay on track, if life would let you.

❧

WHEN Lucy wanted to divert her thoughts from things that might color them dark, she devoted herself to the terraces of pots and artificial beds that made up her roof garden. There were over two hundred plants blooming four floors up above the streets of Kensington and twenty or so small trees. Once a week a young gardener came in to keep things spruce and tidy, but for the most part it was solely her creation and her joy. Today she knew without a doubt that she must prune and weed, repot and plant until her mind had fully absorbed what she had started last night. The kitchen in which she was standing was merely a pit stop en route to full immersion.

Thea was poaching eggs, but just as a second yolk burst its sac, the phone interrupted their silence.

"Oh, fuck it," she said, not sure if she meant the eggs or phone or both. She heard the answering machine click on and Richard's voice enter the kitchen they stood in, but neither of them moved to answer.

"Hello, it's Richard. Just ringing to check that you're all okay. I'm in the office. Give me a call."

She felt confused as she took the pan off the heat and threw the spreading eggs down the waste disposal.

"I broke the eggs," said Thea. "I'll do some more."

"Nice boy," said Lucy. "Not right for you, though, darling."

Thea banged the saucepan back on the stove. She knew she agreed with this assessment, that despite the madness of the previous day Richard was part of a life she was leaving behind, but it wasn't for her mother to say so.

"I'll just have some toast, if that's all right," said Lucy. "I really must get on upstairs."

Thea now took in her mother's dress. Two years' absence had made her slow to pick up Lucy's signals.

"You're supposed to be taking it easy today, Ma. It's too hot up there to work."

"Just a couple of hours," said Lucy, "before the sun gets going."

Thea shook her head in disbelief, then wondered if Lucy had submerged already what she'd told them the night before. That surely wasn't possible. But Lucy's capacity for creating reality afresh might well have parked it temporarily out of reach.

"Last night . . . ," Thea began.

Lucy moved toward a cupboard door and reached inside among the cups and plates.

"There's nothing more to tell, really," said Lucy, her face hidden from Thea. "I know it must have come as a shock."

"Well, no," said Thea, "not a shock exactly. We told you, we sort of knew."

Her mother emerged from behind the cupboard door. She seemed relaxed but far away.

"One always imagines children don't see these things," she said.

"Ma, you had a breakdown."

It was the first time Thea had used the word. Lucy turned to her full on.

"Yes," she said, entirely present now. To Thea's dismay, her eyes looked tearful. "I suppose that's what it was."

Thea resisted the impulse to be cruel. Her mother's vulnerability frightened her. She wanted to shake her and ask her why she thought she'd left the house in an ambulance all those years ago, why she'd spent three months in a mental institution, why she'd left them with their tiny sister and their mad aunts. Did she think she'd been on holiday? Instead she took the cup from Lucy's hand and filled it with tea from the large pot that stood on the table.

Bʏ the time Amy arrived at the hospital to keep her promised appointment, she had lost her composure. She had been confident of her strength, sure that whatever happened to Archie she would rise to his comfort. She saw that she had imagined herself heroic, a tender support to him and perhaps a fighter on his behalf against a medical profession that would see him only as a statistic in its research. But this fantasy deserted her as she walked through the hospital doors. What was she to say to him? What did anyone say in such circumstances? There should be a book or a guide on how to deal with serious conditions. All words seemed loaded and misplaced; it was too easy to be glib or offend.

She found herself quite quickly at the door of his room, so focussed on the question of her demeanor that she couldn't recall taking the lift or walking down the corridor. She shook her head, shocked by this self-absorption. Whatever she experienced, she told herself, its intensity would be so much greater for Archie.

Hᴇ was standing up, facing the window when she entered, his hands on each side of the sill, staring into the office across the street. He turned to face her, back lit by the morning sun, dressed in his clothes, hair brushed. He smiled at her, transfigured in some way she couldn't place, illuminated within as well as without.

"Hi," she said. She put her bag down on the bed and walked toward him. His smile had become a grin, radiant and joyful. But he said nothing.

"You look . . . happy?" she said. She reached to kiss him on the cheek, and he folded his arms around her, bending over awkwardly to keep his groin from brushing against her.

"I'm very happy," he said into her ear. "Very lucky, very happy to see you. It's all wonderful. And where's James?"

She looked around the room, over his shoulder, as if to find the source of his elation.

"He's gone to Aylesbury. He told you. He's back later." Then she couldn't keep from asking, "So what did they say?"

"He—he said I'm fine. There's nothing wrong with me. There never was."

"But how come . . . ?"

"Well, there was a thing, a small lump. But they were able to get at a bit of it and test it. He, Mr. Graham, thought they couldn't. Not without removing a testicle. But they could. And it wasn't malignant. They'd thought it was. It rang alarm bells, that's what he said."

He was speaking over her shoulder, and she heard his words at a distance, bouncing off the wall and around the room.

"But that's wonderful news," she said. "The best possible news."

He turned away from her to look out of the window again.

"It's all going on out there," he said. "And they don't know. They don't know how lucky they are. Look at that one, glued to his screen. He keeps looking at his watch as well. He's absolutely no idea."

Amy was apprehensive now. She had thought that bad news would find her wanting, but this heightened state was beyond her fund of empathy. He seemed different, as if someone new had inhabited his body, a powerful stranger she knew but had forgotten and one, to her secret relief, for whom she felt only friendship and curiosity.

"I'll ring James, shall I?" she said. "He'll be so thrilled." She took out the phone, then hesitated. "But I'm not allowed to ring inside the hospital, I don't think." She could use the bedside phone, she supposed, but a few moments outside would allow her to gather her thoughts, digest this unexpected turn of events. "I'd better not. I'll go outside. I'll stand under the window and you can see me. Okay?"

Archie, his back still half turned from her, nodded.

꒰

LUCY lay in her big chair on the roof in the shade, resting from an hour's exertion. She would meet Michael tomorrow. She'd spoken to him again, this morning, and he'd agreed that above all, before considering anything else, they must sort out the truth, after all those years of lies. She'd talked to Amy and Thea and that was one thing, but would Grace forgive her? Grace who'd grown up without her father. She needed to talk to her, to make her understand how special she was, that she'd been a bond of love between Lucy and Tom, even though Lucy had failed, that Tom had forgiven her for Michael, and that it was the weight of her guilt, not her infidelity, that had helped to kill him.

A fly buzzed in her ear and she waved it away, but the sound remained, increasing in volume. She sat up sharply. The voice was calling again. She'd thought it had gone for good now that she'd let this new breeze blow through, but it was back again, even closer to home, calling for her help, and it frightened her.

⟶

IT was hard to believe he was so close to the center of the city. The roads and pavements were almost deserted, and James felt excited by a rare sensation of emptiness and space. It made him feel high while the passing of an occasional car or bus lent a fantasy of walking the streets in a bygone era. It was hard, out here in the freedom of these avenues, to imagine himself in Patrick's chair, to recall the fear that had gripped him as the wretched lift doors seemed to close forever. As he walked along, his suit jacket over his shoulder, his euphoria moved him to think once more of Grace, and he still suffered a small frisson of embarrassment when he recalled yesterday's encounter. Out of the corner of his eye he saw a young man looking for a taxi in the distance and thought, in his reverie, that it might be Sam, the figure had the same fair wavy hair. But as James got closer, he turned full face, and James could see that this boy wasn't nearly so striking. He felt warm toward Sam today; he was pleased to acknowledge him as Grace's choice. He even thought that perhaps he and Sam were alike in some way, and though he could accept the narcissism of his observation, all the same he hoped that Grace would have the wit to see and to settle for it.

He turned into Abbey Road and on toward Lisson Grove and the station. He was beginning to regret the decision to walk as the sun climbed higher, and he watched enviously as a girl across the street glugged from a bottle of water. He would get one at Marylebone, and a newspaper, and coffee. He would enjoy the trip out, the congratulations, the final sealing of the deal.

He heard the barking before he saw the small dog, which seemed to have broken away from its owner and was racing toward him. A woman was shouting something, and he moved quickly to pick up the leash that was flailing in the dog's wake. He looked up in triumph as he clasped it and smiled at the woman, who made him think for some reason of Lucy, though she must have been at least a decade older. Her face was stricken and her hands were waving at him, raised as if to protect him, to warn him, and he never saw the huge car, though he heard it, too late, as it swung in its manic curve out of the mansion block driveway, killing him outright as the dog ran shrieking under its wheels.

2004

═══

THE ROOM WAS silent now. He could hear her breathing, deep and slow. The street light outside the window flickered before it suddenly illuminated one side of the room. He hadn't pulled the blinds, which was unusual. It was his habit to draw them down before the four p.m. session at this time of year. He couldn't account to himself for what she'd just told him. His mind retreated over the landscape laid out over the three separate hours they had spent together, attempting to review its geography, changed like an old map by a new invading army.

"I'll just . . ." he said, getting up out of the chair and turning from her to disguise the shock he felt. She was sitting with her eyes closed, her tears running down her cheeks, her forearms not quite touching the sides of the chair as if the surfaces were unbearably hot.

"I could ask for some tea, if you'd like," he said. She opened her eyes and tried to smile up at him, wiping her face.

"No," she said. "But thank you. That's very kind."

"So he's dead." Patrick needed to say it aloud. He had a sudden inappropriate urge to laugh at the game he'd been caught up in. But he felt overwhelmingly sad, too, and liberated from his professional constraints. He was surprised to be so moved by the death of a man he'd known so briefly and so long ago, but he could see the dark curly head and the smiling face again, perched awkwardly in front of him, too big somehow for that small room. "No wonder," Patrick added quietly, "that he never came back."

"We were taken to see him," she said, "in the hospital, another hospital, Archie and me, that same day. We went together, then he left me, and I sat with James alone. He was lying on a trolley in a room full of machines, but none of them had been able to save him. They'd sort of half tidied him up, done up his shirt, but two of the buttons had come off. His face was untouched, that was the strange thing. There was no sign of what had killed him. You can't imagine the shock of it."

"No," said Patrick. And not just the shock, he thought, but the overwhelming irony, the notion of some fearful mocking fate.

"It was a terrible, terrible time, a terrible time, for months," she said. "For a year at least. And I was pregnant for half of that, though being pregnant sustained me in some degree. The fact that James had gone, for good, didn't sink in till after Charlie was born. And now, when I look back at the events of that week, it seems . . . well, absurd." She was composed again, her glance rueful, and she turned toward him.

"But that's what life is like, don't you find?" She seemed to plead for his agreement. "That's what redeems its inconsequence, that it can defeat your most careful imaginings."

2004

ARCHIE WAS TIRED from the overnight flight, but he had learned from long experience that, after landing, it was wise to keep to the local clock. Now he stood watching from the house as the man and boy parked on the street outside, and thought, as he never failed to do when he saw Richard with James's son, that he was surprised how much fatherhood suited Richard and wondered if he would have managed so well. He saw Charlie run up the steps, and he moved to open the grand front door of his London home. "Hey, Charlie, Richard," he called down the steps. "How are you? Good to see you." He held Charlie to one side of him while he reached out his arm to clasp Richard in a half bear hug. They heard footsteps on the floor above them as Grace appeared, making an entrance down the staircase, and as he kissed her Richard thought how much more beautiful she seemed to become with each year, and he was glad that he'd known her before the success that now made her unapproachable. Her red hair was sleek and shoulder length, and she had a sheen to her that he'd noticed before on the famous. He wondered if it was just the great care they took of themselves, or whether it was something that was lent to them through the adoration of their public.

"Thea has gone over to see Ma," Grace said. "And the good Dr. Hashemian is asleep. I told him not to go to bed. He'll regret it."

Richard smiled. Grace was so very like Amy, in character at least.

"So you're making an honest woman of my sister at last," she said. "It's about time."

Richard laughed. They all knew that he had not been the reluctant party.

"We're delighted for you both, darling," said Grace. "I did try to persuade Archie to be your best man, but . . ."

"He understands," said Archie, who'd thought it was odd of Richard to ask him. They were good friends, brothers-in-law in effect, but the shadow of James was still present even after all these years.

"No problem," Richard turned to Archie and nodded his reassurance. He thought how Americanized Archie had become. It wasn't just the clothes and the haircut, or even the slight intonation in the voice; it was the ease and confidence that he could remember from the time he'd first met him and which he could see now were a part of his inheritance. He still looked up to Archie, still worked alongside him from time to time, and tomorrow they would officially be family. He'd been with Amy for eight years now, and he loved her and still couldn't believe his good luck.

"So, it's all arranged for tonight," Grace went on. "We'll all go together. We're going to pick Amy up on the way." Richard was only half listening to Grace as she outlined their plans, his mind on his wedding tomorrow.

ARCHIE sat down next to Charlie, who was absorbed in a game on his phone. He was mesmerized by the child's likeness to James. He was pleased, really, he thought, that Amy and Richard were tying the knot. He knew it meant that she'd let James go, let him go, too, if he were honest, that the ghost between them was laid to rest. He looked at his wife, who was telling Richard some plan for a holiday they might all take in the spring. He was glad they didn't live here year-round; he would feel too hemmed in by family. He had retrieved himself in the last few years and was happy to be married to Grace most of the time, but there was still a part of him that functioned best alone.

2004

26 NOVEMBER
HARLEY STREET

—

SHE WAS DRINKING the tea that he'd summoned despite her initial refusal. He was grateful for the knock on the door when it came and the carrying in of the tray, which he took from the curious receptionist. Patrick was standing over by the window watching her, waiting, he thought, for the end, the last act of her drama.

"Why couldn't you tell me the truth?" he asked. "The first time you came."

"I thought I'd find out more this way. And I thought if I told you, you'd send me away, that you'd clam up." She thought about it for a moment. "Or perhaps I would," she confessed.

Patrick smiled at her insight. "I might have been more forthcoming, in fact," he said.

"You left a message on James's phone, a few days after he died," she went on. "He hadn't turned up for an appointment, and when I looked in his diary you were there, just that week, nowhere else, and three times he'd been. I never rang you back. I looked you up and saw you were a therapist, and I couldn't believe he hadn't told me. It was Archie who made me forget it. He said it was simple, that James had some phobia about the lifts at work, that it was just a physical thing."

"That's true," said Patrick.

"And that's all?" she said. "If that was all, why didn't he tell me?"

Patrick sighed. He was unclear as to how to proceed.

"It's never all," he said slowly, "and you wouldn't believe me if I said that it was. But you must remember that your husband came to see me just three or four times. And, to be honest, I can't remember very much about it."

"But he must have mentioned me?" she was almost pleading.

"Mentioned, yes," said Patrick. "But if it's any help, in those few short sessions I don't believe your marriage was central. I mean, in question." He doubted this was true, but it was literal.

She stood up and Patrick looked at his watch once more. It wasn't quite time, but he was more than happy if she wanted to go. Instead she began to walk around his room, peering around the blind at the street below. He was disconcerted by her unexpected movements, but it was too late in the proceedings to challenge them.

"The thing is," she said, turning back, "I couldn't marry again, without seeing you first. I had to see how it made me feel. It was like making contact."

Patrick felt uneasy. He hoped she was speaking metaphorically.

"With what?"

"With James's other life, I suppose, the one he lived without me. You must have been the last person he talked to, properly I mean."

Patrick sat for a moment, thinking. He wanted to ask her another question, but that would be unfair. She needed to hear something from him, but he was unsure what he could give her.

"I sit here," he said after a silence, "and I hear people talk to me about their lives, the intimate events they've experienced, their sadness, and I'm no closer to knowing their existence outside this room than someone I might meet on a plane or over dinner. The only life that's important is the one he lived with you."

"Was he angry with me?"

Her voice was quiet and yearning. Patrick thought how much he liked her in spite of her knowing complexity. Her sadness was as real as the joy she'd presented the first time she'd come.

"I don't think so."

"I thought if I told you, about that week, that it would help me explain in some way to him, explain why I didn't tell him I was pregnant. That's been the worst thing of all. That he never knew. And I'm to blame for that. I took that from him. And I've often wondered whether, if he'd known about the baby, he wouldn't have been unhappy, and somehow he might not have let himself die. That I killed him, just like my mother."

"What makes you think he was unhappy?"

She looked up at him, and he saw the torment in her sadness. Her voice was tight.

"Because in the last week of his life he couldn't talk to me, he came to you. He couldn't tell me what was wrong. That's hard to live with."

Patrick leaned forward and took hold of her hands.

"That's not because he was unhappy," he said. "It was because, like you now, he wanted to protect what he loved."

She was looking at him closely, and he saw some understanding in her eyes. The tension seemed to leave her, and he felt her breathing slowly soften. A church bell sounded in the distance. They had gone the full hour.

"Does Richard know you've come here?"

"Yes, but he doesn't understand. Why should he?" She reached for the tissues and blew her nose hard. "He's just delighted we're getting married at last. I couldn't do it before, even though we've had two more children. That's five including Charlie," she said. "James's Charlie."

"You've had a lot of children for someone who didn't want any more."

Patrick's statement was simple but her answer even more so.

"Death makes you hungry for love," she said. She blew her nose again, then arched her spine, stretching herself as a prelude to her exit.

"That's it," she said. "It's done. There's no more to say."

"One thing before you go," said Patrick. "Why marry now?"

"Because it's time," she said.

2004

Friday 26 November
Kensington, London

THE ROOF GARDEN was immaculate but bleak in November. The pots
had all been wiped clean of mud and a few winter flowers strained
to be noticed in the weak sunshine. Thea was sitting in a chair,
wrapped in a large winter coat and wearing gloves. She watched
Lucy as she tidied and combed out the foliage, her mother's
movements practiced and regular like a form of physical meditation.
She was seventy now, still straight backed with no sign of scoliosis or
shrinkage. Her hair was almost white but still thick and heavy, cut
in a bob that she tucked behind her ears. Thea put her hand up to
her own hair, cut short like a boy's for convenience out in the camps,
and she longed to grow it again, to have it hang down her back once
more. There would be time soon. She and Bahram would have one
more year in the field, and then they would come home.

"Don't get cold, Ma," she said. "We should go in soon."

"You go down, darling. I'll be two minutes. Michael's making coffee." Lucy had been delighted to see Thea, as she had been to see
Grace the day before, but they came and went, these two daughters,
sweeping in from their pressured lives. Amy was the constant. And
tomorrow she was getting married, to Richard, whom Lucy loved
for saving her daughter from despair.

SHE could hear Thea laughing with Michael in the kitchen as she reached the bottom of the stairs, and it pleased her. It no longer felt a betrayal of Tom, as it had at first, in the aftermath of James's death, that dreadful time, when the door had opened and everything bad had seemed to rush over them. She saw them standing by the sink, Michael, bald now and a little round, his glasses on the end of his nose.

"Thea's been telling me that poor Archie was in trouble with Grace the moment he arrived," said Michael.

"Shh. I didn't tell Ma," said Thea. "It's tales out of school."

"What?" said Lucy.

"He'd forgotten some bag she wanted for tomorrow," said Thea. "As if Archie would remember a bag."

"They like to fight," said Michael. "It's their nature. It keeps the marriage on its toes."

"I wish she'd have a baby," said Lucy. "Poor Sam, he couldn't persuade her. Perhaps Archie will have more luck."

"You were going to show me what you're going to wear," Thea said, changing the subject.

"Oh, yes, I will," said Lucy. "But you've reminded me. I want to show you something else I've found, for Amy." She disappeared for a moment, and Thea could hear her opening the drawer of the desk in her sitting room, and she returned with a photograph in her hand. Thea took it from her mother and held it up. It was a picture of James, taken not long after he and Amy were married. He was laughing and pointing, and the resemblance to Charlie was startling.

"I found it last night," said Lucy. "It was right on the top of the box. I can remember that morning. We'd been to the café at Little Venice. It was the day they told me Amy was pregnant with Jonny. I can't remember ever seeing it before. Don't you think that's strange?"

"For goodness sake, Ma," said Thea, "I really don't think you should show that to Amy, not this week."

Lucy looked at her, surprised.

"I thought she might like it. He looks so happy. He was thrilled, I remember, that she was pregnant."

Thea looked aghast.

"But, Ma, don't you remember? She never told him, about Charlie." She wondered if Lucy was becoming senile.

Lucy took the photo from her and looked at it closely.

"I'll keep it here, then," she said. "But he's smiling. And I know you all think I'm a foolish old woman, but I'm sure that he wishes her well."

2004

26 NOVEMBER
HARLEY STREET

HE SAW THEM through the window as he peered around the edge of the blind, careful to stand back, well out of their view. She'd told him as he took her to his door that they were waiting for her, all of them, outside in the street—Archie and Grace, Lucy and Michael, Thea and her doctor, Charlie and the four other children, and Richard. He could see them, pulled up under the street lamp, in a grand limobus of a sort that he'd never seen before. They were going to the church for a rehearsal, then a prewedding supper, as a family.

The street was quite busy now with rush-hour traffic, and the lamps made the clear sky a deep navy blue. Patrick could see two men standing beside the vehicle, one tall, one compact and stocky; they were laughing together, clapping their hands in the cold. The smaller of the two, Richard he presumed, sprang forward to greet Amy, to hug her to him, and as she climbed aboard he heard the other passengers cheer her entry. He caught a glimpse of the boys, who seemed to be wrestling in the back, and then a white-haired woman at one of the windows, who must, of course, be Lucy. There was just a moment when he thought that he saw the elusive Grace Fielding as she leaned across her mother to look up the street then retreat back quickly from public view. The tall man climbed in last and pulled the door behind him.

It was odd to see them made flesh, thought Patrick, as he gazed down through his window, to think that he knew so much about them when they didn't know of or care for his existence. They were so much more than the memories she'd brought him, and he'd felt their separate stories even as she'd told her own. He wondered if he'd helped her at all. He hoped so, and he knew he would always remember her. She had said, finally, what was on her mind, and she had told the truth when she'd said she was happy. He had met enough unhappy souls to know she was right, for the most part, about that. He pulled the blind back into position and sat down in his chair. He felt exhausted and he was glad he was finished for the day, finished now for the weekend ahead, though it stretched in front of him rather too quiet and unpeopled. "An excess of happiness," she'd told him she suffered from, the first time she came. He smiled at her claim and hoped for his own sake that she'd left some surplus behind.

ACKNOWLEDGMENTS

I would like to thank the following for their invaluable help and encouragement: Melvyn Bragg, Liza Campbell, Andrew Goodman, Jane Greenwood, Kate Morris, Judith Murray, Anya Serota and the John Murray team, David Snodin, Deborah Susman, Kathleen Tessaro, and special thanks to Jill Robinson and the Wimpole Street Workshop.

In addition, Lucy Fielding would like to acknowledge the following for the Lifelines they have bequeathed to her: Albert Einstein, Ralph Waldo Emerson, Henry David Thoreau, and, of course, Anon.

About the Author

GILLIAN GREENWOOD is a former editor of the *Literary Review* and was a book reviewer for the *Times* for several years. She subsequently became a documentary film maker specialising in arts and literature. She has made films (for the BBC and Independent Television) with, among others, Gore Vidal, Salman Rushdie, Dominick Dunne, Martin Amis, Margaret Atwood, and Alice Walker.